Wendy Robertson, an ex-teacher, lecturer, and journalist, is currently Arts Council Writer in Residence in a women's prison. THE JAGGED WINDOW is her fourteenth novel in a list which includes contemporary, historical and children's novels. She lives in the north of England.

The
Jagged Window

Wendy Robertson

HEADLINE

First published in hardback in 1999 by
HEADLINE BOOK PUBLISHING

First published in paperback in 2000 by
HEADLINE BOOK PUBLISHING

10 9 8 7 6 5 4

ISBN 0 7472 5978 X

Typeset by CBS, Martlesham Heath, Ipswich, Suffolk

Printed and bound in Great Britain by
Clays Ltd, St Ives plc

HEADLINE BOOK PUBLISHING
A division of the Hodder Headline Group
338 Euston Road
London NW1 3BH
www.headline.com
www.hodderheadline.com

I would like to thank the trustees and staff at the St Deniol's Library in Hawarden, North Wales, for allowing me to research in their wonderful Victorian collection and share in the particularly fruitful quality of peace and quiet in which to write. Also Avril Joy and some of the women of HMP Low Newton who, as fellow writers, have taken an interest in this novel as it has developed alongside the work we did in the prison. Also librarian Gillian Wales for coming up with the answer when I had hardly asked the question. I thank as well my friend Janet Wilson, who, when I was impelled by some unseen force to revert to the simple technology of the fountain pen, saved my life by converting my inkflow into computer files.

To Kendra, Lisa and all those other writers in prison, busy finding their voices 'behind the door' or 'on the out'.

Rose - Mother   Brother Liam
Ellis - Father
Theo
Edward
Casper
Rys

One

Brave White Bird

The street was empty. The boys were late, and that child Theo had been gone for God knew how long. Rose Clare Maichin closed the kitchen door with a click and went to stand by the window. The boys were not yet home, so she must not have overslept. That was something.

She pulled the curtain till it was back tight behind its hook and rubbed the washday steam off the glass pane with her hand. Then she touched her tired lids with a wet finger. Her poor head was still stinging with the shock of waking up from daytime dreaming sleep and finding the fire nearly out.

She bustled now to draw the coals into a delicate pile in an effort to nurture the heat in the dying fire before she could use it for the dinner. A tall gawky woman, with strong wrists and swollen fingers, she moved with speed and economy round the little kitchen.

Of course, her daughter was nowhere to be seen. That child! She was growing wilder by the day, more creature of the sea than helpful daughter. Beating, confinement in the coal hole, nothing would bring her into line. The child would be late for a meal; she got whipped; then she was late again, as though the hard punishment were no more than the mark of a finger on water. In the end Rose Clare had been driven to allow her son Edward to take his belt to his sister. The boy was keen to do this, saying he must take his father's place, meet his father's obligation.

The portly image of her husband Ellis rose before Rose Clare. She usually tried not to think of him, but, still recovering from the befuddlement of her afternoon doze, she found him sitting in her head like a resident frog.

She glanced at his likeness which loomed up on the wall beside the fire. Ellis was small, compact, barely coming to her shoulder. But his head was large and you always thought of him as a bigger man. Thick black curly hair. Rose Clare wondered if it were turning grey now. Nearly eight years since she had seen him, since he had gone to America to make their fortunes.

Well, sure, he hadn't made any fortune but he was still there in America, staying now and then with her sisters in New York. Every two months he sent her a long letter wrapped round a money order. No fortune, this, but small amounts which told her he was still there, still hers. And before the boys started work at the colliery, these small sums had kept the whole house going.

Rose Clare took a cloth from the oven door and rubbed the glass on the photograph till it squeaked. Ellis's eyes were fractionally too close together, it was true. He had this habit of looking closely into a person's face, a trick which could be engaging, even mesmerising. It had certainly mesmerised her into marriage eighteen years ago, just a week after she had served him porter for the first time in her brother's inn on the road to Dublin port.

In those days Ellis was quite the 'big' fellow himself, with his hard hat and his black suit, all scrupulously clean even if a little threadbare. She pictured him as he was then, using his neat white hands to sketch out some new idea in the air, cutting and chopping it as though wielding a sabre.

Yes, quite the big fellow was Ellis, in those days.

The fire was roaring now and Rose Clare placed the pan of stew on the glowing coals. Then she sat at the little table by the window and started to peel extra potatoes and chop some thick ham to add to the bubbling mess.

She kept lifting the curtain to watch for the boys and for Theo. The light was fading. The fact that the boys were late had saved her from the humiliation of not having the meal on the table. But now they were *very* late. Oh, she would rage at them, even Edward, but it was a lucky escape for her.

Edward. She tried to think of the time she had stopped beating and started to submit to her eldest son. In the early days after Ellis left, she had taken to beating them all indiscriminately with the stick that hung behind the kitchen door. It was the only way to keep any order in this house where, without the stick, her voice was not really heard.

Was it two years ago when she stopped? Three? That time when, in the space of a month, Edward seemed to grow six inches and become a man. The boy had just started to work in the mine and was very popular there: at that time bigger than his fourteen years would admit, he was strong and hardworking. The popularity was a surprise to her. She was quite aware that in school and at the pit he had to endure insults for being 'half a heathen', the son of a papist. At least that had hardened him, made him a good fighter. And that fighting strength was admired in the pit.

Edward was a peculiar mixture. He had inherited his father's intelligence and deliberate charm without his weaknesses. It was from Rose Clare that the boy had inherited the tall, rangy good looks which had the girls lifting a shoulder and flirting with him at the slightest encouragement: her brother, Liam, had that same magnetism for women. She caught her breath in a gulp, as hatred flooded through, as it always did at the thought of her brother Liam.

3

His grandparents worshipped the ground Edward walked on; Caspar followed his brother round like a lap dog; even the sly Rhys, the youngest of her three boys, could not get away from under Edward's shadow. It seemed these days that they were all under Edward's spell. Except her, that was. Except the child. Theodora. She was impervious to her brother's looks and his charm. Her indifference pricked and pricked at him till he rose in anger. This brought her in for rough treatment. It was all so inevitable. The child had to learn.

Rose Clare's thoughts meandered on to the day Edward had come in early from work and found her with tears coursing down her cheeks, prostrate across the table, her rosary and her mother's crucifix in her hand. He had taken the holy things from her and put them in their box high on the press. 'Now, Mam, this won't do, will it? Granda wouldn't like it.' It was an old voice for a boy of fourteen years, a voice full of grave authority, an authority which came not from his father but from his grandfather, that raging preacher, that scourger of all heretics, that scorner of the unprofessed: the old man into whose chapel her sons fled each Sunday, to pray morning, noon and night, to chant away the disgrace of having a papist for a mother and the misfortune of having to speak English at home.

She shook the thought out of her head and got the bowls on to the table just as the clatter of boots told her the boys were coming down the yard. 'You're late!' she called, listening to them in the doorway kicking off their boots. 'How d'you think I can run this house if you—'

Edward held up a hand. 'We'd business to see to,' he growled. 'To help a certain sinner to confront their wickedness.'

Caspar giggled and Edward kicked him with his socked foot.

Rose Clare had to wait a good half-hour while the boys stripped to the waist and scoured themselves in the scullery. Then she had to stand to the side as they sat down and ate their basins of heavy stew in silence. When they had finished she gathered up their bowls, saying, 'Our Theodora has been missing for the best part of the day.'

'She has, has she?' said Edward. Caspar coughed and Rhys shuffled his feet.

Here is the water, lapping and splashing through the salt marsh, surging down a million crazes and cracks in my direction. Above me the curlews scratch their last marks on the evening sky, then swoop and settle among their favourite marsh-edged reeds for the night; the distant fishermen stack their last box, stretch their stick-like arms above their heads, and wander, in twos and threes, towards Fisherman's Row. Their growling words of parting hop on the knife-edged breeze towards this place where I am tethered to a stake on the marsh.

I shiver. My teeth are chattering.

The deserted marsh, usually my refuge and retreat, is becoming too dark and too quiet; I start again to pull and push at the hempen rope, but I can't get free. The sky above me turns to gunmetal, sealing its light away, saving it up for tomorrow. The ancient staithes planted around me are sucking in the shadows, taking on the shapes of black dragons, their armoured tails swishing towards me.

Now that the tidal water, lapping forward inch by inch, is over my knees, I lift my foot and kick against the post – to give some purchase while I pull even harder against my tether. I try to lift my other foot out of the water but the river silt, fine and gluey, sucks it back into the quicksand.

The water is about my waist. My teeth are chattering with the effort to hold down the fear which, as much as the rope tethers round my waist, could defeat me. I will not let Edward,

5

wherever he is, have the satisfaction. I will not cry. I will not cry.

Think of other things.

I twist round to peer towards the deserted quay and the town behind it: streets snaking away from the mass of the castle; here and there the glow-worm light of a lantern betrays the route of a single traveller in the growing dark. From time to time the blackened sky flares with the tonguing fire of the ironworks, its crimson glow reflected in the front windows of the ironworkers' cottages close by.

My own father was born in one of those houses. And now! His voice trickles into my head. *Cariad look, the house with two windows at the end, see? Two bay windows because your granda was a 'big' man at the works. The old man worked in that inferno, day in, day out, see? Pouring iron, white as stars, hot as hell, see?*

I feel a little warmer now, my hand seems to lie firmly in my dada's. His singing voice is whispering in my ear. *'No job for a human being, look you, working in those ironworks. But didn't the whole thing give great weight to my da's sermons on a Sunday? It gave him the words, the ways to describe the precise nature of the burning, the suffering of the damned, those despised fallers by the wayside.'*

My father was thrown out of the chapel, you know, for marrying the papist. My mother – she was the papist. The problem is all about beads and crosses and bowing to an altar. And incense. Swinging incense, the intoxication of scent. Maybe I get that from her: I love the smell of things. Poor Mammy. It seems marrying a papist is worse than marrying the devil himself.

But, thrown out or not, my father can sing all the hymns and quote all of the verses of the Bible when it suits him, winning many an argument with holier-than-thou brethren. Like me, he remembers everything.

6

I know all these things about him because, in her softer moments, my mother has told me so. The flesh of him is in her voice. The soul of him is in the long, long letters which come to our house every second month.

Suddenly I feel his hand on my cold face. *'My hand is soft, see? I don't do the work of beasts. No more will you. Isn't that why you read and write like an angel?'* Then just as suddenly his voice recedes and his hand disappears, and I am alone again. And so very cold. Of course, *they* will say I made all this up, my father talking to me and all. This 'making up' is one reason the boys torment me and call me *lunatic*. The reason they turn my mother from me and she sometimes stops me having my supper. So I go to bed hungry on many days. That Edward . . .

I'm not a lunatic. I do know that I really only meet my father in the letters he has sent to us since I was small. I invent his voice and his presence from the tales I hear from my mother. She is especially good at this when the drink makes her sentimental, before she starts on the raging sorrow which comes before sleep. In her voice I can hear the very echoes of his: the cold clean lines of his Welsh coming through my mother's curly Irish tones. It's not difficult for me to conjure him up and make him live inside my . . .

A few drops of water splash on to my head and I put up my face to greet the rain, that soft sister to the sea. I close my eyes and let the rain mingle with my salt tears. Then I gulp and start to sing a song under my breath, a song I've heard my mother sing, many times.

> 'A sorrow for you changing
> Your life, cold your christening
> Brave white bird in rough waters . . .'

Rose Clare peered through the window at the darkening street.

'I suppose I'll have to go and seek her,' she sighed. 'The little devil.'

Edward picked up the prayer book on the windowsill. 'I've a special piece to learn for the meeting tonight. Give me half an hour and if Theo doesn't come we'll go and seek the little devil. Right, boys?'

'Edward . . .' said Rhys, frowning.

'Hear what I say, Rhys! Half an hour!'

Rhys subsided, put his feet up on the fender and watched his thick socks steaming. He had to wait forty-seven minutes before Edward came out of the front room.

I swallow my song as a heavy flesh-and-blood hand grasps my shoulder. I scream and squirm against the hard grasp, retching at the acrid smell of rotting seaweed.

It is a deep, man's voice. 'Hush now, child. Who was it did this to you?'

It's the man from the tar-paper hut.

Halfway between this place and the harbour, a black rock looms over the marsh: on it stands the tar-paper hut, bent slightly skew-whiff by years of persistent offshore wind. The old man lives in the hut: he is very ancient, I think, but it's hard to tell. He smells of the sea, has a big beard, wears three hats and covers himself with a ragged mountain of sodden coats.

I've learned not to worry about the tar-paper man as he strides right past me, enveloped in the stench of rotting seaweed, muttering away and occasionally flinching from some unseen terror over his shoulder.

Apart from this tar-paper man I'm usually left in peace up at this end of the salt marsh. Until today, that is, when the boys came. I fought them hard, but they held me over their heads, my arms flapping like the wings of a captured bird. Then they kicked out my driftwood fire, and stamped on my flowers. How much it roused Edward's fury. He told the others my little stone pantry shelf was an altar. And the fire! That was the worst thing. I love to light fires but our mother forbids it and has whipped me many a time for lighting little fires in the lane by our house.

But today the tar-paper man comes to frustrate Edward's schemes. He pulls at the hairy sea-rope that they tied me with, but to no avail. Then, from a deep pocket, he pulls out a sharp gutting knife. I flinch away. He cuts the rope clean through. I almost fall from the post and he gathers me in his sodden arms. I think I'll choke from the smell.

'Who did this?' My hair, thick and curling as the snakes of Medusa, lashes across his face in the wind. 'Who did this, child? The sea would have taken you sure as Old Harry. Who tied you, cruel, to this post?'

Peering into the distance over his many-coated shoulder, I can see the silhouette of my brothers standing to one side of the castle tower. My oldest brother, Edward, waves his arm at me, then draws his finger across his throat.

I shake my head at the old man. 'I don't remember. I don't remember what happened.' I point my trembling finger. 'Look. There are my brothers. They're looking for me.'

Puffing and blowing as he makes his way, the old man carries me up to the castle, where my brothers are waiting.

'Where've you been, Theo?' says Caspar innocently, his beady eyes sparkling. 'Our mam sent us to look for you.' He turns to the old man, his nose wrinkling at the smell. 'Missing all day, she's been, sir. We've looked everywhere for her.'

The tar-paper man sets me down and keeps me against him as I sway; my cold feet and legs are without feeling. 'Children's games. This child was tied to one of the old staithes. Good and tight. How old are you, child?'

I am watching Edward. 'Thirteen,' I say.

'That's a lie,' says Edward. 'My sister's a terrible liar,

9

sir. Makes up stories all the time.'

'I am thirteen on my next birthday,' I say. 'In my thirteenth year. Mammy says so.'

The old man thrusts me into Edward's arms. 'You need to carry her, young man. There's no use in her legs. First time I saw that white face I thought she was a seagull, a bird bobbing on the tide.'

Edward's hands dig into my shoulders. 'Thank you, sir,' he says smoothly. 'Though you must have the strength of Samson to carry her. She's a heavy lump. We'll get her home somehow. Thank you for your good deed.'

The old man nods and pulls up the collar of his third coat. 'In for a bad night. You get her home fast.' He turns and starts to trudge back towards the tar-paper hut.

Edward releases me and I stagger, then steady myself. 'You're in trouble, girl,' he says pleasantly. 'Our Mam is stotting. And now, getting on with that lunatic! She'll have you.' He turns, nods at his brothers, then sets off round the dry castle moat towards the town. Caspar, always the slave, grins at me and follows him.

It's my youngest brother, Rhys, who hesitates, then goes down on one knee. 'Here, jump on my back, Theo. You'll slow us all down and then Mam'll lam the lot of us. We were already late from work earlier, delayed by you and your dratted fire, and she wasn't best pleased.'

Fires. They burned my mother's father's house around her during the big hunger in Ireland, when the landlords took the roofs and pulled all the houses down. My mother was left unscarred except for a mark of a strange sort in her mind. That was before she went to Dublin and met my father.

When Rhys finally tips me on to the long wooden seat by Mother's fire, my teeth are chattering and my legs are mottled blue. My bare feet are still caked with mud from the salt marsh.

'What is it?' says my mother, wiping her hands on her apron. 'Is it a drowned rat?'

'It's your daughter,' says Rhys. 'Playing the goat out there on the marsh with her friends. Lighting fires. You know how she is about fires. She got herself trapped, tied up and these others, they ran away. That old lunatic, the one in the hut on the beach, delivered her to us like a parcel of fish.'

'The madman?' My mother kneels beside me and I flinch away. 'Still, child, still.' She puts a bony hand on my brow. 'Friends? She has no friends. There never was such a child for being on her own.' Now she leans across to pick up a cloth from the table and starts to mop the muddy floor. 'How did this happen, you silly girl,' she says grimly.

I lift my head and stare at Rhys.

'They were playing crucifixions,' he says. 'And they tied her to a post and left her. Now they're waiting for her to rise again.'

My mother clutches the place where her crucifix should have been and looks behind Rhys for Edward. My oldest brother's very hot on the Lord's name being taken in vain. 'You want to watch it, Rhys,' she says. 'Your brother will not have you saying such things. Holier than your grandfather, he's turning out to be. Where is Edward now?'

'He told you, Mam,' says Rhys impatiently. 'They had Bible class. He and Caspar peeled off, not to be too late for that.'

'After you found your sister?'

'Oh yes, Mam.' Aghast, he was, to find her like that, in the keeping of the old man

He is lying, of course. The truth is Edward sent him home with me, with orders to make sure I kept my mouth shut. Caspar, who's always at Edward's coat tails, went off with him. Rhys takes pride in the fact that he is the least holy of all of them, that pair of hypocrites: *rhagrithwyr*, he calls them.

Unlike them he is no hypocrite. Even so he only defies Edward in sly ways, when it costs little in pain. He will not risk Edward's wrath.

Rhys looks down at me, his ragged fringe of thick hair casting a shadow on his eyes. 'You should see to Theo, Mam. She's wilting there like a dead flower.'

My eyes are sore and heavy and my teeth are chattering. My whole body is shuddering and jerking. And I am looking into a furry blackness. And then I see a ship with sails casting off from the stone harbour.

Rose Clare put a hand on her daughter's cheek. 'You go and get the blanket from my bed, Rhys, and then go off to your Bible class or whatever. Take some money from the box on the shelf.' She lifted Theo's sodden collar away from her daughter's soft white neck and started to undo her buttons.

Rhys obeyed with alacrity. Rose Clare knew her third son well. Pennies from her box would furnish him with a pint or two at the Fettler's Arms; in her opinion this was better sustenance by far than the ravings of Isaiah or sanctimonious readings from the Bible Dictionary.

In his unspoken way, in mirroring her own weakness, Rhys was Rose Clare's ally. Rhys's forbidden preferences, like hers, were known, but not mentioned in the family. Edward did not deign to recognise them, even when his youngest brother rolled into bed beside him exhaling the smell of tobacco and stale hops, and muttering about the heroism of Peredur.

Rose Clare pulled her daughter towards her and, while she flopped backwards and forwards in her arms like a rag doll, she stripped her of her clothes, right down to her little grey-white shift. 'Whaw! Child, you have about you the stink of the sea,' she muttered. 'What's that? What do you say?'

Her daughter muttered something about an old man, then broke into a piping song about a seagull.

'Shh. Shh,' said Rose Clare. 'What a girl you are, getting wet like this.'

But Rose Clare's voice did not carry the accusing, rough tone she usually saved for her daughter. She could tolerate the child when, as at this moment, she was unconscious. In this state she did not display that spark of rebellion which made her mother so angry, so guilty.

She rubbed the sandy curls with a towel, and wondered for a second why she loved this one so much less than she did her sons. Sometimes she thought it was because Theodora was a girl and would be forced to suffer as much as she herself had suffered. Love was wasted on such a doomed creature.

The chill in Theodora's body reached Rose Clare and she started to rub the child's arms and legs with the towel, warming herself with the vigorous action.

Other times she knew it was not that, really. Not that Theodora was a girl. Had she been a boy it would be the same. The problem with this child was the way she came into the world, at the very first.

Theodora's had been a terrible birth: too early, and accompanied by horror. Tucked in behind Theodora like a spoon, slipping out just after her, was an unexpected twin, frighteningly disfigured and thankfully dead. Thankfully dead. So said the old woman who had attended Rose Clare, thrusting the horror away from the young mother's eyes.

After that birth Rose Clare had turned her back on Ellis; the physical passion which had bound them was no longer worth the price. Eight children, four dead. The three who had lived only a short while at least had had names: Rhodri, Glyn and Ellen. They had been baptised by the minister, and had marking stones in the graveyard. But the little one who came with Theo, it was as though she had not been. She had no name and whirled even now in limbo, giving out mewling cries, haunting Rose Clare's dreams.

13

So Rose Clare had turned her back on Ellis. No more. No more. Not like the women in the pit streets here and in the low cabins back home in Ballyhiegue. Rose Clare lived with the daily certainty of purgatory, anyway, because she had married outside her church; the sin of denying her husband his God-given rights was just another sin to be weighted in the one-sided balance. Her own mother had been scolded for this particular sin by the priest and had gone on to have a twelfth and a thirteenth child before she died. Of course, she was a good woman and had died in a state of grace, her weeping children all round her.

Ellis did not 'force' Rose Clare to his needs, as her own father, with the help of the priest, had forced Rose Clare's mother. For a while Ellis tried his charm and his wiles on her: he sang merry music hall songs and praised Rose Clare for her great beauty. But when she resisted him, his eye wandered to other women, easy women about whom she did not ask and for whom she did not care.

Then came the trouble at the coal company. Lies about money and misplaced orders. Rose Clare closed her mind to this. She knew Ellis was light-fingered. He had stolen from her brother Liam to get the money for her wedding ring. There had seemed to her no harm in that. Liam owed her more than he could ever repay. He had used her more than once as collateral in card games, contriving at her humiliation as no brother should.

So in the end Ellis had turned to America, that great enticing whore of a place, that easy woman who promised not only pleasure but riches, if only you responded to her, danced her tune. Rose Clare was left in Wales with the little girl and the troublesome boys. She was left without Ellis, her great love, the one for whom she had sacrificed her immortal soul.

Rose Clare had found it hard to care for this little girl who cried, was fed, slept and cried again. And cried. Once she had

14

picked up a pillow to smother the child, to send her into limbo with her little unnamed sister. But then those pale blue eyes, as ancient as the mountain, had opened and looked up at her mother, and forbidden her to do it.

From that day Rose Clare took more proper care of Theodora and she thrived. From that day, even so, the mother blamed this small creature with its pale face and its shock of sandy hair, blamed her for the yawning space, the black hole in her life where Ellis should have been.

Now, in her arms, the twelve-year-old Theodora coughed and spat, then whimpered again. Absently Rose Clare tucked the blanket round her and lay her back on the wooden bench. She poked the fire till it blazed high up the chimney, then removed a loose brick at the back of the boiler and took out a fresh bottle.

Two hours later, when the boys returned to the house together, Rose Clare was dead drunk, face down on the kitchen table. Theodora was on the floor, the blanket to one side, her body exposed. Her eyes were rolling into the back of her head and she was retching and rattling for breath.

Rhys looked up at his elder brother, trying – but failing – to keep the dark fury, the blame, from seeping out of his eyes.

Two

On the Edge

There is a weight on my chest. I struggle against heavy bedclothes. The smell of cloves and rosemary, which my grandmother carries round her like a cloak, tickles my nose. The dark wraps itself round me, beaming like a black light. It dissolves and I am on the marsh again. I love to play on these flat stretches of land at the edge of the estuary. Twice daily the incoming sea slakes the salty thirst of these broad marshes. The tide creeps up as far as the fishing boats and makes them rock and spin: it licks away at the top of the sea-wall which cups the old harbour in its stony grasp. On stormy days the salt water even sprays the windows of the fishermen's cottages, which stand like a row of dollies' houses, separated from the town by the shining margin of the brand new railway tracks. From where I play the tiny figures of the fishermen and their families are like the stick people I draw with charcoal in the margins of my mother's newspaper.

All my life my heart has delighted in the jingling rattle of the boats as they lurch together at anchor, and the slop of horses' hooves as they make their steady way across the flat reaches of the estuary, hauling light cargo for the boats.

Now I am struggling again, struggling in Edward's grasp. Then Edward is gone and I am tranquil. This sometimes happens when you're in violent reverie. I settle down to have a good think, bringing my powerful dreams into play, and turn myself into a princess tied to the rock before being rescued by Prince Perseus. It's quiet enough for dreaming, out here on the marsh, away from the harassment in the house and the busy streets of the town, which crouches under the looming castle like a sick dog.

Getting away from the house has been even more difficult lately. My mother is forever telling me that now I'm twelve I'm big enough to do the proper chores: to stir the washing, to wind the mangle, to beat the mats on the line, to get my hands black cleaning the range.

But each day the murmuring ripple of the outgoing tide draws me like a magnet, enticing me to slip away from the teeming house and my mother's sullen sleeping face.

That's why I pray for my mother to drink some of that stuff in the afternoons, and wait for her to slide into her heavy afternoon slumber. Then I make my way down here. A blissful escape!

Today, before my game was so rudely spoiled, I had this lovely time on my knees on the salty sand. I like to make patterns, see? Patterns and patterns and patterns. Shapes with seaweed and pebbles, designs with shells and fragments of bleached wood on the coal-spotted sand.

Today, my patterns completed, I build myself a wood fire and put the flowers before it for the fire god. Then I sit back and watch the sky, mottled silver-grey like the belly of a leaping fish, arching over me in a wide sweep. Sometimes I think of this sky as the very helmet on the world. Then the boys come, it seems for the fiftieth time in this dream, and kick out my driftwood fire and stamp on my flowers.

That was before. Now the white light of the hidden sun pulses away its life behind the dense veil of grey cloud. Tethered here, I watch as the waves pursue their leisurely quest

17

up the long estuary, leaping up at the light. The busy sea destroys my patterns of shell and stone.

Across the marsh I can see the oyster catchers poking about among the reeds; they ignore the fussy curlew making dazzling sorties above them. In the distance on the far side of the river the land sits on the marsh like a curl of black smoke.

I dream now about that distant shore where I have never been. It's as foreign to me as America, where my own father is in these days. Through his eyes I see this bright country where the people teem as plentiful as the fish in the swollen nets hauled in here in the early morning. I see the buildings in New York numerous as the honey pockets in a marsh honeycomb. I see him in the tall thin house in New York with my mother's sisters Dreena and Roisin.

Often, it seems to me that my father and grandfather remember everything. Every incident. Every word. I too remember everything I have read, or been told. I remember and, often as not, I write it down. This writing down seems to rouse *their* anger. The boys. I've had many a belting from my mother, and lately Edward, for wasting my time in this way. Most of my scraps of scribbled paper get burnt.

'No. No,' I protest against the burning, and then struggle against the straps that seem to bind me.

'Hush, child.' I can feel my grandmother's cool hand on my brow.

The only time I was whipped by my grandfather was when I asked him whether Zeus and Hera and their Olympians weren't much the same as God and the Holy Spirit. That was when my book of Greek stories – a present through the post from my father – burned merrily in my grandmother's hearth. Like it or not I have set up some heat in that cold house.

I am so tired. So pleased to see the comforting dark invading the edge of my eyes, feel its hand on my brow.

* * *

18

'It's our fault,' said Rhys for the sixth time. 'She could die.'

The three brothers were walking towards the pit in the sulphurous dark of the early morning. On their far right was the estuary and beyond that, where the colour changed from seal to chalk-grey, the sea.

It was said that one of the colliery seams went right under the sea. Some old men could tell the difference when they were underground, could hear the roar of water above their heads. But Rhys insisted that it was all simply a deep dark undifferentiated hole. Edward tried, once, to show Rhys how it was all possible, drawing the land and the sea in chalk on the vertical coal face. But still, Rhys, normally so quick and clever, pretended he could not work it out.

'She'll be all right,' said Edward now. 'Indestructible, that one. That's the trouble with her. You'll see.'

'Still. It's not right. Mam thinks it's her fault. And it isn't. She should know how it happened.'

Edward put out a hand and swung Rhys round to face him. 'Now here's old Rhys, slyboots himself, coming over all honest. I tell you, boy, you keep your mouth shut, see? It was just a bit of fun. And anyway if Mam had looked after her proper, kept her by her, she wouldn't be like that. That right, Caspar?'

Caspar, just behind Edward's shoulder, grunted. 'That's right, Ed. A bit of fun. And Mam not up to the mark.'

'I feel bad about it,' said Rhys. 'Whichever way you look at it, it was—' Rhys's head rang as Edward's fist exploded on the point of his cheekbone. He fell against a tangled hedge that separated the path from a field with three goats in it. 'Hey, stop it will you?' he grumbled. 'I was only trying to say—' Edward's fist rammed the same place again and this time Rhys really did see stars.

Other miners, yawning in the dark morning as they made their own way down the narrow road to the pit, eyed the altercation without curiosity. Fights were not unknown between the men, and these boys were brothers. Best not to interfere.

Edward was standing away from Rhys, brushing his gloved hands one against the other, as though he had touched tar. 'You say one thing to anyone, boyo, and you'll get a worse duckin' yourself. I don't want it known. Do you want me off the list?'

The blessed list. Even at seventeen, Edward's passion and oratory were winning him a bit of a name down the chapel as a preacher. There'd been standing room only that day he gave his piece about the Commandments and the Tablets of Stone. He'd spoken for ninety minutes without pause and had the old ones shouting *Hallelujah!* by the time he had finished. The local committee had put forward a proposal to enter his name on the regular list for the chapel circuit. The word among the wise was that, like his grandfather, Edward Maichin would be one of the great preachers of his generation.

'No need to get churned up,' muttered Rhys, scrambling out of the hedge. 'No need to talk, if you feel that strong about it.'

'I feel that strong. Theo deserved a lesson. And she got it. How were we to know about the freak tide?' said Edward. Then he turned and stomped away down the road, Caspar at his side.

Rhys watched his brothers plod on without moving. He waited for old Owen Charles, who was walking ten yards behind. He liked the old man from whom he was learning the trade of pit joiner. Pit joinery was rough. Any job a pit joiner tackled had to have strength and stamina rather than beauty and elegance. 'Close enough for pit work' was the derisory description for any job which held firm but did not delight.

Owen, the master of such work, trudged towards Rhys. He removed his clay pipe from his mouth and waved it towards

Edward and Caspar's receding backs. 'Difference with the brother, is it?'

'So it is.'

'Brothers sometimes make the worst of bedmates, boy. I tell you that, no matter what is talked about blood being thicker than water. Brothers falling out is as old as time, look you. Consider Cain and Abel.'

My dream of the marsh comes to an end. The second crow of the cockerel cuts like a razor into my head. I rub my ear hard to extract the painful sound. My chest is encased in a corset of lead making it almost impossible to breathe. And I am hot. Too hot. The blankets are scratchy against my fingers. This alien hand presses mine, pulling the blanket back into place. A voice mutters and murmurs above my head but the words bumble together. I rub my ear again. That cockerel seems to have done a lot of damage in there.

My eyes are sealed shut; the messages to open the lids are not getting through. I bang my head this way and that on the pillow trying to jerk my eyelids open. A cool dry hand rubs away at my brow. A voice is saying, 'Ssh, *cariad*, sh!'

That cool hand has done the trick. The bedroom is becoming visible through the long bars of my lashes. Through those bars I can see a man wearing a pale red garment draped across him like a cloak. His eyes, too big for his face, are a piercing blue; his hair ripples down on to his shoulders like golden syrup.

I blink hard and finally manage to open my eyes wide. The hand moves from my brow and pats my shoulder. 'Now then, Theo, back in the land of the living, are we?'

The smooth pale face of my Grandmother Maichin, my *nain*, is looking down at me. I blink at her, then across to the man in red, who, I now realise, is framed in heavy mahogany fingered up with gold. The man is holding a long slim hand

21

out towards a group of people, disproportionately small, in the crowd below him.

I sit up dizzily and look around my nain's back bedroom. 'What am I doing here, Nain?'

She plumps up the white pillow behind me and smooths the hand-quilted coverlet. 'Bless you, *cariad*, your brother Rhys came for me, didn't he now? And you were that bad I got your granda to get old Lew Richards with the gig to come and we brought you here covered in blankets, bumping up the hill. Those ruts are dreadful. I am always saying it.'

Bethany Maichin did not mention the havoc caused by her papist daughter-in-law when they made the decision to bring the child away to the house of her grandfather. She could not say how the woman had made her retch with the stink of berry wine as she held tight onto her daughter. She did not tell Theo how young Edward had to hold his mother by her arms to stop her chasing after the gig. Of course, Edward was a bright creature of the Lord if there was one, and knew what was right.

Protected by a powerful husband, nurtured by the supreme cadences of the Old Testament and the busy virtues of various Bible commentaries, Bethany Maichin saw the complications of life with an awe-full clarity. Her house was clean and bare of ornamentation except for the collection of holy pictures which graced every wall: Jesus on the mount; Jesus raising Lazarus; Jesus washing the feet of the disciples; Moses parting the waters; Isaac in the act of sacrificing his son. It was blasphemous, but not too difficult for Bethany to transpose the face of her own beloved grandson on to all of these images.

I rub away at the top of my arms. 'They roped me to a stake, Nain, and left me to the tide.'

'Who did this to you, *cariad*? When?'

'They did it yesterday. They did it yesterday.' In my head I see Edward standing by the castle, drawing his finger across his throat. 'I can't remember who it was.'

Nain frowns. 'You're muddled, child. Lost track of time in your fever. Haven't you been here in my house a week, not a day? I will tell you, child, that you touched the tip of an angel's wing more than once in that time. We thought we'd lost you to this world, but our prayers were answered and you were saved.' She sighs contentedly. 'Saved in the Lord.'

I wriggle on the bed. Her voice is prim, victorious. Her tranquil face beams down at me, skin as clear as a frost-glazed pond, her hair swept up like the wing of a silver bird. Her eyes, a luminous hazel, are as innocent as a new kitten. But I do not really know her. I only know the name we call her by. Nain.

I don't come to this house to see my nain and granda so very much. Not half as much as Edward or Caspar. But when I do come, these scary pictures on every wall make me want to flee. Sometimes when my nain is in the middle of reading a psalm in that fluting voice of hers I run away, down to the harbour or along the salt marsh trying to get the blank, pretty faces of these holy men out of my head.

For all its confusion and her own dark moods my mother's house breathes a kind of inky life: a relief after this narrow, scrubbed place with its pictures, in pale bright colours, of dead men. This morning, even with my brain hurting with the crowing cockerel, I can sense my nain's satisfaction at my presence here, imprisoned at last in her little back bedroom.

It's a great bone of contention between Mam and these two old ones that she never sends me to the chapel with the boys. Occasionally, Edward has dragged me there, but of course I disgraced myself each time: once by running away during my granda's two-hour hell-fire sermon and clashing the great chapel door behind me; once by capturing a mouse under the bench and placing it in with the pennies in the collection pouch. For this I had to endure pained reprimands from my nain, and being just about kicked all the way home by Edward.

Granda Maichin is much more of a fiery character than my nain. In the right mood he can light up a room like a bright candle. His love of the Lord is no cold thing; it is molten, like the iron he pours from the hoppers at the works. Of course, he really thinks I'm being dragged up to be a heathen, a stranger to the Welsh language; bred without prayer, eventually to writhe in purgatorial torment for being brought up not knowing the Lord. However, he's told my nain, in my hearing, that even that was better than being brought up an actual papist. 'I'll give the Irishwoman that, Bethany, she does not bother herself with the Catholic Church. Mind you, three mile to walk there, three back, too lazy to make the effort, if you ask me. That's the Irish for you,' he says. 'In any case, don't we have the boys? That's the important thing.'

'Is my mam coming for me, Nain?' I finally say now. My tongue struggles with the Welsh. My head aches and the flesh beneath my skin is full of tears.

Nain's lips tighten like the string on a bow. 'Well, *cariad*, your mother has not . . . made any attempt to come, as far as I can see. I have told your grandfather you're better here with us. We can keep you here, no bother. I can take care of you till you get better and you can learn to run a decent house, calm yourself down and go to Sunday School. Your Welsh might begin to sound less like the squeaking of a cat . . .'

I can understand Nain's words fine, but, because in our house English is spoken, Welsh doesn't trip off my tongue so easily. My mother has never learned the Welsh: one reason why she has so few friends here. I sit up straighter. 'My man runs a decent house, Nain.' My face is burning with temper. 'It's clean, and there are colours.' My eye charges desperately

24

round the stark white walls of the little bedroom. 'And she has flowers in jars and a picture of my dada by the fireplace. She'll worry about me. She gets mad when I'm out of her sight – I should know because I've had many a strapping for it. You might think that's because she doesn't want me there, but she does it for my own good, she keeps saying that.' Beads of sweat as big as cherries are forming in my hair and running down my face to be blotted up by the close neck of my flannel nightie.

Nain's dry hand is on my arm. 'Cool, cool, little one. Your mam will know how you are. Rhys will tell her. He calls here at the house every day after work. We've never seen so much of him. Your granda says that boy verges on the ungodly but no one could deny him a kind heart.'

The door downstairs clashes.

'Look, this will be him.'

His footsteps clatter up the uncarpeted stairs. Nain stands up. 'I will go and get you some broth, child. The boy will be pleased to see you awake.'

Rhys's face is still black from the pit. Beneath his ruffled hair a ridge of white skin shows where he's just snatched off his dusty cap. He smiles slightly to see me sitting up. 'Now that's better, Theo.' It is such a relief to hear the English but I don't smile at him. 'Hello, Rhys.'

He glances at Nain as she passes.

She cocks her head at him. 'Oh, the child's much better, Rhys. Woke up good and proper today. She has slept that fever right away.' Her hand is on his arm. 'Nearly mended, I would say.' The door clicks behind her.

He sits in the chair where Nain was sitting before and stares at me. 'You look better.'

'I nearly died, didn't I?'

He shrugs. 'I dunno about that. Granda paid for the doctor to come twice.'

'Nain said the angel wings had touched me.'

'Her and her angels. Sees them more than she sees people. You're not the only one who's a bit of a lunatic in this family.'

I think of hearing my father's voice when the tide was washing around my waist. I can't tell Rhys about that. 'Is Mam all right? She hasn't been here to see me. Nain says she hasn't been.'

His laugh is hollow. 'Do you think she would dare come here? Do you think they would let her in? No. Edward kept her home.'

I press my lips together to stop myself crying. I don't know what this is about. I never cry. 'I want to be home. I don't want to be here.'

'Nain's been very good to you, Theo. You've got to admit that. Watched over you day and night reading you her holy books and drippin' milk into you with a baby's titty bottle.' He pauses and clears his throat. 'To be honest, I get the sense she wants to steal you from our mam and bring you to God like you was some changeling dropped on her doorstep in the dark of night.' His grin now is open. 'Do you know, I sometimes think Nain's more like some old witch than a God-fearing woman, brewing potions to make you stay, conjuring you to give up your heathenish, hoydenish ways.'

I try to laugh with him, then wince as somebody rakes a sword through my chest. 'I don't suppose Mam's bothered, really. Me clear of the house, out from under her feet.'

Rhys shook his head. 'She's glum as an old watchman. Do you know she smashed all the bottles behind the boiler? And sits there by the fire stitching away like mad; a new apron for you, I think. It had patterns of green and red.' He paused. 'She has a candle in the little side window. Edward keeps putting it out and she keeps lighting it. She thinks it's her fault that you were so poorly.'

'You know whose fault it is, Rhys. You should tell her.'

He shakes his head. 'Edward . . .'

'I'll tell her. I'll tell her it's not her fault.' I bite my lip again to stop it trembling. 'I want to be home.' My voice is like the edge of a breeze and he has to bend his head to hear.

'Give it a few more days, Theo. Then Nain won't be able to stop you. Has anyone ever been able to stop you when you want to do something?'

'What about Edward and Caspar?' I look him in the eye. 'Have they been here?'

As he shakes his head his greasy hair moves on to his white brow where his cap has been. 'Not even on Sunday. They went to chapel straight from our house. I'd think our Edward said some prayers for you in that place. They were both anxious enough to know you were well. Me too, come to that.' He laughs. 'Guilt, look you. Nothing more nor less.' He rubs his chin which is beginning to sprout a few manly hairs like scrubby moss on a bare bank. 'I've felt bad about this, Theo. Me following our Edward's lead when I should know better. But I'll not do it again. He's too big for his boots, and a fool in a way. We had a fight over this.' He fingers his cheekbone where an old bruise is turning yellow.

'Who won?'

'Him, of course. So I won't tell nobody about what happened. But I'm finished with him. I'll watch out for you now, too.'

I wrinkle my nose at him but still I find myself smiling. 'I can watch out for myself.'

Silence grows between us and the tick of Nain's clock on the little mantelshelf fills the room.

'Rhys?'

'What is it?'

'Do you think there's a God?'

'Don't be silly, of course . . .'

'They just tell us all that. They say it. But do you feel it,

27

inside? Do you feel Him inside? Do you know He's there?'

He scowls at me. 'You do talk some rubbish, Theo.'

''Cause I don't feel it. Can't feel a thing. Feel more about the fish and the sea. I wouldn't be surprised if Poseidon himself rose from the tide, trailing seaweed and carrying his old trident. I sometimes hear him roar on the wind . . .'

'That reminds me. The old lunatic called.'

'Lunatic?'

'The man who lives in the hut, who saved you from the tide.'

The tar-paper man. I have forgotten all about him. How could I forget about him? My nose itches now as I smell again the rank seaweed and taste the salt which invaded me as he carried me off the shore. 'I want to see him.'

'Mam gave him milk and meat stew. Edward threw him out – sent him sprawling.'

'Tell him I want to see him.'

The sneck on the staircase door rattles and we can hear Nain's plodding steps on the stairs. 'Tell Mam I want to see her, too,' I say hurriedly to Rhys.

'She won't . . .'

But my head is back on the pillow; my eyes are closed. I open my eyes again to the sight of my nain coming into the room, a dish of steaming soup in her hands. 'Now, now, boy, don't you go tiring the child with your talk. Would you like some soup? There is a pan on the fire downstairs.'

He shakes his head. 'No,' he says distinctly. 'My mam will have my dinner ready, Nain.'

She catches his tone, and red patches stain her cheeks. 'Well, go you to your house, boy,' she says. 'And get your dinner.' It's unusual to hear that angry thread in her voice.

But there's no anger in her face when she turns back to me. Her brow is clear and there's a smile on her face. 'Now, *cariad*, a bit of soup and you'll be like a new woman!'

Three

Flaming Dragons

Bethany Maichin wiped her already clean hands on her spotless apron and went to answer the door. She recoiled from the vision before her: a shaggy mountain of clothes smelling of the very essence of the sea. 'What is it, now, what is it?' The Christian in her could not shut the door in his face.

The apparition swept off its hat and bowed a stately bow, exhaling another breath of the sea. Some attempt had been made to clean the face which emerged as a white clown's mask set in a tide-mark of black. 'Mrs Maichin? I am requested to visit the child, the child who near drowned in the sea.'

Bethany clutched the door-post, struggling with the English. 'Requested?'

'The brother came and told me.' His grimy hand held out a parcel of clean sacking. 'I bring a gift.'

She grasped it and the corner fell away to reveal the gleaming rainbow colours of sea trout. She took one step back. 'Mr . . .?'

I am excited to see the tar-paper man from the window and I stumble to the top of the stairs, calling, 'It's the first angel, Nain.' Clutching the banister, I make my way down the stairs.

'Angel?' says my nain.

'He was the first one. He saved me from the sea. Then it was your angels saved me after that.' I shiver.

'Come in, come in,' says Nain to the apparition on her doorstep. She sounds anything but welcoming. 'Close the door behind you. The child has just recovered from her death of cold.' She looks at her spotless kitchen, her white-scrubbed chairs, and sighs. 'Sit down. You too, child. Sit down before you fall down.'

The tar-paper man sits down on my granda's big wooden chair beside the hearth and I sit at the table, leaning on it slightly to stop the dizziness.

'I'll put this fish on the pantry slab,' said my nain. I can see she's keen to escape this sea colossus. She vanishes through the narrow door and we sit silently for a moment, listening to dishes being clashed, and my nain's impromptu, muttered prayers.

I cough, and pull my shawl more tightly round me. 'You saved me,' I say, not knowing really what I want to say.

'I was there, girl,' he says. His eyes glitter in the half-light of my nain's kitchen. 'And you were there, like a white bird bobbing on the tide.'

I cast around. 'It must be hard, living in a tar-paper hut,' I say.

He shakes his head and a fragment of marsh grass floats down on to the scrubbed stone floor. 'It's a fine place,' he says. 'A fine place. A peaceful place.'

My nain's clock ticks and ticks.

'They have gone,' he announces finally.

'Who's gone?'

'The long-tailed creatures.'

'Who?'

'They torment me. The long-tailed creatures are why I came to the edge of the land. I came to escape them. I came but still they tormented me – till the day I lifted you from the tide.'

'And now they've gone?'

'They've gone.'

'The tide took them?'

He nods. 'The tide took them.'

'It came for me and it took them.'

He nods. We sit comfortably now in silence, listening to the mouse-like rustling and muttering of my nain in her pantry.

Rose Clare missed many things about Ireland, but the thing she thought about least and missed most was colour: the vibrant green of the broad fields watered by the persistent rain and nurtured by the bland heat billowing in on the westerly wind; the bright silver of the sea edged pink with the setting sun; the purples and pinks of the hedgerows reflecting the bright cloth of aprons and flash of petticoat and the pot of fresh marigolds by the sink, placed there by her mother to see and smell as she worked in the kitchen.

Here in this country the colour seemed to be bleached out of everything. There were only the greys and sludgy browns of work clothes, faces inked out with the stain of coal. But, worse, a flash of colour could, if you were not careful, give offence. Her own aprons and petticoats, her habit of wasting money on flowers at the Saturday night market had brought early, and pained, disapproval from her mother-in-law. So too did her habit of drinking ale alongside her husband. In those days, though, while she was still happy, she did not drink herself stupid.

Ellis had laughed at Rose Clare's discomfort and she had bridled, saying she would be no colourless bland wretch for anyone. He had laughed more and said he liked her just as she was; he had caught many a chill in his mother's colourless house.

Today, surprised at her eagerness to see her daughter return, and swearing she would never drink again, Rose Clare worked hard in her own house. She gave everything a special polish, put a bright woven rug on the table by the window and on it carefully placed a bunch of primroses she had found on a walk up out of the town. The boys' dinner was bubbling on the fire. She pinned up her own hair carefully and she could feel her red petticoat swishing under her grey skirt. Then she put on her hat – an unseasonal straw – and pulled on her bright green shawl. Over her arm she placed another thick green shawl that her sister Roisin had knitted for her as a wedding present.

She passed her sons in the back lane. 'Your dinner is just to put out,' she said. 'Just takes putting out.'

Edward caught her elbow, grasping her hard. 'Where are you going now, Mam, all dressed up?'

'I've things to do,' she said, wrenching her elbow away from him. 'Everything's ready in there, in the house.'

'You should be home.' He took her arm again. 'Come in with us.'

Rhys stepped close, putting his shoulder between his brother and his mother. 'Now, Ed. You let Mam go.' For a long second they exchanged glances then Edward shrugged. 'It'll be to do with Theo. You're going for Theo, aren't you, Mam?'

'Why not?' challenged Rose Clare. 'The child should be home now. Rhys says she's much better.'

'Nain won't like it,' said Caspar.

Edward dropped her arm. 'Then again,' he said thoughtfully, 'the brat has been ruling that roost too long. No talking to Nain these days, except about her.' He turned without a word and made his way towards the back door, Caspar trailing behind him.

'I'll come with you, Mam,' said Rhys, taking the shawl from her.

She nodded. Then she led him on to the road into town, not towards the ironworkers' cottages as Rhys had anticipated.

'Where to now, Mam?' he said carefully. 'I thought we were going to my granda's house?'

'We're going to get Lew Richards and his gig first, Rhys. They took her in the gig and she can come back home that way too.'

I am still sitting with the tar-paper man, and Nain is still in the pantry, when my mother comes for me in the gig. I want to run to her, to throw my arms round her, but I sit quietly while she wraps me tightly in a green shawl. I am cheered by the glimpse of her red petticoat. Edward'll not have liked that, flashing her petticoat out in the street.

She nods genially enough at the tar-paper man. 'Good afternoon to you, Mr Barra.'

Mr Barra? Is that his name? He should not have a name, any more than fish have names.

'Mr Barra came to visit, Mammy,' I say, muffled now by the scarf she is putting round my head.

'The child should not go.' My nain's chilly voice comes from the pantry door. It seems her prayers have gone unanswered.

'She has a home. She should be in her own home.' My mother's voice is trembling. I have the unusual impulse to cheer her on.

The door flies open. My granda limps in, his massive shape throwing the room into shadow. 'Bethany, what is the gig doing outside?' He is wearing his thick work cap and his leathery skin shines in the firelight. He takes us all in with one sharp glance: my mother, Rhys, Mr Barra and me. I see it through his eyes: the little room choked with people.

My nain says, 'Ellis's wife has come for the child, and this man—'

33

'He saved me from the sea, Granda,' I say, loud and quick as I can.

His piercing eyes turn on me, then back to my nain. 'Will you clear this house, Bethany? I am speaking tonight and I need time to prepare.'

Ever obedient, she shoos us out as though we're ragged chickens and the door clicks behind us. It is something of a shock to be left with no kind words after a week of suffocating care.

It is a fine thing, riding along in Lew Richards's gig, high above the road, hearing the clip of the horse's hooves on the hard paved road. Inside it is a bit of a crush, as Mammy has insisted Mr Barra comes with us. When he says he will get down near the tar-paper hut she puts a hand on his damp sleeve. 'No, no, Mr Barra, sure you must come and eat with us. Warm yourself. My daughter is back home so this is a happy time.'

I have never heard my mother talk like this, without blame in her voice for me. When we get to the house, Edward gives me a black look, grabs his cap and storms off, Caspar following like the lap dog he is. Rhys, Mr Barra and I sit round the table. I cannot eat, but the other two tuck in and eat their fill, my mother watching from her sentinel place by the fire. In the end Mr Barra sits back, wiping his mouth with the back of his hand.

Rhys looks at him over his large spoon. 'Where do you come from, Mr Barra?'

The old man shrugs his massive shoulders. 'I lived in many places. Scotland, Wales, England. Moving for work. I've been in many a workhouse and some few asylums. I lived in many places. London . . .'

'London? Is it bigger than New York?' I say.

He laughs at this, the laugh billowing inside his broad chest like the rumble of a distant storm. 'Bigger, better! London is a fine place, I made good friends there.'

'I'd like to go there,' I say. 'I would love to go to London.'

He laughs, showing blackened teeth. 'Then you must visit my friend in Spitalfields. Horatio Plummer. A fine man.' He cocks an eye at my mother. 'Do you have writing things, ma'am?'

Mesmerised, my mother gets him the pad on which she writes letters to my dada. Her eyes are wide with amazement that such a man should write. With much puffing and sighing the tar-paper man writes down a name and an address, then tears the sheet with a flourish and thrusts it at me. 'There! Get to see Horatio Plummer and mention the name of Euan Barra. He will give you bed and board and fine cheer. A man against the world, is Horatio.'

I peer at the paper. The tar-paper man has a fine looping hand. The name Horatio Plummer fair gallops its way right across the page.

'Wouldn't you yourself be better there in London, Mr Barra?' says Rhys. 'Better than in that tar-paper hut being blown to death on our estuary?'

The man shrugs his great shoulders. 'This is where my demons led, or drove me.' He nods in my direction. 'There was a reason. They led me here to save the little bird. It's good to know there is a reason for things.' He stands up and our kitchen shrinks around him. 'I'll go. All this talk is very tiring. I can do without it.'

We stare at the door as it closes behind him. I look at the paper in my lap.

'Well, he's not an idiot. That's a sure thing,' says Rhys.

My mother moves behind me and smooths the hair on my head. 'And, sure, he's no lunatic. We've much to thank him for.'

That is when I notice the bright cloths and flowers; and the candle burning in the window, lit but rendered invisible in the gleam of the late afternoon sun. Something has certainly changed with me and my mother. I dare not think what this thing is, but things are certainly different.

I must be weakened by being so ill, because there are tears in my eyes. That is a rare thing.

A week later, early one Saturday evening, the tar-paper hut was burned to a crisp. The two town newspapers carried the story and a dramatic sketch of the burning hut. There was talk in the town of the impossibility of burning such a sodden place, but still it burned. They talked of the fact that the man who lived in the hut was mad as a March hare, had escaped from three asylums; that he must have had insane determination to set fire to himself in that way. The constable, poking around in the ruins, found the burned body of Mr Barra crouching over a tin box which was full of charred paper. Nothing was known of him. He had a poor funeral attended only by the Irishwoman, Ellis Maichin's papist wife, and two of her children.

The day after the funeral, the postman brought Rose Clare a letter from her sister Roisin saying that Rose Clare's husband Ellis had embarked for England. She and Dreena had scraped together the money to pay his fare home, as he was in some bother over unpaid debts and – she had to say this – the theft of a watch and silver spoons from a person who had befriended him and given him a roof over his head. He had needed a roof as she and Dreena had thrown him out of their apartment a month before.

His habit of lifting things defeated us here too, Rose Clare. Ellis has great charm but his fingers are far too light. He should be there at home with you. Without doubt he misses you. Anyway, it was send him home or

The figure at the door is hunched against the rain, collar turned high and hat pulled down hard. I think it is the tar-paper man returned from the dead. But didn't I see the cheap deal coffin? Didn't I throw soil on it myself in the bleak cemetery? Now the world wells in on me in waves and I am obliged to hold on to the door-jamb to stop myself falling to the floor.

'Who is it?' My mother's voice comes from behind me and I am thrust to one side, right on to the floor, as she moves towards the newcomer and falls into his arms, touching his greying hair and his thin shoulders and saying quietly, 'Ellis, Ellis, sure there is none of you left. You are all chipped away. Not a picking on you.'

She pulls him in out of the rain and clashes the door behind him. He takes his hat from his head and my mother takes his wet coat from him and he is nothing at all like the tar-paper man. He keeps an arm round my mother and his eyes, bright as night lanterns, survey us all. 'And this must be . . . is . . . Edward, Caspar, Rhys?' He shakes the boys heartily by the hand. 'They are men, look you. I have fathered a breed of fine men. And where is my letter-writer, my little dreamer?'

Rhys helps me to my feet. 'She fainted,' he says. 'She's not been too well, Dada.'

From the shelter of Rhys's arm I examine this short man with his thin cheeks, his large clean-shaven face and his curly grey-black hair. I am nearly as tall as he is. 'I thought you were the tar-paper man. But I see you are not.'

He leaves my mother, takes my hands and pulls me towards him. 'Tar-paper man? Now who's this tar-paper man?'

'An old tramp Theo took up with,' says Edward, his nostrils flaring as though he can smell the old man even now. 'Just an old tramp.' His eyes meet mine and I shiver. Does he hate the old man so much, just because he saved me? Or would he have hated him anyway, dirty, old and smelly as he was?'

'He died. Set fire to himself,' says Caspar. 'Mad as a rabid dog. Good riddance.'

Edward is silent on this, allowing Caspar to say the bad words for him.

I look up at my father. 'Mam and Rhys and I went to his funeral.'

'For respect,' Rose Clare murmurs. Her face is smiling, smiling into his. He still holds me by the hands and shakes me gently.

'Well, dreamer, I am not a tramp. I'm your own dada in flesh and blood.' Then he does something very strange. He raises both my hands to his lips and kisses them. I've seen this in pictures, in some old books, but have never known it in the flesh. My mother, my brothers, they rarely ever touch me in affection. Now he even puts up a hand to push the loose curls away from my face. 'You are beautiful like your mother,' he says.

My mother is smiling broadly; the hard lines have melted from her face. He is right about her beauty. I pull back away from him, nervous at this tender magic, this transforming touch: another thing I have never known. He laughs, drops my hand and moves towards the hearth.

'Now, let me see the fire! There are no fires in the world like a fire of fine Welsh coal.' As he says this I feel I can put out my hands and warm them on him. No wonder he escaped from my nain's cold house as soon as he could.

When my father is thoroughly and noisily warmed we all sit round the table. We look at him, and he looks at us. It is as though he is famished for the sight of us. He holds my mother's hand openly in his and she squeezes his fingers hard. He lights a small cigar. 'Caspar, give me a light from the fire, will you? And, Rhys,' he says, 'look in my carpet bag there, move the books to one side and you'll find a bottle of fine port. A gentleman on the boat . . . er . . . left it behind, and I thought it should not go to waste.'

Rhys pulls the bottle out and sets it at the centre of the table. Silence falls and we look at the bottle, gleaming like a dark jewel in the leaping light of the fire.

'Now then, Rose Clare, you get the glasses and I'll do the honours. We will drink a toast to our family, together again.'

My mother lines up the glasses.

'I can't drink this, Dada,' says Edward stiffly.

'Nor I,' says Caspar quickly.

'Why not?' My father lifts his brow.

'We have signed the pledge,' says Edward. 'Caspar and I . . .'

'What? You can't drink the health of your own da after seven years?'

'I will drink it in water,' says Edward.

'In water,' nods Caspar.

My father roars with laughter at this. 'Wine, my boy! Wine is a living thing! It has the spark of life in its rosy depths. Water is a dead thing. You cannot drink the health of a man in water.'

'Wine is the first step on the road to ruin. The Bible forbids it.' Edward's voice is husky with pure temper.

'The Bible? A fine book. A great book. Read closer, my son. You will read in there about the marriage at Cana. At this wedding our Lord Jesus changed the water into wine. He gave it its spark of life. And then I have no doubt that He went on to toast the health of the bride and groom. Now, Jesus couldn't do that if He forbade us wine, could He?' My father laughs in delight at the thought and my mother chuckles with him.

Edward scowls and stands up. 'I'm not staying here to—'

My father puts a hand on his arm. 'Not so serious, boy.'

Edward shakes off the restraining fingers. 'It's a serious

39

matter, Father, a matter of true conscience.'

'Will you not drink your father's health, son?'

'Get thee behind me, Satan.'

My father chuckles and my mother smiles again. Even my lips twitch. Edward looks younger, smaller. Not boss of the household at all. My grin must have got to him, because he charges past me like a bull and is out of the door in a second and we watch him hare past the window up the street. Caspar makes to go after him but my father puts a restraining hand on his arm. 'Steady, boy. You stay here and drink your father's health.'

And Caspar does. We all do.

Two glasses of this stuff and we go to bed early, not waiting up for Edward. I have to sleep in the cupboard-bed in the parlour because my father will take my place in my mother's bed tonight. I hear the murmur of their urgent chat and laughter above me as I toss and turn on the lumpy mattress. I listen for Edward all night, but I must have dropped off because I did not hear him come in.

Four

The Preacher

Thomas Maichin put down his book and looked over his glasses at his wife, who was on her knees rubbing vigorously at a steel fender which already glowed like burnished silver. When he had made that fender in the forge at the ironworks, he and Bethany had been married one year. 'Happy, is it, Bethany?'

She knelt back on her heels and looked up at him. 'Me? Now why would you say that?'

'To have the boy living under your roof now.'

She regarded him thoughtfully. 'Do you say that, Thomas, because you yourself are content for him to be here?' The word *happy*, such a messy, sprawling word, never crossed her lips.

His eye returned to his book. 'Content. Yes. Content. Hasn't the boy much studying to do? And prayer. Better to do it here than in the house of the Irishwoman.'

She returned to her rubbing. 'There's extra work in the house, of course. The dirt he brings in from the pit. It is quite a trial.'

'The boy gives you money for his keep, Bethany. There is naught against you getting a girl from roundabout to help you. Mr Selwyn Jones at the chapel is injured from the pit and has

41

four daughters on his hands. Two shillings a week and he'd jump at the chance. It would be a great help there. They are needy, that family.'

'We . . . ell, I suppose I could train her to be clean and proper. A lifetime's advantage for her. It would be a favour to Mr Selwyn Jones.'

'So it would.'

Bethany was indeed content. For years she had wanted Ellis's sons under her roof. Now Edward had flown the Irishwoman's coop and was with her here in her house. Her thoughts moved on to her son Ellis. She had managed to keep that one at home until he was thirty. Then he had met the Irishwoman – a mere girl then – out in Ireland, and she had taken him away, with a whirl of that red petticoat of hers.

Bethany had just finished the fender and was sitting on the wooden settle with a basket of Edward's socks and her darning mushroom when there was a rattle at the door and her son Ellis strode in, his shape a dark mask against the precious light from the window.

Ellis placed his hat carefully on the polished sideboard. 'Father, Mother,' he said, shaking his father's hand vigorously and then waiting impatiently for his mother to put down her darning mushroom so that he could shake her hand. It felt slight and papery in his and she used it now to make him keep a certain distance.

They stood looking at each other.

'Home again, boy?' said his father, finally subsiding back on to his seat. No one mentioned the fact that Ellis had been back in his home town for five days now. This was the first time he had been near them. He was ever the coward.

Bethany too sat down and picked up her darning. 'Back for good, then, are we?' She rethreaded her needle.

'Back for good,' he agreed heartily. 'I've been down to Henderson's Grain Merchants and they have a vacancy for

42

a clerk. I am to start on Monday.'

They did not speak of Ellis's hurried departure seven years before. There was no mention of the rumours of unfilled orders and missing money at the coal company.

Ellis moved to stand with his back to the fire, lifting his coat tails to allow its faint heat to billow up the back of his shirt to the nape of his neck. He had forgotten how chilly his mother's house was. 'I see young Edward has found bed and board with you.'

'That is so,' said Thomas.

'There is not a reason in the world for him to leave his own hearth. His own home.'

'He wishes to live his life by Christian rules.' For Thomas, who could stand at a pulpit and bring the wrath of heaven down on whole congregations, this was the nearest he could get to expressing his personal outrage at the sight of his grandson weeping bitter tears as he told of his father's insistence that he should break his holy pledge of abstinence.

'Edward can live such a life in his own home, with his own family. That was simply teasing about the port wine. He should have stood up to me. His faith should withstand such faint assault.'

'His faith is a citadel. As is mine,' growled Thomas.

Bethany looked at Ellis. 'Perhaps the boy feels that now you are returned he can lay down his burden. He has been sorely tried in these years. Responsibility for his sister and brothers. Your family, I remind you. It is time to pay attention to his own immortal soul.' Bethany clamped her mouth closed again and wove her pattern in the sock heel.

'Sorely tried?'

'You may ask the Irish— ask your wife.' She was pleased at her own Christian restraint in not mentioning the Irishwoman's known drinking, nor that of the youngest boy, Rhys, who reflected in many ways his mother's lush excess, nor the wildness of the girl who had nearly died from her mother's neglect.

Thomas coughed. 'You will be pleased to know the miners at the chapel say that young Edward is much respected at the pit.'

'That's very good. Such respect is hard won.' Ellis patted the pocket which held his beloved cigars, but resisted the temptation; yet another appetite to be denied in this self-denying house. An image rose unbidden to his mind of his parents' bedroom: a small space with two great beds, immaculately made with white linen. Between the beds shone two clear feet of cold linoleum, a true barrier against venal appetites. He thought then of Rose Clare's white body lying back, clasping the brass bedrail, luxuriating in his attention.

'Did you hear what I said, Ellis?'

What had she said? His gaze swung to his mother, sitting now on her low bench, her hands busy.

'Edward is making a great offering of service at the chapel. One day he will be as great a preacher as your father. Famous throughout Wales.'

'Vanity, Bethany, vanity!' growled Thomas.

'Everyone says so,' she said firmly. 'They consider him for the list, and there have been requests from other chapels to hear him speak.'

'Good, good. This is great news,' said Ellis, trying to stem the eulogistic tide. Such virtuous fame, he knew, had been his mother's ambition for himself.

'So,' said his mother triumphantly, 'it is very convenient for him, being here, being able to study at the same table as his grandfather.'

Ellis shrugged, giving up. 'Well, as you say . . .'

Bethany rolled two socks neatly together and put them up to join a line on the table. 'And how is young Theodora?'

'She is well. Her head is always in a book, her pen in her

hands. Like Edward she is very quick.'

His parents eyed him silently. Then Bethany said, 'There is a great difference. For him the reading will be his fate, his vocation. For her it keeps her from her proper tasks, her head in the clouds like that.' She heaved a great sigh. Ellis too, to their great disappointment, had spent most of his life with his head in some kind of cloud. Or under one.

Ellis coughed again. 'Rose Clare tells me you took care of the child most tenderly when she was ill. For that I thank you.'

'She nearly died three times. You would have sworn she was dead.'

'Again I thank you, Mother.'

'It was God's will. A judgement, some would say. The child has too much time on her hands. She is too clever. The town school could teach her nothing . . .'

Ellis fought back the powerful desire to strike his own mother. 'Well, God will be pleased that I've found work for her.'

Bethany put aside the concern about God's name being taken in vain. 'Work? She is only twelve.'

'She has the brains of a sixteen-year-old, even if she does not have the stature. There is a new periodical, *Tidal Review*, it's called. I went to see the editor, see? Took some of her letters to show him. The child is a fine writer. She starts at the *Review* on Monday. Clerical stuff.'

'A newspaper, Ellis, I don't think . . . Look, your father says I should get a girl to help me here in the house, pay her money. Why should not Theodora . . .?'

Ellis looked round the pale scrubbed kitchen where in his thirty years of living in this house he had always felt like a rather soiled intruder. Time for some truth. 'The child is very clever, Mother. She has a brain, more so than the boys, even Edward, for his brain is a stiff unbending thing. She has a brain. If you have a brain you have no need to soil your hands,' he finished contemptuously.

Bethany glanced furiously at Thomas, who moved his hand silently to stop her saying that Ellis's cleverness, his brain, had made him see round the corners of the truth so many times and had made him a liar, a thief, a runaway. 'It will do the child good to turn her hand to her own kind of plough,' said Thomas simply. 'We wish her well.'

'I suppose the devil does make use of idle hands,' said Bethany, spreading her own small neat hands before her, admiring their even tapering spread. Then she folded them in her lap and let the silence fill the very corners of the room.

At last Thomas spoke. 'Edward is speaking at the special foundation service the Sunday after next. Six o'clock,' he said. 'You should come to hear him, Ellis.'

'Yes, well, perhaps . . .' Ellis felt himself dismissed. Forty-eight years old and still in some kind of supplication to his cold parents. He picked up his hat. 'Well, goodbye, then. Goodbye to you both.'

His mother stood up and his father carefully placed his wire-rimmed glasses on his nose and fingered his book. 'God bless you, son,' he said.

Outside the house with two bay windows Ellis let out a very long sigh, pulled out a cigar and lit it, then started to walk up the hill. The sun was warming the air after the recent rain and in the distance white foam danced on the tide as it made its inexorable way up the estuary. His heart joined for a second with that ancient traveller, Madoc, setting out in his ship for an unknown country far to the west, leaping aboard with delight at the chance to leave this cold, inhospitable land.

It was quite a shock to find that I had a *proper* job. It seems my father talked to the owner of the *Tidal Review*, a Mr Wainwright. He didn't know him, you understand. Just walked into his office bold as ten monkeys and got me this job. Came home and told me I had to pretend I was thirteen. I was to start on Monday. I was to start at ten in the morning and finish when the office closed, which might be nine at night or even later. Dinner and tea, to be taken alone in my cubbyhole, are included.

I was really angry when Dada said he had shown Mr Wainwright my letters. He just shrugged and said they were a vital tool in persuading Mr Wainwright into giving me this job. He also said my mother was worried about me, thought I had too much time on my hands. Or too much time on my brain. 'Time on the brain is very dangerous,' he said, pinching my cheek. 'The soul goes very sour when there is too much time on a person's brain.'

I've never actually seen Mr Wainwright. According to Mr Gregg, the fussy womanish sort of man who runs the office for him, I am to copy the advertisements in a fair hand into a big ledger and run any errands as required. I can also, in any spare minutes, learn how to use one of the two typewriting machines in the office. There are lots of spare minutes, and there is paper galore to write on. So I type my stories and I put the sheets under my coat to bring them home.

My father bought me a fine new black dress and new shoes with brass buckles. My mother sat up at night and crocheted three different lace collars for the dress and showed me how to put up my hair. This involved a crucifixion of pins but looking at myself in the mirror I know I look older. Fourteen at least. So the lie about being thirteen is not too much of a worry.

The work is easy enough, and after your twentieth piece of copy advertising for a general maid, or the sale of a twelve-piece dining set, or for pills which are the ultimate answer to dyspepsia, I find I can write them blindfold. What I like best are the errands I am sent on. It might be outside into Church

47

Street to buy pies and cakes for some of the clerks. Or down to the railway station to pick up parcels. Or, laden with sheaves and folders, across to the print shops where I have to endure stares and rude comments from the operators.

The pleasure I had not anticipated was the pride I feel when I see words I have copied in print in the paper. Sometimes I alter the copy that comes in scrawled on bits of paper. I make the phrases run smoother, sound nicer. Of course, these are only advertisements, but it makes me read the other articles with an eye to how they could be better.

Sometimes one of the reporters, a Scotsman called Murgatroyd, has too much to drink, and gives me pages and pages of scrawl to make sense of, and to copy in my neat hand. Then he checks them. Then I typewrite them. He never objects to any of my alterations and I have special pride when I see these articles in the paper.

The worst thing is the exhaustion. Each night I plod home and, only stopping to strip off my clothes, fall on the cupboard-bed in the parlour and am asleep in a second. With the exception of Saturday afternoons and Sundays there is no time to go down to the salt marsh, no time for pebbles and shells or the songs of the marsh birds.

Through a mist of exhaustion I am barely conscious of the others coming and going in the household. Mother and Father spend all their time wrapped round each other and the boys are very noisy. The house is so much noisier since Edward went to live with Nain. Still, I take little notice of my brothers or my parents. They are distant puppets in my play. Yet even at this distance I know my mother is happier than I have ever known her, and for the first time Caspar and Rhys are friends with each other. I hear them sometimes, singing as they come in from the public house. Caspar is a fickle creature when you think of it. All for Edward one minute, snuggling up to Rhys the next.

Edward had been very chilly with Caspar for not joining him at their grandparents' house. In the colliery cage and as they passed each other underground, he looked through his younger brothers as though they were made of glass. On his first day at work after he went to live with his grandfather he saw the overman to ensure he would no longer have to work side by side with his brother. Caspar hid his hurt and fixed up to work with Rhys and his mates. The overman tolerated these adjustments. The bond between men who worked closely together was crucial to the safety of any pit. It had to be congenial. In his youth he had seen proximity and temper lead to a death underground more than once, and he vowed never to risk that again.

These days Caspar walked to and from the pit with Rhys. They were often joined by Rhys's master, the joiner, Owen Charles. 'Two of you fallen out with the brother this time, I see?' said the old man one day. Edward had just stalked past them as they plodded on their way home, clogs sparking on the stone road.

'Caspar's been tried and found wanting, Mr Charles,' said Rhys gravely. 'Fallen by the wayside, I fear.'

'Fallen, has he?'

'He signed the pledge and from the minute our father came home he's been drinking like a fish.'

'It's all so much mumbo jumbo, if you ask me. Edward is obsessed.' Caspar's voice was surly. Sometimes Caspar cursed his father for obliging him to drink that first drink. Even as the port gurgled down his throat, making his jaw ache with its tart sweetness, he knew that he and Edward were finished. He was a great one, was Edward, but he was very unforgiving.

'Oh, it's a stony path, that "Way Called Straight",' said Mr Charles, puffing on his pipe. 'Too hard for my old feet, look you.'

That same day Bethany was out when Edward arrived at his grandparents' house. Bethany's new helper, Ellen Jones, daughter to Selwyn Jones, was setting the table. The girl eyed Edward frankly, her slightly protuberant eyes wide open and bold. 'Good afternoon to you, Edward. Your nain is at the women's witness meeting. She told me to set a jug of water to fill from the hot tap for your wash, and your clean things laid on your . . . in your room upstairs.'

'*Bed*, Ellen, bed! Can't you say the word?' He watched her closely.

She raised her chin at him. 'Bed. Bed! I'll say it nineteen times for you if you want.' She could smell the gritty coal-scent of him as he brushed past her to pick up the jug from the hearth. He took it to the pantry and she could hear it gurgle into the dish. He reappeared and flicked the jug across at her. She lunged and managed to catch it safely. 'Fill that half hot, half cold, look you. Then you can come in here an' rinse my hair for me. There was a fall in the seam and my hair's full of dust.'

She filled the jug slowly, carefully, listening to him snorting and spluttering in the scullery. She carried the jug through and he looked up sideways at her through soap-ringed eyes. 'Now then, Ellen, if I bend lower you can pour it, slow, look you, and rinse off these suds.'

He kept his face towards her and as she lifted her arm to pour, she was aware of his eyes on her breasts and her underarm where she knew her dress was torn. 'Slower, slower, stupid girl,' he said. 'There, you've splashed the water. Wasted it! We'll need more now. Go and get another jug, there's a good girl. You can rinse it again. Won't that be nice?'

'I'd like you to come to the chapel and hear him. He is our son after all.' Ellis Maichin pressed his wife's arm.

Rose Clare shook her head stubbornly. 'I will not set foot in that place. You know what they did . . .'

When Ellis had run off to America she had gone just once to chapel with the boys, Theodora straddling her hip. On that occasion some of the congregation had hissed her until finally, red-faced and hauling young Theodora behind her, she had crept away in tears.

'It's a chance to see young Edward doing what he's good at. Don't you miss the boy?'

She looked at him carefully then she shook her head. 'No. I'll be honest, Ellis. I love him. Sure, don't I love them all? But Edward's such a hard, unfeeling boy. In the last years it was like living with a combination of your mother and father rolled into one.'

Ellis smiled slightly at this. 'Heaven forfend. Well, will you mind if I take the boys to hear him, and young Theodora? He is their brother.'

She shook her head. 'How can I mind?'

'They should know their brother, see him at his best. They have their difficulties with him. So why not see him doing what he can do well,' said Ellis firmly.

'Yes. You're right, I suppose.' For a moment Rose Clare wished they lived in another place: Dublin; London, perhaps. Anywhere but this place which was infused with the parched spirits of Thomas and Bethany Maichin.

The next night Ellis came home from work laden with parcels. He unpacked a new dress for Theodora and new suits for Rhys and Caspar; an engraved bracelet for Theo and watches with chains for the boys.

Rose Clare frowned at him as he made a ceremony of presenting the gifts to their children. 'Don't you think your children will look very fine in chapel, Rose Clare? No one to touch them.'

'Yes, oh yes! But Ellis, the money . . .'

51

He winked at her. 'Just a little I saved from America, *cariad*. It's worth it to see them like this, don't you think? Show that lot at the chapel, won't it?'

She nodded, not wanting to spoil the pleasure of the moment by reminding him that he had had no money when he came back from America. Hadn't her own sisters to pay his fare?

The chapel was packed to the doors: women with their bonnets set gently on neatly brushed hair, men with their Sunday hats tucked under their seats. The air smelled of lavender, nutmeg and dust, tobacco, soap and sweat, topped off with just a touch of the odour of sanctity.

Ellis led his family down the aisle so they could sit almost in the centre of the chapel. From here they had a clear view of the wide apron platform and the high central pulpit. Three rows in front of them, also at the centre, they could see their grandfather's massive head and silver hair and the neat black bonnet of their grandmother. Beside them, his blond hair gleaming, his back very straight, sat Edward.

In minutes the chapel was so full that extra chairs had to be placed in the side aisles. Ellis and Caspar sang the first two hymns heartily, word perfect. Rhys and Theo had more trouble with the words and settled for opening and closing their mouths appropriately. Their voices were not missed; the very rafters shivered with the swell of fine voices in robust, joyful unison.

The last note died away and a restrained whisper of anticipation went round the hall as Edward, tall and slender in a new black suit, heartbreakingly handsome with his fair hair wetted and combed to one side, mounted the twelve steps up to the rostrum. He settled his Bible and his notes on the lectern, then made the congregation wait while he looked all round the chapel, up into the gallery and back down to survey them all. His glance passed over his own family without a flicker of recognition.

He opened his Bible at a marked place and read with quiet clarity. "'And when his brethren saw that their father loved him more than all his brethren, they hated him . . .'" Edward turned to another page. "'And He said, Behold, I have dreamed a dream more; and, behold, the sun and the moon and the eleven stars made obeisance to me . . . and his father rebuked him . . . Shall I and thy mother and thy brethren indeed come to bow down ourselves to thee . . .?'"

There was a rustling of satisfaction and anticipation in the pews below him. Ellis folded his arms across his chest. Caspar leaned across Theo to whisper into Rhys's ear: 'Cheek of the devil, that one.'

Our Edward goes on and on and on. My father, arms folded across his chest, is all attention beside me. At first even I, who hate Edward, am mesmerised, as are the hundreds of others, some of whom are moved to shout *Amen!* or *Hallelujah!* when he is in mid-sentence. I think how graceful his voice is; how, standing up there in the high pulpit, he has the beauty of an angel. But he does go on. My head finally jerks forward and I have to stop myself from going to sleep. I have not slept enough yet to mop up the exhaustion of my working week.

Caspar leans his heavy weight across me to whisper again to Rhys. 'The old hypocrite,' he says. 'Not so holy when he sets fire to the old man's hut.'

'What?' says Rhys, in a normal voice.

'Ssh! Ssh!' The hushes come from all round us, and on his pulpit, Edward glares at us, then starts again about the blood of the Lamb cleansing us all, but only when we admit our faults and come to His bosom.

At last the sermon comes to an end and there are nods of

satisfaction and a rustle just short of applause before we stand for a final hymn, the shuffling feet and the swelling voices giving some ease to the bodies and souls held fast by Edward's voice over the last two hours.

With the rest of the milling crowd we stand in the vast panelled entrance to the chapel. My nain glides towards us. 'You will be proud of your son, Ellis,' she says to my father.

'Ah, Mother.' His voice is smooth as cream. 'I wouldn't dream of that. Isn't pride one of the deadly sins?'

I want to clap my hands, shout Hallelujah! But I don't.

She turns her attention to me. 'Now, then, Theo. Are you working hard, child? Keeping away from that long tide?'

I nod. 'Not much time for play now, Nain.'

'Good.' She nods too, her eyes fixing on mine far too long before she goes across to join Granda.

Then Edward comes towards us, the crowd parting like the Red Sea before him. He shakes hands with my father, but barely flickers a glance towards the rest of us.

'Very impressive, Edward,' says my father. 'You learn a great deal from your granda. You must have worked hard at your Bible.'

Edward shrugs. 'It comes quicker every time.'

'You are happy at your grandparents' house?' says my father.

'Never better.' Edward's glance darts past Father to a gaggle of visiting ministers who were coming through the ornate double doors. 'Ah, I need to speak to Mr Askew . . .' and he is gone.

Caspar, ignored, looks after him.

'Come on,' says Dada quietly. 'Your mother will be waiting.'

Out in the road, I turn to Caspar. 'What was it you said about Edward and the hut?'

Caspar shrugs. 'The tar-paper hut? That old holier-than-thou preacher of a brother of ours set fire to that old hut. Two, three months ago. A big can of paraffin oil. Burned like tinder. Tar paper, see? Just before you came home, Dada. No one took any notice, see? Just an old hut burning down.'

My cheeks get hot. I thought I knew what had happened to the tar-paper man. The story was he had burned it by accident and perished in the ashes. For days after the burning I awoke to the memory of how the tar-paper man had cut my bonds and lifted me up the beach. Then in time the memory of the tar-paper man slipped from me. Now it is before me again. I can smell the seaweed.

'That can't be true,' says my father, his brow furrowed. 'Burned it down?'

'I was there. Edward made me keep watch. He didn't know the old man was in it. He said he was in the town.' He pauses. 'I don't think he knew. Said burning the old hut would get rid of the old nuisance. Make him go away.'

I look my father in the eyes. 'The old man. He was the one . . . When I nearly died in the water, you know? The old man saved me from the tide. We must do something. What can we do?'

He looks at me for a long time, then shrugs. 'There's nothing we can do now.'

'We should tell people,' says Rhys. 'All those people in there who think he's John the Baptist for a start.'

My father shakes his head. 'That will do no good. Caspar here says it happened months ago.'

'We should get the constable,' I say. 'He . . . the tar-paper man died because of Edward.'

'The police?' A shadow falls on my father's face. 'Not the police. I couldn't . . . Wouldn't that get Caspar here in trouble too?'

I pull my hand out of his. 'Then we can do nothing?'

He shakes his head. 'No. But don't you worry, *cariad*.

55

That God of his will sort him out.'

'God?' says Rhys scornfully. 'He doesn't believe in all that. Hypocrite, that's what he is.'

'Nevertheless. You wait, something will happen,' says my father, grasping my hand again and striding on, back up the hill to our house. 'Something will happen. You watch.'

Bethany whipped the cloth from her parlour table to reveal a very fine Sunday supper. As no work was ever done on the Sabbath in this house, the feast had been prepared on Saturday by herself and her new little maid Ellen Jones, who was proving helpful despite her slack appearance and her rolling eyes.

Bethany smiled at the murmur of men's voices which penetrated the wall between the kitchen and the parlour. Edward was in there standing at his grandfather's shoulder receiving with appropriate modesty the praise being heaped on him by the chapel elders.

She opened the door. 'There is supper for you. You will help yourselves, gentlemen.'

The men bustled in, continuing their discourse as they came. Edward sat on his grandfather's right hand. There was a short pause while Edward said grace. Then the talk went on and the men ignored Bethany and Ellen as they poured water into the waiting glasses and handed round savoury tarts.

Bethany had to rescue young Ellen when she overfilled Edward's glass and dripped water on to the trousers of his new suit. Edward, with some justification, was rather brisk with the girl and she burst into tears, and had to be pacified with two queen cakes and sent home with a bag of them for her mother and her sisters.

Five

Writing for Mr Murgatroyd

It's hard to realise that it's almost five whole years since my father came home to us from America. In this time you might say our lives have been quite steady. It is during this period I realise just how my mother is besotted with my father and he with her. Twice, though, there has been the problem of a baby which she subsequently 'lost'. What a strange way to put it. As though such flesh and blood creatures were handkerchiefs or gloves. My mother 'lost' three children before she had me. After that, of course, there was my little seal sister slipping away before she could come to life alongside me. As I was to find out, she was 'lost' too.

Of course, these events, these new 'losses' since my father has been back, have been fraught with a great suppressed worry: a worry that was in the air rather than in their faces. The air lightened considerably, became breathable, at the point where these two latest little souls were 'lost'. Naturally they were not discussed at all in the house. I only knew the terrible detail because I was at hand on both occasions and was obliged to help my mother clean up the mess. In her relief at this, however, my mother finally told me about the little seal sister.

'So what was she like, Mam, this other baby?'

'Like?' She stops her scrubbing and frowns. *'Well, she had*

no . . . She had kind of fins. She was like a little seal tucked in there just behind you.'

So I have this shadow alongside me. Perhaps I have my seal sister's memory as well, which is why my memory is so good. And her imagination, so I can dream her ration of dreams. Perhaps as well as this she is my friend, to talk to in my head, so that I have not the need of fleshly friends.

Yes, apart from this tension there has been harmony in the house. My mother no longer reaches for her bottles of fruit wine. Still, she is absent from us in another fashion. She notices little around here now apart from my father. On the occasions when her eye drops on me she is tolerant enough – much more than ever before. Perhaps, being so preoccupied with my work, I am not so much the tiresome creature I was.

I still work at the *Tidal Review* for six days each week. On Saturday afternoons and Sundays I walk the edge of the estuary, watch the birds and the sky and the boats rocking in the harbour. Of course I don't play down there any more. I'm no longer a child. I'd say the only time I really play is when I shut myself in the front parlour and read *Household Words* and *Sylvia's Home Journal*, filched from the newspaper office. Sometimes I write stories about this young girl who rescues her family from Titans with the help of the god Hermes.

They still laugh at my scribbling but in the main they leave me alone. I have a box of typewritten sheets under my bed now, which my mother must see when she sweeps, but she never mentions them. My father in particular is very tolerant, and calls me his little scholar and acts very put out when I won't let him read my current story.

Caspar is blossoming tall and strong but follows Rhys's lead in everything, just as he used to follow Edward. He is a limpet, is Caspar. Now he has stuck himself to Rhys. And Rhys is such a mischief, so they are often in trouble. They have both grown straggly moustaches but Caspar's attempts to grow a beard are singular failures. The boys continue working at the pit although at present the pit is on short time; many men have been laid off.

We see little of Edward. Now and then I catch sight of his blond head at this end of the town. Once I saw him loitering outside the office of the *Tidal Review*. I ran down to catch him up but he got away. My father goes to the chapel and hears him preach. He comes back singing his son's praises, ever the proud father. The rest of us are somewhat uncomfortable at this, but hear him out. Once every couple of months, my father drags us with him to the chapel and then on to my nain's for tea. Here we have to endure Edward's false modesty about his talents and his airy patronage. More than once Rhys has mimed vomiting behind Edward's back which makes me chuckle. This earns me an offended glare from Edward and a rebuke from my nain, who clearly thinks that in Edward she is witnessing the Second Coming. She reads his sermons over and over again. She has more time now as there is a woman who comes in to do the housework. Funny, that, to think of a working man with a maid. But when you think of it, a few shillings a week is easily spared in that abstemious household. According to my father, Nain talks of saving to send Edward to college.

I've been working steadily at the *Tidal Review*. I write most of Mr Murgatroyd's articles now, from notes he has scrawled on scraps of paper. We have an arrangement: he gives me a shilling for every piece I do, as long as I tell no one that I write for him. There is no way I could claim publicly to write them myself. Mr Gregg would dismiss me if it were openly acknowledged that Mr Murgatroyd's pieces were my work.

In the early days I read the pieces out to Mr Murgatroyd and he would shout and knock his stick on the floor when I missed something, or got the balance or the tone wrong.

Now he just leaves me to it and returns even more regularly

to the Wellington Hotel where he holds court with other tall-hatted layabouts in love with the whisky bottle and the deck of cards. Occasionally I visit him there with a note from Mr Gregg about some court case he must attend, or some story he must follow. He is often too drunk to grasp what I'm saying, so I attend to the matter myself and write his article without reference to him. I do them on the typewriting machine, and only return to him for his signature.

The court stories are easy enough. You just need a word-by-word account with an introduction and a conclusion. The other municipal events – the meetings, openings, closings and speeches – are written to an easy formula anyway. Then there are the dramas which can be written as stories, like the accident where a child fell off the railway bridge into the path of the train, or the battle almost to the death between two women over the use of a washing line.

As a journalist Mr Murgatroyd is a fading star, but as an apprentice master he is a great success.

Ellen Jones had two secrets which she hugged to herself like favourite dolls. Ellen was something of an expert on secrets. Secrets were meant to be stored away at the back of your mind. Secrets should not feather the sluggish, oil-smooth surface of life inside a person's family. Showing your thoughts and feelings was against the rules; all except, of course, thoughts and feelings about joy in the Lord. It need be no secret that you were moved to passionate feeling by a man standing on high, dressed all in black, waving a black leather-bound book about like a flail, with which he would sort out the wheat and the chaff. And if you knew you were the *wheat* you shouted out *Hallelujah* and you were saved. You could even faint clean away, entirely drowned by emotion.

This was permitted, and need not be done in secret.

Ellen had never been heard to shout *Hallelujah* within the

four walls of the dark house which she shared with her three sisters and her mother and father. The joyful surge of *Hallelujah* had been called for even less since her father lost his job on the closure of his seam. Since that black day her family had been compelled to accept the well-meaning help of neighbours, and submit to the humiliation of moving to an unoccupied house where the rent man never came.

But now Ellen had proof that every cloud could have a silver lining. One source of this neighbourly chapel charity led Ellen to skivvying in the house of the lay preacher Thomas Maichin. This job gave Ellen her first great personal secret: that she could utter great cries of *Hallelujah* in the scullery, on the staircase, on the landing of Thomas Maichin's house as she fainted with emotion under the attention of the young preacher, Edward Maichin, whose flail was flesh, rather than bound in black leather.

He liked to tie you while it all happened, did Edward. But he let you go when you said sorry for being *the evil temptress*. He liked his games, did Edward, but then he was a man after all.

This was the first great secret which sent Ellen skipping to work each dark morning.

The second secret was the stopping of Ellen's monthly 'show'. In the close confines of the Joneses' house, the girls' menstruation, which happened within days of each other every month, were unmentioned events. The white rags were washed overnight and dried inside the fireside oven, a territory unfamiliar to Mr Jones, their father.

For the last two months Ellen's own participation in the female ritual had been a charade. Her unsoiled rags were washed in the usual fashion each time. But her sister Molly, who shared a single bed with her, had become uneasy, suspicious. The rhythms of her sister Ellen's life were part of Molly's own intimate knowledge of the world. It was not just

61

the washing of spotless rags; the subtle smells and humours of her sister had been striking a wrong chord.

Ellen kept this secret from Edward at first. When she did tell him she was relieved when, after the shadow of shock passed over his face, Edward seemed quite pleased at the forthcoming baby, telling her it was to be a great event. Of course, of course they would get married! But first, first he had two really important sermons to deliver in two pit villages over the river. Then they would for sure get married, humbly ask forgiveness of the Lord and of their families. They would take the opprobrium which would, and justly, come their way and get on with their lives.

Ellen savoured this special secret. Edward Maichin. This wonderful man was hers. Tall and fair and fiery. The catch of the town. That would show all those naysayers who had her already wearing the spinster's shawl, and talked behind their hands about her rolling eyes and stick-like limbs.

The old grandmother would not be so sniffy now, nor the grandfather so distant. The Maichins had no need to be holier-than-thou! Look at Edward's mother, that Godless papist. Edward talked of the Pope as the Anti-Christ. And the father! Slippery as an eel, so they said. And the sister, the one Edward had no time for. The mad girl who wrote in the paper and went into public houses.

No, when the baby was born Ellen would be the chief woman in that family. Not the third snivelling sister. Not the skivvy in an old woman's kitchen. Edward was right. The secrets must be kept for now and she would keep them. She would tip up her three shillings a week into her mother's eager hand and wait her time.

But today, to Ellen's joy, Edward seemed to feel the need to be more open. This time he did not just want to fumble and tie, beat and pierce. 'A fine night!' he whispered when she was washing the dishes in the scullery after his tea. He would meet her by the standing stone on the marsh. They could walk and talk and think of the future.

'Edward!' His grandmother's voice came in from the parlour. 'Will you come and read this verse for me? The light is so poor from the lamp. That girl has made a mess of the trimming again.'

Back home Ellen put on her Sunday blouse in secret, pulling her shawl up to her neck to cover it. Edward had only seen her Sunday blouse from a distance; the pulpit was a very long way from the shadows in the back of the chapel where she and her sisters sat.

As Ellen made her way out through the kitchen, her mother pulled gently at the shawl to reveal the tell-tale collar, then grasped Ellen's arm in a bony fist. 'Best blouse is it, Nell?'

Ellen's face turned its characteristic, unfortunate brick-red. 'Mam, I . . .' Even at twenty-six Ellen's subservience to her mother and her father was all-embracing.

'You will be meeting Thomas Maichin's grandson. Is that it?'

Ellen kept her mouth folded. A secret is a secret.

'He should know better, that Edward Maichin. But then he is a man. A coming one too, at the chapel. And handsome, I'd say. You'd think he'd have the pick of the town. Funny that, you being . . .' She paused. 'Our Molly says . . .'

Ellen tucked her head on her chest.

Her mother's vice-like grip loosened. 'Well, I suppose it is the way of men.' Then she shook her daughter's arm, none too gently. 'But the young preacher will do what is right. Is that not the case, Nell?'

Ellen nodded, her red face stony, then she tore her arm from her mother's grasp and raced away.

Edward was there on the other side of the standing stone, staring out to sea. She ran towards him, put her arm round his unresponding shoulder. The sharp easterly wind picked its way through the space between them and whistled round the standing stone. His chin, jutting against her forehead, was icy cold. Avoiding his clear blue eyes, she spoke into his serge jacket. 'Our ma knows about this baby, Edward. I didn't betray the secret, look. It was our Molly. She senses these things. I kept the secret, I promise you.'

He stood absolutely still for several seconds and she waited for the storm to break. Then, incredibly, his body trembled as he laughed. He pushed her away from him and looked her in the eyes. 'She knows about me, then? That it is me? You must have told her.'

She rolled her eyes. 'No. Silly boy.' This was only half a lie. She did not tell, she just did not deny her mother.

She should have told him. If she had she would have been safe. She should have told him that her mother knew.

'No,' she said. 'I didn't tell her about you. I promise.'

He hugged her and kissed her hard on the mouth. She could taste the salt of the sea wind.

'Well, Ellen dearest, are you feeling warm?' he murmured.

Warm? She was feeling hot. Her heart was pounding. *Dearest?* Her face was even redder with his kisses. 'Can't you see?' she said, rolling her eyes in that way of hers.

'Well, then, I tell you what we'll do. We will sanctify our love, praise our future, under God's own skies, beside His running water.' And he pulled her with him, towards the path which led down to the estuary.

This week my usual Saturday walk down the estuary has brought me the story which will be Mr Murgatroyd's big article for Monday. The end point of my walk is always the great stone on which stood the rackety tar-paper hut. I usually walk there, lean against the stone for five, ten, twenty minutes, as long as the weather allows. I let my mind think of the tar-paper man, and of Poseidon, the god of the sea who would come rising out of the waves, his shoulders streaming with seaweed. I dream of the day I'll go to London and see that friend of the tar-paper man, Mr Horatio Plummer of Spitalfields. I still have the scrawled address safe in my ribbon box.

Then, usually after ten minutes or so of this inner musing, I return home, buffeted by the offshore winds.

But today, by this same rock, in this normally deserted place, I have come upon a cluster of people. They are standing silently in the blustery rain looking down at a shrouded figure guarded by two policemen, one of whom is without his cloak, despite the rain.

I ask the first woman I come to what has happened. 'Well, miss, seems this woman was caught by the tide coming up . . .'

The hair prickles on the back of my neck. I can smell the rank smell of the tar-paper man, see the flash of his gutting knife.

'. . . or walked into it deliberate. Not the first time down here, nor the last. The tide draws people like magnets.' The woman pulls her shawl hard round her head. Her face glistens like a shining skull in the rain. 'Easy enough, look you, to give in to the pull of the water.'

I edge nearer the policemen. I recognise the elder one. It is Sergeant Cobb, not an unfamiliar figure on my forays for Mr Murgatroyd. He knows the old journalist well, and, as a good, abstaining, chapel-going man, disapproves of him. So he is sympathetic with me for having to cope with the drunken Scotsman and recognises the open secret that the articles might just have more to do with me than with him. This fatherly sympathy has proved useful more than once.

'Who's the woman, Sergeant Cobb?' I ask.

He wipes the rain from his eyes and shakes his head. 'Hard to tell, Theodora. Been in the water a time, see? Young woman, about twenty-five, I'd say. From this place I should think. Something familiar about her.'

We look down at her. The toe of a boot, curling like weathered liquorice, has pushed its way out from her black serge shroud, which is really Sergeant Cobb's own cloak. Tied round the ankle is a lick of the hairy rope you see sometimes, down on the beach. The policeman leans down and pulls back the cloak to reveal a face, round and bloated like a pale potato. There is indeed something familiar about her.

The woman beside me gives a little moan and says, 'Sergeant, sergeant! It's Ellen Jones, look you, daughter to Mr Selwyn Jones.'

I blink and look harder. So it is. That little scuttling woman who helps my grandmother in her house. Helped her, I should say now. Her scuttling days are at an end.

There is a commotion behind us and we are hustled to one side while the undertaker's men come with their special stretcher. The way they haul the body of Ellen Jones on to the stretcher – so much puffing and blowing – you would think she were made of lead. One of her arms falls off the edge of the stretcher and they shove it back like so much meat. Then they make a big to-do about hoisting the stretcher from the ground. These men will be used to lifting broken miners on to their stretchers. This small woman cannot be so heavy. But they will have wives and daughters. Perhaps this is what makes her such a heavy burden.

We stand round watching helplessly as the undertaker's cart trundles away up off the marsh side. At last the rain has stopped and, glowing with brassy relief, the sun moves into a small patch of grey-blue sky.

I run to catch up with Sergeant Cobb as he clumps his way back up the estuary into the town. Then I make for the Wellington Hotel to find Mr Murgatroyd. I attract little interest in this dingy establishment. Normally, only women of a certain kind venture here: easy drinkers; easy in other ways as well, they say. I often think of my mother, meeting my father in my Uncle Liam's bar in Ireland and wonder whether, in the beginning, she was a woman of a certain kind.

But here at the Wellington Hotel the men see me as Mr Murgatroyd's apprentice and messenger girl; therefore worthy of a certain shred of respect. I hear only the tail-end of the swearing. I have been jostled once or twice but the regulars reprimand the jostlers and they melt away.

Today Murgatroyd's slender hands hesitate over his cards while I whisper in his ear, telling my tale of dark drama down at the salt marsh. He removes his cigar from his mouth, clears his throat and spits very accurately into the conveniently placed spittoon. 'Mother, father, husband, paramour, Miss Maichin, talk to them! Natural death? Suicide? Not the first one out there on the marsh. Or, ask yourself, is it a darker deed? Now, Miss Maichin! One thousand words precisely. Here by seven o'clock.'

You see how lucky I am in Mr Murgatroyd? Where else could I get such a training in journalism?

He replaces the cigar and looks at the other men round the table. 'Now gentlemen . . .' he says.

Bethany Maichin had her grandson Edward's meal ready the minute he came from his early shift at twelve-thirty. Early finish on Saturday. She had laid the table with a white cloth, polished silver-plated knife and fork, set them parallel with the edge of the table, and placed a cut-glass salt cellar precisely in the centre.

She waited patiently by the fire, oven cloth in hand, as Edward washed and scrubbed himself in the pantry. When he emerged the only sign of coal dust was on the inside of his eye and buried in the cuticles of his fingers. No need to mention it, the coal. She would get a nice mirror and put it in the scullery so he could see for himself. The Lord would not count such a mirror as vanity. Cleanliness was next to Godliness, after all.

She served him in silence. Potatoes, generous slices of lamb, onions and cabbage. Not too much gravy. When she had arranged the food on his plate in a neat pattern, he drew himself up straight and dropped his chin to his chest. Then his hands with their long thin fingers made a cathedral over his plate. Bethany bowed her head. As Edward extemporised a long grace, she silently thanked the Lord for blessing her with two great men to care for under her roof.

Then Edward ate his meal and Bethany sat on the settle crocheting. They talked in a desultory fashion about the chapel and the pit. She enthused about a proposal to raise funds for a chapel schoolroom. This would have great screens which would open into doors to the main chapel so it would accommodate the congregations which were enlarging every week as well as the burgeoning Sunday School.

'I don't know, Nain. There's a chance we'll see no schoolroom built at all. There's rumours flying at the pit about closure. Then people will scatter. If a hundred families move you'll need a smaller chapel, not a larger one.' He moved his empty plate slightly and she started to fill it again.

'Closure?'

'They won't put the money in. They'd need to open a new seam to win more coal. That'll need a new air shaft, new pumping gear. They won't put the money in. Fortunes made easier elsewhere.' He waited while she poured a second measure of gravy. 'I think it will happen, Nain. Give it a week. Best get out before they throw us out, I say.'

'Get out?' She was bewildered.

'Preacher in the chapel – you know? That travelling fellow, Kershaw, Cornishman, he is. He was saying they're recruiting miners for the North.'

'The North?'

'The North of England. There has been some trouble there in a couple of pits and they need new miners not contaminated by the action. There'll be work there a-plenty.'

She sat down hard on the settle. 'The North of England? But Edward! Your work is here. The chapel! You were born here. I was born here. Your grandfather was born here. And his forefathers unto the tenth, the twentieth generation. They built the castle for the English. He has told you.'

'There is work everywhere, Nain. Skilled men. And chapels.' Edward ate his dinner methodically, neatly, as was his habit. The clock ticked. Outside the gate rattled and then the sneck on the kitchen door clicked. Theodora came in, bringing in the cool air with her.

Those two look as though they're sharing some dark secret. The old woman and the young man. They share so much; light faces, light eyes, light hair. Nain's hair must have been blonde like his when she was young. I see now how beautiful she must have been all those years ago, Bethany Swift, born 1812. It says so in her old Bible.

'Well, Theodora, you're a stranger. Feeling better are you?' says Nain. She says that every time I go there these days, although it is years since I nearly died in her spare bed.

Edward takes a sidelong glance at me and attends to the residue of his dinner.

'Sit down, sit down, won't you?' Nain picks up her crochet. 'And to what do we owe the honour?'

'I've come to ask about Ellen Jones.'

Her mouth hardens to a straight line. 'Ellen Jones? Never seen a hair of her since yesterday tea. Wasn't that it, Edward? Went out just before you went for your walk?'

He grunts and places his knife and fork neatly side by side. 'Can't think so, Nain. Wasn't I straight out to the men's Friday

69

fellowship last night. Isn't it the night before you think of?'

My nain screws her eyes up at him and nods. Edward is always right in her eyes. He can do no wrong, any more than John the Baptist or St Peter can do wrong. Then for the first time he turns to look directly at me. For a second I choke on the salt tide, feel the living sea leaping round my knees. 'And why so interested in the Jones woman, Theo?'

I keep my eyes on Edward. 'There has been a death down on the marsh.' I blink. 'Not far from the tar-paper hut. You remember the tar-paper hut, Edward?'

'A death?' Nain's hands are now very still in her lap.

'Ellen Jones. She has drowned. They pulled her out this afternoon. Sergeant Cobb was puzzled why the tide hadn't swept her out. People have been overcome there by the sea and washed up hundreds of miles away before. But there was rope on her ankle. He thinks she may have been tethered. Or somehow tethered herself.'

Edward stares at me and I know he is thinking of the time when I was tied for the tide, and saved by the man in the tar-paper hut. His glance hardens and his lip curls. The silence is finally broken by Nain. 'May the good Lord have mercy on her soul.'

'Amen,' says Edward, his glance at last escaping from mine.

'Is that why you are here?' says Nain.

'I thought you might be upset. Her working here for you.'

'The young woman is with her Maker. Riding in Glory, marked by Grace. It is a reward we may all look forward to.' The soft tone of her voice belies the harshness of her words, but still they are cruel. Has she no ordinary earthly feelings for this woman who has served her faithfully in this house?

I stand up. 'Don't you care? That woman has been working here in your house for years and all you utter is sanctimonious claptrap. The pair of you! Hypocrites!'

'Theo Maichin!' The words explode from my nain's narrow mouth and Edward's chair topples over as he stands up too. He lunges at me. 'What do you think you're saying, in this house?' I dodge away from him. 'Pagan!' he thunders. 'Heathen!' and lunges after me out of the house only to bump into Sergeant Cobb who is standing outside the gate. The sergeant takes him by the arm. 'Steady, my boy. What's this, in full pursuit?'

I stand at the sergeant's elbow and look up at Edward. 'The sergeant wondered if you or Nain knew where Ellen Jones lived? I told him she worked here.'

Edward scowls at me, then looks at Nain who is standing by the back door. 'I have no idea where she lives, Sergeant, but my grandmother will. Nain?' He looks bold and straight at the sergeant, but his hand on the gate is trembling, very slightly.

She tells the sergeant the address and he strokes his pencil down his tongue and writes it into his notebook. 'Thank you, Mrs Maichin.' He salutes, turns smartly and marches down the back street, me scurrying alongside. When we turn the corner he looks down at me. 'That your brother then?'

'Yes.'

'Why was he chasing you?'

'We never got on. Always at daggers drawn.'

'I see. Families! Not the blessing they're supposed to be, if you ask me.'

The children in Carver Street tumbled around the sergeant and Theo, making a procession as they marched down the dirt road at the back of the houses. The news had preceded them. Bulky grim-faced men and flustered women were crowded in the tiny kitchen and a woman – presumably Ellen's mother – was sitting rocking backwards and forwards, an apron thrown over her head to hide her grief.

71

Mr Jones drew the sergeant through into the tiny parlour; Theo sat beside the woman and touched her hand. The woman pulled the apron from her stony face.

'I am Theodora Maichin, Mrs Jones,' said Theo. 'Granddaughter to Mrs Maichin where Ellen worked.'

The woman pulled her hand away. 'Your mother will be the Catholic.'

'My mother is wife to Ellis Maichin.' She held the woman's gaze. 'My grandmother sends her sympathy to you in your loss.'

She hadn't said any such thing, of course.

'A good woman, Mrs Bethany Maichin. The rest of them though, they'll be talking,' said Mrs Jones bitterly. 'They'll all be talking. But my Ellen would never have killed herself. Had not the reason. Even . . .'

'Even . . .?'

'It is not unknown in this town that people should be with child before they marry.'

'She was expecting?'

'Like I say, they were talking already. There will be more talk now. Yet in this row alone, eight women had their first child less than six months after they were married. No one worries about this.'

'And was Ellen about to marry?'

The wrecked face turned towards Theo. 'Seemed for a long time, look you, that she'd be a proper spinster. Unlucky in her looks, my Ellen. Too old for anyone round here. Not blessed like you. Then I knew there was someone, though she kept it a great secret. It happens to some women. As though a light goes on inside and pushes beauty through the skin. Then when I realised about the . . . expected event, I asked her about the man.' She peered at Theo for a moment, then her face closed right up. No need to blacken Ellen, or any other person. Best stay quiet. There would be a time and a place.

72

'But she wouldn't say. Then she went off last night to meet him, assuring me that marriage was in the wind.'

'So she did not take her . . . do it deliberately?'

Slowly the great head moved from side to side. 'No, no. Not my Ellen. An accident, surely.' But she sounded uncertain. Then she started to sob again and flung the apron back over her head and she was just any woman in grief.

Sergeant Cobb came back into the kitchen with Mr Jones. He looked for a second at Mrs Jones; he would get nothing out of her today. He coughed. 'My condolences to all. It will be a hard cross to bear.' Then he stared again at the draped figure of Mrs Jones, shrugged and left the room, Theo following like a pet dog.

When they had finally eluded the last of the Carver Street children she looked up at the big sergeant. 'Mrs Jones said Ellen would not have taken her own life.'

'Father says so too. Unthinkable. Religious, see? Against God.'

'Did he say too she was . . . er . . . in the family way?'

The sergeant grunted. It was hard to tell whether or not it was a laugh, or a mere noise of agreement. 'You're too young to be thinking of such things. A girl like you.'

'Don't think of me as a girl, sergeant. Think of me as Mr Murgatroyd.'

This time he did laugh out loud. 'Well, Murgatroyd, Mr Jones made no such assertion about his daughter.'

'Well, her mother said so. But she said there was no husband. He was a mystery.'

'People have killed themselves for less shame.'

'Not this girl. Not so, her mama would say. Not this one.'

I let myself into the office with my own key and typewrite my report on the machine. In the end, my article is brief. Some point about the ongoing danger of the long tide. Now another body found on the marsh, obviously drowned by the incoming tide. The mystery of why the body was not swept out. Miss Ellen Jones of Carver Street. Further reports were awaited.

It occurs to me Mr Murgatroyd would probably have written the same report about me, about my 'accident' on the marsh. If I hadn't been saved by the tar-paper man, that is. Probably Mr M. would even have been fit enough to write the report himself in those days.

I walk home very slowly, allowing certain images to meet in my head. Me tied to a post in the marsh. Edward. Ellen tied to a post in the marsh. Edward. Edward's hand trembling on the gate.

Then I peer through the window before I enter the house. I can see Edward striding about, talking hammer and tongs to Rhys and Caspar. In our house! He hasn't been here for months. I turn away, hesitate, then make my way towards my nain's house. Perhaps, without Edward there, she will say more about Ellen Jones.

But when I get there, she is in bed and my granda, all grandeur and sorrow, won't let me talk to her. 'The death of Ellen Jones has hit her hard,' he says. 'I've never seen her so shaken.'

On my way home I see Edward but we pass on opposite sides of the road. His head is down and we don't speak. I ask about Edward when I return home. 'He would tell you about Ellen? Ellen Jones?'

'Ellen?' Rhys frowned.

My mother looks up from her sewing. 'Ellen Jones?'

Caspar shook his head. 'No, he said nothing about Ellen Jones, Theo. He was on about the pit. Closures soon. Saying he knows a place where there are jobs for all of us. Up in the North of England. At us about it, he was. Insisting we go.' He frowns. 'I hear the rumours, look you. But no sign of closure yet.'

74

'So what about Ellen Jones?' said Rhys.

'You sit there. I will attend to the door.' Thomas Maichin limped to respond to the knock. Bethany was sitting huddled to the fire, a shawl round her head and shoulders, her eyes bleary with cold.

'Ah, Selwyn!' He ushered Ellen Jones's father in.

Bethany struggled to her feet. 'Mr Jones! We were grieved to know—'

'Sit down, Bethany!' commanded Thomas. 'Mrs Maichin is not well,' he told their visitor.

Mr Jones towered in the little kitchen clutching his threadbare cap. 'Take a seat, will you?' croaked Bethany.

'No, Mrs Maichin, an' you please, I'll be here but a few moments.'

Thomas remained standing and the room seemed full of men. 'So. Is there something we may do for you?'

'I'd like you to speak for our Ellen at the interment.'

Thomas nodded gravely. 'It will be my honour, Selwyn.'

Mr Jones nodded, then made to go. Then he turned back. 'There was something.'

'Yes?'

'Women get an idea in their heads . . .'

Thomas and Bethany waited expectantly.

'My wife and Molly, Ellen's sister, seemed to think our Ellen . . . well . . . she had expectations of . . . well, your Edward.'

'Expectations!' Bethany protested.

'Yes. A strange thing, isn't it? Our Ellen that was born for the spinster's fate. And your Edward, well . . . I thought so too. But then my wife and our Molly, they seemed certain. Fixed on it.'

'Grief,' said Thomas slowly. 'Grief does things to people. Don't see things right, look you.'

75

'Yes.' Mr Jones turned his greasy cap in his hand. 'There's nothing for us here. No work, anyway – and with this affair . . . every time we look at the estuary . . .'

Thomas nodded. 'Heartwrenching, it will be.'

'I could go to my brother in South Africa. Work for me and husbands for the girls, plain as they are. But . . .'

'Thomas!' said Bethany.

Thomas looked hard at him, weighing the unspoken thoughts between them. Then he said, 'I know there will be something we could do. I will help you in this.'

Mr Jones nodded. He did not offer to shake the other man's hand. Gratitude was not appropriate here. He bowed and left, banging the door behind him.

'Thomas!' said Bethany again.

'Silence, Bethany!' commanded Thomas.

When Edward came in five minutes later he found his grandparents kneeling side by side before the Bible which sat on the table.

'What's wrong?' he said. 'What has happened?'

His nain struggled to her feet. 'It's ridiculous. Mr Jones came here and—'

'Bethany!' said Thomas. 'We were praying for the repose of the soul of Ellen Jones,' he said, looking Edward straight in the face.

Edward's eyes slid away from him and sought those of his grandmother. 'Nain . . .'

That was the point when Thomas knew. 'Your grandmother needs to be in bed, Edward. She has caught a bit of a chill,' he said. 'We were just talking. The Jones family need to get right away from here, away from this tragedy. We have decided to help them.'

'Yes. We must,' said Edward. 'We must help them.'

'Mr Jones talked of South Africa. He has family there. We have some money that we were saving up . . .'

'For your college,' put in Nain.

'We must use that,' said her husband firmly.

'Yes, yes,' said Edward, putting an arm round his grandmother. 'Use that. A new start they'll have. We must help them, Granda. We must help this poor family.'

Six

Retreat

The piece of mine under Mr Murgatroyd's name in the *Tidal Review* drew forth several letters from concerned citizens regarding the treacherous marsh. To one side of this was a drawing of the salt marsh, all dark and gloomy and wonderfully atmospheric. I have the original under my bed, in a package under my box of stories.

However, the lack of profound response to the tragedy disturbs me. It seems that the death of a scrubbing woman is a three-day wonder in a town where the deaths of men, from accidents at the pit or the steelworks or on the high sea, are a monthly if not a weekly event. The occasional greed of the tide had been part of people's lives for a thousand years.

The examination of Ellen's body showed her to be pregnant. The coroner speculated that she had tied herself to the post in a last bid to save herself from the tide. Such a judgement saved her from the greater sin of suicide and would allow a respectable burial. Her father was a man of the faith, after all. She came from a good Christian family.

My grandfather preached by the graveside on the text: 'The people that walked in darkness have seen a great light: they that dwell in the land of the shadow of death, upon them hath the light shined.' Isaiah ix 2.

Ellen's mother and two of her sisters stood stony-faced, but her sister Molly moaned and shrieked, and threw herself on the coffin to be pulled off by her grim-faced father. I wanted to shout, to scream, to accuse Edward who was standing by our grandfather's shoulder looking very holy. He had one arm round my nain who, for once, seems wrong-footed by this tragedy, this unexpected death of her little maid, uncomfortable to be reminded of her own mortality perhaps. Held up by Edward, she seemed like a wraith herself. I caught Edward's eye and my mouth started to form some words but my father's hand was on my shoulder and I stayed quiet.

The rumour in the town that Ellen Jones had been going with our Edward was soon dismissed. Her own family denied it stoutly and that was reassurance enough. After all, she was an ugly old maid, and wasn't he the fine lad, the strong lad, chosen by the Lord for the message? Weren't there fine girls in the town just waiting for their chance with him?

I played with the idea of going to Sergeant Cobb to get this thing out about Edward, to tell the story right, even to mention the tar-paper man. I tried to talk about it to Mr Murgatroyd, but my talk of *a person* with suspicions of *another person* was baffling to him in his befuddled state and he reached for his beer glass and waved me away.

Then my father (who had been keeping his eye on me and knew by some intuition what was afoot) cornered me in the deserted office of the *Tidal Review* and made me blurt the truth. He listened in silence and then told me of his own dilemma: some irregularity at the grain mill, it seemed. Oh, he had put far more substance into his job than he had taken out. He was doing the work of two men, after all. But employers were crude in the way they made their calculations, that was the way of their kind. He'd fallen foul of such men more than once.

'So, Theo, if they come chasing after Edward, though he has done no wrong thing, the girl having taken her life in the depths of her shame . . . And the thing about the hut on the cliff. Years ago. Childish speculation merely. Your imagination, your flights of fancy, famous for that, you are. Whatever . . . the spotlight on Edward will mean the spotlight will be on me. If it comes on me, it will be prison. A bit too close to the wind this time, I fear.'

He talked hard at me, it seemed, for hours. In the end he dissuaded me from going to the police. 'He is your brother, Theo. You don't know the bag of worms you open.'

'But . . .'

'I know you and Edward are . . . well . . . not on the best of terms. But would you lie easy in your bed if Edward were hanged by the neck until he were dead? And I am telling you that's what it would come to. Suspicion can be very destructive. And with the old man in the old hut, well, there's no saying what *is* the truth, after all this time, is there?'

'And am I supposed to let it rest at that, knowing the old man who saved me from . . . the sea,' I was going to say *Edward*, but even now I'd not told Da the whole truth. Strange, this, when you think it was my father whom I talked to in my delirium, as I thought the sea would take me. 'From the sea. That old man being murdered and not avenged. And here now Ellen Jones is dead.'

'This is not one of your stories, child. Will you leave your suspicions there? He is your brother. I am your father.'

We had talked until the light outside faded. I jammed my hat on my head and pulled on my gloves. 'I'm not happy about this, Da.'

There was an unusual edge of bitterness in Ellis's laughter. 'None of us is happy, dear girl. What made you think it was about being happy?'

* * *

When his daughter agreed to stay silent, Ellis breathed a sigh of relief. He himself was truly in a fix, and was very loath to have words with the constable on any account. From the time he came back from America Ellis had been popular with Mr Sickert, his employer, and fellow workers at the grain house. He wrote in a very fine copperplate, was extremely clever, and genial in company with his ready wit and his quick, intuitive way of dealing with the most complex things. Mr Sickert used to praise him to his fellow employers: 'A joker he may be but you could never deny his cleverness.'

Ellis solved elaborate problems in his head and worked so quickly that he mastered the chief clerk's job as well as his own in a year. He made a habit of staying in the office after hours and telling Mr Sickert stories about the fine cities of America and the fortunes to be made there.

In the event, when the chief clerk, who was some distant cousin to Selwyn Jones, emigrated to South Africa to find gold in a more concrete form, Mr Sickert did not bother to replace him; he merely gave Ellis Maichin another twenty pounds a year and let him get on with it.

But as the months went on, Ellis's quickness in calculations and his willingness to run errands and pay bills in person started to have worrying repercussions. Bills which were supposed to have been paid were presented again. Calculations which appeared to be correct had elements of unaccounted money buried within them. Ellis's geniality and intelligence weighed lightly in the balance with what was turning out to be not just scores but hundreds of pounds missing. Ellis had his own way of working this out. Wasn't it merely the difference of money he saved by doing the chief clerk's work for Mr Sickert?

But he knew that as soon as the deception was exposed his employer would revert to type and cry *Thief!* It had happened before and it would happen again. And now, here in his home town, it *was* happening again. It was just a matter of time.

We walk out of the newspaper office into Church Street and my father grasps my arm and turns me down the street towards the sea. I pull away. 'I'm going home, Da.'

He holds tight on to me. 'Come, come. I want to show you something.'

I let him lead me down the street, over the railway bridge and up across the high wild grass towards the rearing strength of the old castle. It is in ruins now but in its day must have seemed an Olympus of power to the little people in the town. For all my dreaming of princesses and towers I have never played here. In all the years of playing on the marsh I have never ventured inside. It has loomed over the town, over my life, but I have managed to leave it alone. It has just been here, like the sky and the tide, but for me it does not have their wild attraction, their intriguing, restless sense of change. I've never wished to play inside the castle. One might just as well have played in the barrel of a gun: it has a sleeping danger which makes me shudder.

But today my father drags me across tumbled stones to the tower, through its narrow doorway and up what seem like hundreds of treacherous stone steps. The surface of the wall is crumbling; the sea fret of hundreds of years has larded it with slime and spidery sprouting grass. The damp chill of the place is entering my bones. At last the darkness of the turning staircase lightens and we are before a broken window cut into the deep wall.

'There!' he says abruptly.

We are very high. The jagged window frames a picture of the greens, greys and smoky purples of the estuary. To our right loom the bulky towers of the steelworks and the more distant, delicate tracery of the collieries, the whole weighed down by clouds ineffably stained by the belching of many chimneys. To our left is the frothy anxious movement of the open sea.

'What do you see?' His hand is heavy on my shoulder.

'I see the estuary, I see the sea, I see the town.'

'So what beyond that?'

'Beyond that?'

'Beyond that suffocating hypocritical rabbit warren of a town that you have lived in all your life?'

'Liverpool?'

'Aye. Maybe. Liverpool. And beyond that?'

'America?'

'Aye. America.' He turns my shoulders, makes me face the other direction where even now a train was steaming through the outskirts of the town. 'And here?'

'Chester?'

'So. Chester. And beyond that, London. The centre of the universe. More so than America. A teeming city. All money, all learning, all people of consequence gather there. There a man can choose who he wishes to be.'

I wonder if he means that in that place, lies like his don't count. There a thief becomes honest; a murderer appears innocent by the mere cowardly omission of a good person.

'I know, so. How many times have you told me this, Da?'

'Well then, now I show you the open skies. The open road. When you are ready you yourself should take it. Of them all you are like me. Do not linger. Do not suffocate here.'

I look at him. Am I like him? Are my stories like his lies? Do I hold the truth so lightly that I can live alongside a murderer and not call out, as he has bid me? Is this how stories cross the grain of real life and shriek on the nerves like chalk on an old blackboard? 'You're going off,' I say. 'You're going away again.'

'Well, it seems I must . . .' His voice fades. 'You must stay quiet even when I go, *cariad*. When I'm not here, if you make

83

a fuss about Edward, bad as he seems to you, your mother's life will be hell. You will take care of your mam, Theo. You promise?'

'She won't want me. She wants you. She always wanted you. She was like a man without hands for seven years, without you.'

'She does want you. She tells me so. She is proud of you. I tell you this.'

'And what if I too want to get on a train? Go off to London and be the woman I want to be?'

He runs a soft hand down my face. 'Not yet, Theo. Not just yet. Your time will come.'

A wind cuts through the jagged window like a razor and makes us both gasp. We make our precarious way down the tower and back towards the town. My father parts with me at the bottom of Church Street. 'I'll leave you here, Theo. I have to go and see your nain. There was a message from your granda that she is very poorly. She has been bad since . . . since the funeral. He is worried about her.'

Rose Clare had known for a while, in her heart, that Ellis's eye was straying to other women again. Oh yes, he was fine and loving as ever. Since she had lost the last baby and she had been so unwell, so frantic about not producing another child, he was kind enough to stave off the very final act. They cuddled and kissed and stroked but no seed was planted, no babies made. So she knew he loved her.

But he was regularly late from work now; he went off for walks on his own. In the evening he sat at the table, turning the pages of heavy books which had maps and pictures of men in strange garb. He brought her money and bright scarves which he knew would please her.

She said nothing at this but remembered last time before he went to America. All these things happened then. Then as

84

now there were scarves and trinkets for her, and presents for other women which he would bestow for favours his wife could not give him. In silence too, she worried about the money. He had fobbed off her anxious queries about the money which jingled in his pockets, with airy statements about savings, bonuses and presents from a grateful Mr Sickert. But she knew he was doing it again. Creating the necessity, the imperative to leave again, to be forced to abandon her in this town on her own. And Rose Clare wept inwardly as she returned his smile and stroked his bearded cheek.

So she was only half surprised when a stranger knocked at her door that Saturday and asked for Ellis.

'My husband's at work, at the grain merchant's down on the harbour. He'll be back at three.' Saturdays being his half-day, he usually finished up in the office, then went for a drink with some men at the Wellington Hotel.

The man at the door was clerkly and thin with shiny patches like snail trails on his black coat sleeves. He shook his head. 'My name is Jacob Snaith, assistant to Mr Sickert. I am just from the grain mills,' he said in awkward English. 'I am sent because Mr Maichin is not there and the boss, Mr Sickert, is concerned regarding some accounts.'

Rhys was behind her. 'What is it, Mam?'

'Nothing, Rhys. You go back to your dinner.' She opened the door wide and stood back. 'Come in if you want, Mr Snaith. Look for him. He's not here. We haven't seen him since breakfast.'

The man clutched the light brim of his hat. 'No. No, Mrs Maichin. I will tell Mr Sickert he is gone and you know not where.' She watched him scuttle away down the road and noted at least two twitching curtains on the other side. Then she came in and closed the door and, ignoring the boys at the table, walked steadily upstairs. She looked in the cupboard on the landing where Ellis kept his old carpet bag. It was gone.

She scrabbled through the wardrobe. Two suits of his clothes and three good shirts were missing. So were the books from the deep windowsill.

She sat down hard on the bed, still unmade. It was rumpled and creased by their last night's sleep, by their last sleep together. She collapsed on to her pillow and pulled back again as her head hit something very hard. She put her hand inside the slip and pulled out a wash-leather bag. On to the rumpled bed she poured fifteen golden guineas. She ran her fingers over the queen's face, the ridged edges. Not honestly gained, she was quite sure. She thrust them back into the bag, and the bag back into the pillow slip. 'Stolen or not,' she muttered to herself, 'his last present to me and it's mine.'

There was a rattle downstairs and she jumped as she heard Edward's voice. Surely he had not heard about this yet? About his father's defection? So like him to want to slip back and take charge.

She back down on the bed and closed her eyes, listening to the rise and fall of angry voices downstairs. She lay down and pulled the blanket over her, right up to her chin.

Rhys put his head round the door without knocking. 'Mam, Edward's here. He says Nain's very bad, and that our father has caused it as he has gone off again, bag and baggage. Did you know this?'

Rose Clare closed her eyes. 'Oh yes, Rhys, I knew it. I knew it very well.'

Seven

Travelling North

Within weeks of the discovery of Ellen's body, we are on our way North without our father. The Jones family is on its way to South Africa, so the town has lost two families in the space of a month. Three, if you count our grandparents.

A week after my father left us my grandmother died, of the nasty cold which had hovered over her since the day Ellen died. The next day my grandfather, holding vigil, was found dead in his chair. It seemed to me that the earth was in a great convulsion, expelling so many people. You might say the first ripple was with the tar-paper man, all those years ago. Then there was Ellen and Ellen's baby who made me think again of my own seal sister, slipping in and out of life behind me. Then Dada vanishing down the train line in a wisp of steam. Now Nain and Granda.

Poison in the air.

The old ones were buried together. Edward preached, taking the text: 'Depart from evil, and do good; seek peace and pursue it.' Psalms xxxiv 14.

Beside me Rhys whispered the word in Welsh. *Rhagrithwyr*. Hypocrite. I find myself thinking that Edward killed the old ones too. They had somehow found out about Ellen and were keeping quiet, and the keeping quiet killed them. This is not just my fancy. In my granda's will, his precious savings were left to the three surviving daughters of Selwyn Jones, in three equal parts. Edward, who as Granda's favourite should have benefited, made light of this. He spoke of our granda's natural virtue, of his Christian charity to the Jones family.

We meet looks of bewilderment when we talk of moving because of the pit closure. Rhys says the old joiner tried to make him stay and says the rumours about the closure are not true. But Rhys is not ready, yet, to split from his family.

He pulled at one of my curls. 'I will come with you, Theo. But I'm not a runaway, like the hypocrite Edward, or our light-fingered father. I come to protect you from the rigours of the North. I do hear they boil people and eat them up there.'

I set my lip at that and told him very firmly that I could take care of myself, thank you. Even among cannibals.

So this is how we've landed here at Sheffield station on our way North where, according to Edward, the boys will find work, and according to Rhys, they eat people. Edward is at the far end of the platform, marching up and down in his dark jacket and trousers, his hat hard on his head. He looks every inch the handsome young minister. Rhys and Caspar have gone off somewhere to watch the turntable at work. My mother, grey and haggard – she has aged twenty years since my father left – is sitting beside me on a bench watching our luggage.

I love this station. It is teeming with people from the most ragged to the most respectable. The luggage has labels from all over England and further afield. You can almost smell the tension, the excitement. There is so much to see.

On the opposite platform is an ancient woman, all fluttering draperies, clutching the arm of a big shambling man in his middle years. Too young to be her husband, he must be her son. He towers over her in height and engulfs her small black figure with his girth. His overcut tweed coat glows amber, lit briefly by a shaft of light which has poked its way through the roof-girders down into the crowded station. The old woman talks all the time, her face turned up towards him, waxy as a lily, framed by her neat black bonnet. Now and then her black gloved hand catches his tweed sleeve, guiding him through the crowd with the sure touch of a boatman piloting his boat into the harbour.

On this side of the station my mother, fussed by the alien crowd, starts to babble about our luggage. She insists that I drag it nearer to the edge of the platform, ready to load on to the train when it finally comes. When I have done this I look back and see that the old woman and her son are gone. My gaze returns to my mother, who is stroking the leather straps on the top case, muttering, 'Liverpool-Dublin-New York, Liverpool-Dublin-New York.' She's not right in the head, since my father left.

Now there is a hubbub in the crowd clustering by the iron bridge which arches over the track. Curious, I leave my mother and stroll across to see what it's all about. There, at the bottom of the riveted iron steps, is the crumpled figure of the old woman in black.

I look upwards towards the bridge into the moon face of the shambling man. His wide-open eyes meet my gaze. He holds out the guilty hand towards me, palm up. 'I shook her off,' he says, his full lips trembling. 'I only shook her off.'

The poor soul thinks that he caused her to fall. I have never seen such an innocent face. I shake my head and smile encouragingly as you would with a child. Then I pass by hurriedly, uncomfortable at such naked despair.

Eventually I find myself in a stuffy carriage which smells of rotting greens, sitting opposite my mother. She is faint and retches with the motion of the train and the nasty stench in the carriage. The boys are in another carriage, the train is so full. I watch the big man lifting the ancient woman into our carriage. She sleeps for hour after hour as the train clicks busily on over the tracks. She wakes up and sits very straight. I drag my glance away from her and look out of the window.

I am squashed beside the shambling man who, when his mother wakes, starts to fidget a lot. His bulging eyes are on his mother who sits opposite him, leaning slightly forward, her hands on the silver lion head which is the knob of her stick.

She looks out of the window watching the countryside rush past with avaricious interest, then darts a glance at me. 'Have you been here before?' Her words shoot towards me like bullets.

'Here?' Does she mean here in this countryside which is steaming past the window, or does she mean here on this train which smells of polish, lye soap and coal soot?

'Here!' She fixes me with her gaze. 'In the North of England. Or the North-East, if one were to be precise.'

If one were to be precise! The woman is using words like a broiderer uses her silks. Words I only read, never hear. I salt the words away to use another time myself, in just that tone of voice.

'No!' I say, catching her questioning look at my slowness in answering. 'My mother and I are from Wales. North Wales.'

'Wales.' She frowned. 'You do not sound Welsh. There is something different . . .'

'My mother here, she is from Ireland.' My mother's eyes remain tight shut. 'They say I sound like her.'

'Ah.' She is satisfied now. 'I thought I heard that lilt.'

'You know Ireland?'

'I was in Dublin as a child. My father's family imported tea from the East. Had a company there.'

I find myself telling her about my father, his travels in

Ireland and his travels in America. The words come tumbling out, encouraged by the bright light of interest in those sharp eyes. I even tell her about writing for the *Tidal Review* and the peculiarities of Mr Murgatroyd.

Then the old woman sits back and closes her eyes. She must be made of iron, to get up from such a tumble and act as though nothing has happened. She makes me jump when she snaps her eyes open again and raises her eyebrows towards her son. 'Stephen! My valise!'

He stands up and reaches into the net rack for the velvet bag with its brass clip. Then he places it in her lap as though it is a precious bird's egg and takes her stick from her so she can rake in its interior. Her hand emerges with a silver card clip from which she extracts a card and hands it to me.

I peer in the pearly interior light of the carriage. *Mrs O.D.C. Gervase, Goshawk Shield, Nr Stanhope, Weardale, Co. Durham.*

'Is it a farm?'

'Not quite, but come to see for yourself, when you settle in,' she says. 'You will be welcome, a strong girl like you. There could be work, should you so wish.'

Now she goes back to sleep, her hands quiet as resting rabbits. The man beside her holds tight to her stick.

So, both she and my mother opposite me are fast asleep. With the closing of the eyes both of them seem to have lost any human power; two crumbling bundles of clothes, one in black, with fluttering lace and drapes; and my mother Rose Clare Maichin, dressed in startling greens and red, despite Edward's strictures about neglecting the mourning in respect of her parents-in-law. But my mother is no hypocrite, unlike her eldest son. I am glad she is brave enough to defy Edward. And glad she has kept up with her bright colours even though my father is gone.

The man's pale eyes meet mine. 'My name is Stephen,' he

said. 'Stephen Gervase.' His voice is higher pitched than it might be. 'And this is my dear mother. You can read her name on that card. How are you named?'

'I am Theodora Louisa Maichin.' I put out my hand and he leans over to grasp it. My hand is like a minnow in the mouth of a flounder. It occurs to me that his manners are rather better than those of his mother, who neither asked my name nor told me of his. So I smile at this strange galumphing man. 'I am called Theo. And there by the window is my mother, Rose Clare Maichin.'

'I am not asleep.' Her voice emerges but her eyes do not open. 'Aren't I afraid that if I open my eyes the world will swirl round and I won't be able to catch it as it swings by?'

Stephen Gervase's hand tightens on mine. I can't remember the last time someone held my hand. His hand, large and plump, quite engulfs mine. Enjoying its strange warmth I leave it there while the train lurches and jumps mile after mile after mile. Then in a movement of sleep his hand loosens itself and I pull my hand away and thrust it deep in my pocket, so he cannot grasp it again.

Eight

Settling in the North

The landscape in the North is not so different from Wales when you think of it. Hills and rivers. Pit wheels and black cottages. Ironworks and furnaces. But what is missing here in South Durham is the sea to dissolve it all, to roar in and out and take away the grit, the tight feeling inside.

The town of Priorton, where our last train deposits us, is all right, I suppose. The High Street is brightly painted and busy; lined with shops of all kinds from furriers to jewellers, corn merchants to butchers; the Market Place centres on a big building with towers and a little church resting beside it like a kitten. Graceful houses line the Market Place: on three of them I see discreet lawyer's signs. At one end we pass a fancy gate enclosed by a high stone arch and glimpse a grand house. Not a medieval castle like the looming monster at home, but a large building too grand for this town, outweighing it somehow, just as our castle outweighed our town in Wales.

But then we leave this town in the heavy station brake, and plough up hill and down dale, through smoky hamlets, to the village of Gibsley, which must be all of three miles from Priorton. It is a place with no centre, just three or four pits with their clusters of cottages linked by a broad winding street. This is lined today with market stalls. I wish we had stayed in the place called Priorton. It seems more intricate, less dark.

When we arrive at the pit yard at the end of one of the streets, children without shoes stand in a tight line, eyeing us darkly and listening to the chink of my mother's money as she pays the brakeman.

Edward is cock of the walk in our family now: pleased that my father is gone and feeling that we are all in his hands. His spoiled inheritance from my grandfather is not mentioned. He is peculiar with my mother. On the one hand he is unctuous and caring, on the other sharp and bossy. And she usually obeys. She is like a rag doll bereft of stuffing without my father. I don't want to love anyone, if loving someone as she loves our father makes you half the person when they're gone. I will never love anyone like that.

Caspar and Rhys are lighthearted enough about it all, pleased to be on the move. Caspar is back at Edward's side, his true lieutenant. So Rhys is out on a limb again, on his own. Then I suppose there is me.

Mr Murgatroyd, to do him justice, tried to get me to stay in Wales: to take a room in the town and continue to work for the newspaper. He even came to the house – wearing clean white linen – to suggest this to my mother. He was at his most hearty and persuasive. He even admitted to his own personal benefit from the private arrangement we had. 'Your daughter, ma'am, has a natural gift, and, if I may use a vulgarity, saved my bacon more than once in this past year.'

My mother looked at him as though he were some exotic bird who had alighted on the wrong tree. He pleaded on in his gruff way. I looked at my mother. She was bewildered. 'But she must come with us, Mr Murgatroyd. She is a member of this family. We cannot part with her.' She kept shaking her head.

He stroked his moustache. 'Then I fear my career in print is over. I have lost my own gift to your daughter. D'you see, ma'am? Your daughter was sent as my amanuensis, my surrogate.' She looked at him blankly. He might have been speaking Russian.

Edward spoke up from the corner of the kitchen. 'Let Theo stay here, Mam. We have no need of her. She has never been any use to us anyway.'

'Edward!' My mother was shocked.

'We will manage.' His eyes dropped to the Bible which was flat before him on the table.

Murgatroyd looked at me eagerly. 'See? Your son says...'

But my mother was wide-eyed. Desolate. That was when I decided to stay with her. My father had deserted her, left her to Edward's mercy. He asked me to take care of her. How could I take care of her if I were hundreds of miles away? I shook my head. 'I need to go with Mother.'

I walked with Mr Murgatroyd to the gate. He shook me by the hand as though I were one of his old cronies. 'The best of luck up there in those dark places, Miss Maichin. Some newspaper up there will, no doubt, benefit from your talents. For talent you have, Miss Maichin. The talent for the brief word, the tight phrase, humanity in a sentence.' He grasped my hand tighter and brought his bulbous nose to mine. 'The best of good fortune to you, Miss Maichin. I will hear of you, I am sure. You will make your way.' Then he tucked two coins in my hand and strode off, his cape swirling. I opened my palm and contemplated the two guineas lying there.

In Priorton, I spotted a narrow office front, with iron lettering above, proclaiming *The Priorton Chronicle*. Once we settle in Gibsley I'll go there. Offer my services. Show my examples. But of course they have Murgatroyd's name on. Will they believe me? A reference from him would have been more use than two guineas.

The pit house we're assigned to is tiny. Half as big as the house in Wales. A stepladder to reach upstairs, which is a loft divided by thin boards. A cast-iron oven made locally and a ton of coal tumbled across the yard. No furniture.

Anthony Carmedy weighed up the young men opposite. Three brothers, tall, heavy. The blond one with striking looks: Edward Maichin. The next one more sulky-looking: Caspar Maichin. The narrow one with red hair looked thinner, less fit, he was the third brother, Rhys. But he was the best looking of the lot, despite this: bright-eyed, relaxed, and with an open, ready smile. 'I have two jobs at White Pool,' Carmedy said. 'Last of twenty.'

'You lost twenty workers?' The blond boy's voice was pleasing, low and resonating with the promise of music.

Carmedy laughed. 'Rather careless of me?' He shook his head. 'Fellows too busy agitating their fellow workers. Infected by Chartists and radicals. Lord Chase'll have none of it. They set fire to one of the shafts.'

'Take us all, sir. We'll give more than value for three. I promise you.' The narrow foxy one, Rhys, leaned forward. 'I promise you, sir.'

'At least you all speak English! Not many of the Welsh boys speak English when they first get here,' mused Carmedy. 'This could be helpful, I suppose.'

'Our father's Welsh, but our mother's—' said Rhys.

'English,' put in Edward, shooting a look at Rhys.

Rhys nodded. 'English!' Old Edward was right. The Irish question made everything Irish spell trouble in these times. Talk about agitation. He smiled to himself. And here's old Edward, lying in his teeth again, looking like an angel.

'So we speak both.' Edward hesitated. 'P'raps that would be useful, sir, if you've got a lot of Welsh boys underground? Somebody that speaks both could be useful.'

Carmedy shrugged. 'They pick it up soon enough, to be honest. And, when you think of it, what does a block of coal know in the pit, Welsh from English?' He perched his glasses on his nose and made three marks on his ledger. 'Turn up for the six o'clock shift on Monday. I'll send them a note.' He scribbled on a piece of paper. 'Take that to the clerk in the pit office. He'll tell you about a house, there are houses to spare.'

'Right. That's it.' Edward stood up and put on his cap. 'Thank you, sir.' He offered his hand to the manager. Carmedy looked at it in surprise but shook it.

They walked down the wooden steps on to the hard core of the road made up by pit waste. 'Right, Edward. Got us set on, then!' said Caspar.

'Boyo here nearly lost us it,' grunted Edward, flinging a hand towards Rhys. 'Irish!'

'Our mother is Irish!' said Rhys.

'You don't admit that just now, dolt.' Edward came to a stop. He glared at his brother who, more than his silent sister, more than his fluttering mother, was prepared these days to take him on. 'Stop here a minute, will you? Wait for me.'

'What for?'

'Need to mention something to Carmedy.' He raced back. 'Something I forgot to tell him.'

In the office Carmedy had his head down over his register.

'What is it?'

'I was thinking, sir. My brother Rhys, the one with red hair. He's . . .' he hesitated delicately. 'I was thinking about what you said before about . . . radicals. Well, Rhys, in our last pit he was a bit of a . . .'

'A bit of a . . .?'

'Stirrer. Caused a stoppage once. I hate to say this, but . . .'

'Mm. Now why, Mr Maichin, why would you be telling me this?' Carmedy frowned at him.

Edward opened his eyes wide and looked directly into those of the older man. 'Well, sir, I see it like this. These jobs are precious to our family. I have a widowed mother and a sister to support: our family needs these jobs. If Rhys being a bit of a hothead loses us this, we are in a strange place with no jobs. And, very likely, branded troublemakers.'

'Mm.' Carmedy opened his ledger and put a line through the third name. 'Well, I suppose I must thank you, Mr Maichin.'

Edward nodded and replaced his cap. 'Thank you, sir.'

Anthony Carmedy watched Edward leave, wondering at his motives. Rivalry? Enmity? Carmedy sighed. Thank goodness he only had his schoolteacher sister to consider. No rivalry between them. No jealousy. Just a replication of their parents' quiet life a generation ago.

'What was that all about?' said Rhys suspiciously.

Edward shrugged. 'I asked for coal. I asked if there would be coal at the house.'

Theo and her mother had had to get up at three to light the fire from buckets of coal they had set drying overnight. The wet coal hissed and spluttered and nearly put out the fire twice, but slowly the dry coal won and they had it away. Then it roared. The boys had a hot drink before they went to work.

After the boys had gone they set to in the rain loading the coal in the zinc buckets and throwing it in the coal house. Rose Clare worked alongside Theo well enough for half an hour, then had to lean on the windowsill for breath, the rain streaming down her face.

'Go inside!' gasped Theo, pushing her sopping hair out of her eyes.

'I should help.'

At that moment the back gate opened and Rhys walked in, a sack over his head against the rain.

'What's this?' Theo cocked her head. 'Walk out?'

Rhys ran for the shelter of the scullery doorway and pulled her inside. 'Never got to walk in. They only had Ed and Caspar's name on the list. No place for me. No job for me.'

'I thought it was fixed up. You said it was arranged.'

'*I* thought it was fixed up. I was there when the man said yes.'

'So why not you? Why the others?'

'Something to do with Edward. Deceitful dog. Something he said. Denies it, of course. All outraged innocence. Don't know truth from lie, that one, never mind all his preaching.'

Theo wondered why it was only she and Rhys who could see this about Edward. Even Rose Clare, who was frightened of Edward, thought he was straight and true. Perhaps too sanctimoniously straight, perhaps too woodenly true, but she believed him – believed in him.

Theo peered disconsolately out of the doorway into the rain, which was driving down with razor-edged vengeance. 'That coal heap seems to be getting no smaller.' Rhys grabbed her shovel out of her hands and said, 'Look! I've had a good wetting. I'll take no time to fill this coal. You go and get dry and get Mother to put on a big jug of tea for me.'

She hesitated. Then he shoved her so hard that she nearly fell into the scullery door. 'Go on. It'll take no time, I tell you. It'll work off my temper.'

It took Rhys another three-quarters of an hour to fill the coal, by which time they had his jug of tea made and the fire blazing right up the fire back. He stripped off in the scullery and came dressed just in his vest and pit shorts, his arms, legs and his long-toed feet bare.

Rose Clare smiled her appreciation and threw him an old sheet to rub himself down, and a blanket to cover himself, his handsome face glum.

He sat down in the rocking chair and stretched his feet out in front of the flames.

'No job for you?' said Rose Clare. 'Now that's a pity, Rhys.'

'Ask me, Edward put paid to it,' he said. 'Didn't Theo tell you?'

'Edward? I . . .'

'I tell you, he did it. Said something to that under-manager. I know it. Not that I could ever tackle him with it.'

Theo hit the table. 'I'll tell him,' she said. 'I'll see him,' but her voice was faint. Even she was frightened of Edward these days, knowing what she knew. She tried to push from her mind that he had probably killed twice and in truth he had no conscience.

'Leave it, Theo,' said Rhys. 'Might as well school a viper.' He put his hand out towards the leaping flames. 'I'll go to that town – Priorton, was it? There'll be work there. Above ground I'd wager. Did you see those big shops? Co-operative Society? The workshops? There it'll be an advantage talking English.'

'I'll come with you,' said Theo. 'I want to go to the newspaper office.'

Rhys laughed. 'There'll be no job for you here, Theo. No Ellis Maichin to persuade disbelievers of your talents.'

'Rhys!' Rose Clare sat up straight at this talk of her husband. 'Ellis? Where is he? I've not had a word from him, but he does not know where to send. He'll not be able to find us. We're lost to him, so we are.' Her face was close, focused only on Ellis. The machinations of her son Edward were nothing beside the open wound of Ellis's sudden departure, which returned to pain her many times in a day, driving her ever deeper into herself in search of comfort.

I need my little seal sister for company now, in this dark place. My mother is away in her head into some territory where we can't reach. Edward is ignoring me or treating me like a serving maid. (Serving maid? How did he treat the last one?) Caspar, now cast again in the role of lieutenant, follows suit. And Rhys is like Loki the mischief-maker, sometimes your friend and sometimes a merciless trickster who only cares for himself.

I have used the last of Mr Murgatroyd's two guineas to buy a new coat and a new box of notepaper and new pens but there is nowhere in this poky hole to write. I've had to replace my ink twice and my paper has vanished. I can't make up my mind who has done this, whether it is Edward doing it, to watch me squirm, or Rhys having his bit of fun. But I won't squirm and I'll let none of them have fun at my expense. At least they haven't stolen my picture of the marsh. I will get a frame for it. It will be safer on the wall.

I'm vexed that I have to go to Priorton to get new ink and paper but do not show it. My mother is still worrying at me about my father losing sight of us. 'I have written to Mr Murgatroyd,' I tell her, 'telling him this address, so Father can get it from him when he returns to Wales.' I have also asked Mr Murgatroyd for a reference and anxiously wait on every post. Perhaps the Scotsman is so drunk he has not even read my letter.

It's twelve o'clock when Rhys and I set out. The postman meets us at the gate. Murgatroyd's letter flaps in the wind as I read it. It says all the right things, although the writing is spidery and hard to read.

Rhys and I walk together the three miles to Priorton. Up hill and down dale. My legs are very tired, being more accustomed to the stubby rise of dunes and the falling slope of the tide than these hills.

Atop the last hill, Priorton appears before us, nestling around a winding river. Industrial chimneys and commercial premises tower up above the low rows of houses, poking through skeins of smoke and soot. The spire of the church in the Market Place sets the distance for the blunt and sharp-pointing fingers of other churches and chapels. It must be a very churchy place, this Priorton. The High Street cuts a line through the town as though some hand had marked it with a ruler.

The ache falls from my legs and I start to run, lifting my skirt from my ankles and clutching my hat on my head. 'Come on, Rhys, here is the golden city where we can seek our fortunes.'

'You and your fairy tales. You're quite mad, Theo. Quite mad, I tell you.' But he runs eagerly to catch up. The Market Place is buzzing with stalls, hawkers press us on every side. Fish and vegetables, grain and tools jostle for our attention in the long lines of stalls.

We stop at the corner of the High Street. Rhys winks at me. 'Now then, Theo, I'll start here and go into every shop, every business till I get a job,' he says. 'We'll meet here in two hours. If by any chance I am not here, then I will be working already. You can go home and spread the good news. I want a job before Edward gets off his shift.'

The newspaper office is down a narrow passage into a room lit by a dusty skylight which filters light down on to a large table at which sit two men who look exactly alike though one is twenty years younger than the other. Two tall clerks' desks stand against the walls, and two younger men stand there, scratching away. Through a half-open door I can hear the familiar crank of printing machines.

The father and son shake hands gravely enough with me and introduce themselves as Rupert and Allen Murton, senior and junior respectively. 'I edit,' said Rupert, 'and my son manages.' They listen attentively as I explain my requirements, outline my expertise. They open my folder to see examples of my work.

Mr Rupert Murton holds them up to his eyes. Reads rapidly,

and passes them on to his son. They read five pieces in the blink of an eye. Then Mr Rupert Murton looks at me. 'These are well written. Economy and verve. Hallmark of good journalism, though you wouldn't think so to read some newspapers.'

I look down at my kid gloves with becoming modesty. 'Thank you.'

Allen Murton explodes with a crackling sound which was either a laugh or an ejaculation of disbelief. 'The name here is Murgatroyd. Angus Murgatroyd. Not Maichin.'

I hand over Murgatroyd's letter.

Murton senior holds it up to the light again. 'Yes. Yes. Competent . . . literate . . . forward thinking. But . . .' He looks at me over his glasses. 'It says nothing here about these articles being in your own hand.'

'I wrote them!' I protest. 'On those occasions Mr Murgatroyd was indisposed and I wrote them.'

He shakes his head and leans it back. 'We have many people of talent, Miss Maichin, whose highest aim in life is to write for the *Chronicle*. I have a drawer full of competent, literary articles from earnest hands. Some of them even –' he snorts like a breathless horse '– female!' He shakes his head. 'Now if you had been a young man, we need an extra pair of hands, an extra pen in the office—'

'I could do that,' I butt in too eagerly. 'I worked in Mr Murgatroyd's office. I was in there more hours than he was—'

'Miss Maichin! I don't know about Wales, but here it wouldn't be decent for a young woman . . .' He looked around eloquently at the narrow space. I am aware of the eyes of the young men sliding slyly in my direction. The confidence bleeds out of me. 'Would you be interested in single pieces, then? Single stories?' I ask.

'Stories. Aah. Well. Anything you leave will be very

carefully considered.' He frowned. 'Do you have children's stories?'

My face blank, I invent rapidly. 'I have a lot of stories that I have rewritten from the classic myth.'

He runs his fingers thoughtfully down his ferocious side whiskers. 'Well. The classics? Very edifying. Perhaps there will be space.'

I take a breath. 'What is your rate, Mr Murton?'

'Rate? Rate? Let's see. Could we say five shillings a story?'

I keep my face straight. Inside I am jubilant. Five shillings is more than I would earn, according to the *Chronicle*'s own 'Situations Vacant' column, for a week's skivvying in the parlours of Priorton. It was more than I earned from Mr Murgatroyd.

Rhys is there in the Market Place bouncing a ball off an up-jutting cobblestone.

'No luck?' I say sympathetically, catching the ball.

'On the contrary, sis. Fifteenth business. Fifteenth door. New job, start on Monday. In a nail shop. Ironmonger's. Old woman whose son owns the shop heard the Irish in my accent. She comes from County Mayo herself. Thank you God and Rose Clare Maichin.'

'What will you do? Count nails?'

He shrugged. 'Dunno. Lift things about, I imagine. Make myself useful. Parcel them up. Maybe even count nails. Who knows? How about you?' He sits on a low wall outside a house which has brass plaques for three businesses.

I sit beside him. 'Can you lend me some money?'

'I thought you were getting a job to earn some money?'

'I need some fine paper and new ink. Someone –' I clip him hard on the ear '– has tipped mine out, taken my paper.'

He puts up his hands. 'Don't blame me! Do you think I would do that? Don't they give you paper? To write for them?'

'I am to write children's stories. Five shillings a time.'

'Right. I'll lend you the money if you give it to me straight back when you get it.'

He helps me choose the paper, taking more trouble than I would have expected. We dawdle all the way back – I will not call it home. Neither of us wishes to get back too soon to the dark village of Gibsley.

Nine

A Man to be Reckoned With

On their first Sunday in County Durham Edward dragged Caspar all the way to Priorton, to the Welsh Baptist Church where he presented his letter from the elders in Wales and was welcomed with the cool passion which was characteristic of this community. His eloquence in the discourse after the service was noted and approved, and he was promised a temporary place on their list of lay preachers as a platform to prove himself.

Edward noted the simplicity of the little chapel and the modesty of the people and sensed that this was not where the power was in this town. The Baptist community back in Wales had been the core of the community. If you walked with those men, you knew you walked with men to be reckoned with. From the day he could listen and understand Edward had imbibed ideas not only about the terrible temper and the omnipotence of God, but also the power which He placed in the hands of His chosen ones: power to forgive, to succour, to heal, to punish. He learned most about this hearing his grandfather preach and watching the congregations, where passion and fear, delight and vengeance passed over the still faces like the clouds racing across a sky on a bright day.

Edward did not question the existence of God. Someone

who possessed such power over the human heart had to exist, and those who became His messengers partook in that power. He had noted, in his journeys as a boy preacher, that God endowed some chapel communities with more visible power than others.

So in Priorton he embarked on a royal progress of all the Nonconformist communities. In the end he settled on the Wesleyan community whose membership included tradesmen and businessmen as well as workmen and miners. Many of these were Liberals, very much the powerful party in the town. Among them it was to his real advantage that his English was as fluent as his Welsh. He knew he would have to prove himself more assiduously here: his Welsh credentials were as unreadable as Swahili. But he would prove himself both in the chapel and the Party. It would only be a matter of time.

So he divided his time between the English and the Welsh Nonconformists, and bided his time, before he eventually became, as he knew he would, a leading person in this town, a man to be reckoned with.

I have had to fit my writing in with scrubbing this hovel from eaves to gutter, whitewashing the scullery and kitchen, adapting curtains to fit the tiny windows. My mother and I have had to tie them back in great loops, making them intolerably lush for the tiny rooms. They drop on to the sill and mask even more of the precious daylight. My mother may be incoherent and unfinished in many ways but in the matter of her house (and our clothes, some of which she makes herself), she is particular. The house must be light and bright as human ingenuity can make it, and there must be colour. She throws bright cloths on the back of chairs and puts buttercups in jars. My father's daguerreotype, to one side of the fireplace as always, now has a narrow table beneath it, always with a vase of flowers or grasses of some sort. For me it stands as a kind of altar; I'm sure Edward – very much the master of the household now – has not made this comparison or he would have had it down in a trice. Setting up graven images and all that.

I begin to see that this brightness is my mother's private rebellion – against Edward and his bullying, and very probably against the dull and dreary life she has been forced to lead.

In this house, even my mother's touches and my hard work cannot make it much more than the hovel it is, but in the evening, with the curtains drawn, the fire lit and the lamps on, the kitchen has a welcoming glow. The smells and bright touches, so habitual in the house in Wales, make it familiar. It has become home.

I sit here at the table and write while Edward is out of the way weaving his savage magic in some chapel or other. I have a new hiding place for my paper and ink: behind the boiler in the chimney. Often when I tuck it in there I think of my mother and her fruit wine in the house in Wales. One wonder is that she has not gone back to that habit, now my father is gone. Perhaps, with this last leaving and the need to resist Edward, some kind of iron has entered her, to stiffen her soul.

Down this street we Maichins have been accorded a high regard: my mother and I wear jackets and coats instead of shawls and the boys wear preacher black when they are not in pit clothes. And the windowsills and doorstep are powder-white from my mother's donkey stone.

My story of Loki the mischief-maker is taking more writing than I thought. ('Just a thousand words. To be understood by children,' said Mr Rupert Murton. Easy to say!) Even so these stories of mine will never be read by the children in this pit row. There are no newspapers in their houses. Many of them go barefoot, they are pinched and stitched into clothes once made for older, larger children. Their hair goes unbrushed for many a month, their nails and knuckles set in with grime.

This is so although many of them are red-cheeked, bright-eyed and vigorous, well nourished on potato pie and garden greens. Here the fathers work hard in the pit, their mothers cope in their own ways. In two houses in the row the fathers do work but they drink and gamble heavily as well. In these houses the mothers despair. Only these houses spurt forth children who are hollow-eyed and scabby and look cold on the warmest day.

No, while some of the naughtiest children here would model for a portrait of Loki, not in a month of Sundays would they or their parents read my story. My readers will be the shopkeepers' and traders' children, those who slip about the streets of Priorton on market day, bowling hoops and carrying play baskets to help Mama with the marketing.

Well. So be it. The story is finished to my satisfaction and I am sitting in the newspaper office at one side of the large table while Mr Murton senior reads it on the other. It is like being back at school or worse. Murton junior looks on with open interest. The clerks are standing at their desks with their backs towards me but their rigid attention lets me know they are listening keenly.

He looks up at me. I meet his eye boldly and smile. 'Well, Mr Murton? How do you find it?'

His brows are still knit. Praise evidently is painful. I try a lie. 'The children I tried it on clapped their hands and cried for more. I had to make up three more stories on the spot.' I cast a very appealing glance at the younger Mr Murton.

'Did they, indeed?' He nods wisely but his cheeks redden. He turns to his father. 'The horse's mouth, Pa. If the children like it . . .'

Mr Murton packs the sheets together. 'Not half bad, this. Strong clear expression.'

I try to look demure. 'Thank you. That is very kind.'

Of course they take it. In fact I think Mr Murton is a dolt, squeezing the last out of this encounter. It's my job to get him to do what I want. And I will.

Rhys set out every morning in the dark to walk to Priorton for his job in Berriman's Ironmongery. Even stepping out briskly it took him fifty minutes to walk the miles uphill. The job suited Rhys down to the ground. He relished the daylight streaming down from the dusty skylights as he went about his work in the foundry warehouse. After toiling in the dark galleries of the pit, this was heaven. He loved to wheel the trundling trolleys out into the fresh air of the delivery yard to dispatch nails and iron goods, all neatly labelled, right across the country. Rain, snow, sleet, none of these troubled him. He savoured working under the wide skies rather than folded in the envelope of the earth for days at a time.

Mr Berriman had thirty men working for him. The ironmonger (a large florid man with a heavy neck, who wore chains on his waistcoat) had a passion for iron which was only superseded by his passion for his oboe which he played rather badly in the town orchestra.

Berriman's occupied a great site on Priorton High Street. Facing on to the street was the shop, blatantly graced by very fine plate-glass windows. At Berriman's you could buy anything from a nail, to a gate, to a cast-iron stove. Berriman's had, in their time, made and sold iron staircases, iron chairs, iron tables and iron cradles; they had made iron boats, iron toilets, iron candelabra.

Stretching behind the shopfront was the cavernous warehouse and behind that the forge, which backed on to the road which looped around the narrow back streets of Priorton with their rooming houses and boxing saloons. From that road a great iron gate opened on to the forge which was the fiery heart of the Berriman empire.

Mrs Nathan Berriman, the ancient mother to the oboist,

held court at her desk at the front of the shop. Her desk was made of finest wrought iron and fronted by glass etched with a modern design of hammers and anvils. Mrs Berriman was an O'Connor from County Mayo, and it was she who heard the inflections in young Maichin's voice on that first day and instructed her son to employ him. Here at least the Irish connection was an advantage for Rhys.

Mrs Gerald Berriman, wife to the oboist, was a different kettle of fish. She was very much a town lady, who went as far as Darlington for her bombazine dresses and overladen hats. She called into the shop once a day to greet her mama-in-law and to assert her ownership of her husband in the face of such potent rivalry. The two women were never less than polite with each other.

Rhys had been working at Berriman's for two weeks and had been amused to witness several of these encounters. One day, when he was up a ladder loading a shelf with boxes of nails (being handed to him by Roger Bly who was showing him the ropes), he saw Mrs Berriman junior glide into the shop as usual. But this time she was accompanied by a tall girl with a green hat tipped too far over one eye.

'Oh-oh,' muttered Roger. 'Trouble!'

'Warsat?' said Rhys balancing the last box of half-inch tacks.

'Ruth Berriman. *Miss* Ruth Berriman. Boss's daughter,' he whispered. 'A teasing girl, you might call her. They say she ran off with a circus troupe when she was fifteen. Came back half married to some gypsy.'

'Did she now?' said Rhys, intrigued.

'And a year back got mixed up with a farm lad she met at Priorton market. They say it cost old Berriman fifty pounds to buy him off.'

Rhys surveyed the slender figure at the end of the shop. 'Got off lightly, I'd say.'

'Aye. Mebbe so. They say old Berriman can't get her interested in the stuffed shirts from Priorton. A few more scrapes like that and the stuffed shirts won't be interested in her, spite of her pa's money.'

The two women lingered beside the desk of Mrs Berriman senior. Even at this distance Rhys could see that the young woman and her grandmother were bosom pals: chuckles and talk from the younger one, smiles and nods from the older. And Mrs Berriman, mother to the girl and wife to the son, stood to one side, enduring rather than enjoying the interchange. Then, with her mother, Ruth Berriman made her way through the shop. She looked boldly at the two boys as she passed, then went on through the great iron door to the warehouse, which, for a second, expelled a bellowing clatter of noise, like a yelp of pain, into the more sedate shop area. Her glance had hit Rhys like a blow in the stomach. Her eyes bored into his for a second and her lips tilted in the smallest of smiles. The invitation was clear.

When the door shut again, Rhys felt a loss as keen as hunger.

He decided in that second that he would have that Ruth Berriman. He wanted her. In whatever way, on whatever terms, he would have her. Marriage was not out of the question. Not out of the question at all.

'Are you taking this box today, tomorrow, or God-send-Sunday?' Roger Bly's voice behind him made him jump.

Rhys complied quickly enough but a change had come over him. From that day he started to go to work early and come home late, so that he was almost totally absent from the Maichin house in Gibsley.

Always crafty, he decided, as the first part of his strategy, to court the old woman. So, mimicking his mother's Irish tones, he set to work.

After 'Loki' I have no inspiration for more children's stories,

112

despite Mr Murton's reluctant satisfaction and latent enthusiasm for a children's series. I don't know whether my dissatisfaction is because of the dark newspaper office and the egregious Mr Murton and his son, or my sense that these stories from the myth were out of kilter in this dark place, somehow belonging more properly to the bright skies, white light and blue seas of picture books.

I am so restless here, too restless to put pen to paper properly. But I think the real cause, the real reason I cannot write is Edward. When he is in the house I am too conscious of his presence; when he is absent I am waiting in tension for his arrival.

This week that tension has tightened another thread of the screw. For just this week Caspar and Edward have been on opposite shifts. Edward is on early, Caspar on late. Edward sets off at four in the morning and arrives home from White Pool mid-afternoon, an hour after Caspar sets out for his late shift. Today is Friday. My mother is out at Priorton market. We always eat fish on Friday though it is sometimes condemned in this house as a papist habit. Still, she makes a mouthwatering fish pie.

Today I am waiting for Edward, taking advantage of the light that is streaming through the window to read a book by Mrs Edgeworth, lent me by Mr Murton. I have Edward's dinner warming on the fire top and a dish of washing water is steaming in the pantry.

He has come in. I can hear him puffing and blowing like a walrus. He grunts, 'Theo!' and I take no notice.

'Theo!'

'What is it?'

'Get us a jug of water. My hair needs rinsing.'

I ladle water into the long-lipped jug and carry it by its handle and neck into the pantry. He is kneeling on a low stool, his head beside the tap, over the basin. His blond hair is covered with lather and tiny slivers of bright green soap. His face is streaked and grimed with coaly suds, but he has wiped his bright blue eyes with the flannel and looks at me sideways. 'Is there cold in there? Not too hot?'

'Just warm,' I say non-committally, balancing the heavy weight on my hip.

'I need my hair rinsing,' he says. 'It's full of coal.'

'You could go under the tap like we all do.'

'Cold water doesn't get the soap off. Sticks in your hair all week.' He is staring blandly at me. 'Come on, Theo. This is the least you can do for your keep.'

It is not the first time he has mentioned my *keep*. Well, 'Loki' is one step nearer to solving that problem. The first of many steps. 'Right,' I say, too brightly. 'Dip down.'

He dips down, but still I have to strain to lift the heavy jug above his head. The last drop of water is dripping, sliding down those golden locks when he grabs me. The jug clatters to the floor and everything slows down in a curious way. A chip of enamel flies up and clings to the whitewashed scullery wall, then floats down to the stamped earth floor. I see the soot-grimed soap smeared across his forehead revealing a golden freckle on his pale skin.

One hand clasps my waist and another pins my flailing arms to my side. From where he is kneeling he turns me and wipes his face first this way then that way across my breasts. Then he pushes me right against the wall. He pulls me down to his level, then kisses me full on the lips, the pressure bruising, our teeth clashing. To my horror one hand goes down and lifts my skirt. He drags up the thick cloth and wipes his face and chest with it. I am conscious of my naked legs and ankles and a frozen part of my mind wonders what will happen next.

Then a wave of heat suffuses me and my frozen body melts. I begin to pull at his hair, push him off. He laughs. I stand up straight and bring my fist back and crack him across the side of the head so that his grasp loosens on my waist and he loses his balance. I shoot out of the scullery into the kitchen, closing the door behind me and pulling the settee up against it. I look down at my blackened, soiled skirt, my hands covered with the black scum from his head and his chest.

He is battering on the door calling in a pained voice as though it is I who have done wrong, I who have violated him. I leave him crashing and banging and make my way up the stepladder to the loft. I rake around in my boxes and sort out clothes from skin outwards, right down to corset and chemise. As I take off my spoiled clothes I throw them in the corner. One side of me declares that never, never will I wear these clothes again. At the same time I know I will. Clothes are hard to come by, after all. Even ruined clothes.

Still I hear the dull thud downstairs. I redo my hair and put some of my mother's cologne – brought by Dada back from America – on my wrists and temple. Then I climb back down the ladder, pick up the poker from the hearth and pull the settee away from the scullery door and open it.

Edward is leaning against the wall now, cool as a cucumber. 'About time too, Theo,' he says, his voice silky.

I raise the poker. 'You are lucky not to get this cracked over your head, you . . . you . . . despicable . . .'

He holds a hand up. 'Just let me go and get changed, will you? Can't think what you're doing, messing up the scullery like that.' He rubs his hands together and brushes past me. 'Now, I expect my dinner's got cold.'

I walk out of the house and out of the village, walking blindly on, wondering what I am going to do about all this. I long for the sea: the smell of the salt and the endless charged rhythm of the tide to wash away my fear. Loathing for Edward fills me like bile but the bile is swimming, curdling the milk of fear. All the years in Wales with him being cock-of-the-walk, I was not this frightened of Edward. Even as a small child I defied him and held him in contempt, stood the cuffs and bullyings. But perhaps there in Wales I had my inner life and I had the sea. I had my dreams and the driving tide coming in and washing all the fear and the tension away. In Wales I knew there was a bigger world out there beyond the jagged window. Bigger than Edward. Bigger than all of us, shut in as we were by artificial hills of slag and the ever-moving chains of the winding gear.

But here in County Durham there is no sea. Just a small house in a row of dark houses. Here there is no Murgatroyd to shore me up, make me out to be someone, another self that could be bold and factual on the page, who had respect, self-respect. This was so even if that respect was filtered through regard for a large bewhiskered man who was mortally drunk.

Now alongside the threat of beating and banishment, Edward had added the threat of lust, underscored by the threat of death: the death of Ellen Jones who had also raised lust in his lily-white breast. Part of me was guilty of her death too. Like Pontius Pilate, I had washed my hands of something I felt was surely true but would do naught about. And what about the tar-paper man? Did Edward burn him because of me? Because he took my side?

'Goodness, what's this?' My mother is grasping my hands. 'What are you doing here, Theo, rolling around in the roadway? You'll be ploughed down by some carriage, sure.'

I look round. The afternoon is growing dark. My mother has thrown down her baskets to catch my hands, to stop me chasing this way and that in the High Road.

'Mother.' I pick up her baskets, pleased of their steadying weight. 'I'll help you home. I have come to help you home.'

She looks at me suspiciously but says nothing. She will not pursue the truth, she wants no part of it. As always with her the secret way is safer. She seizes the other basket. 'No matter, I have something to tell you. An amazing thing.'

Rose Clare did have something to tell her daughter: she had a scheme afoot. She had been raised from her numb lethargy for the first time since Ellis left.

The thing had happened in the Market Place. She had done her shopping and was sitting on one of the raised stones beside the market cross before setting off on the long haul back to Gibsley, delighted at least that it was all downhill.

A heavy woman dressed in black had waddled across the Market Place and planted herself in front of Rose Clare, shading the slanting rays of the afternoon sun with a fat hand. Rose Clare was forced to look up. The woman's eyes, small and round, were all pupil, showing no whites. They were like pools of tar. 'Is there something?' Rose Clare said, feeling obliged to say something. The woman was so close to her.

'Oh yes, there's something.' The woman lumbered round to sit beside her in a gale of old food and sweat. The earth seemed to creak as she settled down her skirts. 'You have it around you, shining around you.'

Rose Clare wriggled uneasily and looked behind her, back towards the chattering stall-holders and the restless ponies. 'Round me?' she said.

'Shining out. White and pure. A light you share with all of us. The special ones. You must come to us. We recognise your light. See?'

'Come? Where? Who are you?'

'We're Christians, missis, every one. We hold a little service on a Sat'day night. Saturday, do you see? No interference with any church. Never on Sunday. You'll be Catholic, I suppose?'

Rose Clare stirred uneasily. 'Well, as a child . . .'

'Have no fear. There is no wrong in this. We have a little service for you to contact, to reach out—'

117

'To the dead? It's a sin . . .'

The woman eyed her for a second. 'Not just the dead, missis. To those living who are gone from us. We've had messages from Americky, Australia, Africa, loved ones talking like they were in the same room.'

Rose Clare closed her eyes and saw her own Ellis moving towards her with that rolling gait of his. When she opened them he had gone. 'Where is the meeting? When?'

'Sat'day, tomorrow.' The woman relaxed, slack as a bag of grain now. 'Seven o'clock the room above Velody's Furriers in the High Street. We will be there. All we ask is sixpence for our expenses. Mr Velody is very strict about the rent.' The woman grasped Rose Clare's hands. 'Come. Come! Talk to your loved one . . .' Then she stood up and let go of Rose Clare's hands and they crashed back into her lap. Rose Clare rubbed her hands to force the blood back into them. She watched the woman take her heavy stiff-legged walk into the doorway of the church, where a ginger-haired woman was leaning against the wall, her baskets at her feet. Rose Clare watched the heavy woman talk to her with the same intensity. Another one snared into the meeting, Rose Clare was sure. The woman was a beggar, a charlatan.

But as Rose Clare plodded home with her fish, her husband Ellis rose again in her mind. What trick had the woman used to make her see Ellis? If she could do that perhaps she had other tricks which would let him speak with her. Two months now since she had seen him. Her body ached for his touch, her ear for his speech. She would go to this meeting. But she would not go alone.

'No!'

I cannot believe my ears. She wants me to go to some kind of spook session with her. She never asks me to do anything with her, or for her. We may not be enemies any more, as we were when I was little, but we are in a state of armed truce which involves little fraternisation.

She lifts the net curtain and peers down the mud-packed street. The woman is probably a charlatan. I feel it in my bones that she is. It is just a way of begging, I am sure. But for some reason, for some reason I must go. She pulls the curtain straight and turns to me. 'I can't go on my own, Theo. Please come.'

The room smells of old clothes and wet fur, mixed with lilies and violets. There are only seven or eight people in the room, sitting on chairs pushed up against the wall. Only two of the attenders are men; one of these is so small and narrow he only counts as a half. He is not of dwarfish stature. He only comes midway to my shoulder but is perfectly proportioned. Apart from his old wizened face you would think he was a child of nine.

He struts around as though he is in charge, placing people in chairs; pulling at the cloth on the table in front to straighten it; placing the ginger bottle with its china stopper exactly in the centre, with a clean mug to one side. He makes a great fuss about the tiny lamp, adjusting the wick four times to ensure the correct level of light.

Then he bolts the door through which we have come and settles down on a little stool beside the table at the front. For a minute or two there is pure silence. Then we all jump as the little man bangs the wooden floor with his stick. There is a rattle and a creak and he moves to lift a kind of trapdoor, holding it up while a figure veiled from top to toe in black rises through the space and floats behind the table. There the veil is removed to reveal a woman dressed in a seaweedy green which sparkles in the lamplight. Round her neck she has a rope, heavy as a ship's rope, from which hangs a tawdry crystal star. The little man pipes up. 'Dedicating herself to the service of the assembled company, Mrs Verena Scott.'

There is patter of applause in which I do not join.

I fight down the desire to laugh out loud at this display. Charlatan! What is my mother thinking of?

They sing a hymn and say the Lord's Prayer. The woman invokes the Lord's blessings on these proceedings. Then she sits and holds her crystal tight in her hand. 'A child has been lost.' Her voice breaks and her chin falls on her chest.

Several breaths are drawn in.

'A little boy.'

A few mutters.

'No more than knee high.'

'It's me. It's my young Gerald.' The woman beside me is buzzing with excitement.

'He has gone over, missis.' Verena Scott's voice is neutral.

'Aye. My last lad, missis.'

'He was a good boy. The best.'

'Aye. That's right. Good as gold.'

'No bother.'

'No bother.'

Verena Scott takes a breath. I can feel boredom stream from her like a cloud. She is drenched in it. 'Well, that's exactly like he is over there. He don't want to be no bother there either. He don't like that you are bothering your head.'

'But I miss him so.'

'He says you are not to.' Mrs Scott's voice goes up into a falsetto, no more like a child than a goose's whistle. 'Don't worry, Mam. Don't worry your head about me.'

The woman beside me is nodding vigorously. 'His very voice. His very voice.'

'You hear me, Mam?' the piping voice continues.

'I hear you, son.'

'Find peace close at hand. Find peace.'

'Aye, aye, I hear you, son.'

Mrs Verena Scott's head comes up and her eyes snap round

the company. 'There are many auras beaming around here. Auras of sadness and loss.' She closes her eyes and clutches her crystal. 'I have a man here . . .'

There is a prickling strain in the room as people wait to recognise particular signs so they can take centre stage themselves. 'This man is not much taller than me. His hands cut through the air as he tries to tell me something, to explain. A lot of hair. A big brain. He crosses and recrosses water pursued by demons.'

Rose Clare clutches my arm. 'Ellis.'

'This man is not with us here, yet he is not on the other side. But he is a long way away. He is looking at me through a jagged window. But he lives.'

All around us there is a withdrawal of interest. The people here are only interested in the dead.

Mrs Scott puts her head on one side as though she is listening. 'He says he is sorry. He is definitely sorry about something.'

'So he should be, leaving us high and dry,' I whisper in my mother's ear.

Visibly annoyed by the interruption, Mrs Scott turns and glares at me. Then her fat chin drops on her chest with a slap. 'I can taste the sea. The sea. Floaty seaweed. The fish nibble my ears and my fingers. I see through the green glass. A tide laps up towards me.'

I shudder convulsively and this seems to give Verena Scott more strength. Her voice firms up. 'I can see two children dancing in a ring. "Ring a ring o'roses, a pocket full of posies. Atishoo, atishoo . . ." Two children in a ring but like fishes, holding little flippers not hands. They are happy, do not worry. Be at peace.' The placating voice hardens again. 'But beware that you are not the temptress too and reap the just punishment of all temptresses. Lead us not into evil. Lead us not into evil. Lead us not into evil.'

Two children with flippers.

The little man steps behind her and puts a hand on both shoulders. 'Verena!' he whispers. 'Verena.'

Her head pops up again and she glances round, her eye bleary. 'I have a young man here who had an accident, in the dark somewhere.'

A woman in the corner stirs. 'Our Alfie . . .'

'He is not a young man . . .'

'Not very young.'

'Lost in his prime.' Verena Scott's voice has sunk back in the veils of spooky routine.

I am clinging to my mother's hand. I can feel her bones grinding softly together.

At the end of the – what was it? Service? – we are led in another hymn by the little man who has a fine baritone voice. As he sings he offers his greasy cap and people throw coins in, often more than the requested sixpence. Then we file out. Somehow the little man hustles and shepherds us so that Rose Clare and I are last to leave.

Verena Scott grasps my arm as we pass. 'Thank you, lovely girl.'

I raise my brows, pretending disdain. 'Thank me?'

'Keeps me going.' She winked. 'The odd time it really does happen. The sight.'

On the way home Rose Clare is quite lighthearted and quite dismissive. 'Sure it is a lot of poppycock, all that stuff. I should have known better. The woman's a charlatan, as I say. I do not need that. I know Ellis is truly sorry. He always is.'

But she has been comforted by the bland words of support, as have the other people who sat there. And I am left with the pickle that, very probably, Ellen Jones has spoken to me from beyond the grave to warn me against my own brother. I can just hear his sanctimonious tone, accusing her of tempting him. She knows what he has done to me.

122

'And did you hear the mumbo jumbo about "Ring a ring o'roses?"' went on Rose Clare. 'Children dancing.'

'Just mumbo jumbo,' I say. But I know who they are, the children. They are Ellen's half-born baby and my seal sister dancing below the waves. I march on fast. 'I don't know why you brought me there, Mam. A lot of mumbo jumbo, as you say.'

Ten

Letters

From the first, Edward had hit it off very well with Mr Carmedy, the under-manager at the pit. On pay day in the fifth week Carmedy held Edward back to ask how he was settling in, how he was getting on in the job.

Edward smiled. 'The job is a job, sir. I do my best.'

'I have good reports of your work from the overman.' Anthony Carmedy surveyed the well-set-up young man before him whose good looks shone through the pit dirt. 'And the community. Are you settling in, in Gibsley? The house? You got the coal?'

Edward shrugged. 'It serves. Not so good as our house in Wales, I must say so.' He straightened his shoulders. 'We had a staircase in that house, not a ladder.' He smiled slightly to show he meant no offence.

Carmedy nodded, lips pursed. 'Are you a political man, Maichin? D'you make good use of the vote that was so hard won for you, not so many years ago?'

'Political, Mr Carmedy? I'm much preoccupied with the chapel. Maybe that's political in its own way. Lead men on the righteous way.'

Carmedy shook his head. 'A good and a bad thing, Edward.

If it makes them lie down under the yoke it may not be such a good thing.'

'Jesus saw men as His brothers, yet he knew about rendering to Caesar his own coin.'

Carmedy nodded. 'And what's your persuasion, Edward? How do you vote?'

'Why, Liberal, sir. Always Liberal!'

'Ah! Good man! We've need of upright young men in the Priorton Association. Make your way there. Get into that company, that's my advice.'

'Thank you, Mr Carmedy. I'll follow it. That's good advice.'

Mr Carmedy laughed. 'John George Clelland told me you were a very decent preacher. A preacher of some power. And he should know, as he is a considerable preacher himself. One of reputation too. Mr Stonham, the vicar of St Andrew's, also asked me if I knew you. He tells me you draw people from his pews.'

'I'd not be so vain as to say so, sir. That's for others.' Edward made to go.

'Are you preaching on Sunday, Mr Maichin? My sister and I are Anglican, but we do like a good preacher.'

'Your sister, sir?'

'Miss Carmedy. She teaches at a school in Gibsley.'

'Well, sir, I am preaching out at New Morven on Sunday night. They get a good crowd there. More faces are always welcome.'

'Good. Good. I'm sure my sister will be eager to hear you speak. Injecting variety into the long Sundays is a particular mission of ours.'

Later that day Edward swung along the pit road quite happily. In his head the thoughts tumbled over each other like water over a mill wheel. What a good idea it had been to come to this place. What a good time. Those dolts in Wales with their sly looks and their whispering behind backs had driven him away. But that had led to this place. Then the grandparents had joined the whisperers and betrayed him, dying like that and leaving their money elsewhere. But that too had led him to this place. In this place he could do some good for himself. Things were flowing his way. He could make his mark here. He felt it in his bones.

Good thing, too, to have split his shift away from Caspar. No good having the little runt hanging around all the time, useful as he was. Something else quickened his step. Now, once again, with his father gone, he was master of the household and he was having quite a bit of fun teaching them all their place in it.

I have scribbled this very sentimental story about the childhood of Aphrodite. I am uncertain of the appeal of such a story for the children of miners and tradesmen but I need the five shillings, I want no more dependence on a brother who would do what Edward has done to me.

Mr Murton senior smiles faintly on seeing me. 'Ah! Miss Fairy Story!'

'Good morning, Mr Murton.' I hesitate, unsure of whether to step forward or stay hovering in the doorway.

'Come in! Come in! Take a seat.'

I settle myself at the other side of the table. 'Your story has been very popular, Miss Maichin. Fourteen letters. And Miss Carmedy stopped me in the High Street to give me her considered opinion that it was the most educative story she has ever read in the *Chronicle*.' He laughed. 'I begged to differ, of course, and we had a little chuckle. She does like her jest, does Miss Carmedy. I trust you have a new story for me?'

I sit down and place 'Aphrodite' squarely before him and lay a separated sheet on top of that. 'This one is called "The Childhood of Aphrodite". And on the other sheet is a list of ten more which I will supply at the rate of one a week.'

'Oh, Miss Maichin, I don't know about so many . . .'

I lift the list and smooth it out in front of me. 'Sure, that's no matter.' I am such a liar. 'I'm writing ten anyway for a collection. A London publisher is waiting for them.'

'London.' His eye skims the length of me from my home-trimmed hat to my mended boots. 'London, you say?' He eases the paper back out of my hand. 'Perhaps we will say ten, Miss Maichin. And if the readers' letters keep coming then you may do some more.' He places the list and the story in the drawer to his right. ' But if we are to take dozens of these ahm . . . stories there must be a special rate. Shall we say three shillings and sixpence?'

I cannot grab my list back so I grip the edge of his desk. 'That is not possible,' I said. 'Perhaps four shillings and sixpence. If you're prepared to take twelve of them.'

He puts up one hand, splaying the fingers. 'Four shillings, Miss Maichin. And a secure commission for you for twelve.'

I glance around the room, at the stiff backs of the clerks eavesdropping on this interchange and the round, amused face of Mr Murton junior. 'Will you give me a letter which says this, Mr Murton?'

'A letter? Aren't we formal. Mr Clarence!'

One of the backs turns to reveal the mustachioed visage of a young man affecting middle age. 'Right, Mr Murton. I'll be with you in five minutes.'

'I will wait,' I say. We sit quietly while his pen scratches away. Then Mr Murton blinks and reaches under a pile of papers on his desk. 'Ah. I forgot! This letter came direct to you. The other pile is from more broadly appreciative customers. Two or three of these will go in the paper. And Miss Carmedy, the schoolteacher I mentioned, called into the office. She asked for permission to use your story with her class.' He puts on his narrow wire-framed glasses and reads a scribbled note on his pad. 'Very accessible language,' she says. 'She also asks will there be more.'

I bless my unknown benefactress.

I peer at the letters in the open pile which vary from old pedants pontificating on the benefits of a classical education, to mothers pleased to have such a sweet story to pass the sunlit hours with their dear babes.

The last one, sealed and marked for my particular attention, is in a heavy vellum envelope and carries the faint smell of chickweed.

Dear Miss Maichin,

My son has pointed out a story in the local paper and insists that I write and say how much he enjoyed it. I read the story and must say it had some virtue. We were particularly wondering if you were the same Miss Maichin who travelled North from Sheffield earlier this year. I told him I thought it hardly likely but he insisted. Tragically he is not a very sensible person, but there are times when he can be shrewd, and I thought perhaps this might be one of those times. To remind you: you and your mother sat near us on the train and we conversed briefly. We look forward to your next story and hope that sometime you may visit us up here high in Weardale. You will remember that I extended an invitation on the train.

Sincerely,
Olivia Gervase

'Well!' I say, sitting back.

Mr Murton is discreetly curious. 'Another delighted mother?' he says.

I nod slowly. But I am suddenly thinking of the tiny man dancing attendance on the medium Mrs Verena Scott, just as the huge child-like man had supported Mrs Gervase. Who was he? Her son? Her lover? Her husband?

'Can I take this letter? Can I take it home?' I say, dragging my thoughts back from the image of the seal sister and Ellen Jones's unborn baby dancing beneath the water.

He shrugs. 'It's addressed to you.' He pushes a pile of sixpences across the desk. 'That is for the next story. Here by noon next Tuesday sharp and deadline is like the hangman's rope. It sharpens the certitudes.'

Sharpens the certitudes! What is he talking about?

But I am happier marching home with my four and sixpence in my pocket and the very skeleton of a plan flashing up in my imagination.

I am so bubbling with it that Edward's looming presence at the table, and my mother's shrinking presence by the fire, have no impact on me.

I go to the space behind the boiler by the fire and take out paper and pencil.

'What're you doing?' Edward grunts without lifting his head. 'What've you been hiding away now?'

'I'm getting my writing things from this place. I put them there because some malcontent has been stealing them. Now it is in the open. If anyone steals it I will personally bang them over the head with a spade.' I raise my eyes to his. 'And if it is you, Edward, I will poison every meal that gets in front of you.'

'You are deranged.' But he is flushing. Something in my threat has hit home. 'I don't know what on earth you're talking about.'

'I have a contract now, to write classical stories for children, for the local paper.' I unfurl the letter in its old-fashioned cursive hand, and put it beside the plate. He shoves a forkful of meat in his mouth and reads it. 'You want nothing of this pagan nonsense, Theo. Steer clear.'

'It's what I do. It's my job.'

He overdramatises the laughs and splutters, spraying potato over the table. 'What you *do*? What you *do*, girl, is help your mother organise the house so that I and Caspar – even Rhys – can keep this family going. Seeing' – his eye dropped to the table – 'that our father is too much of a liar and thief to meet his obligations.'

'Edward!' My mother's shout is a cry of pain.

'Mother?' He reaches into his britches pocket, pulls out a sovereign, and throws it on the table. 'Go to McIntyre's and buy me some shirt studs. Someone here has lost me two so I can't go decent to the meeting.'

'Edward!' This time the complaint is weaker.

'Go.'

He has his eye on me and I am scared. I put on my hat again, and stand before the hearth using the ornamental mirror to pin it properly to the lump of hair at the back of my head. 'I'll come too,' I say.

'You stay here.' His tone is powerful, crisp. Like you would use with a dog when you train him.

'Theodora.' My mother wants to placate him.

'I am coming with you.' By exerting a great deal of effort inside my head I manage to keep my voice calm. I will not stay here with him. In front of my mother I will say no more. But he knows.

As we walk along the street my mother looks up at me. 'What is there with you and Edward, Theo? Sure, the boy can be full of himself, but we are all in his hands. He is a good provider, after all.' She pauses. 'And he might be cruel but he is right. Your father has not met his obligations.'

I want to tell her that all of it – the work, the bossiness, the charm, the money – is a way of making Edward fill our world, pushing everything else out. Everything – Ellis, Rhys, my stories, anybody that takes attention away from Edward, who sees himself as a kind of Godhead at the centre of everything.

'This is our bed,' says Rose Clare mournfully. 'And we have to lie in it.'

I march on, disgusted. 'You sound more like him every day, Mother. He's like some kind of plague attacking us all.'

I long to be able to talk to her, to tell her how Edward violated me, how I think he killed the tar-paper man and Ellen, and nearly killed me in the estuary. And I want to tell her that the charlatan, Verena Scott, saw my seal sister dancing in the sand with Edward's drowned, unborn child. But she is wandering along in a world of her own now, no more use to me than a worn-out glove. The secret is kept. It keeps itself.

When we return to the house half an hour later, we are surprised to see that the table is cleared and Edward is sitting at it with a Bible open before him and a notebook at his side. The fire is blazing merrily. As I take off my hat and hang it on the hook, a puff of wind swirls down the chimney and lifts a piece of paper from the top of the flames and spins it into the kitchen on a puff of air. I catch it as it passes and recognise my own writing. 'What's this? What's this?'

'That rubbish in the box.'

'What box?'

'The one under your bed. That scribble.'

'You've been rooting under my bed . . .' My voice rises. I am bawling. 'You went under my bed and got out the box?'

'Yes.' He uses his finger to keep his place in his Bible. 'It's time you put that rubbish behind you, Theo. It only ever made you a laughing stock.'

Numbly, I look at the pile of white ash that floats on the top of the coals. All the sheets from the box – everything I have ever written!

'Everything?' I demand of him now.

He looks smug. 'Everything. You've other ways with which

to occupy yourself these days. This is the grown-up world, Theo!'

I grab his Bible from the table and start to hit him with it, raining blows on his shoulders and head. He backs off a little, a glimmer of a smile on his lips. Finally he grabs my wrist and wrests it from my grasp. 'You'll rot in hell for that,' he says pleasantly, bringing his face close to mine. 'Rot in hell!'

Standing in the corner Rose Clare watched her son like a hawk, noting the spittle at the corner of the apparently calm mouth, the patches of red on the high cheekbones. 'Go to your bed, Theo,' she instructed her daughter. 'Get out of here.'

Rose Clare knew this look on her son's face. She had seen it a generation ago, when her brother Liam took her for his own, before pledging her to his customers as collateral in his wagers.

'Mother!'

'Go to your bedroom, Theo.'

I hear their voices rumble down below: his deep and resonant, hers strident. Then I hear the ricochet of a slap. Then silence. I scramble underneath the bed in the gap where the box has been, and bring out the sheet which has the drawing of the salt marsh on it; the one which went into the paper to illustrate the tragedy of Ellen's death. I sit on the bed clutching the drawing, and decide that she is right. Retreat is the only way with Edward. Get out of his sight or presence or he will do you ill.

I take off my outdoor coat and smooth it down on the bed. The crisp crackle of vellum resounds in my ear like a great gong. I take out Mrs Gervase's letter and smooth it on my hand, then hold the letter up to the scarce light from the roof window, trying to make out the address. *Goshawk Shield. Nr*

Stanhope. Good thing I had not yet placed the letter in my box or it would have gone up the chimney like the rest of my papers; up in flames like the tar-paper hut. Loki's story, Aphrodite's, even they only existed now as part of Mr Murton's world, so temporary and fragile. I will have to copy them from the newspaper to make them permanent again, to make them mine.

There are twelve clean sheets of paper on the gimcrack chest which stands beside the bed which Mother and I share. I take the paper and my precious pen and ink downstairs. The kitchen is empty. I can hear the clash of dishes from the little scullery next door. Edward is nowhere to be seen. Hearing me, my mother comes into the kitchen. 'Edward went to see the Reverend Stonham. Something to do with a Mr Carmedy, although what Edward is doing with a Church of England minister, sure I don't know.' She watched me for several minutes, 'Good heavens, child. What are you doing there?'

'Edward spoiled them. All my stories.'

'You're not to mind him, so!' she says sharply. 'He has these fits of temper. You're to ignore him.'

I notice a bruise on her cheek. 'You saw what he did. He burned everything, Mother, everything. Stories from many years ago. Letters from Dada. From the American aunties.'

She stirs uneasily under my gaze. 'You're not to mind him,' she repeats. 'Without your father we depend on him.'

'We don't. I told you I have a contract, a letter of intent from the newspaper.'

Rose Clare laughs that helpless laugh of hers. 'Contract! For stories! Don't be silly!'

'And I have an offer of work from Mrs Gervase. You know, the woman we met on the train? The one who lives on the farm in the hills?'

Rose Clare throws herself on to the hard chair beside the

fire. 'Farm? You could work on no farm. Farm work is hard and long. Unforgiving.'

I talk on. 'I'll work on the farm for my keep, and keep to the contract for the stories. There'll be more of that. The writing.'

'Edward will not hear of it.' She turns to one side and stares out of the window. 'He'll not hear of you doing that.'

'Edward will not know until I'm gone.' I drop to my knees in front of her and clasp the arms of her chair. 'If I stay he will kill me, Mother.' I turn her face to mine. 'If you stay he will kill you.'

'Kill? What do you say, you silly child. I—'

'He will kill me like he killed the tar-paper man, and like he killed Ellen Jones. Because I offend him. He will kill you because he will make you destroy yourself.'

'Sure, you're a mad one, child. Crazy. Edward says so, that you need protecting from yourself. I'm sorry to say he is right.' She closes her eyes and puts her hands over her ears and shuts me away from her. She wrests her hand away from mine.

I stand up, go back to the table and settle down to rewrite the story of Loki, and 'The Childhood of Aphrodite' from memory.

Eleven

Commerce

Rhys Maichin had never been happier in his life. From her seat in the shop old Mrs Berriman looked out for him every day, ready for their 'bit of crack'. On his mother's orders Mr Berriman had given him the job of selling the ironmongery from a horse-drawn van, to the village shops and farms further up the dale. So on two days a week he wore a brown drill coat over his 'preacher's suit' and travelled up the dale in the van, supplying and taking orders from every ironmonger and general dealer in every village. Even this was more fun than he had thought. Such a well-set-up young man. There was a great charm about him; with his glowing skin and fine bright eyes, Rhys was a welcome sight in the boring day-in-day-out life of small villages. The women, young and old, watched out for him, savouring the refreshment of his ready smile.

When he returned from his rounds he made sure that he hovered inside the shop fingering the small satchel which contained his order book, knowing he cut a fine figure in his black suit. Mrs Berriman said the suit put years on him. 'Makes a man of you, sure anyone would see that.'

'Is there anything I can get you, Mrs Berriman, while I'm still out and about, before I plunge back into the warehouse and vanish for ever?'

'Mm. Yes, now you mention it. Perhaps you'd just call in to Rainbow's drapery and buy me five yards of rose ribbon. My granddaughter asked me to get it for her. She's busy trimming something . . . I forget what.'

He was back in ten minutes, happily clutching the tissue package in the deep pocket of his coat. Roger Bly winked and clicked his teeth at him as he passed, and he winked back. He stopped by Mrs Berriman's kiosk and waited while she settled up with a big burly customer for a pair of iron gates. 'I have your ribbon here, Mrs Berriman!' He took a breath. 'I wondered, does Miss Berriman need it urgently? Perhaps I could take it straight up to the house?'

She stared at him, then a light of mischief dawned in her eyes. 'Sure, Ruth was in a great hurry for it this morning when I left the house. Yes! Take it straight to her. Don't be fobbed off now. Give it into her own hands!' The old woman smiled faintly as the boy raced off, clashing the great glass doors behind him. That would show her nose-in-the-air daughter-in-law; the one who despaired at the fact that the great wealth she spent on her furs and furbelows had to come from something as low as trade, who regretted that her dear husband Gerald had to soil his hands with hot steel before picking up his filthy lucre. And who, above all, perpetually whined about a mother-in-law with money enough to hold a genteel salon every day, who stooped so low as to sit in front of a dirty workshop taking money from common workmen.

At the house the maid wanted to take the package from Rhys but he held hard on to it. 'Mrs Berriman said I was to put it into Miss Ruth's own hands.'

The maid, short, square and ginger-haired, stared at him. He winked at her and proffered a sixpence. She winked back and took it. 'Right,' she said. 'I'll enquire.'

He looked round the hall as he waited. Polished black and white tiles. Glittering mirrors. Heavy frames on paintings of ships and men in civic dress: one of Mr Berriman holding his oboe, his round face beaming. Rhys could hear a piano being played in some upper region: a clattering, angry sound. The piano stopped and it was as though the house sighed with relief. The maid came back downstairs. 'Miss Ruth says I'm to show you into the parlour.' She paused a little too long. 'Sir.'

The parlour was a dark cluttered room, the curtains shut against the invading light. The maid opened these slightly and a blinding streak of light shot across the glittering surfaces to hit the bright brasses which lay crossed like swords before an unlit fire.

'What what what, what what! What is it? Splice the mainbrace! Splice the mainbrace!' The shrieking voice made Rhys jump. The maid went and pulled a cloth off a cage which was hanging within the deep bay window. In the cage was a parrot hunched malevolently on his perch, rocking from foot to foot like a fat man with corns.

'He still jaws on, even with the cloth ower the cage!' The maid smiled at him, showing a gap at one side of her mouth where two teeth were missing. 'Don't mind the Captain, mister. His squawk is worse than his bite.'

'The Captain?'

'Belonged to Mr Berriman's father. That Mr Berriman was a sea captain taking coal to Russia and bringing stuff in from the East. China, I think. And tea. Funny old carvings.' She glanced round the room. 'Place is full of that kind of rubbish. Damned bother to clean.' She put a hand to her mouth. 'Oops.' She winked at him, 'Outta line, ain't I?'

The door handle turned and the maid's face became blank and featureless. 'Miss Ruth, sir,' she said. And she went and held the door while Ruth Berriman, looking elegant in a pale green damask day dress, glided in.

On closer examination Ruth Berriman was not so beautiful

nor so young as he had thought. She must be at least five years older than he was. And her brows were too heavy, her eyes too narrow. But she held herself well and had a kind of fine-boned grace. Her smile was friendly enough. 'Beatrice says you have a package for me, Mr . . .'

'Name of Rhys Maichin, Miss Berriman. I work for your father.' He proffered the package. 'Your grandmother asked me to obtain this for you.'

Ruth Berriman took the packet and opened it, then looped a finger through the ribbon and pulled it out in a tangle. 'You went to the shop to get this?' She was openly laughing.

'Yes. I went to Rainbow's for it. She said they would have it. Is there something wrong? She said you needed it urgently.'

'Did she tell you what I needed it for?'

He shook his head.

'I would hope not. Even she is not . . . that naughty.'

Rhys blushed.

'Oh, Mr Maichin. Have we trapped you between us, Grandma and I?'

He smiled. 'Seems so, Miss Maichin.'

She walked across and opened the curtains further then went to turn the lever on the bell by the fireplace. 'Why don't you sit down, Mr Maichin? I'll get Beatrice to bring us some tea.'

'The shop, Miss Berriman, I suppose I should . . .'

'My grandmother sent you. I'm in charge of you now. No wrong can come to you.' Beatrice was at the door. 'Beattie! A tray of tea, if you please.'

'Right-o, Miss Ruth!' Beattie grinned openly and scuttled away.

Rhys relaxed. He had never in his life been inside a house as plush as this. Here the rules must be different.

Ruth threw herself into a chair, swishing her dress to one side to show a good stretch of ankle. 'You can't think how

138

dreadfully tiring it is, Mr Maichin, lolling round this house, banging away on the piano and taking tea with ostriches and fat hens who call themselves the ladies of this . . .' She paused. '. . . place.'

Rhys smiled broadly. 'Steady, steady, Miss Ruth. Very respectable ladies. Your mother . . .'

'Oh yes. My mother. I am a great disappointment to her.'

'I heard you had run away with a circus,' he said, his eyes meeting hers for a bare second before they slid away.

'And nearly married a gypsy?' She laughed. 'I have heard that story myself.'

'Is it true?'

She shrugged. 'It was wonderful going off and knowing the storm it would cause here, but it was not so exciting as it seemed. The highlight for me was learning to do cartwheels. It was mostly cold, hard and very wet.'

He dare not ask her about the gypsy. 'So it was a relief to get home?'

She shrugged again. 'There was no choice. Nowhere else to go.' She paused. 'So you know what I would like to do, Mr Maichin?'

'What?'

'Well, I would like either to go to America or Africa. Or . . . work in the shop dispensing nails and iron bars, like my grandmother. She has more jollity in a day down there than I have in a month. But I am not permitted. My father says I'm to be a lady, wear shoes and' – she grinned daringly – 'corsets that pinch. I'm to practise scales so that I can accompany him on his damned oboe; I must talk to young men who snuffle through their noses and neigh instead of talk.'

She stretched back in the chair and he noted again her lean elegant frame. She shook her head. 'You should see their surprise, Mr Maichin, and that of their families, when I turn these treasures down one after another. Consider the absurdity of arranging a match between an ironmongery and a flour mill, an ironmongery and a railway shop, an ironmongery and a drapery! Ridiculous, you may say. But the only one who sees that is my dear old grandma, who's rescued me more than once from a fate worse than death.'

'Must be . . . I wouldn't like it, to be sure,' he said.

'No! No! What intelligent person would?'

Someone kicked at the door and Rhys opened it to let in Beattie staggering under a tray laden with a heavy silver tea service.

'Here! Here! Leave it, Beattie!' Ruth patted the low table beside her. 'Now scoot! Run away! We talk about affairs of the world too dangerous for your young ears.'

Rhys held the door for the maid who winked and rolled her eyes as she passed him. There was no doubt she thought her mistress quite mad.

Ruth talked rapidly as she poured the tea. 'No, no, Mr Maichin! Things will have to change here or I will die of boredom. Curl up like a leaf on a dry day. Or run away for good.' She handed him his cup. 'And you will help me.'

He sat back in his chair and took a sip of the tea, which was half cold, with leaves floating on the top. He looked at her over the rim of his cup. 'Why me?' he said.

'Because you are young and very handsome, even intelligent. Because you have taken my fancy. Because you talk like my grandmother. Because it is Tuesday. Oh! No matter what!' she said crossly.

He beamed across at her. 'And how might I help you, Miss Berriman?'

'Where d'you live, Mr Maichin? I'll call on you. I will know your family.'

His mind raced. 'I live in Gibsley . . .' He thought of the pit hovel, then looked round at the glittering room. ' But that's only until I can get rooms here in Priorton.'

'Rooms! Splendid!' She smiled. 'I'll help you find rooms and I will call. We will be friends.'

'Friends? This is very . . . wonderful, but why me?' He had never met anyone, except Edward, who was so managing. In her he liked it.

She shrugged and he noticed now how soft and full her neck was, how smooth her shoulders. 'You? You? My grandmother sends you to me with camisole trimmings' – she said the words without a blink – 'on a day when I am crashing through Chopin, deciding I must commit suicide, run away, or settle to be an eccentric old maid in this Godforsaken town.' She was speaking rapidly, shooting the words out like bullets. 'And you turn up smart and workmanlike in your black suit, an eager hungry look on your face.' She ran her eyes down him from his head to the tip of his toes as he lounged in her mother's chair. 'Handsome in a certain way . . . You'll do, Mr Maichin.' She stood up suddenly and held out her hand, forcing him to tumble to his feet, clattering his cup on to the table. 'Come tomorrow after work. Seven o'clock. By then I will have found you lodgings in the town.' She paused. 'Lodgings appropriate for our needs.'

'Your parents . . .'

'I will introduce you.'

'Your father knows me. Your grandmother knows me.'

'I will introduce you as my intended.' She put out her hand.

Then he found himself doing something he had never done. His father had done it to Theo when he returned from America. It had seemed, then, to be such an extravagant gesture. But now he took Ruth Berriman's hand and kissed it, pressing his lips fervently on its soft surface. He grinned up at her. 'Seems like . . . seems like you've swept me off my feet, Miss Berriman. Is this what you did to the gypsy?'

She dropped his hand and stepped back. She smiled faintly. 'We'll have no talk of the gypsy!' she commanded. 'That is forbidden! Now go! And come back tomorrow.'

The maid Beattie showed him out. 'She's nice, Miss Ruth, sir, but she's mad as Christmas. Gets swept away, like. Tek no notice of her.'

He bounced down the road away from the heavily decorated house. Well, what had he done? Or had she done it? Or had the grandmother done it? Was Ruth Berriman so mad she would completely forget tomorrow what she had said today? Would he be mad to turn up at seven o'clock the following night? They'd probably throw him out on his ear. Oh well. He jammed his hat on his head at a cocky angle. We'll see. We'll see. They could only throw him out once.

I can't tell Rhys of my decision to go and work for Mrs Gervase because he's never here. Caspar has got in with some dog men and is also out all the time. Talks about racing and training but it's mostly drinking and gambling. You hear about his wins but never his losses. Edward has no time for Caspar nowadays.

At least at present I don't have to endure too much of Edward's company myself. He's out at chapel meetings and now Liberal meetings when he's not at the pit. There's been no recurrence of the attack he made on me and he's not touched my papers again. But sometimes when he's eating his dinner I can feel him looking at me through the side of his eyes and I know the threat is still there.

There is some unfinished business before I make my move to Mrs Gervase's farm. I walk up to Priorton with my mother on market day, leave her to look at fish and cabbages and wander the Market Place and the High Street looking for Mrs Verena Scott. First I try the furrier's, where the meeting was held. The assistant, a lemon-faced woman in a long black frock, says Mrs Scott only comes on Fridays to pay the rent for Saturday night, but perhaps I might find Mrs Scott in Mrs

Morpurgo's Tea Rooms. She always has her dinner there on Fridays.

She is right. Mrs Scott sits in the corner of the room like a black meringue overflowing on to two seats, an array of plates before her which would feed four hungry people. I look round and note, thankfully, that her small companion, that strange possessive little man, is nowhere to be found.

I slide on to the seat opposite her and she looks at me over a spoonful of potato. She is not bothering with knives and forks. Rather insufficient for her purpose, I imagine. 'Yes?' she says, concentrating on her potato, chewing it thoroughly, a small bubble of it oozing from the side of her mouth.

'We met the other evening at your meeting, Mrs Scott. I came with my mother.'

'I know who you are,' she said crossly. 'But I'm having me dinner.'

I put two shillings from my precious four and sixpence story money on the table. 'I want to ask your advice.'

She looks sorrowfully at her plate and the rest of the food. 'Can't do two things at once,' she says. She stands up, nearly tipping the table over in front of her. 'We'll sit at another table.' She signals to the hovering waitress. 'Put me grub in the oven ter warm, missis. We'll just take this table in the corner, for convenience, like.'

The hard-faced waitress nods benevolently enough. Perhaps she has benefited from Mrs Scott's wisdom before today. Or perhaps Mrs Scott is just a very good customer, eating four dinners in one.

'What is it?' Verena Scott says, the unctuous desire to please wiped out by the disruption of her earthly appetites.

'What you said as we left the meeting the other day. About—'

'Your story being real? Well, miss, you've no idea how hard it is grubbing a living like this. Folks *want* to know. They

143

want to believe. They are so *needy*. They feed, feed off you even when there's nothing there. And you *give*, give them what they need. But sometimes it's real. Then my spirit takes food, like. I get something back.'

'And it was real, what you said, about the children dancing around under the water?'

She frowns. 'Did I say that?' She rubs the palms of her hands down her greasy coat. 'Here. Give us yer hand.'

I place both my hands in hers. She crushes my fingers together and turns them backward and forwards. 'Yes, yes. But they're strange, these little ones. Minnows. Tadpoles. The unborn, the half-formed.' Now her hands clutch harder at mine. 'But it can't be, lass. One is you but not you. She has your face.' She turns my hands over and strokes the palms, making me itchy and uncomfortable. 'I spoke of danger, did I?'

'Yes.'

'Aye. You're to keep watch. There is raw danger around you. One without let or stay on his ambition. But wily as a snake. Aye. And you're a strange one yourself, come to that.'

'Am I?'

'This man at a fairground, a long time ago. A sailor that'd gone across the world. He told me of an animal which sheds its skin, hundreds of times in its life, becoming new. Renewed. You're like that snake. You will shed skins.'

I laugh hoarsely, disbelieving. 'Me, a snake?'

Her chins wobble as she nods. 'You can change yourself. Make yourself this or that. Throw off the old, take on the new. Shed one skin, show another.'

I shake my head, not quite understanding. She is still clutching my hands. 'There will be great heartache. A tragedy. Yet still you will go on shedding skins.'

I try to pull my hands away. She hangs on. 'You'll give and get great pleasure, but you will pay. There will be balance.

Nature demands it.' My hands feel welded to hers now. They make one thing. 'The sea! Those children were *ring-a-rosying* in the sea. You will be many times by the water. You need the salt water like a man needs blood to flow in his veins. You'll get sustenance from it. I see a creature of the sea. Round head, round eyes. Sliding through the water. Then on dry land, same only different. Trotting.'

'Seal sister,' I say, offering the woman something at last. 'I call her my seal sister. She was my twin. I was born alive, she was . . . not alive.' I stare at our hands, fused together. 'I've sometimes thought I must have killed her, in there. Inside my mother.'

'Aah.' It is a great escape of breath. Then her chins wobble as she shakes her head. 'No. No. She says not that. Who she was was welded to you so that way she lives. She swims around you, helping you off with your skins but because she is there . . .' Verena Scott pauses, frowning. These ideas are very hard for her to handle. 'I think she says that shedding the skins is no danger. She still makes sure that what's underneath is you. And her. And she is on dry land, trotting.'

I wrest my hands away. 'I can't make head nor tail of what you're saying.'

The chins wobble again as she lets out a great howling laugh. 'No more can I, lovely. But would I make up such nonsense? That's what she is sayin', I'm tellin' yer.' The woman stands up, ramming her chair into the wall. 'Lily!' she shouts. 'Get that dinner out. I'm starving.'

What this woman has said is magical, but there is no magic in her. I stay where I am, and watch her settling down again to her feast. She picks up her spoon and looks at me. 'Satisfied?'

'We-ell . . .' I am really uncertain of what to say.

'Well, pet, mebbe you shouldn't have asked?' She heaps potatoes and meat on her spoon and jabs it at her mouth. I make my way out of the café into the street, deciding that she

145

is a charlatan, but a charlatan who now and then hands out a little magic. Nothing she has said will make any difference to what I intend to do, but I still feel that from that gross body with its mobile fleshy mouth I have somehow heard from my little seal sister. And what was that about trotting?

My mother has left me dawdling behind her on the long road back from Priorton. When I turn into our entry, my head still ringing with the strange conversation with Mrs Verena Scott, I come upon one of Caspar's dog men, a hatchet-faced man called Joss Vipond. He's squatting down on his haunches outside our back gate, with a whippet between his knees. His gnarled hands, criss-crossed with blue scars, cradle the fine head as though it is fragile china. Her round eyes, too large for her tiny head, peer up at me with graceful curiosity.

'I'm after thee brother,' Joss Vipond volunteers as I put my hand on the gate latch.

I look down the narrow yard towards the kitchen window. 'Is he in?'

'Thee mother ses he's out.'

I open the gate. Joss Vipond hauls himself to his feet, his knees creaking. 'I brought him a bitch, like.' He lifts the whippet, clutched in a single hand now, up in front of my nose, her delicate paws hanging down. She eyes me patiently, enduring the rough handling with resignation. I put a finger on her brow. Her fur is dark grey with a bluish tinge. It slides past my finger like fine napped grey velvet.

'Thy Caspar shared an interest in the litter, like. Thought he might like one to race. Thoo can tek it for him.'

'He's not home, Mr Vipond. I can hardly take a dog for him.'

'He promised us a florin for her. Took a real fancy for her, he did.' His sharp eyes raked my face. 'She has a good line. Golden Seal and Emperor's Seal in her blood. I have the papers.'

Seal? The dog pushes her head up underneath my hand and looks at me and I am lost. Mr Vipond drops her on to my forearm and she clings on to me, weighing no more than a loaf of bread. I pull her to me and I can feel her fine head against my breast. 'I'll give her to him when he comes.'

'Caspar said a florin. He would give a florin for one of the litter.'

I feel in my pocket and finger the two shilling piece and sixpence I have left from the story money. The little dog starts to shiver. I pull out the florin and thrust it into his hand. 'There,' I say. 'I'll get it from him when I see him.'

He grunts and touches his cap, the deference born, I think, of relief that he has his money. 'Tell Caspar I'll see 'm,' he says and walks swiftly down the back lane with that slightly rocking gait caused by stiff joints from working in the wet. Many miners walk this way.

I hug Seal to me and take her in to show my disbelieving mother. 'That Caspar!' she says. 'Mixing with those gamblers. Sell their souls to make the bet. They would, so! I know them of old. Your Uncle Liam was a gambler.' Her face hardens. 'He would do anything for a bet. We want no dog here.' She peers closer at the dog. 'Mind you, she's well named. Just like a little seal. Look at those eyes . . .'

So the trembling form and the fairy face of the little dog soften my mother's resolve. She finds a large tin basin, lines it with an old towel and places the dog there, stroking her head and her back until the trembling stops.

Caspar roars with laughter when he sees the dog. 'That old devil. That Joss Vipond!'

'He said you wanted her. I gave him two shillings,' I say. 'I said I would get it from you.'

'Want her? Want her?' He picks up the dog and sets her on the ground, then claps his hands. She staggers for a step, then walks across the stone floor. 'See? See that lopsided walk?

The runt of the litter. Her brothers can run but she can't.' He laughs into my face again. 'I'm not paying good money for a runt.'

'But my two shillings . . .'

He shrugs. 'Your loss, Theo. Old Joss must be hard up for a bet, mind you, selling a runt to a soft-minded girl like you.' He lifts the dog back into her makeshift bed. 'Your dog, so far as I can see, Theo. Though I'd drown her rather than race her, if I were you.'

I kneel down beside the fire, my face burning as a flame roars up from newly ignited coal. The little dog looks up at me, fine, wise and old at the same time. Seal grey. Golden Seal. Emperor's Seal. Seal trotting around me. That was what Verena Scott had said. I know she is mine. The living spirit of my seal sister. 'I'll keep her. She can be mine.' The words fall out of my mouth before I know they are in my head.

'A dog?' says my mother. 'Sure, you can hardly take care of yourself, girl.'

'She was sent to me,' I say.

Caspar throws himself into the chair beside the fire. 'More rubbish. Always rubbish, Theo Maichin. Not right up top. Never were. You'll end up in a lunatic asylum.'

'Edward won't like it,' says my mother, a line creasing her brow. 'He won't want a dog here.'

'It's not Edward's dog,' I say. 'It's my dog. In any case, it will be no affair of his. I am going away.'

Caspar whistles. 'Away? To a lunatic asylum?'

'I am going away to work. There was a letter . . .' No, I am not going to explain it. They can make of it what they will.

'Anyway,' says Caspar, eyeing my mother, who is starting to clatter plates on the table. 'All of this is matterless to me. I'm off myself tomorrow. To a new pit in Northumberland.'

'Off?' Rose Clare looks at him.

'Truth is, Mam, there are a few problems about – well,

paying off this big debt for a dog that won that shouldn't 'a. That's why old Joss was wanting money for the dog. He lost on the same wager and there's a man sitting on my shoulder that I owe. A very bad and a very angry man.'

'Caspar, you fool, you young—' My mother's voice carries a rare fury. 'You can't go. You must not go.'

He shrugs, then smiles calmly at her. 'Well, I wouldn't go as far as thieving or even deceiving to get the money. But I will run away. And running away is in the family tradition, isn't that so? Isn't that what Theo's doing? Like our Dada? Running away.'

'Caspar,' I warn. This is not fair.

My mother sits down hard on a kitchen chair, and the three of us freeze for second, like statues in a tableau. Then the back door opens with a clatter and Rhys breezes in on a chill gale of early evening air. He is looking fit and prosperous in his black suit. 'Well, what's this, then?' he says. 'A funeral?'

'It's Caspar,' I say to Rhys. 'He's going off to Northumberland. He's leaving home.'

Rhys leans against the table and peels off his yellow gloves. 'Well, that *is* a strange thing. I'm going to fix up lodgings in Priorton. Nearer to work, and there's such a lot for me to do up there. So I'm off too.'

'And Theodora here, she's off to goodness knows where. She won't let on,' Caspar puts in. 'Although it's a big secret just who'll have the pleasure of her company except for that dog there she's just paid good money for.' His laugh echoes round the silent room. 'Well, Mam. It'll be just you an' good old Edward, then. Grace before meals. Temperance and all that. No gambling. He'll have you living like a nun.'

I look into my mother's face and see the dawning fear. I've not thought of this. Not thought this through. I'd thought of going to see Mrs Gervase, offering my services, earning my keep from her, writing the stories and sending them back to Priorton, perhaps even further afield. But now, looking at her stricken face, I know I cannot leave my mother. Does that mean I must stay here myself? Without even the robust presence of Rhys and Caspar to sand the sharp edges of Edward's presence, haunted by the knowledge of his dark side. Even if only I know what he did to the tar-paper man and Ellen Jones, my mother has seen that dark side too. She has seen it and in her bones she knows it.

'Mam'll not be on her own with Edward. She is to come with me,' I say abruptly, the words out of my mouth before the thought has formed. 'It is arranged.'

In the storm of talk which follows, I notice my mother does *not* say no, that she is not coming with me.

Twelve

High Adventure

Rhys was rather put out; not just by the fresh turn of events at
home. He had yawned his way through the Saturday evening
recital of the Priorton Orchestra, in order to meet Ruth
Berriman on the way in or on the way out. He had called, as
instructed, at the Berriman home at seven o'clock. The little
maid Beattie told him the family were at a concert at the
Temperance Hall. Miss Berriman had said to tell him.

Beattie pushed a note into his hands.

Dear Mr Maichin,
  *I have arranged for you to have two rooms at number
7, Fencale Street. It is a quiet house. Perhaps we will
meet at the concert?*
  R.

As it was, he only caught sight of Ruth through a forest of
serge-clad shoulders and velvet capes which even he could
not penetrate. The sight of his brother Edward sitting in the
front row beside that sallow sister of Mr Carmedy cast him
further into dark gloom and he made off at the earliest
opportunity. At least on Monday at work he would tell Mrs
Berriman he had been to the concert, and hope, at least, the

message would get through to Ruth.

Edward for his part had enjoyed the recital. He especially relished his prominent seat in the front row, beside Miss Carmedy, sister of Anthony Carmedy, who played the oboe in the orchestra with more energy than finesse. At present Anthony's oboe was at rest as he listened with sharp concentration to a narrow man with a shock of grey-blond hair, who was doing some justice to a middle passage of a Mozart violin concerto.

After the concert Edward joined a large company in taking supper with the Carmedys in their tall house on the Avenue: a great opportunity for him to play with gusto the role of the fiery young preacher who wanted to change the world for the better. Looking around, he realised that music was one of the combining forces in this gathering: an eclectic mixture of miners and tradesmen, teachers and shop workers in the cluster of people scattered round the long room. He recognised a good number of faces from the Central Methodist Church. The other combining force was the Liberal Party, which seemed to be the political leaning of most of the people here. The Liberals had been a force back home in Wales, of course, but his grandfather had steered him away from such worldly concerns, always back to the fundamental study of the Word and the Book. These sacred things were not, Thomas Maichin said, tarnished by worldly ambition, as was politics, however innocently embarked upon.

In his life so far Edward had only heard matters of religious doctrine discussed with such passion and intensity. Here it was the Irish Question, the issue of pit safety, and the need to encourage those with franchise to vote.

'You are enjoying our little company, Mr Maichin?' Miss Claris Carmedy, his host's sister, stood before him, a plate of rather stodgy scones balanced on the palm of her hand.

152

'Very fine, Miss Carmedy. Very fine.' He opened his eyes wide and looked fully into the sharp eyes in the shallow-featured face. 'To be honest I'd not thought you'd get such company in a coal town.' He put down his teacup, then took a scone and set it on his china plate.

'Ah, there is such company anywhere, if you seek it out.' She paused. 'My brother thinks you will flourish in its midst.'

'So it seems, Miss Carmedy.' His gaze wandered to the corner where Mr Carmedy, his hand describing arcs in the air, his face red with enthusiasm, was talking to a large man with a heavy neck and a very round face, who had played the oboe alongside him in tonight's concert. Edward was aware now that this was Mr Berriman, Rhys's boss. 'I've not seen Mr Carmedy so enthusiastic about anything. He's a quiet man at the pit, getting about his job.'

She looked fondly at her brother. 'Ah Mr Maichin, that very quietness, that very determination stands him in good stead at White Pool. You see, he talks to the men, represents them fairly to the manager and to Lord Chase. White Pool has had fewer problems than any pit in the county.'

Edward suddenly wanted to puncture that pride, to demolish her complacency. He was resentful of her support for her brother. In his experience, sisters did not support brothers.

'In one way you surprise me, Miss Carmedy. The reason I'm here was because Mr Carmedy was setting on outsiders after the dispute last year. A bad dispute, I heard, with miners sacked outright, and disturbances down in Gibsley. A shaft was fired, so I hear.'

A frown marred her over-wide brow. Then she peered up at him. 'You pick on the one thing which nearly broke my brother's heart, Mr Maichin. There was a problem with a group of miners from Cornwall who had become arrogant, in his view. They had moved from pit to pit for the highest wage.

153

They were beaten down for price. Then there was sabotage at White Pool and Lord Chase insisted they be dismissed wholesale, guilty or not. It was not my brother's choice, I do assure you.' He had offended her and her tone was cool.

'Well,' he said easily, smiling his wide smile. 'It was my good fortune because it brought me here and I think White Pool suits me very well. Mr Carmedy is a very fair man, in my view.'

She nodded, mollified by his tone. 'I understand you're a preacher, Mr Maichin. My brother and I came to listen to you at New Morven. Very powerful delivery.'

'You were there?' He even blushed. He was pleased about that. 'I'm sorry I didn't see you . . .'

'But there was such a crush. You have quite a following. You bring a reputation with you from Wales.'

He smiled slightly but shook his head. 'I'd not admit to such vanity, Miss Carmedy. That crush, as you call it, was eagerness for the word of the Lord. But yes, I do preach. I am called to it, like my grandfather before me.'

She laughed, her long lips lifting above her even teeth for the first time. 'Ah Mr Maichin, my brother and I are loyal sheep in the flock of the Reverend Stonham of St Andrew's. I teach in the Church of England school in Gibsley. We conform, we conform, my brother and I. It is an old habit, a family habit. But only in religion. I understand that you have Liberal sympathies, Mr Maichin?'

'So have you and Mr Carmedy, unlike most of your fellow Anglicans. Always thought they were Conservatives to a man . . . or a woman.'

She laughed again. A deep hearty sound. 'There you have us, Mr Maichin. Now then! Let me take you across to see Mr Glinton. He'll urge you to preach politics alongside religion, if you want a just world.'

Mr Glinton, an elderly man with an old-fashioned high

collar, was sitting in the window seat, smoking a pipe and contemplating the company. 'Mr Glinton! This is the young miner my brother was telling you about, Mr Edward Maichin. Mr Maichin, Mr Elias Glinton, who is a great mover in the Liberal Party here in Priorton.'

The old man hauled himself to his feet and shook Edward heartily by the hand. 'Do you want to get on in this world, Mr Maichin, as well as to ensure your seat in the next? Do you want to improve the lot of all men, even while you render unto Caesar that which is Caesar's?'

'I suppose I do, sir,' said Edward rather stiffly, uncomfortable under the old man's gaze. Elias Glinton was looking at him as though he were a particularly tasty morsel of chicken which he was about to gobble up. But this old man would be useful to him, as would the plain-as-a-pikestaff Miss Carmedy. They had their uses, as most people did.

I am surprised that my mother agrees to travel so readily with me up into the wilds of south Durham. She is not eager but her willingness to do it is sealed by Edward's reaction to our family schemes of flight. He flings off his coat (which carries a spice-and-tobacco scent of somebody's drawing room) and stamps about the cramped kitchen, his fury crackling off the ceiling and the walls. 'Your place is here, all of you! Flight! Flight! The Ellis Maichin solution to the problems of the world. Like father, like sons. Like father, like daughter!'

Rhys eyes him calmly. 'I'm fleeing nowhere, brother. I have a job in Priorton,' he says. 'I take lodgings in Priorton where, if I am not mistaken, I will have a life.' He smiles secretly. 'I was going to ask you if you enjoyed the concert, Ed, but maybe this is not the time.'

'You!' The words drop gently from Edward's hard mouth. 'Job? You do a slavey's job, fetching and carrying, doffing your cap.'

'I see the sky and the sun each day,' says Rhys. 'I talk to people, real people, not hard men whose only way to prove themselves is by feats of strength fathoms underground. I can work. Earn a wage. I can go to concerts, lectures, just like you.' He smiles. 'Maybe not in the front row, though, like some I could name.'

Edward's hands curl into fists. 'You're a coward, Rhys. Always were.'

Rhys grins openly. 'Just so, brother. I don't like to hit people or be hit myself. If that makes a coward then a coward I am.'

Edward turns his attention to Caspar. 'And you! You're better off out of this town. Shame on you! Gambling debts. Bad company.'

Caspar is never happy at Edward's disapproval. 'It's these men, Ed. Sly. Dishonest. Telling lies about me. Making it impossible to stay—'

Edward flicks out a hand, almost catching Caspar's cheek. 'Oh, go! Go! Perhaps you'll not be a liability out in the wilds of Northumberland. Just don't get up to your tricks there. Bad news travels. Remember.'

Edward is always somewhat gentler on Caspar who at least pays him the respect he thinks is due to him. Didn't he seem appropriately ashamed of this self-banishment? That at least was something.

'And you . . .' Edward turns to me. 'What makes you think you can survive with strangers out in the wild? What do you think will happen when they discover that, far from being a good worker, a helpful companion, that you are lunatic? That you hear voices, you tell lies and you are deluded as to your proper place in the world?'

I look him hard in the eye. 'If you think I give twopence for what you think, Edward Maichin, you've another think coming.' I make my lip curl. 'I'm going.'

His hands bunch themselves into fists and he throws

156

himself down on the long settle. 'Well, dear mother,' he says to Rose Clare, who is poking the fire, 'it seems like it is just you and me. At least you won't have these two layabouts to run about after. You can concentrate all your tender mercies on me. But no weeping after your runaway criminal husband, mind you. Or your lunatic daughter.'

She darts a look at my reflection in the ornamental mirror. Her look compounds fear and revulsion in equal measures. For Edward, I think, not for me. 'Edward, I—' she says.

'She won't be here,' I put in hurriedly. 'She's coming with me. The invitation is for her too. She's coming with me up into the dale.'

He closes his eyes, takes deep breaths and opens them. 'Well then. That's it. Not only does my father fail in his fatherly duties, my mother flees her motherly duties.'

'Edward, sure I—' my mother protests again.

He holds up a hand. 'Do not trouble yourself, Mother. Your conscience will plague you, I know, but I forgive you. Just as, long ago, I forgave my father.'

So in the end it is not from my family that I run away: in the end it is my family who flee from my brother Edward. He does not see it happen. All he sees are these bothersome burdens dropping out of his life. I thought he would object, mostly to my mother leaving. After all, she is his body slave; he is not used to taking care of himself. But I see a cunning flicker in his eye and I know he has some plan afoot. He is never defeated, is Edward. In that sense he is very capable of taking care of himself. He will stop at nothing to get exactly what he wants. Nothing.

In the two days before we catch our train up into the dale Edward ignores me and pays court to our mother.

He praises her food and her caring attitude. He makes sure he gets the Gervases' address from her. 'Just in case Father turns up. Don't you know what he's like, Mam?' He promises to write to her every week. 'For I know you will want to know how I am, Mam.' I hear the creak of bridges being built. He is fitting her with a long rein. And me. We have to leave all our nice bits and pieces from the house in Wales, leave all these and only take bags of clothes and personal things.

Edward smiles, talking to my mother, never to me. 'I'll send your things on to you, Mam. When you get yourself settled. No use taking things when you don't really know where you're going. These people could be living in a hen hut up there, you know.'

Later I can feel myself breathing out, relaxing as the train cuts its way through ever more open, more wild countryside. The recent digging leaves raw scars in the hillside where new track has been laid further up the dale. The mean dark villages with their palls of black smoke are left behind, and broad fields of hay and corn open out the country. Clumps of trees, copses, the glitter of a falling stream break the monotony of the lower land.

Then I can see new scars, great basins and shelves of land cut out like putty to win lumps and shafts of stone and marble; raw material to dress civic buildings many miles away. Then my eye lifts and I can see the slow purple surge of rising moorland and high hills which remind me of the sea – much more to do with the gods than the petty commercial interferences of humans. These folds, these lifts, have been here since before man came on earth. And they will survive him.

I have sent a letter to Mrs Gervase, thanking her and her son for their appreciation of my story, and saying that as well as writing the stories I am now looking for work of any kind. If her kind offer still stood, perhaps we could talk about me working on the farm? I told her the train we would be getting, but did not have the effrontery to ask to be met.

The little station is deserted when we arrive and I ask the porter about ways to get to Goshawk Shield, up by Carr's Edge. He looks up at the sky as though an answer will come to him from there. Then he peers along the road in each direction. 'Ah kin get yer a cab, hinny, but they's no sayin' he'll tek tha that far this late in the day. The light's fading, y'knaa. The road's not sure. Good fifty minutes' ride this time o' day.'

I feel my shoulders sag. 'I can't walk that distance. Neither can my mother. I can pay. I could pay someone.' My mother pressed five golden guineas in my hand after we set out this morning. A present from my father, according to her.

'Not a matter o' money, hinny. It's the light, see? An' them tracks up there is unlit and almost unmade. Quarries round every corner here. Holes where God would no put 'm.' He takes off his cap and scratches his greasy hair. 'Mebbe I could get yer a night's lodging an' yer could try tomorrow.'

The high feeling of adventure with which I had left Gibsley and my brothers behind this morning begins to desert me. My mind is a turgid blank.

My mother peers up the narrow road. 'Here's a . . .well, something.' It was not quite a gig and not quite a cart, but something between the two. A kind of high-sided chariot. To it were yoked a mismatched pair: a heavy working horse and a fine-bred horse, more suited to the saddle than the close harness it was heaving its shoulder against.

'Aw.' The porter's tone is a study in suppressed merriment. 'We needn't have worried. Yeh've your transport. A canny chariot, this. Here yeh have sommat that'll feel its way through in the dark. And the driver that could find his way up the Goshawk Shield blindfold.'

The driver signals wildly to us with his whip and yanks the reins so the horses stop at different points making the elaborate cart swerve violently from side to side just close to us, spraying mud in every direction. The porter brushes a lump of mud from his immaculate trousers, salutes and turns to attend to the more obviously important matters of packages for the Priorton Co-operative Society.

'Miss Maichin?' It is the shambling man, the son of Mrs Gervase. He climbs down awkwardly from the cart, yanking back the reins as the smaller horse starts to move on. 'Whoa, boy, whoa. Didn't I tell you?' The tone is plaintive, as a parent might use with a truculent child.

He turns, his broad face beaming, and my hand is engulfed in his large pudgy one. 'My mother said you'd not come. But I assured her – assured her that you would.' He shakes my hand for far too long, as though he will never lose it. I wriggle it away from his grasp.

'Mr Gervase. How very nice of you to come and get us. We'd thought we may be stuck in Stanhope all night.'

'We?' For the first time his gaze drops to my mother, hovering somewhere behind me. 'Mother? There was no mention of a mother, Miss Maichin. This will not do . . .' His eyes fill with tears. 'What will my mother say? There was no mention of a mother.'

I pull myself to my full height, which still only allows me to reach his coat buttons. 'You cannot think, Mr Gervase, that I come all the way here on my own. I cannot think your mother would expect that?' I infuse my voice with all the bossiness I can leach from my memories of Edward at his worst, from Mr Murgatroyd at his most sober. It works.

'Ah yes. Yes.' The man takes out a handkerchief and mops his brow. 'Chaperone! That's it. Chaperone. Perfectly right. Thank you, Mrs Maichin. Thank you. If you will just climb up. Go through that little door at the back, then you can sit forward.' He throws our bags on the roof then flings and ties a canvas over them.

We climb in and settle down behind him. We lean back on

buttoned velvet cushions, our feet up on elaborate footrests. Mr Gervase sits with his back to us, ready to drive the horses before us like a servant, which he undoubtedly is not. Behind him, before us, is a narrow door, open now. When this is shut it should make this passenger space quite a snug haven. On the other hand, the driver up front must brave all the elements. 'This is a very unusual . . . er . . . carriage, Mr Gervase.'

He clicks his teeth. 'Walk on!' he tells the mismatched pair in front of him. 'I can see you admire it, Miss Maichin. My chariot, that's what it is. I designed it myself to take these moorland roads. Needs four farm wheels to take the ruts, but my dear mother insists on her comfort. So I put the two together and had it made up specially.' He strokes the whip across the back of the smaller horse and the cabin rocks dangerously. 'Unfortunately Salmon, the other bay, has an injured leg so we must endure this pair who pull against each other. Now, ladies, I will close this door, for there is a mist about. My mother said I must shut you in, Miss Maichin, though she did not mention your mother. Would it be all right to shut her in, do you think?'

It is a genuine question. He wants permission.

'Yes,' I say firmly. 'It will be quite all right.'

'Thank you.' Relieved, he leans down and closes the door before us, all the time pulling at the reins.

So we are rocked around for nearly an hour in this lurching ship of the trackways. It is quite dark when we turn through some high stone gates, down a track lined with overhanging branches, then through an arch and on to the back yard of a house which looms over us in the darkness.

He lifts our aching bodies down as though we are dolls and leans us against the wheel. 'Just stand there a moment and I'll go and get my mother.'

He shambles off. I put my arm around my mother and pull her to me. She is shuddering, even more cold and stiff than I

161

am. She turns her face to look at me. 'What have we done, Theo? What have we done? This is a mad place. Sure that man's as mad as a March hare.' She jumps and I blink as a great black door in the wall opens and light beams forth.

Mrs Gervase, neat in a day dress and cap, comes forward, a hand out. 'Miss Maichin? My son tells me you have brought your mother! How very charming of you.' Her words are warm, but her tone is cold. We might be paying an afternoon call instead of standing on a blustery moor, having endured nearly an hour of being thrown about in a monstrous vehicle drawn by mismatched horses, who are being led away now by the woman's rather odd son.

Still hanging on to my mother I take the old woman's claw-like hand in mine and shake it vigorously. 'My mother, Mrs Gervase. I am afraid she is about to faint.'

Thirteen

Goshawk Shield

Olivia Gervase considered herself an intelligent woman, and was considered by her narrow band of acquaintants as a *very* intelligent woman. A pity, they would say, about the son, who should have been put away years ago. Wasn't he well on the way to being an idiot? But you could not, they would say, deny Olivia herself was an exceptionally intelligent woman. Not so intelligent, perhaps, to bury herself in the wilds and play farmer. However, if she did insist on keeping the creature with her, did insist on having the idiot son about her skirts, then one could see the logic in hiding away. That way, they could live their crazy idyll out of the sensitive sight of society.

Olivia knew all this and would smile her grim smile at what she thought of as 'the clacking'. But given her much vaunted intelligence, why on earth had she given in to Stephen in the matter of the girl from the train? No doubt she could rue the day.

It had been her habit, in her lifelong mission to bring light to her son's life, to read bits to him from the newspaper. In affairs of the country, he showed no interest. He much preferred the sometimes comically portentous columns of the local paper, and laughed with glee at disputes between housewives over shopping lines, men fined for fighting over dogs, and sober accounts of the doings of the literary and critical societies which were growing like mushrooms, it seemed, in every pit village in the area. What had possessed her to read out the story of 'Loki the Mischief Maker', she couldn't think. Yes. It was the sub-heading about new stories for *children*. That would suit Stephen, for he had indeed the mind of a child. In addition – she had to admit it – for a second she was engaged by the classical allusions. As a girl in her father's rectory Olivia had learned Latin and Greek alongside her brothers and had relished that sun-lit world of certainties, of vengeful gods and flower-laden deities.

Olivia's dream, in those days, had been to have a son who would study such things, become a scholar. Go to Oxford as she (had she not been a girl) would have done. Her son would be a great scholar and she would be his muse. But she was not to have such a son. Very late in life, after a brief marriage to an old clerical colleague of her father, she had given birth to Stephen. And Stephen it was, at forty, who begged her to read him, over and over again, the children's story of 'Loki the Mischief Maker'.

When she frowned over the name of the writer, and said, quite lightly, 'That is such an unusual name. Do you remember the girl on the train, Stephen? I wonder if it is she? Theodora Maichin. An unusual name.'

He had been so happy then, laughing and crying at the same time. 'You told her to come here, Mama. When we were on the train. You remember? You said, "Come and see me." Will she come? Will the girl come?'

She had laughed with him indulgently. In their privacy, when outsiders with their prying eyes were gone, she and Stephen would play their games, have their innocent intimacies and no one would say that she as well as her son were mad. 'Would you be happy if she came, Stevie? Is Mama not company enough for you any more?'

Slowly he shook his head, leaning over to touch her cheek, stroke her hair. 'No, no, Mama. I love you. You are my life. I love my mama.'

She had smiled her satisfaction then. 'So many people lose their children, Stevie, but I still have you to love me.'

'Always, Mama,' he said solemnly.

But later that night, as he tucked her into her bed, before he clumped away to his own room, he returned to the matter of the storyteller. 'In the morning, Mama, if I put your paper and pens all neat on your desk, you will write and say, won't you? Tell the girl to come? The storyteller?'

Later, as she lay in the dense dark which only comes in the deep country, she wondered if people ever knew how equal it was, this strange relationship she had with her son. How, for the great love he bore her, he exacted a price: a keen recognition of his needs.

That time on Sheffield station, when she fell down the railway steps, she had been angry with him. 'No, most definitely no, we cannot go to the zoo.' He had visited the zoo once and focused obsessively on it ever since. She had become quite sharp with him, turned to descend and the steps were there one step before she had expected. The last thing she saw was Stephen's arms thrown out to grab her, his despairing face as she fell. For one wild second she had accused him of pushing her. That was when the girl strolled across; this girl who had now turned up with a mother in tow, a mother who had wild hair, and wore a green skirt with a red petticoat. And now there was a dog. The girl had a dog up her sleeve. Olivia Gervase snorted. As if she couldn't see it.

What had she let herself in for? What mischief was Stephen making now?

The curtains in the bedroom are drawn, and the fire is blazing. I remove my mother's hat, cape, her outer clothes and shoes

165

and put them at the side of the chair by the fire which the little dog has instantly taken for her own. My mother lies back on the double bed, which it seems we are to share. I pull a puffy eiderdown across and she clutches it to her. 'I'll go and find you a hot drink,' I whisper, although there is no one else in the room, or on the landing. As far as I know the Gervases are still two landings and two flights of stairs away.

My mother, white as a lily, shakes her head. 'Sleep, Theo. Sleep is all I want just now. You should get something for the dog.' And she puts her head to one side and closes her eyes, apparently asleep in seconds.

I take off my hat and pat my hair; take off my coat and smooth down my dress. It's the one which Dada bought for me when I first started working at the *Tidal Review*. It has been laundered many times but has a new bertha collar. In those years my shape has changed but the dress still covers me pretty well. My mother, so handy with the needle, has made the adjustments. I change my muddy boots for shoes, take a deep breath and set out to find my way back downstairs.

Moving outside the bedroom is like moving on to a cold continent. I hurry along the corridor back to the head of the staircase, where a small lamp gleams from a chest of drawers. I make my way down two staircases to the faintly lit hall. Then I feel my way back towards the kitchen. Stephen Gervase is there alone, putting china cups on to a tray. He beams down at me. 'My mother says you are to go to the sitting room and I am to bring you tea and orange cake.' He puts a podgy finger on the orange icing. 'See? I have cut three slices.' He holds up a ruler. 'I measured them exactly.'

I go out again into the dark corridor, open two doors on to pitch darkness, then find Mrs Gervase behind the third door, with her feet on a footstool before a blazing fire. This is a very strange room. Small for such a large house. There are curtains covering every wall. It is like a velvet closet.

166

Mrs Gervase lifts her head. 'What, no mother, Miss Maichin?'

'She is tucked up, fast asleep. It was a hard journey for her.'

'Do sit down, Miss Maichin. The journey did not defeat you?'

I sit opposite her on a high-backed chaise. 'It would take more than a journey to defeat me, Mrs Gervase.'

A frown creases the paper-white skin on her brow. 'It is very easy to say that, Miss Maichin. The journey is a treat compared to living up here in the wind and the rain.' She pulls her shawl around her. 'The house is draughty and its occupants are either very old, or, as the world would have it, very mad.'

I smile into that face, despite my sinking heart. 'We come from a cold wet place ourselves, Mrs Gervase, and I'd thought age meant wisdom. And as for mad, I've seen nothing today worse than I've seen in my family. To be truthful, Mrs Gervase' – I open my eyes wide and stare into hers – 'my own elder brother is, I am quite convinced, as mad as a hatter. But mad and cruel, and that's much worse. So far as I can see Mr Stephen Gervase is as gentle as a lamb. A sweet man.'

I watch as she fights back a little smile and recomposes her face into severe lines. 'But we are so cut off. There are no young people around here, except Mavis who comes for the rough work. But sometimes I think, Miss Maichin, she has such old ways. She could be sixty. No companion for you.'

I put my head on one side. 'I have spent my life on my own. I left school when I was ten and it seems like I've been on my own since then. I like it. So I don't mind being on my own and I am not defeated.'

She stares at me for one long moment and it seems she can see through to my bones. Then the neat face collapses and the still of the room is rent with a very hearty laugh. 'Ha! I know that. Not defeated! What we need here at Goshawk Shield is someone who is not defeated.'

'It does seem a long way from everywhere. Everything.'

'No. Not really. Bittern Crag farmhouse is at the far end of the lane. The farmer, Mr Gomersall, manages the land hereabouts for me. Supplies me with eggs and dairy stuff. Up the crag a mile there is another farm, where they run sheep. And two quarries within hailing distance. The place is quite crowded.' She laughs loudly again. 'Stephen and I hate to be crowded. So, Miss Maichin, you decided to come here to help me?'

'Perhaps . . .' I look round the room. I can't tell her that I need this, that I need this chance to get away from Edward. 'I don't quite understand myself. To be honest, I've no skills about the house, although my mother is good at all that. There is little I could do here.' My heart sinks even as I admit this. But I have to be honest with this woman.

'Oh yes there is. I will be frank, Miss Maichin. The farm is very well. Mr Gomersall sees to that. He sends up milk and eggs and bread. He sees to the sheep. Sheep! Sheep, my dear! Dear things are no trouble except at lambing and then Mr Gomersall brings in all his sons from down the dale. The place is full of tiny bleats then. You can't get in their kitchen for boxes of bleating lambs.

'And the house here. The house has been all right. Mavis Gomersall, daughter to the farmer, rides up here on her pony every morning.' Mrs Gervase casts me a level look. 'Can't get help to live in, of course.'

'Why not?'

'Well, d'you see, my dear, they or their mothers, or more probably their fathers, think that my dear Stephen will pounce on them and ravish them.' She laughs, although her laughter is shrill now. 'My Stephen's as likely to ravish that curtain or that fender, my dear. In some ways I would welcome such a danger! Sadly my Stephen is an innocent.' She does sound sad about this. 'Apart from Mavis, Stephen does the rest. As well as that he has his workshop where he carves and makes things. It keeps him out of mischief. But you know what is missing, Miss Maichin?'

I look at her blankly. This woman is a manipulator, like Edward. The people around her are puppets. 'What would that be, Mrs Gervase?'

'A woman's touch. The place is so workaday. There is no diversion. I had thought this retreat up here was ideal for my son and myself. But it seems not so these days. I am restless. He is restless. What we both need is a woman's touch. And, since I see less well now, a woman's eyes.' She smiles her tight little smile at me and I am uncomfortable. 'How nice that you brought your mother with you. We will have twice the woman's touch. Two pairs of eyes.'

I laugh to ease my uncertainty. 'You are more likely to get that woman's touch from my mother, Mrs Gervase. So it is a good job I have brought her.'

Mrs Gervase is not so easy to reckon. She orders things around to suit her, yet there is a tenderness when she talks about that big galumphing son, which only just shows in her tone of voice. There is a slippery softness in her tone, her accent, which I could listen to all night. The words are like silk; the tone is modulated. This is how ladies sound, I reckon. I have not heard it properly before. My teachers in Wales, some of whom were very intelligent, spoke in forthright tones which were clearly, indubitably Welsh. Apart from them, all I ever meet are working people whose voices trumpet their origin like a dunce's label round their neck. How nice to speak without such a label round one's neck.

'Miss Maichin? Miss Maichin? Am I so boring? Have you dropped off to sleep?' Now she is cross.

'No!' I can feel myself flush. 'I was thinking that you

sounded like one of my teachers. I love the way you talk.'

She frowns. 'Well, as I say, if you stay here a week or so . . . We'll see what happens. Do in the house what you wish. Read to me for one hour in the afternoons. That will save my eyes a bit. As you write for the newspaper I imagine you can read?'

'Mrs Gervase! I—'

She waves a hand. 'Sorry, sorry! I have no wish to insult you.'

'I would be happy to read to you.'

There is a pause. 'You will wonder why I want you to read to me?'

I have no idea at all. I don't know how these people behave, what they do in the privacy of their own homes. Perhaps they read to each other all the time. 'No . . . not really.'

'I've had trouble reading for some while. I use a ship's glass most of the time. Now!' She leans forward with a waft of dust and lavender water. 'You must say nothing to Stephen. Any change in me . . . Any slight change and he gets upset.' She pauses. 'He may have an attack.'

'An attack?'

'Oh, don't worry, Miss Maichin. He does not foam at the mouth nor howl like a dog. He cries. Very quietly. He might cry for a whole day. He is so very sad. I do not know where the tears come from.' She takes a crumpled handkerchief from her sleeve and blows her nose. 'And when he is like that I get upset. The older I get the more it upsets me. I used to be able to endure it. Leave him to it.'

I hurry to reassure her. 'Yes. Yes. I'll read to you. And to him, if you want me. That will be no trouble, no trouble at all.'

'Now there is another thing, Miss Maichin. Mavis Gomersall, whom I have mentioned, is with child. Unfortunately no father is visible. Something going on more than shearing sheep at sheep-shearing time, I fear. These gangs of men come and go like will o' the wisps.'

I blink at her. I have never in my life heard anyone speak so openly of the secret things. The things that happen to everyone which no one – at least no one I have ever met – talks about.

'Mavis will be working here at Goshawk Shield for another month. So, perhaps you – and your mother as you so kindly thought to bring her—'

'Mrs Gervase, I want to explain about that. My mother—'

She waved a hand. 'No matter. No matter. She is here, you are here.'

'So you want us to take over from Mavis Gomersall?'

'Yes. Just do it to suit you. I have little interest in matters of the house. But this woman's touch. As I say, there has been something missing. You will supply it.'

'I do have a commission to write more stories for the newspaper. I will need time . . .' I hold my breath. I am taking a risk, I know. On the train she implied she wanted a strong girl. Some kind of skivvy.

Again the fluttering hand. 'Take time! Take time!'

I draw in a deep breath. 'And I will be writing other things. It's what I wish to do, and what I came away from home for.'

That extraordinary loud laugh explodes from her. 'A calling, is it? We are called to write, are we?'

I put up my chin. 'You may wish to put it that way,' I say stiffly.

There is a crack and rattle at the door and I rush across the room and hold it open wide while Stephen squeezes through, carrying an enormous tray.

'Oh Stephen!' A cry of despair from the couch where his mother sits. He places the tray on the sideboard and smiles seraphically at us, first one, then the other. There must be ten cups and saucers on the tray and two full tea services. The orange cake, carefully measured and cut, sits on a crystal cake stand. Beside that is a dinner plate piled high with thick sandwiches, overfilled, if I am not mistaken, with home-cured ham.

'I brought everything,' he says, beaming.

'Oh Mr Gervase!' I splutter, then laugh out loud. 'So you have. You have brought everything except the kitchen sink.'

He nods excitedly. 'That is right.' He comes and places his hot, podgy hand on my arm. 'My name is Stephen. You must call me only this. Stephen. Mama calls me Stephen and so must you. Stephen.' His words are childlike but he, like his mother, has a wonderfully musical tone, which gives the words power over and above their childish intent. There is something very dear about him.

I put my hand over his. 'Stephen. And I'm called Theodora. But my mama, and my dada, they call me Theo. So you can call me Theo.'

He nods again. 'Theo. Sit down, Theo, and I will pour the tea. Theo.'

Mrs Gervase has been watching all this with a still, closed face. She puts a hand out. 'Yes. Come and sit by me, Theo. May I call you Theo?' She smiles suddenly and I realise Stephen's beautiful childlike smile might be as much inherited as a consequence of his simplicity. 'My name is Olivia but I imagine you would find it difficult to call me that. So many years since anyone called me by my given name.'

I am scarlet. She must be mad as well as the son. Edward need not have worried. In this house, by comparison, I am entirely sane. 'Mrs Gervase . . .'

She waved her hand again. 'Do not worry, Theo. I am teasing you.'

Then there is a whole to-do from Stephen about the food. He insists on sharing out the cake and biscuits exactly. We each end up with three tea plates full of cake, sandwiches and biscuits.

Olivia Gervase eyes me over the rim of her cup. 'We will have to eat it, Theo. He is very particular about this. He will get upset if we don't.'

I look in despair at the heap of food.

'It is not easy,' she nods. 'It will not be easy for you here, my dear. Perhaps tomorrow you will return to your home and thank the Lord for your escape from the madhouse.'

I pick up a big sandwich. 'To tell you the truth, Mrs Gervase, I am so hungry I could eat a horse.'

They both laugh at this and we set about the serious business of eating our tea. Despite my determination to keep my guard I find myself telling Mrs Gervase many things about my life. As I munch away and tell the story I spot Olivia tucking the second half of her sandwich and half the cake down the side of the chair. She must have an arrangement with Mavis Gomersall about that. Clearing out the detritus of uneaten meals will obviously be one of the duties I am to fall heir to. I put the last sandwich and biscuit on a separate plate. Stephen is watching me anxiously. I smile up at him. 'Do you know, my Mama will just love these when she wakes up. What a nice surprise for her!'

He beams at me. Then, from behind his back like a magician producing a bright flower, he produces a battered newspaper.

Olivia Gervase sighs. 'It is the one with the story of Loki in it,' she says. 'I must have read it to him forty times.'

'Now you can read it for me,' says Stephen. 'Save my dear mama's eyes.' Then he sits beside his mother on the sofa and takes her hand in his. 'You can read it for both of us.'

I take it from him, draw the lamp on the table closer to me, and start to read it. For the first time I read my own text as a stranger. The story holds together very well. It is a natural story, with its own tension, easy to retell.

The telling seems to take quite a long time, but they both

listen with a quiet intensity and clap delightedly when I finish. The resemblance between them is startling.

I smile my delight. 'There now!' I say. 'I had not realised it was so long.'

Stephen shakes his large head. 'No. No, Theo. Too short.' Tears fall softly down his face. 'No more story.'

I am suddenly desperate for him to be happy. I jump up. 'I have another story. It will be in next week's paper. "The Childhood of Aphrodite", it is called.'

'Yes. Yes,' he says. '"The Childhood of Aphrodite".'

Up in the bedroom my mother is still on the bed, unmoving except for a slight flutter of the lips as she exhales a musical snore. Seal comes across and winds herself round my legs like a cat. She needs a little walk in the yard, I do this, then feed her pieces of the cake before settling her on the bed beside my mother. Then I set about digging the Aphrodite story out of my bag.

Downstairs the two of them, mother and son, are still sitting side by side on the sofa, waiting like eager children.

I am suddenly anxious. 'It is not the same story, Stephen. It is different. It's not Loki, you know.'

'It is your story,' he says.

'Yes. But . . . but you may not like it.'

'I will like it,' he states.

Olivia Gervase nods. 'He will like it,' she says.

They sit there like two mice and nod and clap when the story ends. 'Poor Aphrodite,' says Stephen.

'She was blessed with a son,' says Olivia Gervase smiling slightly. Then in a second she becomes adult again. She is in charge, no longer the child alongside her childlike son. 'Now, Stevie,' she instructs, 'you are to clear away all these dishes. Wash everything and put them in the right cupboard for Mavis Gomersall. Then check that the horses are happy and lock the stables. Then lock the doors, put out the lights.

Theo is tired after her long day.'

We watch as, very clumsily, he puts all the plates and cups back on the tray. I stand up and move to help him. Mrs Gervase shakes her head and flicks her hand to make me sit down again. 'No, Theo. Stephen likes to do his jobs all on his own, don't you, Stevie?' He nods, concentrating. 'He is part of this household, not just a pet kitten to be pampered.'

My brain freezes as I remember Seal, curled up elegantly beside my mother on the puffy eiderdown. I'll have to choose my moment to tell Mrs Gervase about my dog.

We hear Stephen thudding down the corridor. She looks across at me. 'Well, Theodora Maichin who writes the stories, what do you think of my son?'

I look blankly at her. How can she expect me to answer such a question?

'Go on!' The smooth voice persists. 'What do you think of my son?'

I still hesitate. 'I am sorry that he is so . . .'

'Mad?'

I shake my head. Then it all comes in a rush. 'He is such a nice person. So kind and caring. He is a bit . . .'

'Mad?'

'Childlike. But we are all childlike somewhere inside. That is not a bad part of us.' I pause. 'And I think he is quite clever.'

She raises her brows. 'Ah. Clever!'

'Well, he told me he designed that . . . er . . . carriage.'

'So he did.'

'Well, it works. We were very snug in there.'

'So, are you still sorry? Sorry for Stephen, for me?'

I shake my head. 'I am just sorry that people will see him and think he is . . .'

'Mad.'

'Well. Yes.' I stand up, weary of the pressure, desperate for my bed.

'Do you want to know about him? About him and me? Or are you too tired?'

I sit down again, uncomfortable at the confidence. She is slightly mad, I think.

She sits for a second and looks at her hands in her lap, then looks up and tells me a story.

'I did not marry till I was forty. A true spinster, happy in my spinsterhood. Taking care of my father, who was less a vicar than a holy fool of a small parish right above Windermere. I was devoted to him. We had a good home. A good table. We read and discoursed and were quite content. Then one day I woke up and it was as though God had put His finger on me and told me things must change. That I should have a child before I was too old.

'Like the annunciation you might say. But no Angel Gabriel. Of course it was not God's son I was to have but some mortal man's. Naturally the next day I discussed this . . . er . . . revelation with my father, as we discussed everything. He thought it was indeed a sign from God that he had been selfish in keeping me by his side. Then he made it his mission to find me a husband, which he did within the space of one month: a widowed childless clergyman from Leeds. He was a gentle man, not without merit. We were married within three months, I was with child in four, and Mr Gervase lived just long enough to bless baby Stephen and give him his name, before he quit this earthly realm.

'Stephen was a wonderful child, clever, always laughing. I was indeed blessed. Then one day he played with the children of a missionary who had just returned from China and was ill for six months afterwards. I thought he would die. He shrank to a chrysalis. But he recovered, and emerged from the chrysalis. The Stephen that emerged was the Stephen we know today. Quite mad. Quite clever. Quite delightful. A strange butterfly.

'But life out there in Leeds, as he got older, became miserable. He was the butt of much scorn and abuse. By the time he was thirteen we had both had enough. So we took our lives in our own hands and came here. This house has been in my mother's family for ten generations. We've been here since we left Leeds, Stephen and I.'

'And have you been happy?' I could bite the words off. What a silly question.

'Oh yes, Theo. Happy as birds.' She frowns. 'It is harder, though, to be happy, now we are both older. He is nearly forty and I am more than eighty.' Then she flung her hands into the air in that characteristic gesture of hers. 'Oh. Go to bed! Go to bed, girl. You don't need hearts and flowers after such a hard day. Go to bed! And in the morning you will tell me if you will stay.'

I stand up and turn towards her. 'Mrs Gervase, I will stay. You can be sure I will stay.'

So here I am, sitting up in bed beside my snoring mother. Seal is sitting in my lap, her great eyes glittering in the candlelight. The fur on her forehead is soft and fine beneath my touch. 'Oh, Seal. Now what . . .?'

I jump as the bedroom door swings open and Stephen Gervase, rendered large and ghostlike in his voluminous nightshirt, bursts into the room.

I clutch Seal to me, my mind doing cartwheels over the terrible mistake I've made in coming here. 'Stephen!' I say, holding Seal to me like a breast shield.

Then I see that he has two dishes in his hands. There is a small smile on his face. 'I have brought these for the little dog. I thought she might be hungry.'

'The little dog?' I say innocently, as though the creature held to my breast were a doll or a hot-water bottle.

He chuckles. 'You play a joke with me, Theo. You had her

up your sleeve in the carriage and you hold her in your arms now. My mama says we must feed the little dog which was in your sleeve.'

I look down. 'Oh, this dog!'

'I've brought her supper.' He places the dishes carefully by the fire. The flames find their reflection in the trembling milk. 'I cut the ham very small for she is a very small dog.'

I have to tell you that at this moment I feel a spark of love for this great hulking Stephen Gervase. He turns to go, then pops his head back round the door. 'Oh, and Mama was surprised about the dog but I told her it was very small and would take up no room.' He laughed. 'And Mama was very naughty. She said you must keep her up your sleeve or the farm dogs will think she is a rat and eat her!'

I could still hear his roaring chuckle as he made his way down the corridor.

Mavis Gomersall felt that she had come to the wrong house. Quiet orderly Goshawk Shield, occasionally eccentric in its preoccupations, had changed into a madhouse. There was an Irishwoman in red petticoats in the kitchen, a rat-like dog yapping about, Stephen Gervase, normally so quiet, was dancing and laughing around a young girl who (fine-looking, you had to admit) watched everything like a spy and kept writing things down in that dratted notebook.

Mavis brooded on this as she rode (side-saddle because of her condition) back down the hill to her father's farm. There was little she could do about the convulsion in the Gervase household. Her mother would lecture her that she was lucky Mrs Gervase had kept her on so long, with her pregnant at thirty-five who should know better. The real shame in her condition was left unspoken. It was not the shame of 'falling wrong' out of wedlock. That was common enough. The shame was in no one holding their hands up for it, putting a very convenient ring on her finger.

Mavis smiled grimly as she manoeuvred her pony through a patch of boggy ground, made dangerous by recent heavy rain. They would all jump if she really did name the father of her child – if she told Mrs Gervase. Too much trouble to think about. It was convenient to let the legend grow about the sheep-shearer. And within her own family she was treated gentle enough, although in the church down the dale she was now shunned.

She thought glumly of how she would be fixed when the baby came. She could not work for Mrs Gervase. Not for a time. And the two shillings she earned up at Goshawk Shield had brought her some respect from her mother and father. Would they still take note of her when she didn't turn over her money to them on Saturday? She'd known girls turned from the door for less: girls who joined up with gypsies who roamed the dale from time to time, rather than end up in the Union workhouse in Stanhope or Priorton.

That girl and her mother moving in at Goshawk Shield obviously meant that Mrs Gervase was arranging for the time when Mavis herself left. Looking to her own interests. This was so no matter how kind Mrs Gervase had been to Mavis in the past. She had to look out for her own. Who could blame her really with Stephen to care for, blessed idiot that he was?

'But what will happen to me? And who cares?' she whispered as the pony, pleased at the sight of a nice piece of greensward, spiked up to a trot. 'Whoa, boy. Don't you know the condition your mistress is in? Don't want to drop it here on the moor, do I?'

If her mother got on to her about the baby, the sin and all that, she would tell her the truth about the father. That would spike her guns.

My mother and Mrs Gervase are getting along quite well.

Mama has grown brighter through the day. The red petticoat is much in evidence and she has a ribbon in her hair. And what's more she has started to sing about her chores.

At supper, which we take in the little breakfast room by the kitchen, Rose Clare begins to tell Mrs Gervase of her own childhood in Kerry in the West of Ireland where she lived on a farm. 'Not so big as this, mind. No, not at all. The house, bedroom and all, would fit into your kitchen here. But the farm, the land, the seasons rolling round, sure it's always the same.'

'You had sheep, Mrs Maichin?'

My mother laughs at this. 'Sheep? Sure the only animal was the old cow. Potatoes, Mrs Gervase. We had the beautiful, famous, treacherous potato.'

'The famine. I've read of the famine. In the forties, that would be?'

'Fifty-two, we lost our farm.' She looks around the room. 'This'll be your own farm?'

I draw breath at her bluntness. 'Mother!'

Mrs Gervase's cheeks show the faintest pink. 'Yes, my mother's family have had it for hundreds of years.'

'Ah, continuity. Sure there's nothing like it.' Rose Clare nods. 'Us too. Five generations they said. But when three seasons' crops fail and you end up eating the seed potatoes and killing the cow, there's nothing to pay the rent. And the English government takes the landlord to task so he takes off your roof and turns you out.' She laughs. 'Sure and I bet you're the landlord here, Mrs Gervase, so I should mind my tongue.'

'Yes, so I am, Mrs Maichin. But just this land and Gomersall's farm. And I'd never dare to throw Mr Gomersall out, take his tenancy away. His father showed me how to ride and how to fish when I was a little girl. That family have been there for hundreds of years as well.'

The supper table has been weighed down by Stephen with

180

too many plates and dishes. At least he can't overload the food. Mavis Gomersall has left a big pot of stew which is planted in the middle of the table like a tree.

'Mavis is not so happy with us being here,' I say, having endured a week of sulky looks and hurtlings by.

'Mavis is my friend,' said Stephen, and ducked his head back down over his stew.

'Mavis has ruled the roost here for fifteen years,' said Mrs Gervase. 'She knows the house as though it were hers.'

'Sure, she wouldn't want us here, would she?' says Rose Clare. 'I don't blame her.'

'Well, she'll be having that baby within the month,' said Mrs Gervase. 'I was always going to have to find someone else. It just happens that "Loki the Mischief Maker" brought you here.'

'Does she have to leave this house when she's had the baby?' asks Rose Clare abruptly.

'Mother!' I say, shooting a glance at her.

'What are you getting at, Mrs Maichin?'

'If it were her own babe she'd be working with it at her skirts. She could come back.'

'Getting up and down that hill! A baby too!' I say.

'Chaperone!' says Stephen, the word exploding from him like a bullet. 'Mavis stays here with the baby. Sleeping.' He points a knife at Rose Clare. 'Theo's mama is chaperone. Mavis can stay.' He beams. 'She will feel safe from me.' He bends down, a scrap of meat on his fork for Seal.

'Oh Stephen!' I say.

Mrs Gervase smiles. 'As always, Stephen has a solution. You can ask her, Theo. See if she will do it. Come back after the baby's born.'

'Me? She hates the sight of me.'

'All the more reason to do it. Coming from you it might seem like your idea. Don't you think?'

The next morning I beard the lioness in her den. Mavis is working with her characteristic rattling energy. Pans are clattered in cupboards, baskets are dragged out and emptied. The kitchen as large as the whole of our house in Gibsley is spotless and shining, a pot of marigolds on the windowsill. This room contrasts wildly with the rest of the house which is barely dusted once a fortnight. You can't blame Mavis. It is a large space to clean with five fires to service, three beds to make and bed pans to see to. This is quite enough to do in four hours a day. It suffices that she keeps the kitchen in such fine fettle. Somehow it shows that she has respect for herself. Her own space is good and bright.

'Mrs Gervase says you've been here for fifteen years, Mavis?'

'Aye. Me auntie did it before that for fifteen years. And her two aunties before that. And so on.'

'It's a long time.'

'Aye. It's a big house. It'd take six to keep it right.' Her tone is defensive. 'But Mrs Gervase only wants me here.'

'You're right there. How you keep it so nice I don't know.'

'Mm. It's a lot of work, like. But yeh get used to it. Yeh 'ave to leave stuff. More's the pity. It's been a fine house.'

'Won't you miss it, the house, when you . . . when the baby comes?'

She clashes a colander into the water and I jump back to stop it splashing my dress. 'Aye! Yer get used ter things. I like ter come up here. Not under their feet at home.'

'I'm sure, Mrs Gervase and Stephen, they'll miss you.'

'Don't look like it. Ain't that why yeh and yehr ma's here?'

I shake my head. 'No. No. I'm here because of this.' I take the now greasy copy of the *Priorton Chronicle* from the bottom of a pile in the corner. 'I write stories in the paper. It caught Mrs Gervase's eye and she asked me to come. A kind of whim. I have more stories to write. You've seen the little table in the corner of the bedroom? With the papers on?'

'Aye. I've seen that.'

'Well, I have twelve more stories to write like that one.'

'But yer mother . . .'

'I just brought her because . . . my brother has thrown us out and we had nowhere to go.' The truth has its uses.

'Ah.' She pulls up her pinny and wipes the foam off her forearm. She knows about such things, I think. The abrasions of family life.

'When we arrived, Mavis, Mrs Gervase didn't even know my mother would be with me.'

'Aye. Right.' Her eyes, bright and shrewd, survey me from head to toe, recognising our equality, or at this minute her superiority. 'So what's all this about then?'

'Mrs Gervase . . . my mother . . . we thought that, when the baby comes, and you're up and about, you might come straight back.'

'Well, the bairn, me mother's not pleased about it as it is. Talking about the workhouse, they are. But come back? Come back here?'

'Bring the baby. Come and stay here. Live in. With us here you'll be . . . Mrs Gervase says she asked you to live in before.'

'Me da wouldn't let us. The tales about Stephen hereabouts, you wouldn't believe. I telt me da they was nonsense, but he only says I was too stupid to know owt. Says Stephen would jump on us and I wouldn't see the light of day.' She gave out a short sharp bark which might have been a laugh. 'Funny that. Wasn't Stephen that jumped on us, but jumped on I was!'

'Jumped? Mavis!'

'You mind your own business! Water under the bridge.' She folded her arms. 'Live in, you say?'

'So long as your da . . .'

'He has no say over us. Never will, now,' she says sharply. 'Stay? I might just do that.'

'And me and my mother will help. It's a big house, as you say.'

'I thought you was writing them stories of yours?'

'I am. But I have to sing for my supper as well.'

'You're not getting pay for it?'

I throw up my hands, and realise I am mimicking one of Mrs Gervase's gestures. 'Never been mentioned,' I say, 'money.'

'More fool you,' Mavis says, and turns back to her dishes. I am dismissed.

I go to report back to Mrs Gervase in her little sitting room. I almost reel back when I open the door. What had been, at night, a velvet cave, is now ablaze with moorland light. The room is hexagonal and four of the walls are filled with floor-length windows; the fifth holds the fireplace; the sixth the door through which I have come. The view across the fells to the wide storm-lit sky makes me gasp.

'What a wonderful room!' The words are out before I can suppress them.

Mrs Gervase is sitting beside the fire with Seal on her knee. They have taken to each other, the dog and this old woman. She looks at me keenly. 'Do you know what it once was, this room?'

I shake my head.

'The room where they hung the pheasants after they shot them. Then my mother's father had a French gardener, a woman who laid out the gardens. She dug out the fell to make that waterfall. D'you see? She made him put windows in here because it had the best view of the garden. To watch her, I would surmise, because there are whispers of a love affair. And he would sit in here and watch birds rather than shoot them. It was always my favourite room when I visited as a child, and when Stephen and I came to live here, I had the fireplace built and the curtains hung. Now then.' She folds her hands, one over the other on Seal's curving back. 'How has the emissary fared?'

'Well. I'm sure Mavis will come back. I think having a baby, even a baby out of wedlock, has given her some kind of courage. They threaten her with the workhouse so she has nothing to lose. She's not her parents' child any more.'

'Humph! She is thirty-five, for goodness' sake!'

'Younger than you when you had Stephen?' I venture. I don't know where I get the boldness to say this.

'*Touché*, my dear. *Touché*! Do you think it was another annunciation, or do you think it was a browsing sheep-shearer with a Scottish accent which you could carve out of the air with a tree saw?'

This is uncanny. 'I really came to ask you about something else, Mrs Gervase.'

'Now then, my dear.' She is benevolent. Her plots and plans are all working all around her. I must still be careful with her.

'I want you to teach me something.'

'Me, Theo? I am just an old woman. Teach!'

'I want you to teach me to talk like you . . . to speak like you do.'

'Speak like me?' Her ancient eyes are wide, innocent. I can hardly bear her high amusement. Her disbelief.

'Why not? You just spoke of the Scots sheep-shearer in dismissive tones. An accent you could carve with a tree saw. So what do you think of my accent?' I rap the words out, then let the silence hold. Her withered cheeks stain red: with anger I imagine. She will dismiss me for my insolence. Then she laughs. 'Well, my dear, you have a charming accent.'

'Charming!' I say in disgust.

'Well, I can hear Welsh, which is very clear and has some deep tones. And I can hear a lilt that clearly comes from your mother, whose own accent is also charming and clearly very Irish.'

185

'I want to learn to talk without any of that rubbish in it. I want to talk so no one can put a label round my neck. Like a dunce in a corner.'

She strokes Seal's head. 'You want to pretend to be someone else?'

'No. No! Who knows who I am? Do you? Do I? What I know is the minute I open my mouth a thousand people think they know who I am. I don't like that.'

'It happens to us all, my dear, that recognition, false or otherwise.'

'Ah. But what they think they recognise about you is that you have money and standing and are worthy of respect. And that's before they find out a single thing about you.'

'And what do they think about you? When they hear you?'

'They think I have coal dust under my fingernails and very probably make a very good pot pie!'

'Not that you write very fine stories about Aphrodite and Achilles? Or that you talk as though you have swallowed a dictionary?'

'Never that.'

'Well then, you make a good case, I suppose. I will have to be very severe, do you understand? You will not take offence?'

'I'll be a good pupil, I promise you.'

'As a matter of fact you will create havoc wherever you go, you know. No one will know who on earth you are.'

'Good! That's what I want. A bit of havoc. What I don't want is to stay where I am, in some kind of limbo not of my own choosing.'

Then the old woman laughs so hard that Seal jumps from her lap. 'Right, Theodora Maichin. Let havoc commence!'

Fourteen

In the Pheasant Room

Even though she was much relieved that there would be a place for her at Goshawk Shield after the baby was born, Mavis Gomersall was still frosty and distant with Theo, not least because she could not put the girl into any of the available boxes in her head. The boxes had distinct and well-used labels: *Town girl*; *Country girl*; *Young lady*; *Harlot*; *Spinster*; *Widow*. None of these fitted the bookish girl with her neat clothes and sand-coloured hair, her ready smile but eyes that you would not necessarily trust. She was watchful and, Mavis felt, always judging.

However, Mavis, who had survived in her own crowded home where there was no room for an ageing pregnant spinster, knew better than to cross this girl who got on so well with Mrs Gervase and had poor Stevie eating out of her hand. If it hadn't been impossible, (the fellow being an idiot), Mavis would have said that he was in love with this managing slip of a girl.

Mavis had much more time, however, for the girl's mother, Rose Clare Maichin. Mavis herself was quite old in her ways, so the five years' difference in their ages shrank to nothing when she and Rose Clare were together. And, very importantly, Mavis did have boxes in her head where she could place Rose

Clare: *Put-upon woman*; *Victim*; *Deserted woman*; *Despairing woman*. All of these boxes held a bit of Rose Clare, just as they had bits of Mavis herself.

In her first days and weeks at Goshawk Shield Rose Clare wandered about the house and yard, uncertain of where she was and what she was to do. In this time she grew to be comfortable with Mavis and her bustling ways, her practical concerns. She and Mavis would spend any spare time together in the kitchen which was by far the warmest and most comfortable room in the whole house. The public reason for this close association was that Mavis was 'showing Rose Clare the ropes' for when she was away. 'Although,' she said at least once a day, 'I can't see I'll be away more'n a week. Me mam was back in the dairy two days after she had our Poll and our Sadie. I was twelve when she had Sadie an' can remember as clear as crystal.' A shadow crossed her face as she recalled, equally clearly, the shouts of fear and agony that accompanied each painful birth. In the end she had had to pull her pillow right over her head to shut out the screams.

Rose Clare patted the younger woman's shoulder. 'Don't think of it, so. Just think it is a day from your life. The day before, you don't have the baby. The day after you do. All you do is consign the middle day to purgatory, where it truly belongs.'

Mavis closed her eyes and nodded. 'Yes. Yes. I'm sure you're right. Right you are.'

One day they were having a precious cup of tea in front of the blazing fire after a hard morning turning out the back pantries and the old unused dairy, scrubbing and taking turns in singing old songs from the English and the Irish. They had laughed and joked with each other like sisters. Rose Clare felt more at ease than she had for years, in the younger woman's company.

Rose Clare stretched her aching legs before the fire. 'Do

you know I've not had so much fun since I was a little 'n picking praties with me sister.'

'You have sisters?'

'Then I did, before the hunger came and took them, along with Mammy and Daddy.'

'So you're an orphan?'

She shrugged and shook her head. 'No. I have a brother somewhere.' She slurped her tea and her eye strayed to the leaping flames. 'To tell you the truth I don't care for him. I don't care for him at all.'

Mavis looked at her carefully but said nothing.

'And you? You have brothers and sisters?'

'Aye. I'm t'second eldest next to Hermione. Then there's seven more. Second youngest is Poll, the last is our Sadie.'

'Useful on the farm, so many children.'

'Too many, you might say. Our Hermione's me mam's right hand, and t'youngest's fit as any lad, can work inside and out. Ah've allus worked in other folks' houses. Bring cash in, see? Not much cash on farms. All "kind", see? They care less for you when you work away from the farm. Out of sight, out of mind. Out all morning working here at Goshawk. Out all afternoon working for Mrs Crewe at Percy's Leap. Back at dark. Sometimes seems like they're the family and I'm t'cuckoo in t'nest.'

Rose Clare stood up and poured some more tea into Mavis's cup. 'Sure, isn't the tea quite fine, even on a second using?' Mavis had showed her how, with great care, she dried the leaves used once by Mrs Gervase, so she could have as much tea as she liked on second using. Rose Clare settled herself in the chair, pulling the cushion under the bit of her back that usually hurt. 'So didn't you fancy marrying that feller, the little one's daddy? It would have got you out of the house, after all.'

Mavis laughed, a harsh sound without mirth. 'His daddy?

His daddy? A sinner, Rose Clare!'

'They're all sinners, Mavis. Every last one of them.' She thought of Ellis. 'But we can still love them.'

Mavis shook her head. 'Oh no. This one is a sinner. He'll get his punishment in hell. It's me being punished down here, mark you.'

Rose Clare stared at the younger woman and saw again the fiery face of her brother Liam as he held her hands behind her back and made that first excruciating entry into her fourteen-year-old body. 'Be quiet, will you?' He had grunted the words over and over again, over and over, till it stopped. 'Be quiet. You want this.'

'Oh Mavis,' she said, remembering the terror that the pain from her own rape would result in a child. She did not ask Mavis whether it was her father or her brother. She knew it was one of them.

'Nae good sayin' owt, is it?' said Mavis. 'Just get through it, I say. Me mam says this bairn'll go to the workhouse, but I say not. So, coming back up here with the babe . . . that'd be a blessing.'

'Sure, we'll all help you. Help you and the baby,' said Rose Clare, too numbed with Mavis's pain to pile on words of comfort. 'We will all help you, so.'

Mavis nodded glumly. 'Ah have ter think that. If yeh dinnet help, nae one will. Ah'm tellin' yer.'

Mavis Gomersall and my mother are inseparable, which is just as well. At first my mother wandered around Goshawk Shield like a grey ghost, for all her red petticoat. She ate what was put in front of her; she spoke when spoken to. She sat for hours watching Mavis working in the kitchen. Then one day Mavis must have given her something to do and before long they were working shoulder to shoulder, still saying very little at first.

Despite my efforts to be friendly Mavis treats me to glowering distrustful looks. But I have to say she has cheered my mother up. I hear them singing now, even laughing together as they work. Strange that my mother has never sung or laughed with me in all the times we worked together. My father and she sang together. I have heard them many times from another room.

There are signs now of my mother in the kitchen. Extra pots of bright flowers on the windowsill. A gaudy shawl over the back of Mavis's chair. The two of them look up at me like a pair of conspirators as I come into the kitchen. It is as though I am an interloper. They breathe easier when I leave. I know one thing. They don't like my little Seal curling on their hearth, so I have made a little bed for her in the bedroom, beside a fire which I keep up all day. This is her retreat when Mrs Gervase is not petting her.

Although the weather has been fine and the skies are often blue and full of light, the mist on the far hills is waiting to pounce, filling the air with damp which makes my writing paper curl and my ink blotchy.

I take Seal for little walks along the lane but much of the time she rides in my arms, as a consequence of prowling farm dogs who see her as a tasty morsel, I am sure. Aside from the kitchen she runs around the house freely enough, though and her limp is now barely noticeable. She is quite a favourite with Mrs Gervase on whose lap she nestles at least an hour every day. Stephen, seeing her as a kind of liberated extension of myself, treats her very tenderly and, given a free hand, would fatten her like a Saturday porker.

But every time she ventures into the kitchen she is brusquely shooed out by one of its guardians. I rather think they would 'shoo' me out too if they had the courage. I am a willing exile from the kitchen regions. The kitchen is my least favourite place. Apart from the pheasant room, Mrs Gervase's magical retreat, my favourite place is the dining room, a dark foisty place which is rarely used. By custom, the curtains in there are opened eighteen inches during the day and closed at five o'clock sharp every afternoon, summer or winter. The recesses in this room, which flank the magnificent Frosterly marble fireplace, are filled with fine cedar-wood bookcases. Along the back wall is another large bookcase which is nearly twice my height. On these shelves march hundreds of books: tall, short, fat, thin, pushed in together indiscriminately, not even making a physical pattern. They are not organised by alphabet; not by shape or bulk or size; not organised by the subjects in their pages; just there.

I sense the willing but undiscriminating hand of Stephen Gervase.

The first time I really poked around here was when Mrs Gervase sent me to find an American story about a sea captain who chased all round the sea in pursuit of a whale. He was a cruel, demented man who could think only of his quarry, of the death of the whale. I failed to find the book that time, as I shall explain. Later, when I read the story to Mrs Gervase and Stephen, I thought that in many ways this captain was like Edward, born to destroy and murder, yet seeing himself of the highest quality. But in the end I decided that this was not so. This captain had qualities in him that made you pity him, and I have no pity in my heart for Edward.

But that is all in the future. The first time she sent me for the book I couldn't find it. I went back to her, to the pheasant room where she was sitting in the window seat with Seal on her lap, looking out at the moors.

'The room's all higgledy piggledy, Mrs Gervase. You couldn't find a thing in there. It's a real mess!'

Mrs Gervase waves her hand at me. 'That will be Stephen. He did this for me at Christmas. Tidied it up. Two? Or was it three years ago?'

'Well, it's cold and damp and dark and you can't tell one book from another.'

She peers at me in the gathering afternoon darkness. 'Then light a fire – gather lamps! There must be dozens in the house. You claim to be literate, a writer. Sort the books out and find Captain Ahab for me.'

'There is no book there called Captain Ahab, I tell you!'

'There is. Sort the books out. Put them in alphabetical order. Then you will find it.' She lifts her chin and calls, 'Stephen!'

His heavy footstep echoes in the hall and he comes in the room, bringing with him the scent of the stable. 'All the shoes are cleaned,' he said. 'Nice and shiny. And the stable's mucked out.'

'Splendid!' She beams up at him. 'You always do such a good job on the shoes, Stephen. And the stable.'

Stephen cleaned all the shoes in the house every day, whether they needed cleaning or not. Even Mavis, on her morning visits, had to bring her Sunday shoes so they could be cleaned yet again.

'Stephen, I want you to help Theo to sort out the books in the dining room.'

He frowns. 'I sorted them for you, Mama. Your Christmas present.' He counts off on his fingers. 'One, two, three years ago.'

She smiles. 'Yes, and what a splendid job you did! But Theo has some new ideas about how to sort them. Because she is a storyteller, you see.'

He turns towards me, frowning.

'I'll use them to help me write my stories, Stephen.'

All the varied things Stephen does, he does by his own consent. Surprisingly, despite his simple mind, he has some power in this house. He gives me one of his heart-melting smiles. 'Theo will want to do something different, I know it!'

'That's right,' says his mother. 'You go and light a big fire

193

in the dining room and you can both get started.' Seal stirs and jumps from Mrs Gervase's lap, sensing some activity after her afternoon's rest. I gaze into her wise, bright face. Since this little dog has been with me I have thought of my ghostly seal sister less and less.

Stephen and I make good progress. By midnight the dining room, now steamy hot and smelling of crisping paper and drying damp, is a scene of fairly ordered chaos. The big shelves are stripped of books and are being damp-dusted by my mother up a ladder. Two hours ago she put her nose round the door to see what the riot was about and was pressed into service.

The books are on the floor, gradually being sorted into broad types of books. Each dining chair is stacked with ever-refining categories such as flowers, nature, religion, farming, ancient history, modern history. One small stool even has a growing pile on the subject of witchcraft. The dining table is for stories of every kind, from Bible stories and fairy tales to novels just purchased in very recent years. One of these is by a man with a fancy French name, and (for I dip and dip as I sort) is about a man who mesmerises a girl into being a great singer. I make up my mind on the spot to read that one. There are plays, some with astonishingly worldly wit by Oscar Wilde, about whom I have read in the newspaper. There are magazines, going back years. *Good Words*, *Sylvia's Home Journal*, *Household Words*, *Judith's Journal*. A feast of reading. There is a box of papers, including one wrapped up in string, which has pictures of this house, of Goshawk Shield, from another age. Tucked underneath it are plans for the garden, all stretches of shrubs and waterfalls. The signature on the bottom is French and is a woman's: Pauline de la Carrière.

Now at last we place the final book on the final pile and the shelves are dusted and polished. Stephen looks round the room with pleasure. 'Now we put the books on the shelves,' he says.

I stretch my arms above my head and look at my mother who is leaning on the back of a chair which is probably holding her up. 'No, Stephen. We will put them all wrong. We're too tired.' The springing chime of the clock in the hall twangs out twelve strokes. 'It is tomorrow now!' I said.

Stephen put his hand to his mouth, his eyes wide open. 'Mama! I have to tuck her in!'

My mother and I exchange glances. She smiles at me openly, without reserve, I think for the first time in my life.

'You go and check she is well tucked in,' she says. 'Sure, haven't you been a great help here? Your mammy will be pleased with you, so.'

'Yes. Yes. I'll do that, Mrs Maichin. Will I do that, Theo?'

I nod. 'Just go and check, Stephen. She's probably fast asleep.'

We watch him shamble out. 'Poor feller,' says my mother softly.

I smile at her, then decide not to make too much of this moment between us. It could flee at a glance. 'Well, Mother, I'll just damp the fire down and put the fire guard round . . .'

She takes her cue and wipes her hand down her apron. 'Yes, yes. I'll shut up the kitchen and lock the door.'

I am halfway up the stairs when I realise that Seal is missing. I go back to find her curled up beside the dining-room fire on a cushion discarded from one of the chairs to make room for a pile of books. I pick her up. She weighs no more than a bag of sugar in my arms. 'Come on, lazybones. We need our bed because we have a hard day before us tomorrow.'

The next day Stephen and I set to, right after breakfast. By noon we have all the flower books and animal books on the bottom shelves and Stephen has begun to learn the alphabet. So anxious is he to help me that he is sorting them out by the shape of the letters which begin the name. Then he starts naming them very quickly, picking the same letter out later in the author's name, or the book title.

'Did you never learn to read, Stephen?'

My mother brings us a tray of milk and biscuits and we sit side by side on the hearth rug before the leaping fire. She sits down in the chair, the tray on her knee, watching us with bright eyes. He drinks his milk noisily and thirstily and crams a biscuit in his mouth.

'Did you never learn to read, Stephen?' I ask again.

He shakes his massive head, then speaks, spitting biscuit in every direction. 'No. I am too stupid, you see, Theo. The first schoolmaster explained this to Mama. Too stupid. So Mama says no matter. I can do many other things. She knows this. I can make machines. Carve wood.'

'Would you like me to teach you to read?' I must be mad to offer, when you think of it.

He shakes his head, chewing on his second biscuit. 'No. Too stupid, the schoolmaster said.'

Can you believe that I persist?

'It would be so helpful to me if you could read, Stephen. Would you try with me?'

He finishes the biscuit and drinks off the milk. I seem to be waiting a long time for his answer. Finally: 'I will learn from you.' His voice is troubled. 'But will you whip me if I am stupid? Like the schoolmaster?'

I laugh loudly at this and take his big hand in both of mine. 'Your mama is right, Stephen. It doesn't matter a jot. You can do so many other things. But you're so much older and wiser now. Perhaps you can do it. And if you can it will be a great honour for me to be your teacher.'

His large eyes fill with tears. He pulls away his hand and races from the room with his awkward gait. I put my glass back on to the tray and look across at my mother. 'I made a mess of that, didn't I?'

She shakes her head. 'I don't know where you get it from, this persuasion, but it's not from me.' She picks up the tray. I am warmed by her praise. 'Is that you finished? Mavis and me are checking the bottled fruit so I know what's what when she's away.'

I haul myself to my feet and start to look through the story piles on the table, flicking through the pages, admiring the typefaces, the fine engravings, the detailed illustrations on the magazines. My eye is caught by a coloured illustration at the front of one book. It is the prow of a ship, rearing out of the water. Standing at the helm is a man with the stance and demeanour of a captain, eyes too large for his face. Beside him is a henchman with an evil-looking trident. In the water, distorted by the proportions of the picture, lurks a great whale. I turn to the title page.

Moby Dick; or, The White Whale by Herman Melville. I skim the first few pages and the name jumps out at me. *Captain Ahab*. I am still smiling my delight when the door opens and in comes Stephen, dry-eyed.

'I talked to Mama,' he says. 'She said that you can teach me to read and I will not be stupid this time. Do you know what she said, Theo?'

'No.' I am smirking with double pleasure now. 'She said it was not I that was stupid, it was *he* that was stupid. The schoolmaster.' He starts to laugh his hoarse, unformed laugh. 'She said he was as stupid as a day-old piglet. Is that not funny?'

And we laugh together as old friends do.

It has taken me a week to get the dining room right. My mother and Mavis have had the big curtains down and, having shaken them, washed them in the big pot in the wash house. Stephen and my mother and I had to help to wring them in the yard. My mother and Mavis put blankets and sheets on the big kitchen table and ran a relay of irons to iron them smooth.

Stephen and I clean the tall windows which look straight out on to the fell, and stay up the ladder to rehang the curtains. We banish four small tables and three chairs to the attics. We keep two chairs for the fireside and open the dining table to its longest, place it end-on to the largest window, so that daylight streams on to it.

Mavis tuts away at this so much, about the sun ruining the wood, that I have to listen. 'Well,' I say finally, the very image of patience. 'We'll cover the table. Have you anything big enough to cover it, which I can put books on, which will take inkwells and paper and will stop the sunshine attacking it?'

She vanishes, to return with a huge velvet curtain over her arm. She shakes it, then spreads it across the table. The light falls on it, showing the faded streaks where it must have hung at some window for years. It is a very friendly curtain. 'It used to be in the big drawing room, when Ah just came here.' She smooths its surface with an almost tender hand.

'That's perfect, Mavis.'

'Perfect, Mavis,' says Stephen.

She reaches in her apron pocket and produces a ball of garden twine. 'Ah thowt mebbe the curtain'd move on the polished wood. Under the books and papers, like. So it'd need fixing.'

So, as we watch, she sets about tying the velvet to the table legs and stretchers. She fiddles with the tension across the top to get it just right, and somehow manages to pull the velvet back up again over the ties, like a mother pulls the flounce of her daughter's knickerbockers to cover the elastic. It looks quite smart.

When this is done to her satisfaction she vanishes again and comes back with two fine but very old-fashioned lamps which she spaces along the centre. 'Tha'll not want to strain thee eyes after dusk, Theo, writing them stories.'

'They're wonderful lamps, Mavis.'

She shrugs. 'They were here when I first came to Goshawk as a lass. They cast a good light. Just need to keep them properly trimmed.'

So that is how Stephen and I have acquired our lair. He lights the fire every morning, as he lights all the fires in the house. Then he hastens off to do all his mysterious chores and his carving.

I stay here right through the morning, writing the last of the Greek stories for Mr Murton. And I must confess that I read in here. Books, magazines. How could you not read in such a place? I started with *Moby Dick*, reading on and on until four o'clock when I go along to the pheasant room, to read to Stephen and Olivia Gervase. I read ahead, so I have an idea of what will happen. The overwhelming sense of the sea in the story makes me ache, makes my whole inside cry out for the tide which fed the rhythms in my head and was my refuge as a child.

When I have finished my own reading of *Moby Dick*, I race ahead on my own. I take the books away and read them right through the night. *Kidnapped*. And another by the same man about a doctor who is a good man but who takes an evil potion and becomes a wicked murderer. I am very struck by this and am reminded, again, of Edward.

King Solomon's Mines; all sorts of bits and pieces by Rudyard Kipling who has been out in India a long time; an amazing story about a machine which a man invented, which took him into the future. And there are plays: some old ones by William Shakespeare, of course; some by Mr Wilde, as I said; and some by Mr Bernard Shaw. These are really modern. About real people. The plays are so easy to read that you can hear the people's voices in your head. You can read them much quicker than the novels.

I ask Mrs Gervase if she has seen the plays and she laughs

heartily, shaking her head. 'No, no, I have not been in London for many years, Theo. Some of these are new plays. I have them sent from London. Some of them I've not even read myself yet. You read them and tell me their story.'

What I discover, in all this reading, is that you can write what you like, about quite ordinary people. Extraordinary things happen to them, but they are still ordinary people. So ideas start to cook up in my brain which are not about Aphrodite or Loki in their sunny realm. They are about young men and women who grow up as I have done, trying to make their way in the world. Like that French woman gardener, I suppose, travelling from France in the throes of revolution to this Northern lair to practise her art.

So, I spend the mornings reading and writing. Stephen comes at twelve o'clock and we struggle with our letters for an hour before we have our mid-day dinner, all together including Mavis, in the breakfast room. The hours between two and three Stephen and I spend in the pheasant room with his mother. He shows her proudly what he has learned. Then I read poetry to her for half an hour when she corrects my speech mercilessly. She only does it during this half an hour, not during Captain Ahab or other stories. Not during the normal intercourse in the rest of the day. In this I think she is very clever.

However, for this half-hour she is merciless. 'No, no, my dear. Loosen your jawline. Think of it as on a very soft length of wool . . . loose, loose. Mobile.

'No, no, my dear, your voice is locked in your cheeks, your nose, it should come from your chest, your throat, pure as the note of a flute!

'No, no, my dear, you forget how the words are made. You have entirely forgotten the letter g . . .

'No, no, my dear, you are making your tone too hard. It has hobnailed boots on.'

It has been agony. I yearn to tell her to stop being so rude.

After that it is a merciful release just to read to her. I am supposed to read to her for an hour, but after forty minutes both she and Stephen are fast asleep, so I mark my place, stop reading and have five minutes shut-eye myself. Then, on the hour, I wake them both up and we make a foray into snippets from yesterday's *Times* and *Priorton Chronicle* which have been brought up by the post boy. I have usually read *The Times* first, to find nice bits and pieces for the two of them. I have learned a good deal about the affairs of the day through doing this and am disturbed by how profoundly ignorant I have been heretofore. It is not always easy to understand and I can feel my mind fumbling, like Stephen is fumbling with his letters. The *Priorton Chronicle* I don't prepare. It is easy to pick up tit-bits on the spot in this paper. Easy to scan, easy to précis.

This was the reason for one of the two surprises of today. The first surprise was Stephen producing from his various pockets all the letters of the alphabet carved in smoothly sanded boxwood. Mrs Gervase and I exclaim in delight and we ask him to sit them along the windowsill in order. There is a bit of a flurry when we discover that the P is missing and his eyes fill with tears of disappointment. 'I did it, I did the P,' he insists.

'Your pockets. Look in your pockets!' I instruct. We look in every pocket. No P. 'Turn round!'

He turns round and round, then Mrs Gervase claps her hands. 'It is there, Stevie, caught in the lace of your boot.'

He hooks it out with his long thick finger and puts it in its place in the order. 'There!' he says. 'Not stupid, huh?'

I pat his arm. 'You're clever, Stephen. You learned quickly.'

'Well done, Stevie. Well done.' Mrs Gervase beams.

We proceed to the *Priorton Chronicle* and read about all sorts of things in the locality. Then, glancing again at the front page, my eye falls on a small engagement announcement.

The engagement is announced between Ruth Berriman, daughter of Councillor G. A. Berriman, of Priorton, nail merchant, and Rhys Michael Maichin, of Wales. The wedding will take place at St Andrew's Church, Priorton, on 1st September 1899.

'Come on, my dear. What are you staring at? Read it out.' Mrs Gervase is watching me very closely.

I read it out.

She frowns. 'Maichin? You know this man?'

'I should. It's my brother,' I say. I stand up. 'I must go and tell my mother.'

She flicks her hand. 'Yes, of course. Go and show it to her.' Her kindness is instant but I sense a tension, even an anger in her. Perhaps she sees this incursion from the outside as a threat.

My mother is sitting dozing before the kitchen fire and takes a bit of waking. 'What? What is it? Ellis!'

I shake her shoulder. 'No. No, it's me.' I wait till she has shaken herself awake, blown her nose, and is looking at me expectantly.

'Well, Theo, what is it?' she says crossly.

I show her the paper. 'There.'

She reaches into her apron pocket for her wire spectacles, and spells out the words on the page. 'Ruth Berriman. Who's that? Berriman?'

'Wasn't that where he went to work? Berriman's?'

'September. Will we go to this wedding, Theo?'

I shrug my shoulders. 'We haven't been invited.'

She starts by shaking her head angrily, then starts to sob, finally she throws her apron back over her head. Some savage hand clutches my heart as I remember Ellen Jones's mother mourning her lost daughter in just such a way. My mother's words confirm my thoughts. 'This is no family. To be sure,

202

this is no family. Getting married and not a word to me.'

I stand there awkwardly not knowing, after nearly eighteen years, how to take her in my arms and comfort her. Then I comfort her in the only way I know how. 'I'll write him a letter and ask what he is up to. I will tell him we will go to his wedding if we are invited. Then the call is with him.'

The apron comes down and she uses it to rub her red eyes dry. She sniffs. 'Well, sure, that'd be something.'

'And' – I manage to put my hand on her shoulder – 'whether or not he invites us, we'll go and gawp at them like townspeople. Like strangers. We'll show them!'

She smiles weakly. 'Oh Theo. Sure, we couldn't do that.'

'You watch us!'

I go off there and then to write the letter, seal it carefully and address it to *Mr Rhys Maichin, care of Berriman's Ironmongery, High Street, Priorton, County Durham*. Then I go to Stephen's work shed where he sitting painting his alphabet blue by the light of a storm lantern. 'I've written a letter to my brother, Stephen. I want you to take it down to Stanhope tomorrow to post it for me.'

He nods, his eye still on the letter Z he is painting. 'Yes. I'll take it tomorrow for you, Theo.' He doesn't look up.

'What is it, Stephen?' I shake his shoulder. 'What's the matter?'

'Mama says I must be careful. She says you may go to the brother's wedding and not come back. I must be careful. I cannot learn to read now.'

I turn his heavy face towards me and look into his wide eyes. He twists away. 'Look at me, Stephen!' Finally his eyes return to mine. 'I may go to the wedding, I may not. He is my brother. But if I do I'll come back here the same day. I promise. I truly promise.'

'Promise?'

'Promise!'

He looks at the letter in my hand. 'Will you write down the promise?'

How can this strange man know me so well? 'Yes. I'll do it right away.'

He nods, satisfied, then holds up a blue-painted M with rusty pliers. 'Do you like my M in blue?'

'It's lovely.' I pat his shoulder. 'Lovely.' Walking swiftly back to the house I know that, brought up as I have been, I don't know very well how to love. But I think, lunatic that I am, that I love this Stephen Gervase. Certainly more than I love my brothers, or my mother, or my father.

I burst into the little sitting room in high temper, and corner Mrs Gervase. 'How dare you? How dare you say that to Stephen? That I would go?'

She sits up straighter in the chair. Seal jumps from her lap. 'You are above yourself, miss! What on earth are you talking about?'

'Stephen! You told him I'd not come back if I went to Rhys's wedding.'

She sighs a sigh which must come right from her tiny old-fashioned high-button boots. 'I have to do this for him, Theo. The depths of his disappointment, when he is truly disappointed, are terrifying to witness. In that state he might cut his throat. So I must prepare him. Let him down gradually, if not gently.'

It takes some seconds for me to absorb this and as I do my temper quite leaves me. 'I didn't think . . .' I say.

'No, you didn't, my dear. But then you are very young.'

'I'm sorry. Sorry.' I back out of the room. 'But I wouldn't let him down, you know. I would never let him down.'

I go to the dining room, now very much my work room, and turn up the lamps. On the velvet-covered table I lay out my best paper and my pens and inks. I spend a few minutes poking the fire and am suddenly aware of Seal at my skirts. I pick her up and look into her wise little face. 'So, seal sister. I am a dolt. A thoughtless dolt. My mistake is I think I'm perfect. I can teach Stephen, I can please Mrs Gervase, I can make my mother happy, I can transform this house. But I'm wrong. The old woman, she's had Stephen all these years and has made him a happy, busy man, mad as he is. She's protected him where many, even I, would've put him away and forgotten about him. And I have the effrontery to read her the riot act because she continues to do the same.'

Seal struggles from my arms and, using the stools and chairs as stepping stones, leaps on to the table and settles down on the velvet, her body curled up. With her watchful eyes as the centre, she has the appearance of a curved shell.

I sit down and in my very best writing I write a note to Mrs Gervase saying I know that I am very young but promise to stay here for two years and even then will not leave without her consent. I print Stephen's note. I WILL COME BACK FROM THE WEDDING. I WILL ALWAYS COME BACK. I PROMISE. I sign them with a flourish and walk across the hall to the pheasant room. As I open the door they both look up sharply and for a second the two faces – one small, withered and neat, the other large and square – look terrifyingly alike: innocent, wary and at the same time very wise.

I give them each their letter. Mrs Gervase flicks her eyes over hers, gives a small smile and tucks it in the velvet carry-all that moves around the house with her. Stephen opens his, and frowns down at the paper. I sit behind him and we spell the words out together. He smiles his wonderful smile.

'You promise?' he says.

'I promise,' I say. 'Now will you post my letter? Tomorrow?'

Fifteen

An Appropriate Arrangement

In the event there has been a lot more to do in the last twenty-four hours than post letters. Stephen's chariot, as it careered away from the house, did carry the letter in Stephen's pocket. It also carried me and my mother, desperately hanging on to the prone figure of Mavis Gomersall who was shrieking and groaning, clutching at us with terrifying power. I knelt in front of her in the crashing, rocking chariot, holding her forearms, staring into her sweating face.

'Wait, wait, my darling.' My mother's voice was low. I've never seen her so calm. 'Wait till you get to your home.'

But Mavis didn't wait. Her body shuddered, her hand clutched at me and I felt as though I were drowning in the tide. 'Oh Mavis!' I held her and our sweat and tears mingled as she screamed and screamed. The baby came out, I know not how. My mother pulled off her shawl and wrapped it up somehow despite its being still attached to its mother.

Mavis became quiet now, slack in my arms. 'Is she . . . he . . .?' she gasped, her eyes half closed.

'A girl, a fine baby girl,' my mother assured her.

'Poor soul,' said Mavis. 'A life of pain!'

'No, no!' I protested. 'It's good. Who'd want to be a boy?'

Mavis began to convulse again.

'Here now, Theo!' My mother's voice was sharp, authoritative. 'Get down here. Take the baby.'

I get down in the little space in front of the seats and take the shawled baby from her, still trailing its bloody cord. Then there is more blood.

'Another one?' I whispered, horrified, thinking of my seal sister.

'No, no,' said my mother, bloody but calm. 'This comes away afterwards. Perfectly natural.'

The babe mewed and chirruped in my arms like a captured bird. 'She's lovely,' I said to Mavis who was lying back on the pillows breathing heavily. 'Her little hands are perfect.'

'Well, that's something!' said Mavis and closed her eyes.

The chariot rocked to a stop.

'Thank God,' said my mother. 'Now give me the baby, Theo, and run! Get the mother, the sisters. Tell them the baby's born but the cord's not cut. They'll know what to do.'

The Gomersall women, junior and senior, came rushing out in a flurry of aprons and rattling talk which I did not understand. They shooed us out of the way and descended on the chariot. Hermione, the eldest, was dispatched for a big yellow towel and a thick grey blanket. In the towel she wrapped the baby who was crying lustily at being cut free from her mother. Then Stephen was deputed to carry Mavis, bundled in the blanket, into the house. The other sister, Sadie, stayed swabbing out the chariot as though it were just another job on the farm – like mucking out the byre.

My mother and I made to follow the procession into the house but Mrs Gomersall, short and thickset, casually blocked our way. 'Thank you, ladies, for your help, but as yeh can see, there's more hands here than we know what to do with. Ah'll send Stevie out to take yer home.' Then she turned her back on us.

'Mrs Gomersall?' my mother called anxiously.

The woman turned. 'Yes?'

'Mavis needs a doctor. It wasn't straightforward. She . . .'

'Aye. Don't you worry about our Mavis, missis. We'll tek care of her.'

So we were left, leaning against the chariot, being battered by the wind like orphans in the storm, waiting for Stephen to come and drive us home. I could feel my mother seething beside me, muttering under her breath.

'What's that, Mother?' I shouted in her ear.

She looked up sharply at me. She had forgotten I was there. 'Mavis wants nothing here,' she called above the wind. 'Nothing. She, nor that babe. It's a bad place.'

'But this is her home, Mother. Her family.'

'Her family's where the trouble started,' she said grimly. 'It all started here.'

I had no chance to ask her just what she meant because at that point Stephen came out, ashen-faced.

'Mrs Gomersall says I must take you home,' he said. 'Straight away. But Mavis is very poorly.'

I pushed him towards the chariot. 'Let's go home, Stephen. Haven't we done what we can do? Come on, Mother!' I had to drag my mother into the chariot's damp, smelly interior. I felt that if I let her go she would make a break for it and wrest Mavis from her mother's arms.

I think only Mrs Gervase had a good night's sleep that night. My mother and I took turns in waking each other up, tossing about in the big bed as though it were a ship in a storm.

The next morning at eleven o'clock there was a knock on the door. Mother and I came through from the kitchen. Mrs Gervase, who was hovering restlessly in the hallway, opened the door. It was Mavis's sister Sadie, balancing a washing basket on one hip and a milk can on the other. I wondered why she had come to the front, not to the kitchen door.

Mrs Gervase opened the door wide. 'Come in, Sadie, come in!'

Sadie walked in and placed the basket on the hall table which her sister had polished a hundred, a thousand times. Her face was grim, and her eyes were red-rimmed with crying. 'The worst of news, Mrs Gervase. Our Mavis's gone. Gone to her Maker. Seemed to rally for a while, but then went right back. Hung on right through the night and . . .' She coughed, put the milk churn on the floor and wiped her face, nose and mouth on her sleeve. 'And . . . passed on, like.'

Mrs Gervase sat down hard on a hall chair and I went to stand by her. From behind me my mother said, 'And the baby?'

Sadie straightened her shoulders. 'Well, the bairn's survived sure enough. Lusty. Better that she went with her mother, though.'

'Sadie!' Mrs Gervase rapped the word out.

'Well, ma'am, begging your pardon. No one knows who the da was. Some sheep-shearer or gypsy. She was a queer'n, our Mavis. Not that you speak ill of the . . . Well, like my da says, you could never tell what she was up to, our Mavis.' She sniffed. 'Not that it matters where she's gone, poor soul. She's in a Better Place.'

Silence settled on the hallway like a thistle cloak. Then Stephen clashed through the door in his outdoor boots. 'I got Mavis's pony for you, Sadie. Tethered her to the back of your cart.' He sniffed, trying and failing to stem the drip of tears.

Sadie looked from one face to the other. 'There is the matter of the bairn,' she said.

'The bairn?' I said.

'Me mother'll not have it in the house. Says it can go down to the new workhouse in Stanhope. She says it's nothing to do with us, that bairn.'

'What?' said my mother. 'Mother of mercy, girl, what are you saying?'

'The child's a . . . b— was born out of wedlock to a man we do not know. Perhaps even Mavis didn't know. And Mavis is gone.'

'Sadie Gomersall,' said Mrs Gervase grimly, 'you should be ashamed of yourself.'

Sadie set out her lip defiantly. 'Not me who should be ashamed, ma'am.'

Mrs Gervase raised her stick. 'Get out! Get out!'

Sadie made for the door. 'What about the bairn, ma'am?'

'What about it? You said it was at the workhouse.'

'Not yet. Not yet. Summat our Mavis said just before . . . before . . . like, she went. She telt us, she said, not to forget it was a Goshawk Shield baby.' Sadie glanced spitefully at Stephen. 'We did think for a second it might be. But decided no, not possible.'

Mrs Gervase was striking her stick on the floor now. *'Get out.'*

Sadie flew through the door then poked her head back round in. 'The bairn. It's in the basket. Mebbe you could get it down to Stanhope workhouse for us.' Then she slammed the door behind her.

Right on cue, from the washing basket, came a lusty wail. I pulled away the towel that was lying on the top and looked down into the bright red, crying face of Mavis Gomersall's daughter.

Sixteen

Honourable Intentions

Rhys Maichin could not quite make his mind up whether he had bowled Ruthie Berriman over with his charm, or she had bowled him over with her energy. But the months since they had met had been a dizzying round of meeting, flirting, confiding, creating a private language of jokes and allusions. These soon encompassed everyone around them, including her ponderous father and her snobbish mother, her skittish grandmother, his landlady on Fencale Street, the people at the forge and the general hard-working populace of Priorton.

Having, in her forwardness, lowered the barrier to enable Rhys to leap across from his level of worker to her level of merchant's daughter, Ruth took charge of everything to make sure that whatever she wanted, happened.

She firmly established their scandalous state by visiting him openly in his rooms in Fencale Street. This led to a summons to Mr Berriman's cluttered office at the foundry, and a laborious enquiry about Rhys's intentions.

'The most honourable, sir. The most honourable. I . . . er . . .' It was difficult to say the words. 'I love Ruthie with all my heart. She has quite bowled me over.'

'Aye,' said Mr Berriman drily. 'She has a habit of bowling along in her own sweet way. She is the plague of her mother's life and I must admit I have not seen it as my duty to get her under the whip. It seems that when I was looking elsewhere she turned from a lively little spark to a very self-willed young woman.' He pulled at his beard. 'Do you know, in my house – in my own home – she has even made an argument that women – women, mark you! – should vote shoulder to shoulder with menfolk. We have women in the local councils now. Can't tell you what embarrassment this causes, my boy. Once,' he said gloomily, pausing to select a cigar from a box on his desk, clipping it and lighting it, 'once, she ran away with gypsies and was away a month. Her mother took to her bed.'

'Oh dear,' said Rhys, hoping this was the right thing to say.

'Oh dear, as you say!'

'What happened that time, sir?'

'Chief gypsy brought her back. They couldn't tolerate her – he called it mannishness. That was probably the worst embarrassment of all. Rejected by gypsies.' He sighed heavily.

'I can imagine!' said Rhys, stroking his own chin where his beard would be – if he had one.

'No beating the nonsense out of her,' said the other. 'Tried it once. She bit me in two places. I still have the scars.' Rhys could not for the life of him think what to say about that.

'And your family, sir,' said Berriman. 'Where are they?'

Without blinking, Rhys said, 'They live in Wales, sir. We were born there. My father was coal factor for a big company. These days he works in America.' He paused. 'My mother, as Mrs Berriman senior will tell you, was Irish. Her people were in the licensed trade.'

'And what has brought you to this part of the world?'

'My brothers, Edward, Caspar and I were miners. We came here for work. The town where we lived was failing. Two pits shut. You've met my brother at Mr Carmedy's, I believe.

Caspar works in Northumberland.'

'The preacher? Aye, I hear tell of him. Interested in music too. Elias Glinton has his eye on him for the Liberals, I gather.'

For once Rhys blessed Edward and his overwhelming ambition. 'Yes, sir. My brother.'

For a few minutes Berriman seemed buried in the serious business of drawing in smoke and blowing it out. 'So!' he said, finally raising his eyes and looking straight at Rhys. 'You want to marry my scapegrace daughter?'

This was the first Rhys had heard of it. Of marriage as such. 'Well, sir . . .'

'How old are you, boy?'

'Nineteen, sir.'

'Do you know she is twenty-six years old?'

'She told me twenty-four.'

'Oh yes. And she is a liar as well.'

'Er . . . lying about your age is what women do, sir. It's common. Er . . . so I'm told.'

'Ha! Defend her, do you?' Berriman flourished a smouldering cigar towards him. 'Defend her? Play the gallant, do you?'

Rhys flushed. 'Well, sir. I must. I . . . I . . . am very attached to her. She is a very fine woman. Like no one I have ever met.'

'Hum. There is something in that.' Berriman threw the half-smoked cigar into the smouldering fire grate. 'Engagement now, Maichin? Married in one month. That is the agreement?'

Rhys's brain was racing.

'What do you say, sir?' Berriman's tone was brisk. He was frowning.

'Yes, sir. Yes indeed. I'll be the happiest man. The happiest.' He injected fervency into his voice.

'I doubt it. I very much doubt it.' Berriman was round the

213

desk now, looming over him. 'I do not envy you, sir. I do not envy you at all. Yet for myself I relish the thought of a quiet house.' He shook Rhys by the hand. 'The very best of luck to you, son, the very best.' He went back round the desk. 'Now you'd better go and tell Ruthie's grandmother. She has had no small part in all this. Prepared the way for you.'

Closing the door behind him, Rhys stood in the dusty corridor, his brain reeling. Did he really want this? Did he want it? Was she playing a game with him? Father so well-off that, even after the famous dalliance with the gypsy, she could have any stuck-up stiff neck in the town. And that same father visibly relieved to have her off his hands. Even if that meant letting her go to an ex-pitman six years her junior who didn't have sixpence to his name.

Rhys thought again about Ruth's bright piercing eyes, her long slender frame. Did he really want this? He set off along towards the shop with a little skip. Of course he did. He couldn't fool himself. There was nothing but good for him, in this scheme, whatever Ruth's weird intentions.

Old Mrs Berriman grinned merrily at him as he approached her kiosk. 'Well, young sir, are we full of beans this morning?'

'You knew! You knew what she's been up to. He, Mr Berriman, said you had prepared the way.'

'Know? Anyone within five miles of that house knew. Such screaming, such ranting and raving! Such spitting and gouging. Imagine Ruthie as Gentleman Jim Corbett and the combined strengths of those two as John L. Sullivan. Bare-knuckle fist fight and she won hands down! The more they raised their voices, the quieter she became.' There was satisfaction in the old woman's voice. 'The more set on her own way.'

'Sure, I bet you were a great referee!' said Rhys, thinking that if Ruthie were really like her grandmother, their marriage would indeed last a lifetime, whatever her strange ways.

'Oh no.' The old woman's high pompadour hair trembled as she shook her head vigorously. 'I was on her side from the start. And they knew it, though they didn't say a word to me.'

'I'm very grateful, Mrs Berriman. But why me?'

She put on her wire-rimmed glasses and surveyed him top to toe. 'Because I knew the first time I saw you that apart from being very handsome in a foxy way, you're clever enough, and most importantly you have the smell of the street, the workshop about you. Good working blood.'

'Well, thank you very much!' said Rhys, angry for a second.

She put up a half-mittened hand. 'No. No. Sure it is an honest compliment.' She chuckled. 'You should have seen some of the charmers Ruthie's shown the door to. Solicitors' sons. Doctors' sons. Millers' sons. Railway kings' sons. Milksops all. Two generations away from real work. Look round you at this shop. Look back away over the foundry. Milksops have nothing to offer here. But you do.'

Rhys thought his brain would burst. 'I can't really take all this in. Me and Ruthie get on, you know. I like the time we spend together. I had hopes . . .' He'd had hopes, in truth, of getting her into bed, although he'd not yet succeeded. 'I had hopes that sometime in the future . . .'

She shook her head. 'The future's now, Rhys, with our Ruthie. Now or never.' She leaned under her desk and pulled out a small box in tooled black leather. 'Now then. You take a look at that, my boy.'

He opened the box. There, nestling in cream velvet, lay a ring: a great loop of dark gold set with garnets and diamonds in a fetching flower design. 'What's this?' he said suspiciously. 'It's brand new.'

'It's your engagement ring. To give to Ruthie.'

'She might not like it.'

'She will. She chose it.'

He snapped the box shut and nonchalantly put it in his overall pocket. 'Right,' he said, not knowing quite what else to say. 'Right.'

'Just one thing, Rhys, my boy. Just watch yourself. Our Ruthie is a big handful, to be sure. But if you harm a hair of her head, or make her unhappy, or betray her in any way, I'll string you up by your . . . by your heels.'

'Oh my grief,' he said, clapping his hand to his head. 'What chance do I stand with two of you?'

She smiled broadly. 'Not a chance in heaven or in the other place, my boy. Not a chance.'

He stumbled through his day's work, suffering more than one reproof for a wrong count or dropping things which were very difficult to pick up. Thank goodness he hadn't had to go on the road today. He'd probably have ended up in South Shields instead of Durham City.

Ruth came to the shop at exactly five to seven, five minutes to closing time. She was wearing a tightly buttoned coat in emerald serge, and a very stylish hat which swept low to one side.

'Ruthie, what have you been up to? Your father . . . your grandmother . . .'

'I know,' she grinned, looking extraordinarily like her grandmother at that moment. 'I've arranged it all. Now take off that dratted overall.'

He slipped his shop coat off and picked his jacket off his peg, conscious of the other lads watching him with a combination of amazement and contempt.

She took the shop coat from him and threw it under the bench. 'The last time you'll wear that thing,' she said.

Then, arm in arm, they walked through the warehouse and the shop under the gaze of the whole staff. Someone at the far end of the shop whistled, 'Ta rara boom de ay'.

At the door Rhys panicked and pulled away from her.

'What is it, Rhys?' She grabbed his arm. 'It'll be all right, dear boy. I promise you.'

'No. No,' he said. 'Wait here. Wait for me!' He raced back through the shop.

There were jeers from the other lads as he reappeared. 'What is it, Taffy? Lost yer spunk, have yer?' one of them shouted.

He grabbed his work overall from under the bench and rescued the ring box which was still in the pocket. Then he grinned at his persecutors. 'Nah. The lady needs a ring. Wanna see?' He opened the box and they crowded round. There were one or two whistles. 'Whoa, Taffy. Yer a bliddy dark horse, ah'll say that for yeh.'

She was waiting for him outside, more anxious than she would have cared to admit. 'What was that all about?'

'Here, stand still in here.' He pulled her into a shop doorway. 'You'd better get this on your finger. If I lose it I don't know who'll horsewhip me first, you, your father or your blessed grandmother.'

She put it on and they kissed each other so vigorously that her hat was pushed from her head, only being saved from falling to the ground by the delicate net which was caught under her chin. Around them, late shoppers were clicking their tongues in disgust at such an exhibition of vulgar behaviour. They kissed on, oblivious.

After that they took each other's hand and raced to his room in Fencale Street, banged the door behind them, drew the curtains, and made love for the first time. It was nearly an hour later when Rhys pulled the sheet over them and, battling to stay awake, said, 'That's not the first time you've done that, is it?'

She was rehooking her corset with practised efficiency. She laughed. 'A bad lookout for you if it was. That was a bit of a surprise. You hardly . . .'

'I've been saving myself for you, beloved.'

She threw a pillow at him and got on with her toilette. 'You'll do, Rhys Maichin. You'll do.' She went to the narrow mirror and started to pin up her hair again. 'Now. The wedding. One month on Saturday.'

He pulled himself up on his elbow, still trying to stay awake. 'So your da says. I just do what I'm told.'

'I took the notice to the *Chronicle* today so it should be in tomorrow's paper. We'll be married at the Wesleyan Church and have a wedding breakfast at the Gaunt Valley Hotel.'

'There's grand for you.'

'Mm. Now, your family! Will they come from Wales?'

'Bit of a long way,' he said slowly. 'I imagine they wouldn't want to make the journey.'

'But there is your brother, the preacher! He can stand for you.'

'Yes,' he said, his heart sinking. Edward would enjoy making trouble. 'But I thought maybe Robert Bly, from the foundry. He's a good sort. I've got to know him since I've been in Priorton. Edward will come, of course. But not to stand for me.'

She looked at him through the mirror. 'Do you not like your brother?' She pulled her dress over her head.

'Well, seeing as you ask, no.'

'Here, can you fasten me up?' She backed on to the bed and he began the long business of fastening the buttons with fumbling fingers. 'Well, to be honest, the time I met him I thought he was a pompous prig, if a stunningly handsome one.'

'He is. A pompous prig. And he's not stunningly handsome. He's a snake. No snake is handsome.' Rhys scowled.

'Right. You know best.' She was fully dressed. 'Now you get dressed.'

He groaned. 'I'm tired. All I want to do is sleep.'

218

'No, love. We have things to do. Get dressed.'

He stood up, pulling the sheet around him. She laughed. 'Oh for goodness sake, Rhys, after what we've just done, you play the modest virgin?'

He dropped the sheet but he dressed in double quick time, with his back to her hearty giggles and cynical eye. Then, when they were both respectable and fully clothed, they clashed the bedroom door behind them and moved through to his sitting room. Ruth set about poking the fire into life. 'Now then, call Mrs Miller and ask if she would bring up a tray of tea.'

'What? Did you see her look as we walked through?'

'Call her!'

He leaned over the banister and called. His landlady answered very quickly, then grumbled at his request. Still, she was back at his door in five minutes with a tea tray. 'Good afternoon, Miss Berriman.' She prided herself on her manners. 'And how are you today?'

'Very happy. Very happy.' Ruthie jumped up. 'Oh, Mrs Miller, you're the first to know. Do you see this?' She held out her hand. 'We are betrothed, Mr Maichin and I.'

Mrs Miller peered at the ring, then looked back at Rhys in his threadbare preacher's suit that had seen many better days. 'Lovely, I'm sure. Congratulations to you both.'

'Well, Mrs Miller, the wedding will be in one month on Saturday and you'll have your invitation in due course.'

So, Mrs Miller, who had come up the stairs in high dudgeon, muttering about people who were no better than they should be, despite a good family name, went back down the stairs quite mollified, saying it was different, after all, if there was to be a marriage. Anyway, with the theatre in Priorton she'd had theatricals in those very rooms more than once. And the behaviour of those Johnnies put the billing and cooing of Mr Maichin and Miss Berriman quite in the shade.

The following Saturday Mrs Miller brought up a letter for Rhys. He recognised Theo's writing. He turned over the muddy envelope and noted the three red spots on one corner which looked suspiciously like blood. He read the letter and thought suddenly that while he had to have Edward at the wedding he'd much prefer to have Theo there. Even his mother. He wondered how his mother would get on with old Mrs Berriman. They would probably scratch each other's eyes out. But first he had to tackle Ruthie. 'I've had a letter from my sister, Ruth,' he said, after they had made love.

'From Wales?'

'Well, no, it's the strangest thing. Seems she's found a post with some lady farmer up the dale here. Kind of companion, as far as I can tell. She saw the announcement in the paper and writes to enquire.'

Ruth clapped her hands. 'What fun! She must come. She must come to the wedding. Did you know we have sent out eighty invitations?'

'That is seventy-nine for you.'

'Well, it's not me inviting the world and his wife. It's my mother, electrified at the thought of having a wedding at last.'

'I don't know why she's bothering. She has no opinion of me.' He'd endured two stiff, icy suppers in the Berriman household this week, with Mrs Berriman junior at the head of the table.

Ruth touched him on the cheek. 'Quite the contrary. It's I who've deprived her of the dynastic wedding.'

'Dynastic?'

'You know, ironmonger to banker, or ironmonger to baker. We've robbed her of that. As for you, you seem to have emerged from Celtic mist and she doesn't know where to place you. But still, she'll have her grand do and fill the occasion with her gaggle of acquaintances and small town cronies. Let her have her feast. She's even having it in the church for a better show. Doesn't suit my father, being a staunch Wesleyan, but there you are,' she said indifferently. 'And we can get on with our lives.'

She could hear Mrs Miller, now their confidante, banging and clashing fire irons downstairs. 'Oh,' said Ruth. 'I forgot to tell you. I've found the sweetest house on Victoria Road. Big rooms. Quite as big as those on the Avenue, but less of them. Walking distance from the foundry and the High Street. What do you think?'

He shrugged his naked shoulders. 'Your money. You please yourself.'

She put a soft finger on his lips. 'Sulking, are we? Do we have a problem with Ruthie's money?'

He pulled her down beside him and ran a hand down the side of her face. 'I have no problem with the money, no problem. But I am here somehow like a . . .'

She kissed his brow and his cheeks. 'Like a . . . ?'

'Kind of hired horse.'

She spluttered. 'A hired horse.' She surveyed the naked length of him. 'Like a stallion, you mean. Or a concubine.'

'Ruthie, you are so . . . such a . . .'

'Woman of ill repute!'

'To put it mildly.'

She rolled lightly on top of him, holding herself away from him. 'Only ever in private, dear. But that's what you like, dear, isn't it? All that dammed-up Welsh passion, released at last.'

He groaned and reached up to press her to him. 'Of course I like it.'

'And one day' – she pulled herself away again – 'one day, Berriman's, all that caboodle, will be yours . . . ours. Is that not worth all that clatter, with my mother floating around pretending even to herself that I've married a viscount or something? Isn't it worth it?'

221

'Yes. Yes.' He buried his head in her hair. 'But wouldn't you say that would make me a man of ill repute?'

'Yes, please,' said Ruth.

Seventeen

Town Wedding

So here you find me on my way to my brother's wedding togged up in a guest outfit which is a glorious amalgam of a dress of my own, topped by a pelerine from Mrs Gervase's wardrobe, and a hat of my mother's retrimmed by her with flowers from two of Mrs Gervase's hats. They assured me I looked fine. However, it's all very well stuck up there in the wilds just seeing each other, thinking we look 'all right'. Mirror image ragamuffins, all of us. Look at Stephen. Like something from a circus.

I have a feeling, from the glances I am treated to on the train, that this outfit is not quite all right. They are not quite smirking but they are certainly looking twice.

My mother and I received quite a nice personally written invitation from this Ruth Berriman. A bit gushing, but who knows what you would write to some unknown future sister-in-law whom you've never seen, who lives in the wilds? To be honest, I'm pleased not to have to miss this special occasion for Rhys. He's not perfect but he is the only one of my brothers I recognise as kin. The distance between my mother and myself is only just closing a bit. After that business in the chariot I think she is a saint but we go on just as before.

She's not coming to the wedding. Mavis's baby is

commanding all her attention. She was very sad about Mavis but in the presence of the child she smiles. She dances her around the kitchen floor and sings nursery songs to her in the Irish language, songs I have never heard before. She gave me a message to relay. 'Tell Rhys and his new wife about Mavis's baby. Sure, they'll understand. Rhys has a soft heart like his da, so he has.'

I've never been in an Anglican church, although I have been in several chapels which seemed large at the time. But this place is as large in comparison as a mountain to a hill, a great oak to a blackberry bush. And it's bright with candles. Unless I am mistaken there is a sweet smoky smell which must be incense. My mother would be at home, here, with her rosary and her love of sweet smells. I wonder, though, about Edward. And our nain. She would have thought we descended into the first circle of hell to cross this threshold.

There must be a hundred people in here but the whisperings, rustlings and creaking of stays are blotted up in the echoing emptiness of the place. I creep in just at the last and, stretching my neck, can see Rhys's upright figure and auburn head at the front. Three rows back, Edward's tall square frame is unmistakable. I wonder if I should just see the service through and run. These people with their feathered hats, serge-coated backs and fat stomachs are nothing to do with me.

There is a rustle at the back and a wheeze of violins at the front and people turn round. An old tramp wanders in, and after a whispered discussion with the tall clergyman, takes a seat in the very back row. The music tails off somewhat, until a mere echoing trill of the flute apologises into the air. Then a tall man steps forward with his violin and begins a very sweet passage.

Another rustle and a satisfied a-a-h at the back, and the bride walks slowly up the aisle. She is taller than I thought, and no beauty. But the tight grey silk dress shows off a narrow waist and a fine bosom. The man on whose arm she walks is a great bull of a man, sweating wildly, his tall silk hat clasped under his arm like a cocked gun.

In the service the singing, the prayers and responses seem to go on for ever; even so they have a soft and pleasing rhythm to them. I wish I knew what to say, how to join in. How much better this is than the wild shouts of *Hallelujah* which we were allowed in my grandfather's chapel.

Then it is all over and everyone relaxes. It is as though a wire has been broken. Rhys and – what is her name? – Ruth turn, link arms and make their way down the central aisle, nodding and bowing as they recognise people to their left and to their right.

When they get to me Rhys's face splits into a grin and they stop. Ruth looks at him enquiringly. He draws her towards me. 'Ruthie, this is my sister, Theodora.'

She smiles and offers her hand in a straightforward, almost mannish fashion. Her glance just flickers up towards my hat, then down to my face again. 'Theodora! Down from the hills! I am so very pleased you could come. You will be at the wedding breakfast at the Gaunt Valley Hotel?'

I rescue my hand. 'Yes. Yes. I'll be there.'

And the procession moves on, giving me a chance to look over the great and the good of the town of Priorton. Furs and feathers, pearls and heavy gold watch chains are much in evidence. Here and there appears a more workaday body dressed in black, weary, well-brushed Sunday best. My brother Edward walks by, a fluttering spoon-faced woman on his arm. I don't know whether he sees me. He certainly doesn't turn his head my way.

The church is gradually emptying. I sit very tight wondering if there is another way out.

'Well now, young Rhys has got his feet under a great table!'

225

a deep voice resounds in my ear.

I swing round and there beside me is the tramp. Or more properly there beside me is my father who has grown a beard as big as a gooseberry bush and has leaves and grass stuck to the greasy arms of his jacket. 'Dada!' The ferocity of my whisper almost frightens me.

'Theo! Just got here on the back of a flour wagon. Went to the address your mother sent back home. Seems the birds had flown. Man there told me Edward had moved. Went there and a woman told me he was attending his brother's wedding in this church.' He cast a grubby hand towards the bright altar with its crucifix and embroidered altar cloth. '"Thou shalt not make thee any graven images". Your nain will be turning rather crossly in her grave.' His eyes twinkled.

I fight back the desire to smile. 'Dada, we'll have to . . .' I look to the back of the church where the exit is dammed up by the flood of congratulation and rejoicing on the part of a hundred guests. The clergyman is striding back down the aisle, his vestments flying behind him in a wind of his own creating. I stand up. 'Sir!' I say.

His spade-shaped face, set in a benign mask, turns towards me. 'Yes?' he says, just short of brusque.

'I would like to take my . . . this gentleman out another way. He . . .' My mind turns revolutions. 'He is feeling unwell.'

The face bestows its beneficence on us, first one, then the other. 'Ah. I see. Follow me!'

We get up and follow him down the aisle. He makes some sign with his hands before the cross, then takes a smart, almost military turn to his left and leads us through a half-lit corridor-like room smelling of candle wax and old sweat, then he opens a door to the outside. 'Through here,' he says briskly. 'There is a small wicket gate which will lead you back to the town. It is quite hidden from the front door.' His tone is reassuring.

I hustle Dada through the crowded churchyard. My face as

I turn it to Dada is whipped by a chill wind. 'Well?' I say.

'Hit on hard times, dear girl. Thought your mother might need me.'

'Need you!'

'Well. I need her, shall we say?'

The miserable tone in his voice strikes a chord in me and I take his arm. 'Now then, Dada. We'll get you to a barber's to get that bush off your face, then the Public Baths. Then we can talk.'

I feel more like his mother than his daughter as I drop him at 'Harold Quincey, Barber', an establishment seamy enough to accept even the business of an unkempt tramp like my father. I pay the barber before I rush away to the pawnbroker's on the next corner. Here I root through left-behind clothes till I find a white shirt, black suit and shoes which I know will fit. I bargain the price down to eleven and sixpence. Then I race down to Rainbow's Drapers and buy appropriate underthings and socks, hiding my blushes by talking airily about my grandfather who is out of fettle at the moment.

My father, now neatly shorn and recognisable, is waiting for me as I race back, laden down with brown paper parcels. 'Now!' I say. 'The lady in Rainbow's says the Public Baths are down at the bottom of Princess Street. I'll sit in these tea rooms – see them? I'll wait for half an hour for you there. There are newish clothes in that bundle. Put them on. Put that stuff . . .' I wrinkle my nose. 'Put the stuff you're wearing in a bin or on a bonfire or something.'

'Theo, you sound different. Very grand, look you.'

'Go!'

'I go. Give me ten minutes!' His eye is gleaming; he is enjoying the game.

The man who comes through the door of the tea room half an hour later is unrecognisable from the man who stumbled into the church an hour ago. Very much the coal factor, the man of minor business. He sits down, drinks a cup of tea with evident thirst and beams across at me.

'Now then, dear, transformed, bossy daughter, shall we go to this wedding?' Sitting there, apart from the smell of mothballs, he looks no worse than at least a quarter of the wedding guests who trooped past me down the aisle. He glances up at me, his eyes sparkling. 'Was there no hat?' he says.

We pick up a bowler hat from the pawnbroker's on our way up the High Street to the Gaunt Valley Hotel. There the waiter shows us into a spacious private room where people sit round long tables munching and talking. As we walk through the door a hush falls over the company and every eye is on us.

'Here we go,' says my father through the side of his mouth and, taking my arm, he marches me right to the front to where Rhys is sitting, his bride on one side and a haughty-looking woman with an ostrich feather hat on the other. Rhys gets up from his seat. I will swear there is a look of genuine pleasure on his face. 'Father! Look, Ruthie, my father has come!'

Ruth looks up, her face quite beautiful with mischief. She leans her body too closely across Rhys to shake my father's hand. 'Mr Maichin. And how was America?' Her voice resounds in the room.

He lifts her hand to his lips. 'Very fine, Mrs Maichin, very fine!'

And then she sets about disrupting the whole of the front table, making a space for me and my father. Chairs have to be brought. Cutlery. Plates. There is a flurry of sweat emanating from pressed suits, the low tenor of annoyance. The string quartet pauses briefly in its labour then saws on with greater gusto. The same fair man leads, his fingers moving like butterflies over the neck of the violin.

I find myself facing Mrs Berriman, Ruth's mother, who

smiles thinly in my direction and proceeds to spear her ham with her silver fork and cut it into tiny bits with her knife before piling it onto the corner of her plate.

I try just once with her. 'This is a very fine wedding, Mrs Berriman.' The voice that comes out of my mouth is the new one: the one I have been practising with Mrs Gervase each afternoon. I can feel a ripple of interest passing along the row.

She answers. 'Ruth is our only daughter,' she says, spearing a potato and cutting it into small cubes. 'We always planned a fine wedding for her. The town expects it. But, under the circumstances, it is even more necessary.'

I start to spear my ham and chop it into little bits and pile it onto the edge of the plate. Wasting food is catching. 'So how would these circumstances,' I enunciate, loosening my jaw and using my lips as I had been taught. 'How would these circumstances make any difference, Mrs Berriman?'

There is a hearty laugh on my left and I turn towards an old woman, dressed in black with a frilled purple cap. 'Sure, if the circumstances had been different, Miss Maichin, wouldn't our sweet Ruthie have married into flour, or iron, or the railways?'

Mrs Berriman puts down her knife with a crash. 'Miss Maichin. We did not introduce you to Mrs Berriman senior, Ruth's grandmother.'

My hand is grasped in a muscular claw. 'The omission was quite deliberate, Miss Maichin,' she says smiling. 'My dear daughter-in-law much prefers my room to my company. It is her curse.'

'Mother!' Mrs Berriman picks up her fork and starts her stabbing again. 'Your own mother, Miss Maichin, she was not able to come?'

'I'm afraid not, Mrs Berriman. A close friend of hers has died, leaving a new baby, and my mother has the care of her. The baby is frail herself.'

229

'Sounds like a good mother to me,' says the old woman on my left through her potato.

'So, are you Rhys's full sister, Miss Maichin?' says the younger Mrs Berriman, wresting my attention from her obviously disliked mother-in-law. 'Is he your full brother?'

'Full brother?' I find myself frowning. 'Of course he is.'

'Well, you must forgive me for saying so, my dear, but he doesn't sound the least bit like you. The way you speak.' In her voice there is a pleading *be on my side* note.

'I can't think what you mean, Mrs Berriman.' Then I stuff my mouth with the piled ham to stop my voice betraying me, or Rhys, any more. To my right I can hear guffaws and tinkling laughter as my father becomes his most entertaining self for the benefit of Ruth Berriman. On the table leading down I catch sight of Edward sitting beside the mild-faced woman. He's lifting a glass of wine to his lips and taking a long deep gulp.

It seems all of us have come a long way since our life in Wales.

'I can't think when I've been to so fine a wedding, Edward. You must be proud of your brother.' Claris Carmedy prodded at her ham.

The glass hovered an inch from his lips, he sipped carefully again then put it down on the fine linen cloth. 'Yes indeed. Miss Berriman is a fine girl,' he said. The truth was he'd been seething since he had heard the news from Anthony Carmedy at a Liberal meeting. Carmedy had laughed. 'Now that'd've been a good catch for you, Edward. Mr Berriman is a staunch patron of the Party. You could have got far with such patronage. Your brother has done well in the marriage stakes.'

Edward's ambition had evolved in the months since he had been in Gibsley. He was relishing his growing respect as a lay preacher, but had been drawn into Liberal affairs by

Carmedy's enthusiasm and the patronage of Elias Glinton. He had begun to realise that fame inside the chapels was a hollow thing. It was not, as he kept reassuring himself, that the Lord was not as potent as ever in his life. He still believed, as his grandfather had taught him, in the all-encompassing power of the Almighty. He knew, as his grandmother had taught him, that the Lord had a special place for him at His table. That He understood sacrifices had to be made so that he could take that place, that the Devil's tempters and the wicked ones had to be dealt with. The Lord understood. And now He was placing in Edward's head the understanding that the real power to bring the world in the ways of righteousness lay in politics, which opened the world to any outstanding man. More so in these days in a small town where the top players were mere tradesmen, only second or third generation from the work bench themselves.

'I can't see that,' he said now to Carmedy. 'I'd rather get somewhere by my own labour than clinging to the apron strings of some woman.'

'Quite so,' said Miss Carmedy to his right. 'In any case, it seems that women will be making headway on their own behalf within the decade. There is suffragist activity here in Priorton. Even in Gibsley village there was a meeting—'

Edward laughed shortly. 'Come, Miss Carmedy, you must be joking! Those women are deviant, have no sense of the real world, frustrated, strident . . . St Paul says let the women be silent. It is better so.'

'Really, Edward!' she said, bright red patches on her cheeks. 'Perhaps with more years and much thought you might come to think of their cause without such strong aversion.'

His own pale cheeks reddened and he waited a second for his anger to abate, then he said to her, 'And did the married state never appeal to you, Miss Carmedy?'

Carmedy, on her other side, leaned forward and laughed.

231

'You don't think I would have allowed that, do you, Maichin? My help-meet, my best friend, my dear sister deserting me? On no. I fought off all contenders.'

'There were two sound offers,' said Miss Carmedy drily. 'They were both plug ugly and bullies to boot. Even the company of my irritating, untidy, forgetful brother was preferable to that of such Neanderthals.'

'Oh Miss Carmedy!' Edward allowed his face to look stricken. He cursed the wine which must have made him drop his guard and attack his best ally. Or perhaps it was the sight of his sister in her silly over-decorated hat talking on the top table to the Berrimans, as though she were one of them. Or perhaps it was the fact that he was stuck here between some riveter from Berriman's foundry and Miss Carmedy. He would have liked to be over there on Carmedy's right next to the Liberal MP and Elias Glinton. 'Oh dear, Miss Carmedy,' he repeated, flashing his charming smile and looking apologetic. 'I have been too carried away. What I must say is if all these women were as—'

She put up her small, finely shaped hand. 'Spare me, Edward! Spare me the eulogy. All I ask is for you to listen to their arguments for equity and justice, and not leap instantly into condemnation.'

'I will, Miss Carmedy. I will,' he said meekly.

'Now, Edward. Tell me about this sister who has just joined us. She must be the one who writes those excellent stories in the *Chronicle*. Did I tell you I use them with my class?'

After the meal we are ushered to another large room and set around small tables on spindly chairs. The string quartet is playing and there is a piano, large as a small carriage, on a large dais. The line of ivory keys sets off the glossy black casing. I have never seen such a wonderful thing close to.

Someone has been fixing things behind the scenes because

I am ushered to a table to sit with my father and Edward. Rhys joins us for a few minutes before going to the table where he is to sit, in isolated splendour, with his new bride. (They lean towards each other and laugh; they look happy at this moment.) But first he shakes hands with my father and a thunderous Edward, and then grasps me in a hearty hug and treats me to a smacking kiss on the cheek.

'Well then, here we are!' he says cheerfully. 'What a pity Mam cannot be here.'

'Did she write to you about the baby?' I ask, knowing very well that she did.

He nods. 'Very Christian of her, I would say, taking on someone else's child.'

My father sits up straighter. I notice the collar of the pawnshop shirt is digging into his neck. 'Baby? What's this about a baby?' he says, very tense, looking at me.

Rhys laughs, and it is not a nice laugh. 'Don't worry, Dada. It is some other poor woman's baby. A woman that died.' He smiles knowingly at me as he says this.

My father sits back and relaxes into his velvet-covered chair. In that moment I realise that no one around the table, not one of his children, has the least bit of respect for our father. The sentimental thing to say would be that, despite this, we all love him. To be honest I don't think even this is so. As a child my father had a touch of magic: he was the traveller who went to the lands beyond the jagged window. The adventurer. The storyteller. But now all of this is gone. The edge of his charm is patent, as over-used as a London umbrella. His stories are half true, half fake, half remembered, half contrived. He himself cannot remember which half is true. The only true thing about him is his love for Rose Clare, and this we only witnessed when he was there, when they were together. It was as though the two of them were up on a cloud and we had to strain to see them. And even that love for her did not stop him from betraying her and leaving her bereft. What respect or even love could be left from all this?

'So how did you get in with such a . . . such a fine family,' says my father, looking fondly at Rhys. 'These are prominent people, if I'm not mistaken.'

Rhys shrugs. 'I work in the shop which her father owns. We met there and we got on.'

'So you left the pit?'

Rhys glances at Edward, who is staring at his cup of tea as though his stare will freeze it to a jelly. 'I left the pit. No future at the pit. Working for a master. Better be your own master, look you—'

'If,' interrupts Edward, 'you can chase the master's daughter and marry her.'

But Rhys will not be riled. He smiles very directly at Edward. 'If that, as you say, brother.'

'And what of you, Edward?' asks my father. 'The pit suiting you, is it?' .

'The pit's fine,' said Edward. 'At least that's men's work, away from women's skirts. I'll be promoted to overman before the year's out. They say that I'll be the youngest in the country.' His modest tone belies his words.

'Excellent,' says my father blandly. 'And no doubt you are the leading light at the chapel.'

Edward shrugs. 'I preach in two different chapels on a Sunday. I have requests for up to thirty miles away.'

'Well done, son. And in the pit it's manager you will be, in time.'

Rhys coughs and pulls down the cuffs of his brand-new linen shirt to even their line. 'What our Edward is too modest to say, Da, is that not only is he a leading light in the dark chambers of the pit, he's a bit of a glimmer in the Liberal Party too. Running for the local council, is it, Edward? He'll be chairman of that in five years.'

234

'Well, my boys . . .'

'Of course,' says Rhys smoothly, 'that comes easy if you chase the skirts of Anthony Carmedy and his sister, whose oldest friend is Elias Glinton, a power with the Liberals hereabouts.'

Edward leaps to his feet, the chair scraping back, his hands rolled into fists. 'I'll show you, Rhys, I'll show . . .' Heads turn in our direction. I grab Edward's arm and force him to sit down again. I look at Rhys. 'Isn't that Ruthie waving at you, Rhys? You shouldn't desert your wife on her wedding day, now should you?'

We watch Rhys weaving his way through the maze of little tables, shaking hands with first one of them then the other. I am struck again that this is a very mixed company. The Berrimans are certainly not snobs. I smile at the thought. They can't be snobs or we wouldn't be sitting here ourselves and Rhys wouldn't now be taking his seat in the place of honour beside his bride, daughter of Councillor Gerald Berriman, leading citizen of Priorton.

'So what is that secret smile for, Theo?' says my father, watching me keenly.

'I was just thinking that you hadn't asked me about my success in this town, Dada. You've a daughter, you know.'

He frowned. 'Your success?'

'I've had several stories published in the local paper. They're taking every one I write.'

'Only children's stories,' shoots Edward. 'Theo's usual rubbish. Can't think what the editor's thinking of. Space to fill, I suppose!'

At this I turn my chair so I am sitting with my back to him and concentrate on the concert, which is now beginning on the dais. A large lady with a deep bosom and a silk-embroidered scarf around her head announces that she will sing three German songs of love. I am amazed by this, that

235

she should sing songs in a language I cannot understand. However, as the trilling notes emerge from her trembling mouth I am moved to tears and decide that the voice is like that of the birds. It is sent straight to the heart without the intervention of language. Next the violinist plays a solo accompanied by the pianist, then it is the turn of a flautist.

Each performance is greeted by a storm of applause. I feel I could listen to it all night, but catch sight of the longcase clock in the corner and realise that we are about to miss our train back to Stanhope. I whisper in my father's ear, and he whispers back that he will say goodbye to the happy couple. I hiss that he can't, as he will spoil the concert, and I drag him out of the room without a backward glance at Edward.

It is pitch black when we arrive in Stanhope station but the faithful Stephen is there with his chariot. Stephen is overwhelmed with pleasure at meeting my father and shakes his hand for so long that my father has to use his other hand to release it. The chariot rocks and slides but gets us to Goshawk Shield in good time.

Stephen marches into the house, shouting that Theo's father is here, Theo's father is here! The dog barks. The baby cries. Seal is the first to reach us, skittering across the tiles on the hall floor and leaping up into my arms like a gazelle. Then my mother follows her down the stairs, the swaddled baby crying in her arms. She peers into the pools of lamplight which barely illuminate the hall. 'Father? What are you saying, Stephen?' Then she catches sight of my father, and stands stock still on the turn of the stair. 'Ellis. It can't be . . . How can it be you?'

He runs up the stairs to her and they are one, he in his black pawnbroker's suit, she in her voluminous nightgown, the baby between them. I put the disappointed Seal down on the hall floor, and move swiftly up the staircase and rescue the baby. My mother and father hardly notice this, clinging together as though for dear life.

By the time Mrs Gervase, in her mannish silk dressing gown and nightcap, has joined us, the baby has stopped whimpering and opened her eyes, which are round and wise, like those of Seal who is scratching away at my feet, annoyed at her displacement. A vital charge rushes through my body. It is as though I am seeing the baby for the first time.

'Well now?' says Mrs Gervase. For a second it is hard to tell whether she is annoyed or just curious. Her tone is distinctly blank.

'I am sorry, Mrs Gervase. My father, he came to the wedding, and I thought I should . . .'

She sways a little and replants her stick to improve her balance. 'Well then. That is quite right. Your mother seems pleased to see him. So it is quite right.'

The scene being played out halfway up the stairs is proof of that. Feeling our attention at last the pair come down the stairs and my mother introduces my father to Mrs Gervase. The old woman smiles graciously. 'You are welcome, Mr Maichin. Now then, perhaps for tonight you could sleep in the spare bed in my son's room? Tomorrow we will do some juggling around to make you more comfortable. Welcome! Now, if you will excuse me . . .' She has such dignity. Such composure.

Holding the baby on one shoulder I walk along the corridor with her. 'This is very kind of you, Mrs Gervase.'

She shakes her head slightly. 'Nothing, my dear. Nothing at all. Perhaps if you could put some coals on the bedroom fire? It is suddenly rather chilly in there.'

She half rolls, half jumps into her high bed, and I place the baby beside her while I tend to the fire. When I get back to her she is tickling the baby's face and watching the neat mouth. 'This is a very nice baby,' she says.

'My mother says she is perfect. Perfect in every way.'

237

'What is she called?'

I shake my head. 'I don't know. She has no name. We just call her Baby.'

'She has to have a name, Theo. It is indecent to have no name.'

'Yes. I suppose she should have a name.'

'We will have to register her. The Gomersalls appear to have wiped the slate clean as far as Mavis is concerned. They've never been near since Sadie dropped the baby like a parcel.'

'So what shall we call her?' I look down at the baby. What a responsibility it is to give a person a name. A person has her name all her life. Her name is who she is. How could Rhys be Rhys if he were not called that name? How could Rose Clare be Rose Clare?

Mrs Gervase is stroking the little, perfect hand. 'When I was expecting Stephen I was sure he was a girl, you know.' Her voice is strong, young for a second. 'I chose Susan for his name. Do you think that we could call her Susan? This baby?'

'That's a very nice name. Not usual.'

'Shall we call her Susan Cornford?'

'Cornford? Where on earth does that come from?'

'My name when I was a girl. My father's name.'

'Won't she have to be called Gomersall?'

'Yes. Yes.' The point irritates her. 'Susan Cornford Gomersall. That's it. But she will be known as Susan Cornford. What do you think?'

'It is a very nice name.'

So Susan Cornford Gomersall has now become part of this strange household at Goshawk Shield. My father too has settled in, but for how long, the gods alone can tell. I am struck now with the difficult thought that, unlike the baby, my father brings with him a tension, a sense of danger. And in that, although the gentlest and weakest of people, he is like my brother Edward.

Eighteen

A Small Mouthful of Pure Happiness

In the end it is Stephen and I who go down to Stanhope to register the baby. We call at the Gomersalls' to tell them what we are about. The old man with his dreary side whiskers and round face is sitting in the kitchen with his hat and gaiters still on. Mrs Gomersall, gaunt and stony-faced, is at the table, up to her elbows in bread dough. Sadie and her sister Poll came in from the yard smelling of the byre, wearing their clogs.

We are met by a wall of disinterest. They ignore the baby. 'Do what you will,' growls Mr Gomersall. 'Gie the lass the death certificate,' he says to his wife, who wipes her floury hands on her bleached sacking apron, scampers to an overstuffed bureau in the corner and extracts a newish envelope from the pile of greasy paper.

They do not even ask how we will name the child.

On the way back across the muddy farmyard it occurs to me that the powers that be will not let Stephen and me register the baby. Surely you need a member of the family to register her? I trek back to the farm kitchen and they look up, unsmiling, as I enter the open doorway.

'I think I will need one of you with me. To register her.'

They look blankly at me.

'I don't think they will let me register her. I think it must be family.'

'It's nowt to us, that bairn,' the father grunted. The women glance at him, all feeling scoured from their eyes.

I look at him, then at the strained faces of the women. 'Would you rather the child had died with the mother? Do you wish her in purgatory? To burn in the flames? To writhe in torment?' My grandfather would have been proud of me.

'Jess . . .' Mavis's mother risks a hard stare at her husband. 'It's only decent. The child . . .'

The old man grunts, then nods at Sadie, standing by the hearth where she has been stirring something in the pot. 'Get thee coat on, lass. Thoo can gan wit' 'er. And tek our Mavis's paper from the doctor. Sure to ask for that.'

Sadie is silent for the first mile or two in the chariot. Then she puts a hand across and lifts the veil from the baby's face. 'She is a fine li'l lass,' she says.

'Yes,' I say enthusiastically. 'And smiles! She smiles all the time.'

'Not like her mam then.' Sadie drops the veil. 'Poor li'l thing.'

'She's fine,' I say defensively. 'Well looked after. My mother, all of us. We look after her.'

'Let's hope so,' she says glumly. 'Poor Mavis. Poor innocent lass.'

And I leave it at that, not wanting to know what else she may say. Her attitude has certainly changed.

It turns out that we do need Sadie there as the next of kin, and she is pleased to be so important. The man writes *Mavis Gomersall, deceased* and *Father unknown* in the appropriate columns. The town of Stanhope feels bustling and full of itself after the stillness of the moor. The castle is planted foursquare in the centre of the village, curiously domestic with trees clustered at its skirts like children. We stand there, me clutching the certificate, Stephen clutching the baby, Sadie hunched and wide-eyed on the busy pavement. Then suddenly she bursts out, 'The bairn needs a blessing. She needs a baptism. She needs excluding from the devil and all his works.'

A strong phrase.

'Baptism? There must be a chapel here.'

Suddenly Sadie is all energy. 'There's a church. We go to church, not chapel. A rector.' She is pulling me along the narrow pavements. 'We have a rector. And a curate.'

We disturb the curate at his meal. There are stains on the napkin tucked under his chin. He is annoyed, but recognises Sadie. This is the man who, only weeks ago, buried Mavis. He strides back into his square hall, scolding Sadie for not bringing the baby earlier, for abandoning her to sin. He has, he says, expected one of them long before this. He vanished, then returns without his napkin, but dressed in his long coat and cloak, round hat in hand. 'Now then!' he says. 'We must go to the church!'

Which is how Stephen and I, with Sadie, become Susan Cornford Gomersall's godparents, renounce the devil and all his works on Susan's behalf, and welcome her into God's family. There are candles on the altar. I can see the scandalised hurt in my Granda Maichin's eyes at what he would see as a papist place.

After the ceremony the curate becomes affable and insists we return to the vicarage where he gets his housekeeper to bring us sherry in the hall, so we can drink the baby's health. He does keep us standing. I look longingly at a heavily carved chair. I would love to sit down. Susan Cornford Gomersall is getting heavier by the second.

I choke a little on the sherry, wondering what my Granda Maichin would think of me taking alcohol with a man of the cloth. It would certainly confirm his dismissive contempt for the degeneracy of the Church of England ministry.

We drop Sadie back at the farm. She stands there in the mud, holding the door of the chariot. 'If ah ken get away, is it all right if ah cum up t'see the bairn?'

'Yes, yes,' I say eagerly. 'Please come.'

Stephen grins at her. 'Come and very welcome,' he says.

Ellis had settled in very well at Goshawk Shield. Theo moved out of Rose Clare's bedroom, to another bedroom, taking the baby and the dog with her. So Ellis and Rose Clare had their own room. They went to bed early just to be alone. They did not make love because Ellis loved Rose Clare too much to risk a pregnancy. But they clung together, each acknowledging the unspoken truth that this time together, like all the others, was temporary.

Ellis proved to be a cheery member of the household, whistling as he helped about the place, cleaning windows which had been untouched since Mavis had gone, cleaning out stables so that Stephen could concentrate more on the workshop. Theo encouraged him to scythe the grass in the neglected garden, creating a way down to the pool below the waterfall. He and Theo pored over the old garden designs of the French woman gardener, finding new treasures to excavate.

Some days Ellis saddled up Samson and went down to Stanhope for the newspapers and paraffin and other essential supplies. He even saddled up Samson and went down to Stanhope when there were no supplies to get. He returned with little gifts and gewgaws for them all except Mrs Gervase of whom he was very uncertain. She met his charming sallies with an absent abstraction which made him wary.

Stephen became more clumsy, more unsure of himself with another man in the house. When Ellis came into a room or outside into the yard where he was working, Stephen would gradually escape and go down the garden with his clippers and his scythe, anxious to be on his own away from this bubbling, fizzing little man.

I don't know what is the matter with Stephen. He had been coming on so well with his reading, but that all seems to have come to a stop now. In fact he's not as good as he was a month ago. He worries about this, that I will call him stupid. But I don't.

I try out all my children's stories on him and he always gives them his seal of approval, and delights when it appears in print. I am secretly sketching out a much larger story, based on the lady gardener coming to this dark northern realm. I show this to no one.

We've finished with Captain Ahab now. I have not read it all to them. After I finished reading it to myself I wrote a series of short summaries, which I read to them to get on to the exciting bits. I was sorry to leave behind this great battle between a flawed man and the savage spirit of the sea.

We have proceeded to *King Solomon's Mines*, an amazing adventure, full of mystery and intrigue. Stephen loved this one and asked me about the story at other times in the day, as though he were slowly digesting it like well-relished food.

I then move to the tales by Mrs Linton: Eliza Lynn Linton, stories of powerful emotion. Mrs Linton writes very fully but seems to understand the lives of ordinary people. This gives me hope that one day I may write such stories. All the time now, matters of ordinary life are going into my brain as text, as sentences on a page. They will wait there until I am ready.

Mr Murton at the newspaper wants more children's stories, and I have letters from people across the region who take pleasure in the stories that appear in the paper. I have a letter from Mr Murton himself who mentions that he has a friend in Edinburgh who would publish the stories as a collection. It is not yet clear whether I would be paid for this or would have to pay for it myself.

My father, when he can take his eyes from my mother, listens to me read the stories and comments on my fine accent. He is interested in the publishing enterprise, and one day, having ridden out early with Samson, returns with four magazines in his knapsack. He throws the magazines on the kitchen table. 'Another place for your stories. I read some in the Gaunt Valley Hotel. If you couldn't do better than that I'd eat my hat.'

'You were in Priorton?' says my mother sharply. She is sitting in the rocking chair, soothing Susan to sleep.

'Yes. I was just taken with the fancy,' he says easily. 'Stabled old Samson in Stanhope and went down in the train.'

'It's too dull for you here, Ellis. Sure, isn't that the truth?'

'No, indeed it isn't, dear woman.' He smiles at her with devotion.

I read some of the magazine stories to Mrs Gervase and we decide that they're very good but similar to each other. Courage. Beauty. Daring. Danger. Resolutions. These are served up every time. (My lady gardener story has all these things.)

Mrs Gervase claps her hands as I list these things. 'There you have it, my dear. You see what they do! You shall write one and read it to us and we will send it to one of these magazines and they will publish it, and you will be famous!'

'Famous!' says Stephen, clapping his podgy hands.

'No. No.' My cheeks are hot. Seal jumps on to my knee and nearly displaces the magazine. It takes me all my strength not to tell them about my big story, the one about the French lady gardener. I have been reading about the French Revolution and have decided that she comes here as a refugee from the Terror.

'Yes. Yes,' says Stephen. 'Special stories.'

I go off and spend all my spare time in the week writing, thankful that my father is here to help my mother. My only chore is to have Susan in her cradle in the dining room as I work. She gurgles and chuckles and watches Seal as the dog stalks around the room on her regular inspections.

My magazine story is, I suppose, a mixture of the legend of Aphrodite and George du Maurier's novel *Trilby*. A girl grows up on a farm with a beautiful voice which goes unrecognised by her uncaring family. One day in spring, a musician, who is walking the country for a rest cure, calls at the farm for a drink of milk and hears her singing in the dairy. He is entranced by the voice and is convinced he can make a famous singer of her. So he takes her to the city to great teachers and she becomes famous. But in winter in a dark region of the city she is waylaid and left for dead by an attacker. She recovers, but she starts to pine for the green safety of her county and her lark-like voice reduces to a frog's croak. Her lover abandons his city fame and returns to the country with her. Here they live simply, he giving music lessons, she back in the dairy singing again like a lark.

Mrs Gervase and Stephen love the story. My father likes it, suggesting one or two changes. Fewer words here, a brighter image there. 'Now let them see it, *cariad*. Copy it in your very best hand and send it off. See, there's an address at the beginning of this magazine. Write a letter and tell them about the stories in the Priorton newspaper, and that these will be published in a collected edition of children's stories. Just to show you are not a beginner.'

'Should I?' I look at my mother.

She shrugs. 'Your father knows about these things,' she says. 'Where d'you think you get it from, this way of making words work for you?'

'And I think,' says my father, 'you should go down and

see that Murton fellow and say you're interested in the children's collection. But at their expense. They'll easily make money from it. Talent you have, isn't it?'

So I copy out the magazine story twice and decide to go down to Priorton to post it. And combine that with a visit to Mr Murton at the newspaper. And I could call to see Rhys. Not Edward of course. No point in that. No point at all.

Rhys wore his preacher suit every day now for his work at Berriman's. He was finished with brown overalls, even though he still made the deliveries right up the Gaunt Valley, calling at shops and farms as per his order book. Three mornings a week he sat beside old Mrs Berriman and helped her with her account books and learned the way the shop part of the business was run.

Ruth was amused at this. 'Granma's books are her Bible. She never lets anyone see them. You should be honoured.' Ruth called in at the shop when she knew Rhys would be there and talked with Rhys and her grandmother, even her father when he was around.

To everyone's surprise Ruth was 'settling down'. Despite her suffragist leanings she found she was relishing the role of mistress of the little house her father had bought them. For her it was another game. She had enticed young Beattie to come with her as maid so she did not need to soil her hands in this new game. Each night she had Beattie lay the table very beautifully for when Rhys came home. Rhys, ever the quick learner, soon mastered the plethora of forks and how to loop the napkin to his second button.

Ruth was on better terms with her mother now that she had a separate household of her own and did not have to play the child. Her days were filled with making the little house more fetching and filling it with the latest gadgets. Their evenings were full of the varied amusements which Priorton could provide. There were two theatres, one which provided serious drama, the other with the rather jollier flavour of the music hall, sometimes even circus presentations. Then there were the musical occasions: quartets, trios, chamber orchestras, *Lieder* singers. They could have gone to something every night had they chosen to do so.

Now and then Rhys would throw up his hands and tell her he had married her, but seemed to have married a whole town and could he have her to himself for a single night please? Her appetite and his willingness ensured that they made love most nights and he arrived many mornings at work with shadows under his eyes. These brought ribald whispered comments from his former workmates, who had a healthy disrespect for his new station.

Edward cropped up in their lives quite frequently as they made their social rounds. A councillor now, he was invited to most town functions, and often attended, at the elbow of Elias Glinton or Anthony Carmedy. He did not make a beeline for the newlyweds unless Ruth's father was with them. At such times he made their presence an excuse to get into conversation with Mr Berriman, to talk over Liberal and town affairs. Sometimes he was with Claris Carmedy, as he was one night they attended a chamber concert at which both Ruth's father and Anthony Carmedy were playing the oboe.

'Do you think those two are attached?' said Ruth one night at the intermission, clutching Rhys and nodding to a corner where Edward and Claris were deep in conversation.

'Attached? Well, she's . . .'

'Plain? But she's clever, and a very nice person.'

'She's years older than him.'

Ruth smacked him, hard, on the arm. 'As I am than you. Six years, remember.'

He caught her hand and kissed it. 'Sure you'll be young and daft when I'm old and grey.'

She wrested her hand away. 'But what do you really think? Are they attached?'

'I'd not thought about it.'

'It's not really suitable, is it?'

'Why so?' Although not liking Edward himself, he was stung to his defence. 'He's the handsomest man in this room. And he's a caring man. Councillor. Aiming for manager at the pit. A good catch for anybody, I'd say.'

Ruth shook her head. 'I wouldn't trust him as far as I could throw him. A cold fish. Cruel, I wouldn't wonder.'

He laughed contentedly. 'Well, the fish that you landed is your willing slave, but no genius. And is not so much a cold fish as . . .'

'As a snuggly squirmy one.' She brought her lips close to his ear. 'Can we get away from here, dearest boy? Time we were tucked up in our nice inviting bed.'

'Not to sleep, I hope?' he murmured.

'Never,' she said fervently. 'Let's miss the second half.'

Edward nodded to them curtly as they left, arm in arm.

'They make a very loving couple,' said Claris Carmedy thoughtfully. 'An unexpected pairing which works admirably. Ruth Berriman seems to have settled down very well.'

'I suppose she keeps him out of mischief,' said Edward sulkily.

Claris picked up his tone. 'What about you, Edward? Would you not like to meet someone? Surely there is a nice young woman who—'

'No,' he said curtly. 'There is more to do than dally about in that fashion. It's . . . well, it's embarrassing.'

'Oh Edward, have some charity. Everyone goes through that stage.'

'You didn't,' he said.

She smiled gently. 'No I didn't. But I have Anthony, don't I?'

'It's not the same in one particular.' The crudity slipped from him, unleashed by Rhys's insolent demeanour.

Her cheeks stained an unflattering purple. 'Edward, I don't think . . .'

He recovered, and put a gentle hand on hers. 'Forgive me, Claris. Perhaps I envy Anthony his good luck. A loving sister is so much more desirable than a demanding wife. I was never blessed in such a fashion.'

'But you have a sister, surely!'

'Sister?' He laughed shortly. 'She was never a blessing. More a changeling.'

'Well,' she said. 'I can be your sister. We are together so much these days perhaps I should adopt you as my brother.' The crudity was forgotten.

'Perhaps I should marry you. Then it will all be in order.' It was a statement, not a tease.

She laughed. 'Now, you don't think Anthony would permit that, do you?'

'It would be nothing to do with Anthony, if we decided,' he said grimly. 'What if I asked you?'

She stopped laughing. 'Edward, it is unthinkable. I am fifteen years older than you. And so plain that it would be remarked on. It is remarked on already.' She paused. 'Anyway. I am content, as I have been for years, to be Anthony's friend and help-meet as well as his sister.'

He made himself relax and smiled at her. 'Well then, my dear Claris, I'll have to content myself to be your adopted brother.'

'Good,' she said, beaming.

'And you won't tell Anthony I made this ridiculous suggestion? It's our secret?'

'Never!'

'Now then, hadn't we better go in and listen to him playing his blessed oboe?'

Later Edward turned down the offer of a lift home, said he needed some exercise so he would walk. He walked home by way of a dark district of Priorton called Little London and availed himself of the services of a discreet young woman with whom he had become acquainted. She, for an extra sixpence, didn't mind how rough you were with her.

The Murtons, father and son, make me more welcome in their office these days. A seat is drawn up for me. I am offered coffee. The children's stories are very popular, so popular that I am running out of myths to adapt. But they get many letters of approval and insist that I dig out more stories. I can invent myths if I like, says old Murton.

'What about English stories,' I suggest. Mrs Gervase has a lot of English history books on her shelves. 'King Arthur, perhaps? The Knights of the Round Table. Robin Hood?'

Rupert Murton rubs his hands. 'The very thing, Miss Maichin,' he says heartily.

We agree on ten children's stories from English history.

'Learning by the back door, Miss Carmedy calls it,' says Murton senior, slurping his coffee. 'She thinks it is very good for the children. They are making a scrapbook of them.' He paused. 'Now then, Miss Maichin, about the proposed collection. I am in correspondence with my Edinburgh friend about this. He says, for a contribution of fifty pounds, he can make you a fine edition.'

I shake my head. 'Out of the question, Mr Murton. I have no money.'

'Perhaps twenty pounds?'

Again I shake my head. 'You heard what I said. I have no money. None at all.'

'It does not appear so,' he says sulkily. 'You are the picture of affluence, Miss Maichin, if I may say so.'

I smile as sweetly as I can. 'Mr Murton,' I say. 'There is

no point in the world in being poor and looking poor, is there?'

'Bravo!' Murton junior claps his hands.

'Well then.' Rupert Murton picks his pipe from the desk and starts to puff on it. 'What say we ourselves make the contribution of fifty pounds and advertise and sell it from the *Chronicle*?'

'And retrieve your fifty pounds?'

'Yes. Well . . .'

'What will I get out of it?'

'Well . . .' He puffs on his pipe and then takes it out of his mouth and looks at it as though it is an alien thing. 'Well then. After we have our fifty pounds we will share the proceeds.'

'Half and half?'

He sighs. 'Half and half.'

Pleased with the outcome of this meeting, I make my way down the street to Berriman's Ironmongery. I don't know where Rhys lives. I don't know whether he'll be in there at this time of day. But suddenly I have the desire to see him. To know how he is. I wouldn't have said I was fond of him before but now I have an urgent need to claim kinship. I don't quite know why.

In the shop Rhys introduces me again to the old woman, his grandmother-in-law. Her hand clasps mine in a grip as strong as a man's and she says she is pleased to meet me. 'I spoke with you at the wedding, but you ran away before we could get acquainted. You wore a . . . er . . . charming hat.'

I have to smile at this. 'It was a bit overdone, I suppose. We thought it very fine before we set out!'

'Our mama is keen on loading on a little bit extra as far as decoration goes,' put in Rhys. 'Always did.'

'There you have it,' I say.

'Sure, I must say I thought it was very jolly,' said Mrs Berriman. 'Now, Rhys, get off that stool and take your sister to see your wife. She'll not have much time, coming down from the hills.'

At the house Ruth is up a ladder in the dining room, putting up a set of curtains. She looks prettier than she did at her wedding. She shakes my hand heartily and turns to Rhys and gives him an embarrassingly close embrace. 'Your sister is lovely. I thought so at the wedding and I think so now.'

'I hope you don't mention the hat,' I say gloomily.

'The hat was—'

'Don't mention it!'

We all laugh at this and they show me round the house, every nook and cranny, pride oozing from them. I have the unusual desire to cry in the presence of their delight. Rhys is happy and I suppose I must be happy for him.

He asks about our father. 'Settling in, is he, up there?'

'Seems to be, but . . .' I glance at Ruth.

'But we both know him, don't we? There's no telling . . .'

Ruth, looking from one of us to the other, says, 'Well, he seems very charming to me. Good company.'

I turn to Rhys. 'Dada's been here?'

He nods. 'A few times.' He stares me hard in the eyes and I don't ask the question which is on the tip of my tongue. Our father has been here and has borrowed money from Rhys. I know it.

The little maid brings us tea and I am treated to tales of life in Priorton and the vagaries of Ruthie's mother, Mrs Berriman junior, who sounds like a bit of a harridan. They make me laugh and their happiness is a tonic. The splendid mantel clock strikes four and I gather my gloves and bag. 'I must go. I'll miss my train.' They protest but in some ways it is a release at last to get away from their energy, their oneness. Pure happiness can only be digested in small mouthfuls.

Nineteen

A Scandalous Proposal

'She never asked about Edward,' said Ruth, shutting the door behind Theo. 'Isn't that strange?'

Rhys shook his head. 'No. Those two hated each other, look you. Couldn't bear the sight. Even when we were small. She was too quiet, too bright, too defiant for him and he was always playing tricks on her.' He paused. 'And not very nice ones too. Tried to get her to rise, like a fisherman playing a hook, see?'

Ruthie shuddered. 'Ugh. Someone just stepped on my grave there.'

He laughed. 'Well our Edward's alive and very much kicking.' He pulled her into the parlour and sat beside her on their new plush sofa. 'Seeing as we are on about my weird family I want to tell you something. Things have happened so fast this has slipped further and further to the back of my mind.'

She nestled close to him. 'What is it? You're all descendants of the ancient kings of Ireland? Or is Mr Gladstone your uncle twice removed?'

He laughed, and kissed her hair where it dropped on to her cheek. 'No. No. Just that there is another one of us. My brother Caspar.'

She sat away from him. 'Is he dead? Is he mad?'

He laughed and pulled her back to his side. 'Not at all. He's working, in Northumberland somewhere we believe. We don't know where. He promised letters but none there came.'

'Well, it's very strange—' She was interrupted by the long peal of the doorbell.

It was Edward, a dark outline for a second against the late afternoon sun. Rhys opened the door more widely. 'Edward! Speak of the devil! We were just talking of you!' He led Edward into the parlour. 'Ruthie, look who's here! Weren't we just talking about him?'

She held out her hand towards him and he shook it warmly. 'Good to see you, Ruth.' He glanced around the glittering clutter of the room. 'I thought perhaps it was time I called on you.'

She patted the couch beside her. 'You are welcome, Edward. You have just missed your sister.'

His face darkened. 'Theo! I thought she was up in the hills.'

'Seems she gets down here now and then,' murmured Rhys.

'She had to go to the newspaper office,' said Ruth. 'Have you read those little stories of hers? Charming!'

Edward shook his head. 'To be honest, Ruth, I've more important things to do with my time than read children's stories.' Then he shrugged, as though throwing something off his shoulders. 'Well then, what about you two?' He smiled at Ruth. 'You are a very lucky man, Rhys.'

Ruth laughed out loud. 'If I didn't know you were a man of the highest principles, Edward, I'd say you were after something. Wouldn't you, Rhys?'

Rhys looked at the two of them on the couch. They were easy and comfortable. He wondered just what Edward was up to. 'You're lucky to have caught me, Edward. I only came home because Theo called at the shop.' His tone was abrupt.

Edward continued to smile at Ruth without looking at Rhys.

'Yes,' he said. 'Lucky, that, wasn't it? I was on early shift so I walked here after work.'

Ruth leaned over to pull the bell by the fireplace. 'We must get you some tea, Edward. It's a long walk all the way up here from Gibsley.'

When I get back to Goshawk Shield all chaos has been let loose. There is no word about this from Stephen who says nothing while he drives me up there in the chariot. I hardly notice his unusual silence: my mind is full of Rhys and the wonderful change in his fortunes. And my own equal fortune, living here with such benevolent people, writing my stories, my mother and father by my side.

My mother is sitting in the kitchen with her apron over her head. I rush to baby Susan's crib, but she sleeps sound, her full lips have a bubble clinging still to the corner. Seal is winding her way round my feet wagging her tail.

I shake my mother's shoulder. 'What is it?' I pull at the apron to find her staring up at me wide-eyed. 'What is it?'

'He's gone.'

'Who's gone?' Why do I need to ask?

'Ellis. Walked off with his pack. Down the hill away. I saw him at the far gate. I ran after him but he was gone.'

I grip her shoulder tightly. 'Oh Mam. How can he do this? He is so bad.'

She stands up. 'There's worse.' She leads through to the dining room and opens the cutlery drawer. 'Six silver knives and forks. A wine server. Three silver snuff boxes. All gone. He has taken them.'

'Did you know this at once? Did he leave a note?'

She shakes her head. 'No note. But his clothes are gone. All that marks his presence here. When I saw that I went straight to the silver drawer. I don't know why. But then I do know why.' She sits down hard again, throws her apron back over her head and rocks back and forth.

In her crib Susan starts tó wail and thresh her arms and legs about. I pull her up, hold her against me and she is quiet. My mind is racing with the enormity of just what my father has done. Stealing is no new thing to him, we all know this though no one ever mentions it. But by this act of stealing he has not only disgraced himself, he has made sure my mother and I must go from this place we have made home. He has destroyed us as well as himself.

I wrench the apron from my mother's head again. 'Stop wailing, will you?' I say crossly. 'Have you told Mrs Gervase?'

She sits up, startled. 'No. No,' she says. 'No. I was waiting for you! Stephen knows. At least he knows Ellis has gone. He knows something is very wrong. I don't know that he understand about the other. The silver.'

'Here. Take care of Susan.' I thrust the baby into her arms. 'And pull yourself together. It's your fault, you know. You shouldn't have let him stay. You know what he's like.'

'But I love him,' Rose Clare whispered. 'And he—'

'Doesn't love you enough not to spoil your life for you. Or mine, either.'

Mrs Gervase beams as I come into the pheasant room, saying how much she has missed the reading today. 'So amusing, Mr Kipling's tales of India. I've been looking forward to it all afternoon. I—'

I stop her mid-sentence and tell her my tale of woe. I do not embellish it. The smile leaves her face. A silence grows up between us like a sharp thorn. Then she says, almost too gently, 'If you just leave me now, my dear. I have to think about this.'

'Mrs Gervase, I will pay. All my savings . . .' I blurt the words out. 'But the value must be so much. I'd not have that in a year. Two.'

'Just leave me, dear.' She closes her eyes.

Dismissed, I stumble out of the room, crashing into Stephen, who is standing in the doorway. 'Theo?' he says, tears in his eyes.

I push him to one side. 'Oh Stephen! It's all too bad. Too bad.'

Whole, painful days have passed and nothing has been said. Mrs Gervase has been charming but distant and I've not had the courage to offer to read for her. Meals have been silent and we have all become very interested in baby Susan. She is the only neutral territory now between us. I start to sort out my clothes and other things in my room ready to pack. I wonder what will happen to Susan now. She must come with us, but that will compound our difficulty.

Mrs Gervase has kept Stephen at her side. He casts agonised looks in my direction and I smile and shake my head. I am as fond of Stephen now as I am of my dog Seal. And that is certainly fonder than I am of any of my brothers. Or my mother and father for that matter. But my mother, my embarrassment, and Mrs Gervase's distance is creating a chasm in the house. Soon none of us will be able to leap it.

Stephen shambles into the kitchen as my mother is preparing our midday meal. The watery sun is shining through the narrow window on to the plain table in the breakfast room. The cutlery is neatly arranged and the roses glow in their jug at the table centre; Seal is holding court from the chair by the fire.

Stephen turns his troubled face to me. 'My mother says she will take her dinner in the pheasant room if you would be so kind.'

Humbly I prepare the tray. At the last minute my mother, with Seal winding her way round her legs, plucks a rose from the crock and puts it in a little glass on the tray. I raise my glance from Seal to my mother. The glance she exchanges with me is one of apology and appeal and it comes to me like a thunderbolt that my loyalty should be to her, not to Mrs Gervase. That she is more injured by this than either the old woman or me. For a second I dissolve to the seventeen-year-old. The daughter. It is a while since I felt so young.

'The tray looks lovely, my dear.' There is neither strain nor blame in Mrs Gervase's voice. As I place the tray carefully on the low table beside her, she banishes the awkward mistress-and-maid performance by patting the sofa beside her. 'Sit here, Theo. Sit by me. We have to talk.'

I sit beside her and, avoiding her glance, I pour her tea. She takes the cup from me and looks me full in the eyes. 'You look as though you have the woes of the world on your shoulders.'

I mumble. 'Me? I couldn't be in a worse situation. You know that.'

She shakes her head. 'It is difficult for you. In some ways it is not your affair at all.'

'We're going away,' I burst out. 'We have to go. We can't stay, my mother and I. We'll take little Susan. My mother—'

'I am not sending you away. I will not do that.'

'I know that. It makes it worse.'

She takes a sip of the tea, ignoring the hearty dumpling stew on her plate. 'There are one or two things I want to do, Theo.'

'What can you do? What can anyone do? He's my own father and he deserves to be put in prison. But I don't want him there.'

'No. They're terrible places, my dear, prisons! I visited one once. On a mission with my father. A living purgatory. Made one ashamed to be part of this condemning world.'

'How could my father do this? How could he do it to us?'

'In that matter I am in agreement with you, my dear. Not

the silver. I have no attachment to those things. But I must admit I find it hard to think how he can do such a thing to you, to your mother, even while it seems that he has great affection for you.' She pauses. 'Perhaps it is a compulsion, like that towards drink, or gambling.'

I hang my head. His shame is mine.

'I have decided . . .'

I lift my eyes to look at her. She is throwing us out. Quite right. She'll have to get Sadie Gomersall up to take care of the house. Sadie has been in and out a bit lately. She's not so bad about Stephen as the others . . .

'Theo! Are you listening?' The old voice is sharp.

'Yes. Sorry, Mrs Gervase.'

'I don't know what you have decided to do, but first I will pay you and your mother up to date.'

I am frowning now. 'Pay?'

'Yes. How many months have you been here? I have offered you no wages.'

'But, Mrs Gervase . . .' The household expenses were generous. From the first we had been grateful for a roof over our heads, for a congenial life.

She puts up a hand and gives me a cotton purse which seems overflowing with golden guineas. 'I have worked out wages for your mother as housekeeper. You were more difficult. I decided you were both lady's companion for me and governess – if that is not too ridiculous a word – for Stephen. He reads quite well now.'

'But . . .'

'What is in there is quite fair for these services. It is no great sum. You can stay or you can go. If you go this money will help you. If you stay, then you will feel more secure.'

'But the silver . . . My father . . .'

'That is in the past,' she says firmly. 'We were in danger, for a moment, of your father's . . . er . . . weakness affecting

260

us all.' She waves her hand, in that characteristic gesture of hers. I am dismissed. Despite her earlier kindness, I see that I am not her friend. I have no illusion as to that. 'Now, my dear, you will need to discuss all this with your mother.'

I am at the door when she calls me back and hands me an envelope. 'I have written something on this paper which has been on my mind for a while. It is a matter too delicate for speech. If you would read it in a quiet moment I would be grateful. If its contents are of no interest then I do not wish to discuss it with you. If the contents raise your interest then you will come and perhaps we can talk.'

I thrust the letter in my pocket and make my way back to the kitchen. My mother is thrown into floods of tears of relief at Mrs Gervase's action. 'Ah, then. Sure, things can go on as before, Theo. Our place is secure? Wait! We must make it safe.' She grabs the cotton bag and puts it on a high pantry shelf.

I shake my head. 'No, we can't stay. It's too difficult. It will be a lump under the carpet, the thing that Father did. There's money here but not enough to replace all that silver. We'll be stumbling over that lump under the carpet all the time. We must go.'

Stephen is ploughing his way through a mountain of potatoes, tears dribbling down his cheeks. 'You can't go, Theo. You, Rose Clare, you can't go as well,' he said. 'You must not go. Who will read the stories? There will be no one to mind the baby, take care of the house. And Mama will miss the little dog.'

I restrain myself from putting my arms round him. Hugging him. From the hearth Seal pricks up her ears and looks at us with her gleaming eyes.

There is a great clattering on the door and Rose Clare jumps up to open it for the post boy, shivering in the drizzle outside. Post boy is a bit of a misnomer. He is fifty if he is a day. She

261

pulls him in and he brings a breath of the damp afternoon with him into the warm fug of the kitchen.

'Nice fire, missis,' he says, rubbing his hands. 'Weather out there like a wet donkey.' He slaps his post bag on the table and removes his caped coat. 'Tied up old Theseus in your stable. That's all right, Mr Gervase? Feeding alongside your old Samson.'

If he has post for us the post boy makes a stop here, the furthest delivery on his round, to warm up, take a drink and a bite before he sets off back down the valley. While my mother pours foaming milk and cuts bread for him he unbuckles his bag and slips out two letters. 'One for Mrs Ellis Maichin . . .' With a jolt, I recognise my father's loopy hand. 'And one for Miss Theo Maichin.' This is an unknown hand.

He sits down beside Stephen and eats and drinks with lip-smacking appreciation. I watch my mother carefully as she opens the envelope, takes it to the window to read. She turns and silently hands me the letter and another piece of paper which it contains. A pawn ticket.

My dear Rose Clare,

You know I love you more than life itself. There is so much joy being near you. But these old feet of mine are so itchy. I am a person of the town and the city. The countryside is bland and unforgiving to my eyes, too green, too brown, too dull. I need the bright lights. You will forgive me for the disgraceful manner of my departure. You will see from the enclosed that I borrowed the items rather than stole them.
Love always, from your husband Ellis Maichin

I look blankly at my mother. The post boy is chewing away at his bread, his bright eyes observant. I pull my mother into the pantry and close the door behind us. 'He has pawned it.

262

The silver. He did not sell it,' I whisper fiercely.

We stare at the ticket. My glance moves to the cotton bag of guineas, our wages from Mrs Gervase. We could never have bought back the silver but now we can redeem it. If we redeem it our wages are gone, and we will set out into the world with naught.

'We must redeem the silver,' whispers my mother, unusually firm. 'She must have it back.'

'Then we have nothing left. Nothing to start again elsewhere.'

'So be it. We will start again here with Stephen and Susan Cornford,' she says. Then she puts her hands on my shoulders, strong hands, used to work. 'I'll tell you one thing, Theo. Your father may come back again. Indeed he will. But I will not take him back. Never more.' I look at her and I realise that it is not only I who have grown up in the months at Goshawk Shield. There is a firmness about her. 'There is baby Susan to think about, after all,' she says.

'Sadie Gomersall—' I start.

She shakes her head. 'That family hate this child, hate anything to do with Mavis. Their guilt. Don't you realise it is some man in that family was the cause of Mavis's pain? No sheep-shearer. No gypsy. The father, the brother . . .'

I find myself blushing. I think of Edward and feel sick. All this kind of thing has passed me by, so preoccupied am I with myself and my stories and my simple reflections. I know about flirtation and romance from my reading. I do not think of this kind of passion in the context of raw physical encounters. This suggestion that a brother . . . a father could do such a thing brings me up short, despite that horrible thing Edward did to me.

'We need to stay. To take care of Susan,' she goes on firmly. 'And if ever . . . ever Ellis comes back he will be turned from this door. I promise you.'

263

She does love Susan. This girl child. She loves her like she has never loved me. In a strange way this is a comfort to know she is capable of such loving. It was not for me to experience, but it is still a comfort.

Back in the kitchen the post boy is standing steaming by the fire. 'Need to be off now, missis! Back down to Stanhope before light fails, that's my aim.' He dons his scarf and heavy cape and pulls his hat down over his eyes.

Stephen is sitting watching my mother and me like a fat owl. I go and put an arm round his shoulders. 'I think we must stay here at Goshawk, Stephen. We can get your mother's silver back from the pawnbroker with our wages and have a clean fresh start.'

He turns from where he is sitting and hugs me round the waist, his face in my chest. It is like the embrace of a child. I disentangle myself. 'Now, set the post boy down the lane. He'll want a word with you about the horses.' This occurs every time the post boy calls. This talk about the horses. No need to make any difference today.

My mother begins to clear the table, her steady actions radiating a kind of content. She rearranges some flowers in a jar. I sit down at the table, pick up the second letter, lost until now in the drama of the post. It is from Miss Bell, editor of *Judith's Journal*, who finds my story charming and fresh and will be happy to publish it. She encloses a cheque for two guineas in payment for same. She will be most interested in any further stories I care to submit. I stare at the cheque.

'Is that money?' says my mother over my shoulder.

'Yes. Two guineas.'

'How do you make it into money?' she says suspiciously.

'Bank,' I say cautiously. 'You have to take it to a bank, I think.'

'Which bank would that be, then?'

* * *

264

In the end Mrs Gervase solves the bank problem. Delighted that we really are going to stay and intrigued by the payment by the magazine, she announces she and I will travel down to Priorton soon and I can open an account at her bank, which is Backhouse's Bank in the Market Place. It seems I will have to leave the two guineas in the account, but that will be no bad thing. Sometimes when I am with Mrs Gervase I feel old, as old as her. Sometimes I feel very young, nearly as young as Susan Cornford. This is one of the times.

I go to bed quite content, and lie in the dark with Seal by my side, listening to the rain pad on the roof with the feet of a cat. I stare into the darkness, thinking of my story in print, lines of print and a dramatic illustration. Read by thousands. *Theodora Louisa Maichin*. I can see my name underneath the title. Then I see another story. And another. In the next room I can hear baby Susan whimpering and the murmur of my mother's voice as she soothes her. Seal stirs and jumps down from the bed and goes to join them. It is a long time since my mother shooed Seal out of her kitchen.

In the middle of my half-dream I shoot up in bed. In all this day of letters I have forgotten the one Mrs Gervase thrust into my hand. I turn up the lamp, retrieve the letter from my dress pocket and leap back into bed. The fire is out and the room is chilly. With all the business today I've forgotten to keep it stoked up. I'm usually more careful than this. Two days up here in the dale with the fire out can leave you with ice on the inside of the window and chapped cheeks and a blue nose when you wake up.

The letter is two pages of closely written text. The first page is the story with which I am vaguely familiar. Mrs Gervase's own life as the daughter of a rector; her brief marriage and the birth of Stephen, a joyous day for her. But when Stephen fell ill, how her need to be a mother had extended to forty-odd years of the nurturing you give a very small child.

And old as I am now, Theo, I am still concerned for him. I could die very soon, and they will take him somewhere and lock him up for his own safety and the safety of others.

I have a proposal for you. It may seem scandalous and disgraceful, in which case you must ignore it. Do not mention it again and things will go on as before.

I wish you and Stephen to marry. That will ensure that his life will continue as before. It should not be a physical union. Simply, you will remain the friends you are today, but each of you will have legal protection after my death.

If you do this I will bequeath you half of my worldly goods and Stephen the other half. If, three years after I die, you find the life unbearable you can make what arrangements you care to for Stephen, and go off with your inheritance and do what you will. I will not blame you from beyond the grave, but will applaud you for taking up the challenge, however briefly. I feel I can trust you with the confidentiality of this proposal, and hope that you will not be too shocked at my temerity in making it.

I tuck the letter under my pillow, turn down the lamp and slide down in the bed. I close my eyes and contemplate my world turned upside down for the second time in twenty-four hours. Stephen! I love Stephen as you would a little brother. But, marriage!

This thing from Mrs Gervase sets my mind in a turmoil. But the last thought before I drift into sleep is that Ellis, my justly maligned father, is also the cause of whatever success I have in my life. It is he who made me write for Mr Murgatroyd, who applauded my storytelling. It is he who got the magazine, made me send my story away. And now here was a proposal from Mrs Gervase more fantastic than any story even I could write. How my father would laugh.

Twenty

The Violin-maker

'Your brother called today.' Ruth poured Rhys a glass of water from the crystal jug.

'Edward?' Rhys scowled. 'That's the third time. He can come to the shop if he needs to see me. Tell him.'

'He said he would wait for you, then he went.'

'What's he up to? He's after something.'

'He was just being polite. He'd come down to Priorton on some business for the council. So he said he would call.' She served him his beef and his potatoes. She had enjoyed the visit. It was Beattie's afternoon off, so she had made the tea herself. Edward had followed her to the kitchen and sat talking to her as she did it, his feet stretched out on the fender.

Rhys shook his head, frowning. 'I'll go and see him. He gets things in his head, does Edward. Don't trust him an inch.' He picked up his knife. 'Don't trust him.'

She smiled at him. 'Oh Rhys. That's all childhood stuff! We're all grown up now. I did bad things when I was a child. I was a very naughty girl, you know.' She glanced complacently round the cluttered dining room. 'Edward thinks our house is lovely. Says I . . . we've done a lovely job.' He had said other, more flattering things, but she was not about to tell Rhys.

Rhys looked around his parlour, used now to the crowded splendour. 'It's a home. What can he expect?' What Rhys most enjoyed these days was the buzz of life in the foundry and the front shop with old Mrs Berriman. Where the hard graft of the pit had worn him down and defeated him, the bustling life of commerce was suiting him down to the ground. His quick thinking and sly mind was well suited to this business. 'You're in the house too much,' he said abruptly. 'You should come down to the shop and give your grandma a hand or go out visiting.'

She pushed out her bottom lip. 'There's so much to do here to keep this right, with only one maid. And there are callers to deal with.'

'Like Edward, you mean? I'll soon stop that!' he said sharply.

Her plain little face became plainer, darker. 'You will not do that! You will not! What is wrong with you? He's your brother.' Edward had told her in sorrow about all the problems with Rhys when he was younger. About the wickedness, the immorality, the lawlessness. 'Of course, dear sister-in-law, that is all behind us. With my guidance, which I know he resents, and your good influence, he is a changed man these days.'

Ruth's heart had leapt not at the words he said but at the sulky challenge in his eyes. Her heart leapt with that old delight in risk, in defiance and adventure. Rhys's earnest anger was nothing in comparison.

The next day Rhys made sure he was obliged to make a call at an ironmonger in Gibsley which gave him the opportunity to call on Edward at the house where he lodged with the widow of a former Wesleyan lay preacher. Edward was just scrubbed and clean from the pit, wearing braces but with a collar and tie. He smiled slightly when he saw Rhys. 'Ah, brother! An honour!'

269

'I understand you wanted to see me. You have called at my house three times,' Rhys growled.

'Just social calls,' said Edward easily. 'I happened to be in Priorton and was concerned about your wellbeing and welfare in a brotherly fashion.' He threw a scrap of paper across the table. 'Letter there from Caspar. Toiling away in a pit near Glasgow. I've written back to him saying things are looking up a little here. In fact I read that they were looking for lead miners up the dale. Gave him Theo's address.'

'She might not like that, Edward. Caspar's a rascal. Trouble in store for her? Is that what you're after?' Rhys stood in front of the fire, watching his brother as one would watch a snake.

Edward shrugged. 'Just the hand of friendship, brother. We are all alone in this world, but blood connects us. Theo has her duty.'

Rhys stared at him, then shrugged. 'No matter. I am here about you. I don't want you to call on my house when I am not there. Do you hear?'

'But how do I find you? You work so many hours at the foundry. I call to see you and you're not there.'

'Sundays. You can call on Sundays.'

Edward shook his head sorrowfully. 'That is impossible, Rhys. I am riding to chapels all over the county. Every Sunday. Much call on my preaching, these days.' He paused. 'Did Ruth complain about my calling on you?'

Rhys moved towards his brother. 'No. She is too polite for that. And too bamboozled by your goings on. It is I who complain. Me! Keep away from my home. I tell you this.'

Retrieving the silver is not as easy as I had thought. The weather has defeated me three times: the first time in the guise of a thick mist, impenetrable as a nun's veil, rolling down the hill, slipping across the river and up to the sills of the pheasant room, wrapping the house in a close grey blanket.

Stephen shook his head that day. 'No, no, Theo. Samson will not go forward in such mist.'

'But once we get down to Stanhope, Stephen, the train will be running, I am sure.'

Stephen's look of gloom darkened. 'But there is something else, Theo. It is me. I cannot go forward in the mist. I am afraid. Faces stare at me.' His protruding lower lip trembled. I looked at his gloom now in a different light. What if I were his wife? The words echoed through my head.

'But the road is there, Stephen . . .'

'Once, in such mist, I went off the bridge into the river. That day the ford was ten feet deep. That's why I went by the bridge. There was thunder and the horse bolted and the carriage we had then shot over the parapet. That was when I made the chariot, after that.' He shrugged his massive shoulders. 'Mama says I was lost for two or three days. Swirled down the river and wandered the moor. I cannot remember how long I was in the water. I can only remember I was afraid. And voices spoke to me, out there in the mist.'

The next time we were prevented our journey by the rain which fell like a thick curtain, sweeping down from the crag with rattling fury, splashing off the roofs and the windowsills in torrents.

But today will be the day. Last night there was an early autumn frost. The white light from the pale sky glints off the hoar frost edging the ruts in the road, and outlines the fences and stones in the walls with crisp silver.

'It should be fine enough to travel today, Stephen.'

'Mud underneath!' says Stephen gloomily. 'Soft mud.'

'We must try!' I say in my most bracing voice. In fact I will not settle until I have that silver back in the house. On the surface, the household is relaxed again. Susan is taking more notice of things every day. My mother is settled, she is

271

restless not like those other times my father left her. She sings. She makes me smile. Perhaps this final misadventure of his has put him down, at last, in her esteem. Whether it is Susan who has achieved this, or Goshawk Shield, I don't know.

Mrs Gervase is her usual, faintly distant, intelligent self. But as yet I am stiff with her and it is not so comfortable as before. Her proposal drums away in my head. But the house is almost too busy, bubbling like a steam pot. The baby is fretful and Seal is barking and squeaking and skittering about. I have a real desire to get away and the silver is as good a reason as any.

So, bumping along in the chariot, I am quite content. Seal is with me, along for the ride. She is tucked under my arm inside my cloak, a heavy, old-fashioned garment dredged (with her agreement) from the back of Mrs Gervase's wardrobe. My hat, however, is my own: a green felt with a curling feather and a small cluster of violets. It reflects my jaunty, jaunting mood.

The train is on time and, having waved goodbye to the disconsolate Stephen, Seal and I settle down in the lurching carriage for the journey to Priorton, content with the rhythm of the train which sings the song of escape.

Opposite me are a farmer and his wife. The man, with his heavy, decent jacket and his muddy gaiters, is half a head shorter than his wife. His features are drawn to the centre of his face like a fold in the moor. Deep-set eyes peer over a strong jutting nose and narrow pinched mouth. His skin is coarse-grained and leathery, polished to a harsh red over the cheekbones. The woman's face is blank and flat, her stringy hair pulled greasily back under a very plain bonnet. She is younger than him. Perhaps ten or twenty years. Hard to tell. Her high-buttoned serge dress is covered by a home-made cape. This garment is decorated bravely with bands of velvet cut from some other dress. The stitch runs are still there, like

272

the footsteps of a fly. The woman's hands are flat and separate on her knees. They do not touch each other. They are raw red, the knuckles too large, the wedding ring almost buried in puffy fat.

Watching them, soothed by the rhythm of the train, my mind moves on, to that strange proposal from Olivia Gervase for me to marry Stephen Gervase and . . . what? Become a dale farming wife? Could that blank-faced woman with ruined hands be me? Could I be her? Could that closed-in colossus of a man be Stephen? No. No. For we are different people, Stephen and I. But the drive of their lives in the last thirty years is the same as that in our lives in the next thirty years. The drive of the seasons. The rain and mist on the fell. The ice cutting into your hands, carving keens, swelling joints.

I shiver slightly.

'Aye, it's a bit parky, the day,' says the woman, who has been watching me as closely as I have been watching her. 'Days, whole days and not gettin' out.'

I nod fervently. 'It took me three goes to get down to get the train,' I say.

'Coom down off the fell, have yer?'

'Yes, from Goshawk Shield.'

The woman raises her sparse brows. The man shifts his trunk-like legs a little.

'Aye,' says the woman, 'they say Mrs Gervase has outsiders in there. Living up at the Shield.'

'Yes. That would be Mother and I. We live there. Work there.'

'Pity about that son of hers. Always was a pity.'

'Stephen?'

'Mekkin' her hid hersel away like that, from the town and from other folks. Hid herself up at Goshawk. Stranger from a strange place, set up at Goshawk. Her mother, old Mrs Cornford'd not be pleased. House in that family for hundreds of years. But it is different with that son here. Keeps herself to herself, you know. Too good for the dale. Goes to none of the gatherings.'

'Josephine! Ha'd thee whist!' The admonition cracks out of the old man's narrow mouth like a whiplash. The woman closes her own mouth and settles back in her seat. Ten minutes later she tries again. 'Nice little dog yeh've got there. Like a little *ornament*.'

I stroke Seal's fine head. 'Yes. Her name is Seal.'

'No more'n a pup, I should say? Whippet, isn't it?'

'She's nearly grown. They don't grow much bigger than this. So I'm told.' I stroke Seal's fragile head.

'Well I never! I seen them dogs racing at Wolsingham Show. Quick as lightning, little as they are. Now on the farm we only have working dogs. No time for—'

'Josephine! Enough, I tell you,' the old man barks. The woman subsides, her ration of allowed conversation complete. I glance out of the window at the land racing by. *Three years* the letter said. I'd only have to stay with him for three years. That was the bargain. My heart is in my boots. I fear I may not have the strength for this. Three years. Is that too large a price to pay for a lifetime's security, for myself and my mother? My mind races on. If I do this thing, won't Mrs Gervase be stealing my life as surely as my father stole her silver? The thoughts whirl round and round in my head. I need someone to talk to about this. I'll call on Rhys and Ruth. Perhaps I can talk to them.

I have to wait a long time in the pawnbrokers while more affluent jewellers' business goes on the other side of the thick plush curtain. The worst thing about this place is the smell. I suppose it comes from the parcels of clothes neatly labelled and stacked on these shelves to the left: delivered on Monday to be collected on Friday, money and goods moving round in an ever-whirling dance of poverty. The old man must make quite a living out of it.

But it is not the old man who comes through the curtain but a much younger man. His neat face (narrow, intelligent, not unlike a horse) is topped by a brush of grey-blond hair. He looks vaguely familiar.

'Now then,' he says. 'Is there something I can do for you?' His voice has a deep sweet tone, like black treacle. It is as though someone has hit me with a yard broom. My brain races, my body trembles, clutched by the sight and sound of this man.

There are romances a-plenty in all the books I read to Mrs Gervase. Joy! Gladness! Heartfelt declarations of love! But as I look at this man it is like a large key turning in the lock and a door swinging open, never to be closed.

How very ridiculous.

'Well!' The fine eyebrows are raised. 'You wish to pledge something?'

'It was another man. I dealt with another man before.' I am mumbling like a schoolgirl before her master. 'I bought clothes from him. For my father.'

'My old uncle? The poor old boy is ill. He usually does the pledges. The jewellery and the musical instruments are what I deal with.' He pauses, staring at me, discomforting me with his close attention.

The bell pings next door. 'Now then!' The tone is brisk. 'Do you have something to pledge?'

I am offended that he could take me for one of those poor people pledging the coat off their backs for a few days' respite. I glare at him, but no words will come.

'If you please!' he says crisply. 'I have customers waiting next door.'

I hand over the tickets. 'I wish to redeem these items of silver. I have the money here.'

He returns with the silver, folded in green baize inside a

card box. 'I noticed these items when I was doing the shelves.' His crisp tone has changed. It is less certain, less commanding. 'They are very fine pieces, unusual crests.'

'It is the crest of the Cornfords. A Gloucestershire family originally, back in the middle ages,' I say abruptly. 'The pledge was an aberration. A mistake.'

'Aberration?' I see him raising his brow at the long word and want to slap him.

'So please.' I place my sovereigns on the counter. 'Will you wrap them safely for me?'

He busies himself with string and brown paper. 'And this Cornford family, is that your family?'

I cannot tell whether he is being respectful or just mocking me. I resent my burning cheeks. 'No it is not. I work for Mrs Gervase at Goshawk Shield, up beyond Stanhope. She was a Cornford once.'

'Ah. I see.'

He thought it was I who had stolen them. I stop the tumble of embarrassing explanation falling from my mouth. I glance around. 'Are you a jeweller? Is this your place?' Now he can be on the spot.

His grey-blond hair falls forward as he shakes his head. 'No. Though the jewel-making is a great craft. My uncle, when he was young, had great skills. But now with his stiff fingers he is reduced to selling other people's stuff. And –' he looks round the dark cubbyhole – 'this pledging business.'

'So what is it that you do?' I persist, trying to punish him for his rudeness.

'Well. Mostly I make violins with another uncle up in Newcastle. I am down here to help this uncle while he is ill.'

I am caught, despite myself. 'You *make* them? It is hard to think of anything so . . . complicated and so beautiful being made.'

He flushes. Now I have got him! 'It's the best task in the

world, because a violin goes on and on every time it is played, beyond the life of the maker, or the player.'

'And do you play?'

'Very occasionally I play in the Priorton Orchestra.'

'Fancy!' I say.

'Fancy!' he laughs. 'Just fancy.' He pushes the heavy package over and puts the guineas into a felt bag under the counter. 'Well, Miss . . .'

'Maichin.' I know now where I have seen him. At Rhys's wedding. In the church and at the reception. Playing his violin.

'Well, Miss Maichin. You have redeemed your silver.'

I reach the door.

'If your Mrs Gervase ever wants to sell some silver, I'm sure my uncle . . .'

'No. No. I am sure she won't.'

'Miss Maichin?'

I turn. 'Yes.'

'I was admiring your hat. It is very fine.'

I clash the door behind me and stamp my boots hard along the pavement. He must think me a real fool, probably a thief. Even worse, he thinks me a comic fool with a clown's hat. I reach up and tear the bunch of flowers from my hat and throw them in the gutter.

I am not stupid, of course. I know what is happening to me. I am wishing I am tall and beautiful, that he admired my elegance as I stood there. This tumble of feeling is new. I've never taken much notice of boys. The three brothers I have are enough *boys* for anyone. And sly and strange as they are, they are all the *boys* I have known. The only romance I have ever experienced has been between book covers, between ladies and gentlemen who are the conjuring of someone's imagination: less real even than Loki the mischief-maker, and the beautiful Aphrodite, who has at least come to me mouth to mouth, down a hundred generations of storytellers.

But this violin-maker, whose name I do not even know, has impressed himself on me in this fashion. Of course I will never see him again. The whole thing is hopeless. I'd as well marry poor old Stephen and be done with it.

Rhys's wife, Ruth, seems pleased to see me, takes my hand and draws me into the house and calls me *dear sister*. She makes quite a fuss of Seal and insists the maid, Beattie, brings the dog a bowl of water. She plies me with coffee and fairy cakes and questions me about life at Goshawk Shield. 'They speak of Mrs Gervase down here in Priorton. Her family, the Cornfords, were well known here. The good people quite resent that she doesn't join in events these days. But they say she has a mad son.'

'You mean you've been checking on me, where I am?'

'We . . . ell,' she says. 'When I'm asked about you and I say where you are, they're bound to say, to tell me, aren't they?'

'Well, what do they say? About Mrs Gervase?'

'Just that Mr Gervase married her when they were both old, he a crusty old man in holy orders, she an old maid. Then they had an idiot child and the old man died and she came back up here to her mother's house in the hills with the idiot child . . .'

'That must have been nearly forty years ago. Stephen is forty. And he's no idiot. They have never met him. How can they think they know this?'

'Oh, they know. What they don't know they invent. Mouth to mouth it's passed.' She paused. 'Is it true he's a gibbering idiot, foaming at the mouth? This son of hers?'

'No, it's not. He's very nice. A loving son. And very helpful. He carves wood. He's just a bit slow.'

'So an idiot, really.' Ruth is pleading for confirmation, so she can go back to her gossips with fresh tit-bits.

'Not at all,' I say crisply. 'He can read and write. He's shy and reserved; a very gentle man. Kind. And clever is some ways.'

Ruth raises her brows. 'Seems you like him yourself.'

'You could not help but like him, if you knew him.'

She nods thoughtfully. 'Of course there'll be money there. They say Mrs Gervase has money.'

I survey the heavy parcel of silver at my feet. 'I know nothing of that. I just work there.'

'So what is it that you do, dear sister? Housekeep? Cook?'

Strangely enough I find myself unable to take exception to her tone. It is naked curiosity, interest, like that of a child surveying a new toy. There is an openness about it, a clarity. She is a strange woman herself and does not really baulk at strangeness.

'No. My mother does much of that. Housekeeping and such. But that's because of the accident of my being there. She came with me and there is need at Goshawk for her skills. What I do is . . . kind of . . . entertain Mrs Gervase. I read to her. Write some of her letters. Organise her books. And I do my own writing. She encourages that, takes an interest.' I feel I should defend Mrs Gervase. I do not mention teaching Stephen to read and write, this would surely be a betrayal. 'I have just delivered some new stories to Mr Murton on my way here.'

'Mm,' Ruth says thoughtfully. 'I wish I had such a pleasant companion as you. It can get so dull here.'

I laugh. 'I'm not a performing parrot, you know. It can't be dull here.' I glance around the busy room. 'In this town? There's so much to do: the music; the theatre.'

'But Rhys is out at business for so many hours. Dawn till well after dusk. I suppose I should be glad he has taken to it all so well, but—'

As if on cue, the front door clashes and Rhys bowls in. His

eye drops on to me and he smiles broadly. 'Ah. Visitor!' He shakes my hand. 'Down from the hills, Theo?' His hand goes to Seal's fragile head. 'You still have the whippet, I see?'

He kisses Ruth on the cheek. 'The best hostess in Priorton, my Ruthie.' In the past months he seems to have become taller, more solid; his voice has dropped a note. He looks older. He is a man who has found his niche. Ruth is watching him with the warm proprietorial glance of a mother whose child is coming on very well. I wonder if Ruth really likes this. It would not suit me.

My mind goes back to the violin-maker and I have a vision of a room with a blazing fire, with half-made violins hanging from the rafters and me sitting in a chair, spectacles on my nose, reading a book. I shake the thought away. 'So how is it, Rhys? You look very well.'

'It is all fine, Theo. As you see.' He glances across at Ruth. 'It must be family day today. I've been down to Gibsley to see old Edward.'

'Edward?' I realise how much I hate even the name.

'Seems well set up there. Lodging with a widow who takes care of him like a baby. He has all our old furniture heaped up there in two rooms.'

'What was it, Rhys?' Ruth's voice is sharper than I have heard all afternoon. 'Why did you go?'

'Just a word. Wanted a word with him over a matter of business.' His tone is easy but she frowns up at him.

The grandfather clock strikes. I stand up. 'I have to go for the train.' Rhys picks up my parcel of silver. 'Whoa! This is heavy. Been stealing the crown jewels, Theo?'

'Yes. That's right. That's my job. Chief companion and jewel chief.'

Something in my tone catches him. 'And Dada? How is he up there in the wilds?'

'He's gone. Vanished in the night.'

He places the heavy package carefully in my arms. 'And there were things to retrieve from such a situation?'

I nod. 'Yes.'

'And how is Mam?'

He expects me to say that she has fallen apart.

'Gone wild again at the loss of our father?'

'She's very well this time. There is a lot of work for her up there. The house. And there is a baby now to take care of. Left there by a maid who died.'

'And the poor woman's idiot son to watch,' put in Ruth.

Anger finally sheets through me at this. 'No. I told you, Ruth. Stephen's not an idiot! He is a kind, sweet man, hard-working. He loves his mother. He is a good son.'

'So you say,' says Ruth shrewdly. 'But when she dies, they say he will be in an asylum as sure as shot. Too much of a handful without a mother's restraining hand.'

'Now then, Theo,' says Rhys hurriedly. 'I'll take you to the station in my new gig. Had it made at the Co-operative Society. You should see their coach-work workshop. Artists they are. Artists!'

They both fuss me as they get me into the gig but I sense a coldness between them. It seems the pure happiness is fading already. Is true love so short lived?

When Rhys got back to the house Ruth was fussing over the supper table with the maid. When she finally got upstairs to change he was lying on the bed in his braces staring up at the ceiling. She took off her day dress, shook it vigorously and hung it in the cavernous wardrobe. She stood beside him, her grey silk basque showing off her fine shoulders and neat figure to advantage. She ran her fingers over his brow. 'So did you disagree with your brother?' she said softly.

'Yes. No. I just told him he could find me at the shop if he needed me. Not to bother you.' He kept his eyes closed. 'He played the blamed man, of course. He's good at that, Edward.'

She bounced on to the bed beside him and his eyes flashed open. 'Now!' she said. 'Beattie says the beef will be ready in twenty-five minutes.' She put an arm across and turned him towards her. 'There is just time.'

'Ruthie!' he groaned. 'I am worn out. Just leave it.'

'Worn out with going to see your big brother?' She bit his ear and he flinched. 'We'll see about that.'

He sat up straight, tumbling her from him in a very undignified fashion. 'I forgot!'

'Forgot what?'

'I should have warned old Theo. Edward has set Caspar on her, see? Told him there's work up there in the lead mines, he has. Theo wants nothing with Caspar turning up on her doorstep. Trouble there.'

She pulled him down beside her. 'Forget about Theo,' she said.

Stephen is waiting for me at the station, almost asleep in the front of the chariot, every fold on his broad face illuminated by a streak of late sunshine. I touch his knee and his eyes flick open. A look of pure pleasure lights up his face like a lamp. 'Theo. You are back!'

As I settle beside him, my parcel of silver at my feet, Seal on my lap, I realise that the pleasure is not one-sided. When I defended Stephen to Ruth this afternoon, I was offended in a very personal way. It was not just the injustice of what she was saying but the fact that she was saying this about someone I genuinely liked, perhaps even loved in a way. Why am I thinking this way? Would I be thinking about this if I had not met the violin-maker? But I do like Stephen, and not *despite* the fact that he is eccentric and strange. His strangeness is all in the parcel of what I like about him. Without that, in many ways he is less of a person. More of a shadow.

My mother helps me put the silver back where it belongs. She shuts the drawer with a click and turns to smile at me. 'Sure, it's a nice thing to do, to put things in their proper place,' she says. 'All that business is finished now.'

After supper I go along to the pheasant room to take the day's papers to Mrs Gervase. She is on her couch by the central window as usual. The great landscape behind her is darkened to a shadow, a black halo behind the tall lamp on the table.

'The silver is back in place,' I say, glad, even proud to get the words out.

'Good. I had no doubt.' She looks at me speculatively. 'You know, I could very easily have redeemed it myself. There was no need . . .'

'No,' I say.

'Well.' She pats the couch beside her. 'Come and let us read of the affairs of the world beyond Goshawk Shield.'

'Mrs Gervase.'

'Yes.'

'I've been thinking about Stephen.'

There is a silence.

'Stephen?' she says.

'When you . . . if you were no longer here, Mrs Gervase, what would really happen to him?'

The narrow shoulders shrug beneath the black shawl. 'Of course I will try to safeguard him. Solicitors. Lawyers. But I know in my heart they will put him in one of those places where people are put. People like Stephen who frighten those around them, and who themselves are frightened of shadows. I will put safeguards in place but he is not clever enough to retain them.'

The clock on the narrow mantelshelf ticks away.

'I am very fond of Stephen, Mrs Gervase.'

'I know.'

'I would be sad if that happened to him.'

283

'You would be powerless to do anything about it, my dear. Now!' she says briskly. 'What is happening in the world?'

I put down the newspaper and smooth it on my knee. 'I was thinking about the letter you gave me. Did you mean it? Everything you said?'

'Of course I did.'

'It doesn't seem fair.'

'Not on you, I agree. You're very young.'

'No. No. I could leave after three years. You say this.'

Mrs Gervase shrugs. 'It would be three years more security than he would have had. And, anyway, who knows what you would really decide, in the end?'

Outside the windows the fells have closed in, right up to the long sashes. Carefully, I pull all the curtains so that we end up in a chamber of velvet. 'I think I'd like to do it, Mrs Gervase. What you suggest in the letter. I'll meet your proposal, if Stephen . . .'

'He will want it,' she says firmly. 'He loves you dearly. That is clear for anyone to see.'

'And,' I pursue, 'it will be only . . . we will live as we do now.'

'Yes. That is clear. He'll want no other. He is a child inside that great frame.' She takes my hand and holds it firmly in hers. 'I want this, my dear girl, so that my beloved son does not end his comparatively happy life locked up in some small room reeking of misery. I do not want him wived and bedded in the conventional way. It is not appropriate.' She pauses and the tick of the clock is there, muffled now in the circle of velvet. 'There is this place, my dear, and what is in it, not a great deal of money. You will not be wealthy. Not in the world's sense anyway. You will have security and the opportunity to write your stories. He will have his life here at Goshawk Shield and his friend Theo beside him. That is all.'

There is tension in her voice. She is waiting for my answer.

I find myself nodding. 'I think I should do it. He has been on my mind all day. I met someone . . .'

'Someone?' she says sharply.

'A violin-maker. He . . .'

'What about him?'

'He made me think of Stephen. And what you propose.'

'And?'

'And if Stephen himself wants it, I'll do it.'

She lets out a long, long sigh. 'That is, if they let us do it. You know the legend that he is an idiot? They would not let him marry if he were an idiot.' She smiles slightly. 'But his being able now to read and write should make a difference on that score.' She takes my hand in hers. 'There'll be an uproar, my dear. But you are to take no notice. No notice at all.'

Twenty-One

Wedlock

Mrs Gervase was right in a way. There was a subtle, almost unspoken, uproar, but an uproar it was. Quite a three-day – well, a three-week wonder. We were stared at in the street, and the rector, with extreme politeness, refused to marry us.

In the end Stephen and I were married in a little church about ten miles from York, by special licence, by an old friend, actually a protégé, of the late Reverend Maupin Gervase. Stephen, happy and proud in his new suit, beamed right through the day. He knew exactly what was happening and told me several times he would love me all his life and he would carve me some wooden spoons with pictures of Seal on them. He spoke his part in the service as we had practised, his modulated tones encountering and rolling over the ancient phrases with relative ease. I stumbled more myself, aware of making bizarre promises which I knew would not be fulfilled. I suppose you could say, though, that worshipping him with my body was making sure he got his dinners and was physically fit and well. Not quite the kind of body-worshipping my parents indulged in, in the length of their marriage. My mother, who had been uncertain at first, entered into the spirit of things, little Susan Cornford chuckling away in her arms.

That day was quietly merry and life since then, back at Goshawk Shield, has gone on just as before. In fact it has been better. I, more confident now, move about the house with some authority. I have sold four stories to the magazine and seen my name in print. My own name: Theodora Louisa Maichin. Not the name borrowed in the bizarre contract I have with Mrs Gervase. I am getting on with the longer story about the French woman gardener: Pauline de la Carrière.

My mother also seems to have firmed up, grown in stature. She runs the house like clockwork with the daily help now of Sadie Gomersall, who reports back to the wider community that, though Stephen Gervase and the Welsh girl are wed, it seems to make no difference: they sleep in separate bedrooms. Sadie takes a scared kind of interest in baby Susan.

The wedding announcement in the *Priorton Chronicle* a week after the event resulted in quite a flush of visitors at Goshawk Shield. First, Rhys and Ruth, in best bib and tucker, made an official call. Ruth, after being somewhat fazed by the informal state of affairs in the household, entered into the spirit of things, clearing the table and washing dishes alongside Rose Clare, talking to her mother-in-law as though they were intimates. Which they are not, of course.

Rhys tackled me about marrying Stephen at all, but I became angry with his suggesting that my nature and motives were mercenary.

'. . . not that I am blaming you, Theo. It's a hard world, and . . .'

'No! Rhys, that is not why. The reason is because, as Mrs Gervase said, Stephen will be abandoned when she dies. She is over eighty. I like Stephen.'

'You can't say this is real, this marriage? I don't—'

'I am fond of Stephen. As I am of little Susan Cornford. I will protect him as I would protect her. As I *will* protect her.'

He shook his head at that. 'You always were a little crazy,

Theo. Now I am sure you are. Perhaps you and this Stephen are well matched.'

My next caller was Edward, who knocked on the front door and marched in, stamping his feet and looking round like a proprietorial squire. I introduced him to Mrs Gervase and Stephen, then left him in the kitchen with my mother until it was time for him to go back down for his train. All the time he was in the house Seal clung to my heels, shivering.

'I hate to say this,' said Mrs Gervase, watching him stride down the path, 'but that is a very unpleasant young man. I much prefer the other brother.'

I was easy enough with her by then to laugh with her. 'There is something wrong with all of us Maichins, Mrs Gervase. None of us is quite right.'

She chuckled. 'I suppose you're correct. Or else how would you end up at home in this madhouse?'

My next visitor is much more important and is the source of much more grief. At first I do not recognise him under the weight of his cape and the shadow of his brown slouched hat. I open the hall door to its full width to let the hall light fall on to him and I begin to make out the narrow intelligent face, the thatch of grey-blond hair. 'Hello,' I say, nervous of I know not what.

'Miss Maichin? May I come in? I have something . . .' He follows me in and places a case down on the floor.

'Perhaps . . .' I hold up my hands for his cape and he swings himself out of it and places it in my arms. I lay it carefully across a hall chair. 'This is a long way to come, Mr . . . er?' My brain freezes; I do not even know his name.

'I'm called Lytton. James Lytton.' He shakes my hand heartily. 'I know your name as it was on the ticket. And the address because you mentioned Goshawk Shield.' He glances around the dark hall. 'An old place, this,' he says.

I nod and wait in almost miserable silence to know what

he wants here. I set my face smooth so the turmoil doesn't show.

He looks around. 'Here. Can I put this on the table?' He lifts a long leather-bound carrying case and places it on the gleaming mahogany. Then, with the flourish of a magician, he clicks it open. Inside, lying on the blue velvet, is a finely wrought violin, its satiny wood gleaming in the light from the hall window. 'Take it out, look at it,' he urges.

Bewildered, I lift it out. My fingers run across the silky wood, trace the deep curves. I hold it closer to my eyes. I can smell fresh wood and some kind of rosin, sweet like the smell of toffee. On the curling edge of the instrument, outlining its sensuous shape, is a line of decoration in inlaid wood. At first it looks like an abstract pattern, but when I bring my eye closer to it I see it is a line of interlocking seals. 'Seals.' I lift my eyes to his which are watchful, slightly anxious. 'How did you know?' I say hoarsely.

'Know what? The inlay? The pattern on the edge? Won't help the tone, but I wanted to make this one special. I tried several times to make a pattern of the dog in the inlay. But I failed. Then I remembered what you called her. Seal. A seal was much easier.'

'Why?' My brain is racing. How can a man whom I have met for just a few minutes have done all this?

'Why?' he shrugs. 'It does not do to ask that question too often. I was driven to do it.' He glances round. 'Could we sit somewhere, do you think? It's been a long journey. I led my little horse down to your stable yard. A man came and took it.'

Still carrying the violin I lead the way to the dining room. This room is my private space now, with its books strewn all over the place and the fire blazing high.

I place the violin carefully on the table by the books and then sit in a chair. 'What is all this about, Mr Lytton?'

'I was driven to it, as I say. I have been very industrious since we met. I am known to be good at this violin business. Perhaps the best in the North. I had just finished one and I had these woods prepared. Once my uncle was better I got on with it.'

'Why? Why did you do this?'

'I can only think, Miss Maichin, that some power, some deity greater than us had ordained that our relationship shall not be as the flotsam and jetsam on the sea, but shall light on some bright permanent shore . . .'

I am laughing. 'Do you always talk like this, Mr Lytton? All such nonsense?'

He smiles, pleased, I think, to have made me laugh. 'It's not nonsense. I've not worked hundreds of hours on this thing, burned the midnight oil for you in the service of *nonsense*.'

'I can't take it. You're a stranger.'

'Yes, you can take it. It was made for you. Being a stranger does not exist between us. We were fated to meet.'

Now I am moved. I allow the great heave of recognition inside me a second's acknowledgement. 'We can't be. We are separate . . .'

'I want you to come with me. To Newcastle, to see where I make them, these eternal beauties.'

'I cannot. My place is here.'

He looks towards the door. 'Go and get them, your father and mother. I will explain . . .'

I cannot tell you when last my heart was so heavy. I shake my head. 'That's not how it is here.' I walk across to the door, put my head round, and call for Stephen. In minutes he is shambling across the hall in the big felt slippers he wears when he takes off his yard boots.

'Stephen, this is Mr James Lytton.' I see the man survey this figure before him, of the man who recently took the reins of his horse and led it to the stable.

'Look what Mr Lytton has brought me, Stephen!' I hand him the violin, which he takes as one might take a holy chalice. He touches the strings and feels them resonate, rubs the tips of his fingers down the polished wood. His face breaks into that wonderful smile which is like the sun coming from behind a cloud. 'Very fine work,' he says. I can feel the ripple of shock in the other man at Stephen's cultured tones. 'Very fine work indeed.'

I put it safely back on the table. 'Stephen works in wood himself. He carves, and makes things from wood,' I say, 'so he knows good work when he sees it.

'Stephen,' I say, 'shake hands with Mr Lytton.'

I watch Lytton's tough, slender hand being engulfed in Stephen's.

'Mr Lytton,' I say quite brightly, my head held high, 'this is my husband. Stephen Gervase.'

So that was the beginning, the middle, the end of what may have been a great friendship, and more, between me and Mr James Lytton. We were civil enough. So much passed between us without words. He took back the violin when I pressed it on him, and placed it back in its case as one would place a stillborn baby in a coffin. The image of the seal sister rose in my head for the first time for many months. The physical self of Seal, my little dog, has long supplanted the ghostly image of my sister in my imagination.

James Lytton came into the kitchen and ate bread and cheese and a foaming tankard of milk. He conversed in his strange overblown way with my mother and paid his respects to Mrs Gervase. He looked at Stephen's carved spoons. He petted baby Susan. He stroked Seal. He went to the workshop to see Stephen's new project which was a little bookcase for me to use in the dining room. It swings round to show a different face, depending on which book I may want.

I walked with him down to the big gate, his horse clopping on the long rein behind us.

At the gate he turned to me. 'Why?' he said. 'Why did you do this?' He did not need to elaborate.

'It seems, it seemed like the right thing to do. Stephen is such a good person. And his mother is so very old, and was worried about his care when she died.'

His face was drained of colour, his jaw stiff and over-controlled. 'It is such a waste,' he said. 'You should have waited.' He mounted his horse, went forward on the path, then swung round the horse's head and came back. He delved in a deep pocket and brought out a battered posy of violets, the bunch I had taken off my hat and thrown into the gutter in disgust as I left him that day. 'I suppose you should have this. I retrieved it from the gutter.'

I kept my hands behind my back. 'No. You keep it,' I said. 'You keep it.' I turned swiftly and ran towards the house before he could thrust it in my hands.

Back at the house I ran upstairs to my bedroom, and from the window watched him and his horse until they reached the road junction at Bittern Crop Farm. Then I threw myself on to the bed and wept, beating the pillow with my fist in frustration and temper, mourning a whole stretching lifetime which, by a fluke of time, I had missed.

It is months now since I put pen to paper. I have been in some black place, weeping inconsolably with no immediate cause. I have left food on my plate for days at a time. I have snapped at my mother, even at Stephen, with no just reason. Even Mrs Gervase – whom I cannot bring myself to call Mama, despite her requests – has looked anxious. Only little Seal and Susan Cornford have been spared my miserable outbursts. But today is fine and I have dusted my table and brought out my pens. The will-o'-the-wisp appearance of James Lytton seemed to put paid to such a lot of things, most of all the pastimes of my childish days. In this black state writing has seemed such a childish thing.

Even so, the days since James Lytton's visit have been long and busy. Mrs Gervase had a chill at the end of the winter but seemed to pull through. Afterwards, however, she became more fragile, almost transparent in the crossbeam of light in the pheasant room. My mother is rounder and bonnier than I have ever known her, steadier and more content than any time when my father was with her. Stephen can read bits of the paper himself now and is more loving in his innocent way each day. He has made no attempt to translate our legal state into greater intimacy, though his love for me shines out of his every innocent action. He worries that I do not write. His main concern, though, has been for his mother. Her mind is still bird sharp and she watches proceedings with great perception, but her body is shrinking before our eyes, her skin becoming more translucent.

It is because of his persistence that I have taken up my pens again. He was disappointed when my children's stories dried up and would not be put off by Mr Kipling's *Just So Stories*. 'But your stories are best. Why are there none of your stories?'

Stephen's anxiety must have affected my mother, who every week dusts off the long table in the dining room, replaces the velvet cover and lays out my paper afresh. The events of the day of the violin have taken on a distance now, although when I close my eyes I can see James Lytton's face almost in the flesh.

What I can't get rid of, can't dig out of my soul, is the finality of what I have done, the depths of my stupidity. I am not fit to be let out of the nursery.

Despite her fragility Mrs Gervase is serene, relaxed and happy. She is forgetful now and then, not quite sure whether she did a thing today or yesterday. I now have my bank account at Blacklock's Bank into which is paid not a wage, but an 'allowance', at the insistence of Mrs Gervase. I don't spend it, of course. What could I spend it on, up here in the wilds? Some nights I lie awake, thoughts whirling round my head. I make up my mind that the next day I will go down to Priorton, call at the jeweller's and make enquiries about a bracelet or a locket. In this way I might happen into conversation with James Lytton or even his uncle, somehow to make a bridge between this impossible situation and real life.

The next morning I take one look at Stephen's open countenance and the wild plans melt away. One morning I hardened myself not to allow my dream to fade; even more determined to go, I made excuses to my mother, saying I wished to get a present for Mrs Gervase. One day, I even had my coat on, ready. But then Seal went missing, and when we finally found her shivering in the corner of the barn, it was far too late to set out.

But it was Stephen who got me back to this table today and put my pen in my hands. After breakfast he came to the kitchen door. 'Come, Theo. I've something to show you,' he said.

He led me across the garden, under the windows of the pheasant room. Glancing up, I could see the white face, the sketched salute of Mrs Gervase as she sat in her customary place in the window seat.

He led me down the small ravine where the river trickled jumping and spurting over man-made stone obstacles, built especially to make the water surge and leap, catching and reflecting the dense light of the moor until it settled in the waterfall pool.

Stephen jumped across the river at a narrow point and held his arms out for me to follow. I slipped across, my gloomy thoughts lifting in the presence of the gleaming water and the white expanse of sky.

'Now!' he said proudly, and led me round a high stone. Behind it someone, obviously Stephen, had been scything and clipping the brambles and the high growing thorns, opening a way into a narrow valley, a rocky pencil-shaped hollow which was completely hidden before. The turf had been cut, creating a rough carpet. There, almost blinding in their colour, were hundreds, even thousands of spring bulbs, lurking by rocks, sprouting out of the turf.

I dropped to my knees. 'Stephen. This is a vision.'

He pulled me to my feet. 'More, Theo. There is more.'

He had hacked his way through to the far end of the little valley and, entwined here and there with creepers, was a double seat carved in the stone. We sat side by side in the seat and looked back to where we had come from. In my mind's eye the creepers and the brambles were all gone. In their place grew shrubs and low plants which complemented rather than competed with the grandeur of the stone. The plants dipped and reflected in the river as it moved through the space, stilled now and then into pools where the current tugging underneath did not disturb the surface.

I took a deep breath.

'Mama says a lady came from France . . .' he said.

'Yes, there are papers. In the dining room. I have seen them. Mademoiselle Pauline de la Carrière.'

'And see, Theo! I couldn't read this. There are words here.' He guides my hand towards some writing which has been carved into the side of the seat. *Pauline de la Carrière made this garden for the delight of Joshua and Susan Cornford, and thanks them for the sanctuary of Goshawk Shield.*

So of course here I am. I am back here at my table with Pauline de la Carrière's plans before me, her letters and notes in a neat pile. I have dusted down the poor beginnings of a story which I made those months ago. We have decided, Stephen and I, that he shall remake her garden to her design and I will tell her story – or my version of her story. Mrs Gervase is delighted at our project and talks of getting a gardener up from Stanhope to help.

Stephen is very wise. The darkness I feel inside, the mourning I felt for my lost life, the life I might have had, is receding.

I write my story and am daily taken on a tour of the reawakened garden. I push, push the notion of James Lytton right to the back of my mind. I write all the daylight hours and into the evening. The pile of paper, neatly written, with only the occasional change, grows by the day.

Our contentment is broken one Saturday by the appearance of my brother Caspar, who has put on a great deal of weight and is very much the worse for wear. He greets me with slobbering affection and he cries when my mother moves towards him. She is quite pleased to see her son but, like Edward, I feel he is better out of our sight and out of our minds. Nevertheless, we are civil enough, we give him a great big dinner and wait while he thaws out by the fire and tells us of the desperate times he has had working as a miner up beyond Middleton in one of the lead mines.

'Just believe me, Mother, the coal pits are bad enough, but here the wet, the cold makes it so much worse.' He gulps off a great gulp of fear. 'And there is little comradeship, so far as I can see. And –' he lowers his voice as though he is revealing some very shameful thing – 'these fellows knit. *Knit!* No occupation for a man, I can tell you that. They knit as they walk to the pit. They knit as they walk home. And they don't go home each night, living too far away. They sleep in a freezing kennel not fit for dogs.'

'How long have you been there?' says my mother.

'A week. No more. And that's enough.' He glances around the warm kitchen. 'Well . . .'

'Are you going back down to Gibsley?' I say hurriedly.

'There'll be work in the pits there.'

His smile is barely civil. 'In a hurry to get rid of me, isn't it, sister? Me frozen and chapped with all the cold?'

'You cannot stay here,' I say stubbornly. 'We are only . . .'

He shoots me a hard glance. 'Only what? I have it from Edward you are married to the good Mr Gervase. Mistress of all she surveys, isn't it, Mam?'

'Edward should mind his own business. I tell you that.'

Anxiously my mother crumbles bread on her plate. Then Caspar catches sight of Seal in her basket. 'Ho. So you kept the runt?'

'She's not a runt.' I am offended. 'She is fine and fit. No trace of a limp. She runs like the wind when she wants to.'

'Is that so?' He leans over and scoops her up from her basket. With enormous dignity she endures the way he pokes and stretches her limbs, pulls out her ears. 'Aye. Thrown it off,' he says thoughtfully. 'Sometimes they do, you know.' Then very gently he puts her back in her basket. She stares patiently at him for a second, then closes her eyes and feigns sleep.

'You can stay tonight,' I say abruptly. 'Then you must go down to Gibsley. I believe Edward has good lodgings. You can join him.'

'And Rhys has a big house in Priorton now. Perhaps he could put you up.' Rose Clare is as eager as I am to get rid of him.

He shrugs his heavy shoulders. 'I would do this, and willing, but unfortunately I do not have any money. Those lead miners may be knitters but there are one or two unforgiving gamblers in their midst.'

'I'll give you money,' I say grimly. 'Enough for your fare and to keep you for a week, until you get some work. But you should go down there. It is dull here.' I glance at my mother. She, too, is thinking about my father Ellis for whom also

Goshawk Shield was much too dull.

He nods. Thank goodness. 'You are too kind, sister. Too kind.'

'And when you see Edward,' puts in my mother, quite sharply, 'you may tell him he must keep my things safe. He has my things. My furniture.'

I had forgotten. Forgotten all about the chairs and the clock, the ornaments and the pictures. 'You should have them here now,' I say. 'We are staying here now. Always.' My heart sinks to my knees at the finality of my own words. What have I done? At Goshawk Shield always? With great lumbering Stephen. Always?

She looks at me closely. 'Yes. I suppose we are.'

My mother makes Caspar a bed in one of the empty bedrooms; we feed him a hearty breakfast which is more like a dinner; I press five guineas in his hand and we wave him off in the chariot with relief. It takes me quite half an hour to get back into my imagined story of Pauline de la Carrière. At times, as I pursue Pauline through the tale, it is as though I am her, fleeing from the French pursuers who were once her friends. I dream it. Unbidden to my mind comes Mrs Verena Scott's assertion of my being like a snake throwing off skin after skin, ever becoming a new person. Perhaps that is what I do when I write someone's story. Become that person for however small a time.

I am pulled back to my present-day self with a jolt when Stephen brings in a cup of milk to 'help me to write the story', as he puts it. As he places the tray on the table beside me he announces, 'Seal is lost. She is nowhere to be found. I have looked all round the buildings, right down into the new garden. She is nowhere.' His tone is mournful. 'I hope that the farm dogs have not eaten her. Mama said, a long time ago, that the dogs would eat her.'

I stand up, pens scattering to the floor. 'No, Stephen. It's not that. I'll tell you what's happened. That dolt, that thieving, robbing brother of mine has stolen her.'

'Oh dear,' he says. 'Poor little dog. Thieved and robbed, no less.'

Within an hour I am on the last train to Priorton out of Stanhope. It is late and dark when I arrive. I will have to stay with Rhys tonight and go on to Gibsley first thing in the morning. With a bit of luck I'll catch Caspar before he has sold Seal to one of the dog men. Above all I want to box his ears, and in my present mood, if Edward plays up, I'll box his too.

Ruth welcomed her sister-in-law with open arms. 'A stranger! You're too much a stranger. How nice that you come to stay.'

Theo handed over her hat and cape. 'I arrive so late that I have to impose on you. I must go to Gibsley in the morning. To see Caspar. He has stolen my dog.'

'Stay! Stay! This house is like a tomb. I think Rhys has forgotten where he lives. Either that or he has fallen in love with my grandmother and must spend his time with her.'

Theo was too preoccupied to note the genuine rancour in Ruth's voice. 'Have you seen Caspar?'

'Caspar?' Ruth wrinkled her nose. 'He came here a couple of weeks ago. Stank of beer. Rhys gave him money to go to find work in the lead mines.'

'Yes. Then he came to us . . .' She told Ruth about Caspar's visit. 'And as he left us he . . . stole . . . my little dog Seal. Seal is missing anyway, and I feel sure Caspar has taken her. I'm going to get her back from him tomorrow. He is staying at Edward's, I think.'

'Edward?' Ruth pursed her lips. 'Edward would not approve of Caspar stealing your little dog.'

Theo looked at her sister-in-law for a second, arrested by the certainty in her voice, the familiarity.

'You see a lot of Edward,' she said suddenly, a statement rather than a question.

'Not so much,' said Ruth, her cheeks pink. 'Just now and then. He comes into Priorton on council business.'

The truth was that she was enjoying the tension, the sweet risk. Edward called every week now, on Beattie's afternoon off. His was a reassuring, flattering presence. Nothing untoward had happened between them, although he had led her to understand his passion for her, unrequited as it was. She had avoided telling Rhys anything about the visits. He got into such a fuss about his brother. Edward had explained to her why. How, as a child, Rhys had been jealous, and had to be saved from himself more than once. How Edward himself had tried and tried to keep him on the straight and narrow. How much he admired the way Ruth had tamed Rhys, made a decent man of him. The fact that he was a little neglectful these days could be understood and even, perhaps, forgiven. He was swept away by his new importance at Berriman's and would not imagine the effect on Ruth, who should be treasured, not left alone in the house uncared for.

I have been saved from the long walk down to Gibsley by the offer, from Ruth, of her little gig pulled by the horse which she and Rhys keep in the livery stables at the bottom of Fencale Street. I practise driving it by delivering her back to her house in Victoria Road. She is quite pressing that she should come with me down to Gibsley, but I resist. There will be a fight, I know, and Rhys won't want Ruth party to it.

Rhys himself, in very late from work last night, was pleased enough to see me, but seemed too preoccupied with matters of business to be more than surface polite.

It is Ruth who is more interested in my mission, wishes more involvement herself. I can sense a hunger, a restlessness in her, an eagerness to share. But I turn down her kind offers.

There is a certain matter of business between me and Caspar. And Edward will be on hand to stir up more trouble. I want no witness to that.

Twenty-two

Racing Seal

By the time I am halfway to Gibsley I have mastered the little gig and the horse that pulls it. I let her trot on, oblivious of shouts from the brake and cart behind me accusing me of blocking the way with my slow passage. The streets of Gibsley seem even smaller and meaner than I remember, the pall of smoke is denser over the many chimneys dominated by the great industrial edifice of the ironworks.

I have to stop the gig twice to ask the way. By people's reactions to me I begin to realise that I have leapt a fence now and am somehow stranded on the other side. The man and woman I stop to ask are not deferential (too bold and confident for that). But they call me 'miss' and look at me with that tentative mistrust always offered to outsiders, to people of an alien sort. The fact that they shake their heads and disclaim knowledge of John Street could be, of course, another way of putting me in my place. I catch up with a more formally dressed, tall man making good pace down the main street and pull up the horse (with some difficulty) to ask him. It is only when he turns round I realise that it is James Lytton. 'Miss Maichin!' he says. Then the bright look on his face fades. 'Mrs Gervase now, isn't it?'

I am hot. 'Mr Lytton, I didn't realise, didn't think it was

you. I'm looking for John Street,' I hurry on. 'I've asked two people and you'd think I was asking for Timbuktu.'

He puts a foot on the step and leaps lightly in beside me. 'I'll show you,' he says. 'I know John Street.'

Awkwardly I manoeuvre the gig; timidly I tell the horse to walk on. Courteously he tells me to turn this way or that until we turn into John Street, a very neat row of respectable houses with bay windows. We stop outside number seventeen and I draw a deep breath, preparing to face Edward and do battle with Caspar.

'Are you on a difficult errand?' says James Lytton suddenly.

'Well . . .' I find the whole story tumbling out, about Seal being my companion, my soul mate, though a flawed whippet, about my brother who has so wickedly stolen her because she is no longer crippled and may be a racer.

He puts a hand over his mouth, covering, I know, a smile. 'Well. That should be no trouble. Just demand what's yours.'

'You don't know my brothers.'

He jumps off the gig and holds out a hand. 'I'll come in with you and supervise fair play only.'

I feel that he is laughing at me, but cannot refuse his help. Still, I avoid his hand as I clamber off the carriage. I am too aware of him already. His body beside me as we drove through the streets was almost too much to bear. My heart is so heavy. I wish now I had not met him.

The woman leads us upstairs to Edward's sitting room. He is fully dressed and is fiddling with a small case on the table. 'Theo! What is it, I am on my way out . . .' I am treated to no welcome. There is no indication that he hasn't set eyes on me in a long time. His eye falls on James Lytton, standing behind me. 'Ah. Who have we here?'

'This is James Lytton, Edward. He guided me through the streets to find this place.'

Edward frowned at him. 'I've seen you before, Mr Lytton.

The Priorton concerts. You play the . . .'

'Violin.' James Lytton stands easily in this small space.

'And what are you doing in Gibsley?'

'Same as you. I live here . . . well, my grandmother lives here and I stay here when I'm not up in Priorton with my uncle. Or in Newcastle, where I have another uncle.'

'Yes. Yes.' Edward, not having discovered the value of this other man, is forced into politeness. He makes a great effort to be civil; he sits down in a chair by the table. 'Sit down, won't you? Is there something you need, Theo? Is there something wrong?'

I stay standing. 'Is Caspar here?'

'No. Yes. He stayed here last night and is off somewhere today, some gambling enterprise I shouldn't wonder. I have told him he may only stay till Saturday.'

'Where is he now? You must know.'

'He'll be down with the dog man. He had a dog with him. A scrawny whippet.'

'That's my dog. Seal. Didn't you realise?'

He shrugs. 'All dogs are the same to me. Yappy things. That one was yapping all night. Kept me awake for hours. Should be destroyed.'

Hands curled into fists, I take a step towards him, only to be pulled back by the hard hands of James Lytton. 'Where do the dog men go?' James Lytton's voice floats over my shoulder.

'I'm told they race behind a pub called the Haunted Dog on Collier Street.' He looks insolently into the other man's eyes. 'You cannot be a dog man, Mr Lytton, or you'd know so yourself.'

James Lytton takes my arm. 'We'll go there, Mrs Gervase. Your brother will be there. We will get your dog and go.'

'Are you and my sister good friends, Mr Lytton?' says Edward, snapping his case shut.

'Mere acquaintances,' says Lytton. 'I was there on the road and Mrs Gervase was enquiring the way. We have met through business –' I waited for him to mention the silver cutlery and the pawnbroker's ticket – 'I sold her some jewellery in my uncle's shop. Some months ago, if I recall.'

'You are in business?' Edward's interest sharpens.

James Lytton shakes his head. 'My uncle's business, as I said. I am a maker of violins.'

Amongst all this I am tickled by this 'Mrs Gervase' person. Surely that's not me? Then I flinch slightly as Edward leans towards me. For a second I think he is going to kiss me on the cheek. He whispers in my ear. 'An easy woman, is it? A whore? My, you have grown up, Theo!'

My hand comes up to slap him and he grasps it hard, pushing me away from him. I fall back into the arms of James Lytton. Even in the middle of this ridiculous drama I am too conscious of his strong arms, his hard hands. His long body. He puts me behind him and faces up to Edward. 'That's enough, Maichin,' he says curtly.

'Now, now, Lytton. All I did was stop her slapping me. We're old sparring partners, my sister and I.' He smiles seraphically. 'We are all family here.'

There are no women in the crowd milling around on the half-acre of stamped-down turf at the back of the pub. The crowd consists mostly of working men, indulging in a bit of risk, a bit of enjoyment before the afternoon shift. There is a sprinkling of men in matching suits and bowler hats. The straight course is crudely marked out with home-made flags and the finish is cut out of the turf and marked with powdered chalk. Half a dozen men are lined up at the winning line, crouching down. One of them is Caspar. There is a roar at the other end of the track and the dogs are let loose. The men shout, shout for their dogs. I grasp Caspar's shoulder. He glances up, sees that it's me and growls, 'Leave off, Theo, will yer? See! She's coming!' He starts to roar for his dog as do the other men on the line. 'Come on, lass! Come on!'

I can see Seal at the front of the pack, shooting forward on her gazelle feet. Pulled into the thing despite my anger, I shout, 'Come on, Seal!' She leaps forward even faster. She gains a foot, now a yard, in front of the field. She wins easily, passes Caspar, and leaps up into my arms. I pull her to me, and look up for Caspar, ready to kill him. But he is gone, collecting money and pocketing it, from a gaggle of men by the fence. He comes back beaming. 'Not quite the runt after all,' he says. 'Give her here.'

I hold Seal closer to me and turn my shoulder against him. Both Seal and I are trembling. 'You stole her, you . . . you barbarian!'

He makes a grab for her but I turn my back altogether. He wrenches me towards him, his hoarse voice in my ear. 'She's mine. You were keeping her for me. I've a fellow over there offered me ten guineas for her. You and me can go halves. Clear profit.'

'You never paid me. She belongs to me. She is not for sale.'

Seal yelps as he shakes us both. Then he is pulled off me and when I turn round Caspar is on the ground and James Lytton is standing over him. Caspar raises himself up on his elbows. 'No need to be sticky, Theo.' He cocks an eye at the man looming over him. 'So, who have we here?'

'My name is James Lytton.' James dusts down his sleeves and offers a hand to Caspar and pulls him to his feet. 'Mrs Gervase and I are friends.'

'This is my middle brother, James. He stole my dog.' I move to his side. 'I'm going back now,' I say. 'Back up the dale. And I am taking Seal with me.'

Caspar leaps towards me again and puts one hand on Seal.

306

I take a step back. 'No!'

'Oh, just give us her for a fortnight, Theo. A month. She'll make our fortunes.'

'She's going home.'

'Home, is it? A kennel in the wilds?'

'It's my home now,' I say. 'More home than I've ever had.'

He shrugs and half turns his head. Another race is starting. 'Suit yourself,' he says. 'It's your loss.'

James Lytton and I make our way back to the gig through curious, staring men. He sets himself behind the reins and I clamber up and put Seal on my lap.

Lytton makes a kissing noise with his lips and the horse moves forward. 'No love lost between you and your brothers,' he says.

'Never was,' I say. 'I have another brother in Priorton, Rhys. He's a bit different. But not too much.'

We make our way down a narrow street. There are women brewing their gossip in doorways. Children are skipping or lying on stomachs playing with marbles.

'Do you belong in this town?' I venture.

'My grandmother does. I stay with her sometimes. Most of the time I live in Newcastle with my uncle, helping with his music shop there, making my violins.'

'How can you play with the Priorton Orchestra, then?'

'By arrangement. Most people who play are amateurs. For them, these tradesmen and craftsmen, it is a fine pastime. For me, it is my profession. They pay me to play, so now and then it's worth my while to come and stay with my grandmother and play with them.'

'Are you a good player?'

I can feel his shoulders shrug. 'Better than the pastime players, but not good really. Not good enough for the best orchestras. I am the very best at making them, though.' The best violin maker?

I laugh. 'So very modest!'

'I know I am good,' he says. 'I have won prizes. In London and Paris. Strangers think so, so I must be good.'

'A bit like me, I suppose.'

'Do you make violins?'

'No. Nothing like that. I write stories. And strangers tell me they are good. So I think perhaps they are.'

Now I find myself telling him about the Frenchwoman. The gardener called Pauline de la Carrière. 'I know so little about her. There are the garden plans and some letters between her and the Cornfords. The rest I have read in Mrs Gervase's history books about the revolution and the Jacobins. All this kind of thing. But I write of Pauline's adventures and she trips through the pages, drawing the characters around her from the shade into the light. She is safe and satisfied with her work.'

'A strange thing to do, write a story half true half made up. Is it finished?'

'I have nearly finished it, I think. The garden is all there, the waterfall, the Secret Place. She has met the Cornfords and made a kind of acquaintance with Rupert Cornford. But she has quarrelled with him now and he is gone off to France. So perhaps it is not quite finished.'

Drops of rain start to fall and he pulls a waterproof cover from underneath the driver's seat. I place it across my knee, spreading it on his knees as far as I can.

He glances down at me, rain sliding down his face. 'Would you leave me at my uncle's place?' he says. 'Can you remember? The bottom of Princess Street?'

'Yes. Yes. It's on my way.'

The roaring of the storm takes away our voices, but through the noise and the wet I am very conscious of him, his shoulder and the length of his thigh beside me. Outside the jeweller's shop he thrusts the reins into my hands and with one leap he is gone from my sight. I slide Seal under the blanket and wearily lift the reins on the horse who raises her head and plods patiently on in the rain.

Ruth has a fine supper ready for us. She seems surprised that Rhys is early from work. He roars heartily at the tale of Seal winning her race and tells me I should enter her myself in races. I shake my head. 'She's not a money-making machine, she's a . . . a . . . person. I wouldn't put her to run a race any more than I would put you to run one.'

'But aren't I in another race, Theo? The race to make Berriman's the best ironmonger's in the North?'

Ruth meets my glance and shrugs. I suppose this eager work-fiend is hardly the boy she married. He tucks into his meal with gusto and I note, from his lengthening jowl and his thickening waist, that he is looking more the affluent tradesman than ever before.

'And will Caspar stay? Will he work at the pit?' he asks with his mouth full.

'I asked him that, but Edward refuses to put a good word in for him at White Pool, just as he refuses to share his lodgings with him more than a few days. They are not close. Not these days.'

'You can hardly blame Edward,' says Ruth. 'I'd not like Caspar under my roof either. All that drinking and gambling.' She sounds uncharacteristically prim.

Rhys unhooks his linen napkin from his waistcoat and sits back. 'If I didn't know Ruth better, I'd say that she had a soft spot for old Edward,' he says complacently.

I look from one to the other. There seems to be some game going on between them. Ruth's eyes flash dangerously but she replies sweetly enough. 'Your family is my family, dearest. Even Edward, for whom you seem to have an unwarranted dislike. He's well liked in the town. He is a hard worker. A caring man, they say.'

Rhys winks at me. 'Ah, but the town, and you, dearest Ruth, don't know this caring man like I do, or like Theo here knows him. Tell Ruth what an odious creature he is, our Edward. Go on, Theo.'

I'm saved from answering this by Beattie clashing through the door with an empty tray, her dark looks letting me know that my extra presence has delayed her home-going for at least an hour.

Later, we're just about to repair to our beds when the doorbell rings. Tension sharpens the air in the room; late callers are unusual. To my great surprise Rhys ushers James Lytton into the little sitting room. 'A caller for you, Theo. It seems Mr Lytton has a package for you.'

My confusion is covered by introducing him to Ruth, who mentions that she has seen his performances with the Priorton Orchestra. 'Perhaps I shouldn't say it, Mr Lytton, but your playing is in a different class from these scrapers and puffers who make up our little band.'

'They are very earnest, Mrs Maichin. Good souls.'

She laughs heartily at this. 'Good souls! No greater insult could you give them, Mr Lytton. No greater insult.' She touches the silver teapot, which is cold now. 'Would you care for tea, Mr Lytton?'

'No thank you, Mrs Maichin.' He turns to me; I can feel my jaw so very hard and a slight pain in my back. I sit rigid as a poker.

'The instrument, Mrs Gervase. I have brought you your violin. I thought you'd like it with you for your return to Goshawk Shield.' James Lytton places the violin gently on the sofa beside me. 'It is in full working order now. The string is repaired.' He smiles easily at my brother and sister-in-law. 'Mrs Gervase took a fancy to it in my uncle's shop, but the string needed adjusting.'

I cannot protest or thrust the thing back at him. Not in

front of these two. I put a hand on it. 'Thank you, Mr Lytton. I will treasure it. Is there a charge?'

He shakes his head. 'No. The original payment holds. The adjustment was only a small one. The envelope inside there will tell you of its history. You should keep it with the instrument.'

When he is gone Rhys picks up the case and opens it. Ruth clucks over the violin. ' A very fine instrument. He makes them himself?'

'So he tells me.' I'm trying to stay calm. 'Though I have no way of finding out if this is so.'

'Have you known him a long time, Theo?' says Rhys, his voice flat and calm.

I shake my head. 'Just once in the shop when I bought it, and then today. The . . . er . . . string. They kept it to fix it.' I leave it like that, appearing, I hope, to lose interest in the topic. Later, having said my goodnights, I stand in my bedroom and open the case again. The wood is like silk under my finger. Seal stands on the bed watching me with her wise eyes. The smell of shellac permeates the still air of the room. The tacky newness of the instrument shines out. A letter sticks out of a pocket in the velvet lining. There are three sheets. Two of them are notes and designs regarding the making of the instrument. *Maker James Lytton Esq., Newcastle*. The third sheet is a letter to me.

Theo.

This was made for you so you must have it. One day, no matter how distant, I will play it for you and you will hear how sweet it sounds.

'Now that was a strange thing.' Rhys Maichin sat up in his bed, watching his wife brush her hair in preparation for its night-time plaiting.

'What was a strange thing?'

'That fellow bringing Theo the violin.'

'She had bought it from him.'

'She can't play the violin. Nor can anyone up there in the wilds, unless it is the old woman. Certainly not that idiot Theo has taken on for a husband.'

'It's a whim. Your sister is the sort to have whims. Marrying the idiot was a whim.' Ruth tied a yellow ribbon to the loose plait, threw off her dressing gown and slid into bed beside him. She touched his shoulder and ran a hand down his cheek. 'Perhaps they are in love. Your sister and the violin-maker.'

Rhys pulled away slightly. 'She is married.'

Ruth laughed. 'You cannot call that a marriage. Your sister is as pure as the driven snow.'

'And you would know that?' said Rhys sulkily.

'A woman knows these things.' She edged closer to him. 'And who is to blame her, looking for . . . fulfilment? She has a husband who, to all appearances, is a child.'

Rhys turned away from her, heaving the blanket to his shoulder. 'I must sleep, Ruth. I have an early start in the morning and this has been a long day.'

She turned down the bedside lamp and slid further down the bed. She closed her eyes and breathed deeply to allay the depth of her disappointment, to dull the craving she felt at the very base of her stomach. Never mind, she consoled herself. Tomorrow is another day. More important, tomorrow afternoon was Beattie's afternoon off.

'They say you're a councillor now, Ed?' Caspar put his boots on Edward's fender and watched the steam drift upwards, then into the chimney as the soles dried off.

'They say right.' Edward was fiddling with his new pipe, a gift from Claris Carmedy. He tapped down the tobacco, then applied a paper spill to get it alight, sucking and puffing as the surface of the tobacco began to glow.

'Good, is it, being a councillor? Telling folks what to do?'

'It's hard work. But, seeing as you ask, you do have your finger in some very important pies. You get to see how things run, even get a say in them.'

'That'll suit you. Always liked to run things, didn't you, Ed?'

Edward had the pipe drawing now. 'Someone has to do it. There's plenty of lazy folks around won't offer to do a thing. Moan about the work. Say they do enough work at the pit or in the shop.'

'Aye. And I can see you'd make a good fist of it, Ed.'

Ed peered at the bowl of the pipe. He took a good draw on it then coughed. He had tears in his eyes when he finally spoke again to Caspar. 'What is it you want, Caspar, wheedling round like this? Spit it out.'

'I want a job, like I told you, Ed. Think again, won't you? Put a word in for me at White Pool and I'll be no bother, I swear it.'

Edward shook his head. 'Impossible.'

'Ah go on, Ed. I want to stop my wandering, I promise you. I'll be as good as gold. Things here've quietened down a lot. Gamblers dispersed, I promise you.'

They both looked hard at Caspar's steaming boots for a while. Caspar picked them off the fender and pulled them on, lacing them tight. Then Edward tapped the bowl of his pipe on the fender. 'I thought there was work up there in the dale with the lead miners. You could live up there with Theo and Mother. Keep an eye on them. Seemed like a good scheme. They shouldn't be there on their own.'

Caspar shook his head. 'They shuffled me out fast as they could, Ed. And that's such a big, grand house. They want for nothing, the pair of them. Mean, grasping they are. Worse now Theo has the upper hand. Anyway, that lead mine was a grim place. Wet. The people like damp moles from under the ground. Not like coal miners at all. I'd rather go on the parish.'

Edward gave up on his pipe and put it on the mantelpiece. 'The parish?' He shook his head. 'There is a councillor who's manager at White Leas pit, near New Morven. I'll put a word in there for you, if you like. You can live across in New Morven. Lots of houses empty there since they moved the ironworks across to the coast.'

Caspar grinned and stood up, hopping about a bit, his soles burned by his overheated boots. 'Good man, Edward. I'll be off your hands in a wink.' He paused. 'So what do you do, Edward, apart from the pit, the church and the council? No lady in your life?' he said cheekily.

Edward swallowed the words which would have put his brother in his place. Instead he said, 'There are lots of ladies who are dying to be in my life, Cas. Every day it is intimated to me . . . but no. Women require rings and allegiance. A millstone round a man's neck.'

Cas, catching the flavour, was emboldened. 'And what do you think of Rhys's wife? Haughty madam that one, look you.'

Edward blinked at him. 'Ruth? I know nothing about her,' he said slowly. 'She is quite a clever woman, I am told. No beauty, I grant you.'

Caspar poked the fire. 'Cold as a block of ice, I'd say. I'd pity poor Rhys if he wasn't such a pompous bastard.' He awaited the tirade from his pious brother at his language, but when he looked back at Edward his glance was far away; it seemed he had not heard.

Edward sat down as always on the chaise longue and accepted the cup of American coffee Ruth had made with her own hands. 'So inconvenient, Beattie having this afternoon off,' she said, lowering her lids over her long eyes. 'Now, Edward, tell me the gossip about those powermongers on the council, those old hypocrites in the chapel.'

He stared at her for a moment, then shook his head. He patted the horsehair sofa beside him and said, 'Sit here, won't you, Ruth?' The sun behind him created a halo of his fair hair. His pale eyes pierced her. His hand reached towards her.

Obediently, she sat beside him.

He took her hands in his, first one then the other, and squeezed them hard. He leaned forward. 'What you really want, Ruth, is . . .' he whispered in her ear.

She blushed, but she did not struggle.

'Say yes to this?' he said.

She shook her head.

'Say yes!' he commanded again.

She smiled slightly, loving the risk, enjoying the dare.

Then he pushed her hands behind her, held them in a tight grip with one hand and forced her hard back on to the couch with the other. His kiss was deliberate, even cold, bruising her lips with his teeth. But she could not deny the flood of feeling that started at the nape of her neck and ended up at her heels.

Still holding her tight he looked round. 'Now where shall we make ourselves at home in this comfortable house of yours? Will you show me?'

She shook her head, her eyes gleaming.

'Shall I drag you?'

She nodded, a smile showing at the very corner of her mouth. Now the game would begin.

Twenty-three

Storm Clouds

When I returned from Priorton Mrs Gervase was not well, not well at all. She had been fragile for some while, but now she began to lose track of time, sometimes she even lost track of her words. She slept many more hours in the day than she was awake. In the following few weeks the doctor rode up to Goshawk Shield every other day. Mrs Gervase dealt with him very well, as her equal, even her inferior. In her lucid times she had all her old authority. But her skin was pale, almost translucent, and each day her eyes seemed to become bigger and brighter in her face.

She insisted that the routines of the house remained the same. Susan Cornford was brought in her cot to gurgle and spit in the sunshine streaming through the bay windows. From time to time Mrs Gervase put a frail blue-veined hand to touch the plump hand of the child. Grey skin beside pink.

I read to Mrs Gervase each day at the usual time. A troubled Stephen read bits to her from the newspaper, his brow furrowed from the effort. Then she asked him to put her bed in the pheasant room. 'It's awful, Stevie, being stuck in that stuffy bedroom all day!'

Rose Clare and I took turns sitting with her in the Pheasant Room through the night. She insisted that the curtains be left open so that the night sky, the moor, the occasional glittering array of stars seemed to fill the room. On my mother's nights in attendance she built the fire up because, she said, of the draughts that invaded the room from the windows. I was aware, though, that the dark was too much for her. Too velvety and suffocating, even with the single candle we allowed ourselves for illumination.

But me, although I kept the fire in, I left it low and sputtering so that the dark could envelop Mrs Gervase and me, its embrace as engulfing and as natural as that of the sea.

'Can you say the Lord's Prayer, Theo?' Her voice is strong and clear.

It is my night to sit with her. The fire, low and dropping, fills the air with the smell of burned pine cones. The darkness of the moor is all around us and above it the piercing glitter of the stars, in immaculate formation in the night sky. I am sitting at a small table writing by the light of a single candle.

'Can you, Theo? Say the Lord's Prayer?'

I make my way across to her. 'Yes, I can. That and the Twenty-third Psalm, if you like.'

She puts her hand on the crocheted coverlet. 'Say them for me. Say them both.'

I kneel by the bed and say them in the firmest voice I can find. 'Our Father . . .' My words go out through the panes of glass across the moors and up, up into the sky where now the moon and the stars have vanished behind gun-metal cloud. My voice fades and I think she is fast asleep, but when I move to stand up her hand clutches me still.

'Would you like me to send Stephen to get the rector, Mrs Gervase?' She is worrying me now.

She shakes my hand. 'I know that my Redeemer liveth, Theo. I know it. I would not be my father's daughter, my dear father's daughter, else. He came, you know.'

'Who came?'

'My father.'

'When?'

'Last night . . . the night before . . . I cannot remember when. He knelt there where you kneel now and told me of his Father's place, which has so many mansions.'

'Well, he would know, Mrs Gervase, wouldn't he? Being a clergyman.'

'Your mother too, she was here saying rosaries, so I am well looked after.'

'A rosary? I thought she'd lost her rosary. My brother Edward took it from her.'

'You don't lose such things. You should know better than that. I loved him, you know. Loved him with my heart. With all my heart. The love of my life.' Her voice is a mere breath on the air, the hand which clutches me a fragile claw.

'Who? Stephen? You love Stephen?'

'No. My father. He was so good. Such a good man. We were so happy.' She seems to doze again but now I dare not move. I want to go and shout for my mother, for Stephen, but I dare not.

Her eyes snap open. 'Stephen too! I love him. Do you love him, Theo?'

'Yes. Yes.' It is true. I do love him. 'He is a fine person.'

'He has been a great companion to me, just as I was a great companion to my father.' The hand clutches harder. 'Take care of him, Theo.'

'Always,' I say. And I mean it. I am engulfed with sadness at the stumbling departure of this fine old soul. The hand clutches me again, pulls me nearer. 'I want you in this room,' she whispers.

'I am in here, beside you, Mrs Gervase.'

'No. After. You must bring your table here. Your stories.'

Now there are tears in my eyes. 'You can't say this.'

The claw-like hand grasps my sleeve and shakes it. 'Do as you're told, girl.' The voice is firm, like the voice I first heard on the train.

She has survived another day. The rector comes in the morning and we can hear his booming reassurances from the hall outside. Ten minutes later, with much bustling and many bland words, he goes off in his carriage, made muddy by the farm tracks.

It is much later in the morning when we are all gathered in the pheasant room. Stephen is tending the fire, carefully piling coal on coal, one by one. My mother is by the bed, a bowl of bread and milk in her hands. Susan Cornford is sleeping peacefully by the bed, in the birchwood cot made for her by Stephen. Seal is sitting on the bed, and Mrs Gervase is stroking her. I am standing by the window looking across the moor. A shimmering veil of grey cloud is moving swiftly from the tops down towards the Goshawk boundary. I shake my head. 'Isn't it wonderful how you can see weather here, moving towards you minutes before it happens. Look at this cloud. Just look!'

My mother stands up. Stephen heaves himself to his feet and comes across to the window, shovel in hand. We watch the weather come, feel the patter of ever heavier rain on the yard, the thunderous reverberation as it hits the great roof of Goshawk Shield. Then as quickly as it comes it departs and we can see sun again, glittering white on the steel-grey of the horizon.

'It's so beautiful!' I say. There are tears in my eyes.

Then Seal barks her small yelping bark and we look towards the bed. She is licking Mrs Gervase's creased powdery cheek. My mother walks quickly to the bed and closes the old woman's eyes. 'She's gone,' she says. 'Gone from us. A lovely way to go, so 'tis. No struggle. So very quiet. The old lady is gone.'

319

Stephen stands by the bed. 'Mama,' he says. 'Mama!' He touches her shoulder. 'Wake up. Mama, wake up!'

I swallow hard and go to take his arm. 'She has gone, Stephen. Gone to sleep always.'

He shakes his massive head. 'Mama will wake in the morning. She will wake then.'

I search my mind desperately. 'The cloud,' I say at last. 'We were looking at the cloud. Remember? The cloud came down and swept your real mama up to heaven with it. All you see in the bed is your mama's shell. Like the shell of an egg when it is broken and the chicken steps out.'

He looks down at the body. 'Mama's shell,' he says.

'Yes. Your real mama is in heaven.' As I say the words I don't even know that they are true. I am a heathen compared with my mother, who is kneeling by the bed muttering the very ancient prayers. I am a heathen even compared with Edward who is the bad one and has thoughts of purgatory. But I am pleased with the idea of the cloud coming to take her. It satisfies me. I think of the sea taking Ellen Jones and the baby inside her. The sea, like the cloud, is a natural thing, coming to comfort and nurture its own.

Stephen rubs his hands down his trousers. 'I have a box for her. In the back of the shed. I have a box for when she goes to heaven. She told me to make it. She drew it for me. Said when she went to heaven she would need a box. It will need the last polish. I will do that. I will polish it.' He walks heavily to the door and closes it behind him.

Mrs Berriman senior put on her outdoor mittens and pulled her outdoor hat on top of the linen cap she wore in the shop. Rhys looked up from his ledger in surprise. The old woman never left early. 'Is there something wrong, Grandmother Berriman?'

'Wrong? Not a thing, my dear. Nothing at all. You just

keep adding those columns till they balance. I have an errand. Sure, I'll be back in a blink of your eyelid.' She swept off in a swirl of dust and lavender.

Ruth was waiting for her in the dark interior of the railway station buffet, a brown earthenware teapot standing before her. 'Now then, Grandma! A mysterious note! An assignation! Tell no one!' she said brightly. 'What is this?'

The old woman handed her coat to a hovering waitress and settled herself comfortably in the wooden seat. 'Will you pour the tea, Ruthie?'

Ruth poured carefully, eyeing her grandmother with an amusement edged with caution. 'So what is it, Grandma?'

Mrs Berriman lifted her cup and stared at the steaming liquid. 'You have a caller, Ruthie,' she said slowly. 'Wednesday afternoons. Fair, tall. A man, naturally. He calls every Wednesday.'

Ruth kept her face perfectly smooth. 'What's this, Grandma? You've had your spies on me, have you?'

'This is a small town, Ruthie. The woman who lives opposite you used to make my hats for me before her hands became too stiff. She was in the shop buying a new fireguard and just happened to mention how well you had settled in Victoria Road. And how very popular you were. So many callers. But just one, regular as the ticking of a clock, on Wednesday afternoons.' She sipped her tea. 'I'm supposing young Beattie has Wednesday afternoon off, like she did when she worked for us on the Avenue?'

'You know she does.'

'Who is it?' said the old woman, placing her cup none too gently in its saucer.

'Have you spoken of this with Rhys, Grandma? If so . . .'

Mrs Berriman shook her head so vigorously that a lock of her carelessly pinned grey hair escaped from her hat and landed on her lined forehead. 'There is so much to be lost

here, Ruth. Nothing to be gained. Who is he? Who is this . . .
interloper?'

Ruth tried to laugh. 'Grandma, it's only Rhys's brother
Edward. He works shifts and he preaches on Sunday. It is the
only time . . .' She stared at her grandmother but it was Ruth
who dropped her gaze first.

'And does Rhys know? Surely Rhys would like to see
his brother?'

'They are not well suited. They are bad friends.'

'If Rhys is bad friends with his brother, then you must be
also.'

'I can choose my own friends, man or woman. My woman
friends visit me, why not my brother-in-law?'

The old woman put a lace-mittened hand over that of her
granddaughter. 'You know this is silly talk, Ruth. It is not
possible and must be discontinued. You didn't know what
you were doing. Word is not yet really out into the town about
it. It can be mended now.'

'Can it?' Ruth stared into her empty cup. She knew
perfectly well what she was doing. What she had done. Married
one brother on a whim and playing perverse games with
another on a soft Wednesday afternoon. Her marriage might
just be as misbegotten and mistaken as that of her sister-in-
law who had married the idiot.

'It must be mended, child,' said the old woman sadly. 'Rhys
is a very good boy, you know.'

'Grandma!' said Ruth suddenly. 'Did you . . . were you
ever . . .?' The words stayed in the air between them.

Mrs Berriman sat very still for a moment. 'There is so much
energy, Ruthie. We have so much energy. Hearth and home
are not enough for the likes of you and me. That's why I went
to the forge, to the shop to work, to get rid of all that energy.
There is excitement, life there. Fire, in more ways than one.
You should come too. Sure, it will blow some of those

dangerous cobwebs out of that head of yours.'

The following week, to her mother's great dismay, Ruth Maichin went to work in the forge. She sat by her father in his office, by her grandmother at the till, and began to accompany Rhys on his rounds. Her father was delighted, but Rhys did not take too kindly to the perpetual presence of his wife at his workplace. He liked her at home, playing the good wife.

Even while Ruth teased Rhys about this, mocked him that he had fallen for her because she was *not* one of those home-bodies, Ruth worried that, for the first time in her life, she had stepped out of her depth. Oh, she had always *liked* to stray: from her father into the arms of the gypsy and now from Rhys into the arms of his brother! But the gypsy, hard as he was, was in no way as bad as Edward. Not half so threatening.

Yes. Her grandmother was right. Hard work at the forge was an attractive retreat from these dangerous games. Rhys's gentle worship might not stir her to such heights as his brother, but she had grown to like him very much. To love him, in her own way. In fact she liked him more than anyone she had ever known.

The retired milliner who lived opposite the Maichins saw the young fair man knocking in vain at their door. She reported back to her cronies that someone had nipped that in the bud, and a good thing too, even if the young man in question was a preacher. And a councillor too, so they said.

The funeral was a small affair. Just my mother and Stephen and I, and Sadie Gomersall with baby Susan on her hip. The baby likes Sadie; is quiet and smiling in her presence. The doctor came on his big chestnut horse which he tethered at the church gate; the rector stood before us uttering words about a life well lived, and a devoted daughter, a loving wife and a loyal mother. No hymns were sung and later we stood by the open grave in the blistering cold, listening to further words of majestic condolence.

Small announcements in the *Priorton Chronicle* and the Leeds and Carlisle papers brought forth letters on stiff paper laden with sympathy and commiseration. These letters, addressed to Mr and Mrs Stephen Gervase, gave me a jolt, reminding me yet again of the impact of this fragile, determined old woman on my life.

One letter was written on much thinner paper. It was addressed to Mrs S. Gervase only. It said simply: *My thoughts are with you*, and was signed James Lytton. I went to my bedroom and opened the violin case and took out the violin. The strings were loose but I flicked the wonderful, waisted shape with my finger and it resonated for a moment with a melodic *thrumm*. That was when I cried. I cried for Stephen. I think I cried for my old brave friend. But mostly, I think, I cried for myself.

Stephen came and found me like that and then he started to cry as well. He continued to cry for three days and nights. He cried like a child, without disguise, his hands by his side, tears dropping from his eyes, till I was sick of the sight and sound of tears.

In the end I was cross. I was very severe with Stephen; I told him to wash his face and feed the horses and then come back because I had a job for him. In my voice I could hear the ire, the faint desperation of Mrs Gervase when her son finally exasperated her too much with his childish obsessions.

Stephen shuffled his feet, heaved a deep sigh and plodded off towards the scullery.

'Sure, there's no need to talk to the poor feller like that,' said Rose Clare from the corner of the kitchen table where she was spooning oatmeal into the glossy pink mouth of Susan Cornford. Since Mrs Gervase's death the child seems to have got beyond her pure baby self, and is looking at the world with eyes too wise for her months.

'So how would you stop all that blubbering?' I said crossly. 'He's like a fountain.'

'Sure, they'll dry up when they're ready,' said Rose Clare calmly.

'Mother, he's been crying for three days. There's a tear factory in there.'

Her spoon arrested in her hand, she said, 'It's a hard woman y'are, Theo. A hard woman.' There was a faint smile on her face.

I slammed the door behind me and made my way to the pheasant room. Seal was there, sitting on the window seat looking out at the garden and the moor beyond. She had kept guard there since Mrs Gervase was carried out in her box. The bed was still in its place, stripped bare except for a rug across its flock mattress. It looked like an alien insect in this room of velvet and glass.

The decision came to me as clearly as if Olivia Gervase had reminded me herself. Hadn't she told me to do it? I went softly from the room, followed by Seal, who was barking now with excitement. I called Stephen from the kitchen. 'Come on, Stevie! We have work to do.'

As soon as we started to dismantle the bed, his tears started to flow again. I took his arm and shook it. 'Stop!' I commanded. 'Stop crying. Your mama would not wish it. She would wish you to stop crying while we move this bed back to her bedroom. We can make it up again for her there.'

In the bedroom we made up the bed again and dressed it with sheets and pillows. When we were finished Stephen surveyed it. 'Now I will light a fire in here,' he said. 'She would be cold.'

'Yes,' I said. 'But you can do that afterwards. First I want you to help me lift my writing table into the pheasant room. Your mama told me to do this, Stephen. She told me that after she went to heaven I had to put my writing table in the pheasant room and do my writing there.'

His face brightened for the first time in weeks. 'Will you write stories again?'

'Yes. I think I will.' My mind was whirling on now. The story about the Frenchwoman first, then another big one! Perhaps with a younger, imagined Olivia at the centre: a young woman devoted to her father but enticed away by a young clergyman who was temporarily attached to her father's parish . . .

In an hour the room is set up. My table stands in the centre draped with the velvet cloth, its pens and papers neatly stacked. Some useful books are lined up in the revolving bookcase which Stephen made for me. Here, unlike the dining room, the light streams in from every angle.

My mother stands beside me, surveying the bright space. 'I don't know how you could work here. The place where Mrs Gervase . . .'

'She told me to do this. She'll look over me. Bless me if you like,' I said. 'I'm sure of that.'

I don't really know what Stephen thinks of it and at the moment I don't really care. I want to take possession.

Mrs Gervase has been as good as her word and has confirmed her promise to me in her will. Half of the estate is held in trust and administered by her solicitor until I have been married to Stephen for three years. After that it will be wholly mine whatever I do. Already I have made up my mind that three years would make no difference. My real pledge with Mrs Gervase has become a lifetime's pledge.

She was a very clever woman. She knew that once I took Stephen on I would not leave him. I do not love him as a husband: he is more precious than that. I love him as you love a child who adores you and by that very adoration binds you to him with bonds of steel.

So I have set to work in the pheasant room. I sometimes feel Pauline de Carrière sitting beside me, her voice in my ear. What with her in one corner, Mrs Gervase in the other and Seal's wise eyes gleaming at me from the hearthrug, I am surrounded by ghosts. But the Frenchwoman's story is telling itself. The pages slip away under my hand one by one: they are a pleasure to write. Stephen often sits here by the fire with some small toy he is carving for Susan. He stares into the flames and whittles away. Occasionally he will heave a sigh which seems to come from his boots, but I ignore him and carry on writing. As each chapter is completed I read it to him and we walk the paths and avenues of the garden which were hacked out by Pauline's hand. We stand on the little cliff which overlooks the waterfall and the lagoon. We pick our way through to her secret places.

Stephen has became as familiar with the Frenchwoman as he is with my mother or Sadie Gomersall. It is as though in inventing Pauline de la Carrière I am giving him another ancestor – a fresh Cornford – to replace his own mother.

The story completed, I write to Miss Bell of *Judith's Journal* and ask her advice. I need someone in that arcane world of letters, which is as distant from me as a star in the sky. I need a name, someone to whom I can send the story.

I read the letter out to Stephen, and show him one of Mrs Gaskell's novels from the shelves of the dining room. *North and South*. 'It will be like this, Stephen. Hundreds, even thousands of people have this book on their shelves, just as I have it on my shelf. And they will have my story on their shelves too. *The Frenchwoman's Garden*.'

He claps his hands. 'Mrs Gaskell writes her stories and you write yours. Mrs Gervase writes *The Frenchwoman's Garden*. On thousands of shelves. Bravo, Theo. Bravo!'

I find myself blushing now, at my presumption and his

enthusiasm. I reach up to kiss his round cheek. 'But that is a secret, Stevie! A secret between you and me. Don't forget now!'

'I will remember, Theo. A secret between you and me.'

Twenty-four

A Child in the Family

Susan Cornford is sitting up these days, holding her fat arms out to anyone who passes. My mother lets her play now on the kitchen floor. She rolls across, fast as lightning, if offered some sweet thing or enticement. Stephen puts her on his shoulder and walks out to the barn with her. There he sits her on the back of the somnolent Samson, or lets her ride 'horsey' on the stall. They are good friends.

One day he comes back without the child and we have a wild run across the farmyard to find her bawling her head off in Samson's manger. She is naked, her clothes draped across the beams. Stephen smiles at me. 'Susan wanted a bath,' he says.

Unfortunately Sadie Gomersall is working at Goshawk and it is she who gets to Susan Cornford first. She picks up the baby and soothes her, grumbling away to my mother who is close behind her. 'It's not right, Mrs Maichin. He shouldn't get his hand on the child. It's not right.' But Susan Cornford has come to no harm and I explain very carefully to Stephen that this must not happen again.

Later in the day Sadie Gomersall returns to the house, her mother puffing and blowing alongside her, with her very large brother behind. My mother and I are in the kitchen with

Stephen, teaching him how to play gin rummy. The Gomersall family crowd even this large space. I stand up and, tall as I am, I am dwarfed by these people. My mother is behind me, Susan Cornford in her arms. Stephen still sits at the table, putting the cards in neat piles.

'What is it?' I say.

'We're come for the bairn,' says Mrs Gomersall. Her voice, sullen and low, is like lead in the still air of the room. Behind me Susan Cornford yelps as my mother grips her tighter, retreating further into the corner.

I shake my head. 'Why would that be, Mrs Gomersall? Why would you want the child now when you wanted her in the workhouse not so long ago?'

The woman glances at her daughter.

Sadie blushes. 'It's Stephen, Mrs Gervase. Stephen shouldn't have his hands on her. Look what happened just this morning.'

'That was an accident. A bit of forgetfulness. It could happen in any family.'

The brother speaks up. 'Yon's not fit. Not fit to be out.' He glowers at Stephen.

Stephen, who seems just to notice them, stands up, the chair falling back behind him. 'Reuben Gomersall!' he says, smiling his delight. 'What a long time it's been since you were up at Goshawk. Last spring, or was it the spring before, when we had the sheep?'

Mrs Gomersall exchanges glances with her son, who leaps forward and has Stephen by the jacket in a second. He brings his head back and butts Stephen in the face, like a goat. Stephen is on the floor and the man is astride him punching him in the face with big hammy fists.

'Go on, get him, Reuben!' Mrs Gomersall shrieks. 'Not fit to be in a decent household. A perversity.'

Reuben. I should have realised. He is the one. Reuben.

The one who forced himself on Mavis Gomersall like Edward tried to force himself on me. The shock which has turned me to stone now melts to nothing and I reach for the longest and heaviest of the fire irons and take a step towards Reuben, where he is kneeling on Stephen, beating the lights out of him. I grab the farm lad's greasy hair and pull back his head. He sets still a second, then starts to struggle. I bring the iron right on to his cheek. 'Just stop that, will you?' I look up at Sadie and her mother who are uneasy now, moving towards me. I raise the fire iron. 'I will belt him so hard that his face'll never be the same. I promise yer.' I say this through gritted teeth, my fine speech so carefully coached by Mrs Gervase has melted away.

Sadie scowls. 'Some lady!' she mutters. 'You!'

'Who said I was a lady?' I pull Reuben's head further back, and steady myself for the blow. 'Stephen! Get his hands!' I order. Stephen's hands come off his own bloody face and take charge of Reuben's flailing mitts. 'Tell him to leave off!' I am looking Mrs Gomersall straight in the eye. 'Tell him!'

'It's not right, that lunatic having charge of a child, Ah tell yer. Not right,' says Sadie again.

'Get up, Reuben. Leave him,' the old woman mutters.

Reuben half stands up and Stephen scrambles from beneath him. I still have his hair, Stephen still hangs on to his wrists. I pull his head down at an awkward angle. 'Now tell them.' I thrust the poker in his face. 'Tell them about Mavis. Tell them it was no sheep-shearer got her with child.'

'I knaa nowt about what yer sayin',' he growls, but the corner of his lips puckers to a smile.

I pull back the poker, fully determined to smack that smirking face.

'Theo!' my mother's voice warns me from the corner of the room where she is sheltering with Susan Cornford. 'Sure there's no point in injuring the poor feller, is there? To be

331

sure his mammy must know that this poor child here is a family affair, no outsider involved. Mavis told me so herself. Plain as the nose on your face, 'tis.'

Reuben stops struggling and I can hear a gasp of protest from Sadie. But as I look at Mrs Gomersall's dour countenance I see no flash of surprise. There is, more, a flicker of relief.

'Come away, Reuben,' she grunts. 'We got carried away, some. Come away. Let him go, missis.' She looks me in the eye.

I release his hair. 'Let go, Stephen. Let the man go.' Stephen lets his hands drop and Reuben leaps away.

Mrs Gomersall is already at the door. 'Coom on, lad.'

Sadie is looking from one to the other. 'Reuben! I . . .'

'Coom on, lass.' Her mother raps out the order. 'Thee's the byre to see to.'

Then the kitchen is free of them and seems very empty. My mother comes out of her corner. 'Poor Sadie,' she says. 'Sure, she knew not a thing about all that.'

'The mother knew, you could tell.'

She shakes her head. 'What mother would stand for that?' she says.

I stare at her and think about Edward's cruelty to me when I was a little girl. How I could say nothing? 'Some mothers never know,' I say. 'They are not told or they do not see.' She blushes at me and I hope she is remembering when she thrust me away from Edward, the night I heard him slapping her from the room above. But still she says nothing.

Stephen is heaving himself from the floor. The blood dripping from his cut eye and his nose is mixing freely with the tears which are pouring down his face. 'I am bad!' he says. 'I am such a bad person. An idiot. I am very, very bad. The punishment is just.'

I drag him to the table and make him sit down. There, he

puts his head in his hands and sobs. I lift my eyes to my mother. 'All this is so hard.'

She stares at me a second before she speaks. 'Well, didn't you take it all on "for better for worse"? Sure this is the bit they call "the worse".'

Later, when we have bathed Stephen's cuts and packed him and Susan Cornford off to bed, my mother and I have a quiet few moments by the fire. She sits stitching a red pinafore for Susan Cornford; I sit with Seal curled up on my knee.

'We need to make Susan ours properly,' I say.

'Oh. Have no fear, they'll not be back. You showed them the door.'

I shake my head. 'For one moment I thought they would grab her from us, and we'd have no redress.'

'Redress? Now that's a fine word.'

'We will go to Priorton and get a lawyer to arrange it properly.'

She shakes her head. 'Not without some kind of permission from the Gomersalls. Paper, you need. Proper paper.'

There is a rattle on the back-door sneck and out of the night comes Sadie Gomersall, bonnet on one side, sporting a black eye and weighed down on one side with a heavy bundle. 'I've come to stay,' she says.

I stand up. 'What?'

'Sorry for causing a ruckus this afternoon. Really I am. Got the wrong end of the stick, seems like. That Reuben! I could kill him. To think of him and our Mavis . . . Now Polly, if I ain't mistaken.'

'What makes you think you can stay here? A while ago you were calling Stephen an idiot and me anything but a lady.'

She hangs her head, and her bonnet slips further down the side. I struggle with this great desire to laugh. I keep my lips prim. Then Sadie heaves a great big sigh. 'I'll say sorry to Stephen and sorry again to you. Wrong end of the stick it was. I feel . . . like . . . protective over the little one and . . . our Mavis you know . . .'

'Ah, let the girl stay,' says my ma from her place by the hearth. 'Doesn't she have real feeling for young Susan no matter how she's been mistaken over poor old Stevie?'

Sadie looks at me again with such a hangdog expression that this time I do laugh. 'Oh come in, Sadie. Hang your coat up and come for a warm.' I resume my seat.

'I'll work for my keep, honest I will,' she says.

'So you will,' says Rose Clare. 'This house eats work like a starving dog its food.'

I wait till Sadie's settled. 'We were just saying we'll need some signed paper from your family about Susan Cornford. I want her ours by law. We had a shaking this afternoon.'

She shakes her head doubtfully. 'There's sense in that, making it legal. I can't see . . . don't trust papers, none of them.' Then she brightens. 'There is one way. Bitter about that house, my da is. Talks about it being three hundred years in his family and still not his own.'

'What? Buy Susan Cornford for the price of a house?'

She shrugs. 'A notion! One way to be certain to my mind. If you want to be that certain.'

So Susan Cornford becomes ours for the price of Bittern Crag Farm. Sadie acts as the go-between and I write the two contracts out in my best hand. One paper talks about the farm and its outbuildings, though not the land. (The Gomersalls must still rent this from us). The other paper mentions an agreement that Mr and Mrs Stephen Gervase should adopt Susan Cornford Gomersall.

Of course the Priorton lawyer chuckles at the simplicity of my papers. It all becomes much more legal, with Priorton lawyers drawing up proper contracts and Mr Gomersall signing it, with much grumbling, in their office. I sign it willingly, as does Stephen when I explain that Susan Cornford will become ours to care for just as his mama cared for him. My mother is delighted and makes a celebration cake for us to eat when we return. Both Susan Cornford and Seal are wearing ribbons filched from the summer hats of Mrs Gervase.

When I am in Priorton to see the lawyer I call at the house in Victoria Road. Rhys is out on his travels, but Ruth is in. She is full of beans. The house is dusty but she talks of the shop and the forge and how much her mother dislikes her daughter working in this position, which rather adds to its charm for Ruth.

Sadly, since taking a beating from Reuben, Stephen has had attacks of melancholy as bad or even worse than when his mother died. He has ceased his carving altogether and will not read the newspaper. He seems frightened of Susan Cornford and will not settle in any room where she is. Worst of all he has taken to sleeping in his mother's bedroom. He pretends he is not doing this, but all the household knows about it. For such a kind, transparent person to deceive us he must be so sad. But it would be unkind to burst in on him in the middle of the night to prove that it is so. I do not want to make him seem like a fool to himself. Mrs Gervase spent the whole of her time with him saving him from making a fool of himself to others.

The painstaking process of making the final copies of the Frenchwoman's story is making my fingers and back ache, so long have I to sit at the table in the pheasant room. Miss Bell has written back to me to say that normally a publisher would need three volumes even to consider a novel but the man she had thought of had seen my other stories and was prepared to look at this one with an open mind. Would I post it, or would I take it? If the latter she would be delighted to see me.

Before receiving this letter, actually going to London was the last thing I had in mind. But now the thought is burgeoning in my head like a fast-growing strawberry. Wherever I turn, another strand is sprouting.

'With child?' Edward, at the door of his lodgings, struggled to put on his coat.

'Can I come in, Edward?' said Ruth. She had waited for his sulky tirade to stop, for the fading of his injured tone on the air, and then told him her very special news.

He cast a glance into the gloom behind him. 'Not really possible, I fear. My landlady is a strictly moral person. Is that your gig? We can ride somewhere and be private.'

They were silent as they made their way along the road out of Gibsley and up towards Priorton. When they had gone three silent miles Ruth reined in and turned along a narrow road by the priory wall, finally coming to a rest under the branches of an oak tree overburdened with a very successful late summer leaf.

Edward alighted from the gig and handed her down. Then he glanced in both directions along the deserted lane. 'So, Ruth! There is a child on the way?' His voice was chilly – he was so distant from her he might as well have a brick wall around him. There was even an echo in his voice.

'Indeed there is a baby on the way.'

'And Rhys must be very delighted.'

'Rhys does not know yet.'

'Then I am honoured, dear Ruth, that I am the first to know.'

'It is your child, Edward,' she said, watching him closely.

He took a step back from here and folded his arms. She noted the purple scars on the back of his hands and black rims on the inside of his nails. No pitman could rid himself properly of these things. Stigmata. Now how had that word got into her head?

The only sign of tension about him was a slight tic on his cheek, caused by the rigidity of his jawline.

'Did you hear what I said?' she said sharply, looking into the far distance at the ring of hills which cupped Priorton with such tender care.

'I hear you, Ruth. How do you know it is mine? Couldn't it be fathered by any one of a dozen lucky fellows humming around Priorton looking for a homely hive?'

'What?' Her head went up like a questing bird.

He towered over her, then he leaned close to her. 'If you say this bastard is mine I will denounce you to Rhys, and to the valiant, smug citizens of Priorton. As well as that I will denounce you as an extortioner, an obsessive. I will not admit to being closer to you than the other side of your teapot! *Never.*'

She raised a hand to strike him, but he caught it in a painful grasp, twisting it back. 'A violent extortioner! Perhaps that would sound better.'

She pulled her hand away from him and scrambled aboard the gig. 'You're hateful, Edward Maichin. Your brother is worth twice you. You could not lick his boots.' She lashed the horse, who started and whinnied at this sudden assault, then set off at a careering gallop, rearing upwards as Ruth pulled the rein to turn him full circle and return the way he had come.

For a moment Edward watched the dust thrown up by the wheels, then put his hands in his pockets and followed the gig at a leisurely pace. Perhaps he should have let Ellen Jones live. This was much more fun.

'You must be with child.' Mrs Berriman surveyed her granddaughter's pasty face. 'If I was another kind of grandmother I would send you home on the spot.'

Ruth breathed hard, trying to stop her gorge from rising again, which would entail another rush to the little washroom at the back of the shop. 'With child?' she gulped. 'Is that what you think?'

337

Mrs Berriman nodded. 'Never more sure. How long is it since you showed?'

Ruth blushed. 'Well, I have missed twice. But I have been so busy . . .' Her eyes were wide; too innocent.

'A baby!' said Mrs Berriman. 'Thanks be! What a thought!'

Ruth hitched herself on to the stool beside her grandmother. 'Now then, these monthly stock reconciliations, how did you say you did them, Grandma?'

The old woman put her head down over her books, thinking furiously.

'With child?' Rhys's eyes swept down his wife's slim figure. 'A baby for us?'

'Yes. I think so. Grandma thinks so.'

He grinned. 'Well I never! I am bowled over. Truly bowled over!' He took her in his arms and waltzed her round the little sitting room.

'You're pleased?' she said, when she was finally allowed to stop to get her breath back.

'Yes. Yes. When?'

She blushed. 'I'm not quite sure, but it will be in the spring. I have not . . . well, you know . . . I have missed it once.' It was an easy lie.

He grinned. 'That weekend we went on the train to the sea? Then!'

She nodded. 'Then! That is most likely.'

He led her to the sofa. 'Now you must rest. You must be careful. No more forge, no more shop—'

She sat up straight and threw off his hands. 'What? You couldn't be more wrong, dear boy. Grandma was telling me that she worked in her father's shop right up to the day my father was born.'

'Oh, Ruthie. You're impossible.'

'Aren't I?' She grinned at him and kissed his nose, then

sat down opposite him. She watched him eat his dinner with his usual relish. Yes, he was the one. The safe one. The safe bet. A woman with a child needed a safe bet. And Edward Maichin, for all his magnetism, was too much of a cruel gamble for any woman. Worse than the circus man, and that was saying something.

Rhys was the one for her. No doubt about that. She could think that now, and at last she could mean it. She could.

Twenty-five

A Capital Time

London, I must tell you, is a place so full of people that it is as though all the people in the land have gathered there to do business, to pursue their fate. They heave together shoulder to shoulder on the pavements, wheel to wheel on the roads. Many of the roads are wide enough for five carriages, then they narrow to space for two, then for one. People dodge the omnibus and the tram which are like monsters at a carnival and wait for no man. In one alleyway I saw a single donkey pulling a milk churn. It had a hard time getting through; it stumbled to one side then another in weary response to its master's whip.

And the smell! Burned paraffin and soot, rotting fruit, week-old sweat, sour milk and old perfume. You have to gulp them in to forget them. It is worse even than the sooty smell of Priorton after the clean air of Stanhope. I stare like any provincial as grand ladies, dressed to almost indecent excess, are handed out of their smart carriages, I ogle at the rush of men in dark suits and high hats. I am ashamed to say that I recoil as I come up against the poor people with their overworn clothes and bare feet; greasy hats and caps and the scarves round their necks which were once bright red or blue. Am I becoming a snob? No. It is the strangeness of the place that makes me feel this way, I am sure.

And the strangest thing about this press of people is that (apart from the costers and the flower-sellers who speak to you like your sister) these individuals walk around the streets as though they are alone. They look over your shoulder or way to the side of you, never at your face.

But all this is exciting, and does not trouble me because it turns out that I have a companion. This is despite the fact that I set out alone with my bag in one hand and a heavy parcel containing the Frenchwoman's story in the other.

Stephen was very good; he understood that I should do this journey. I explained carefully to him about the people in London who would make my story into a proper book. We took proper books down from the shelf again and considered which books would be most like mine. He made me repeat several times that I promised to return as soon as I could.

He insisted on coming right down to Priorton with me so he could see me on to the train. It was he who spotted James Lytton. 'See, Theo! There is the man who makes the violins.'

I swallowed and looked towards the railyard where James Lytton, hat on back of head, was talking to a carter who had a load of wood bursting out of the canvas covering on his waggon. Before I could stop him Stephen lumbered across and shook him heartily by the hand. He almost dragged him across to see me. 'See, Theo! Here he is. The violin-maker.'

James Lytton grasped my hand in his thin strong fingers. 'Mrs Gervase. You go on a journey?'

'I . . .' My voice squeaked to a stop.

'She goes to London,' said Stephen proudly. 'She goes to take her big story so they will make it into a proper book. Like Mrs Gaskell. *Mrs Gervase*. The new writer.'

'A publisher?' James Lytton's voice was very polite. 'That is very good.'

I shook my head. 'Not exactly. Mrs Bell who has published

my stories in her magazine has arranged a meeting with a man who may publish it.'

'And you take your little dog?'

I looked down at Seal who was patiently waiting to take her seat on the train. 'I couldn't leave her. We have never been apart since I have had her – except for the time she was stolen. She takes up very little room.'

He laughed. 'One look at those soulful eyes and the publisher won't be able to resist.' He looked from her eyes into mine.

'Come on, Stephen,' I said, turning away swiftly. 'I must get on the train or it will leave without me.'

I changed trains at Darlington, and was just settling down in the empty carriage when the door opened and James Lytton leapt in. He nodded, took off his hat and placed it on the rack, and sat down opposite me. 'How good that we meet again.'

The long journey to London was a journey from darkness into light, from childhood to maturity, from isolation to companionship. And yet it was so very ordinary in a certain way.

The first hour was dedicated to polite muttering and long silences. My brain was turning and turning, rejecting the coincidence. I looked quite desperately around the empty carriage, at the closed door. Until the train stopped at York, there would be no getting out, no getting in. 'Where are you going?' I asked abruptly.

'London,' he said, stretching his long legs out before him.

'You have no luggage?' Only his hat was in the luggage net.

He took out his large silver watch. 'I just made up my mind to come an hour ago. After we spoke on Priorton platform.'

I could find nothing to say. For quite a long time the only sound we could hear was the click of the train on the rails and the rustle of my dress as, I must admit, nervously I moved my feet about on the dusty wooden floor. In the end the silence was too much to bear even for Seal. She jumped off my knee, stretched her legs in the narrow space between the seats then jumped on to James Lytton's knee.

'Seal!' I protested.

He put a protective hand on her head. 'Leave her. She's making me welcome. She is telling me I must tell the truth.' He kept his eyes on her as he stroked the fine thick fur. 'The truth is, no sooner did Mr Gervase tell me you were to go to London than I felt I must go too.'

I was grateful that his eyes were on Seal for my cheeks must have been scarlet at his admission. I could say nothing.

'And I paid the porter a handsome emolument to make sure that no one came into this carriage.'

'Mr Lytton!' I finally exploded into words.

'Would it cause you too much pain to call me James? I know we aren't much acquainted, and perhaps we never will be better acquainted. We never meet. We never will meet, in the ordinary way of things.' At last his eyes engage mine. 'And if I could call you Theo, I'd count it an honour. If not that, then I will call you Miss Maichin. I cannot bring myself to say Mrs Gervase. It is a fault in me, I know. But I can't.'

My eyes were steady on his. 'Theo is my name,' I said.

Thereupon, as the train stopped and started, stopped and started we told each other the story of our lives. After York passengers entered and left the carriage until we reached London. From their first appraisal of us they took us for travelling companions, so deeply were we in conversation.

I learned of his life. The early death in a river accident of his mother and father; his upbringing by his mother's brothers, bachelors: a maker of instruments and a silversmith. How he himself had chosen to make violins which were bought by violinists all over Europe and which won competitions for

343

the delicacy of their craftsmanship. How he liked to play occasionally in small orchestras, to keep his hand in and to allow him to test his instruments in practice. There was a deal of travelling involved. Around the Northern region. Edinburgh. London. Once or twice even Paris.

I took a breath. 'And your wife, James,' I said. 'Does she not travel with you?'

He shook his head. 'I was married once. But my wife was laid low with a fever that engulfed her for five whole days. She recovered from the fever, but it left her so frail that a year later she caught a simple chill and died.'

The grim simplicity of his words was almost too hard to bear. 'I am so sorry, James. It is very sad.'

He shook his head. 'It was twelve, thirteen years ago. You might say all my sadness has gone into my work; it has been dissipated in the fine turn on the curve of the neck, the elegance of the inlay. That is all my life consisted of for many years, till you came into my uncle's shop.'

I was embarrassed at this and, as the train was stopping at yet another station, I made a great to-do with Seal, saying that she must attend to her toilet with a quick walk to a private place on the platform.

When we returned, the carriage was full, but he had kept a place for me beside him. When he spoke, his voice was very quiet, his breath tickling my ear. 'Your turn now,' he said. 'Tell me about you.'

So then in the anonymity of a crowded carriage I told this man more about myself than I had ever told anyone. It all came tumbling out. About the sea and the salt marsh and the looming castle. I told him about the tar-paper man. I did not tell him Edward had nearly drowned me, nor that he had really drowned Ellen Jones. That would have been too much. I told him about my father who could charm the birds off the tree with one hand and steal their eggs with the other. About my mother who loved him but had spent most of her life in chill exile from Ireland, which was her heart's home.

How Susan Cornford was making a difference even to her, making her gay, young again. Then I had to tell him about Susan Cornford, omitting of course her dubious parentage. That was a secret for her alone.

'And Mrs Gervase? Stephen?' he prompted.

So I told him the story of my marriage. It sounded quite ridiculous, half whispered in the busy hum of the carriage.

'A kind of bargain?' he said, his voice quite sharp.

'She was concerned what would happen to Stephen. That they would put him in an asylum. She was a fine woman. I liked her very much in the end.'

'A hard bargain. I hope you think it worth it. You are very young to have made such a bargain.'

'The bargain was only for three years.' I paused. 'But I could not do that to Stephen. I would not do that to him. I love him.'

'Love him?' It was a gentle prompt in a stony voice.

'I love him like the dearest of brothers. I would never desert him or let them take him to one of those terrible places. Even after three years.'

'And he loves you! Anyone can see that.' His hand moved from Seal, who had again taken possession of his lap, to my arm. I looked uneasily around but the other passengers were all either sleeping or deep in their own talk.

'He trusts me,' I said miserably. 'He trusts me.'

At the next stop he took Seal for her walk and came back with a bunch of roses still wet with recent rain. 'The guard keeps a fine garden,' he whispered. 'I told him these were for my sweetheart and he gave them willingly.'

We said very little after that and I dozed off from sheer exhaustion. When I woke up his arm was through mine, and his hand was on mine, and he was fast asleep. I stayed very,

very still, for fear this wonderful moment would pass.

At King's Cross Station he was very businesslike. This place was so huge and noisy that I clutched Seal to me in a fright. It was James Lytton who told the cabman where to go and helped me down in a narrow street beside a great temple of a building which he told me was the British Museum.

'Where are we?' I said, looking along a street of tall houses illuminated by the glow-worm light of a few street lamps.

'This is Montague Street. There are lodgings here, where I stay when I come to London. Mrs Muswelhome. She will find a corner for us.'

'Us?' I said. Seal yelped as I clutched her even harder.

He glanced up and down the deserted street then touched – just touched – my cheeks. 'It is the most proper house, Theo. Mrs Muswelhome is a most proper woman.'

So it proved. The niche she found for me was a small bedroom close to her own on the first floor. The niche she found for James Lytton was in the attics.

We did sit side by side at the busy dining table. James asked me quite politely if I had slept well and I replied in the affirmative. It seemed that he slept well too. He offered to take care of Seal while I went to visit Miss Bell with my manuscript. 'It's Bedford Square, is it not? Seal and I will walk with you there and leave you to the tender mercies of Miss Bell.'

I shook my head. 'I will go myself. The landlady will give me directions . . .' I had not become so besotted that I had become a child to this man. I would find my own way.

'Mrs Berriman! What a surprise.' Claris Carmedy helped the old lady down from the gig. Mrs Berriman senior nodded to the young man who was driving and he clicked his mouth and told the horse to walk on.

'I am just back from school,' said Claris, bringing out her

346

key to open the door. 'Come in, come in.'

The house was warm, despite the chill day. Claris poked up the fire in the sitting room and settled the old lady on one chair, herself on another.

Mrs Berriman refused polite offers of tea and got straight to the point. 'I'm here on a matter of delicacy, Miss Carmedy.'

Claris frowned. 'Delicacy, you say?'

'My granddaughter Ruth is, as you know, married to Rhys Maichin.'

Miss Carmedy smiled her crooked smile. 'Of course. Ruth's mother was kind enough to invite Anthony and me to the wedding. A very fine occasion.'

Mrs Berriman nodded impatiently. 'Yes. Yes. Fine is as fine does.'

Miss Carmedy smoothed the velvet tie on her modest dark red dress. 'So what is this matter, Mrs Berriman?'

'You are acquainted with Edward Maichin?'

Miss Carmedy smiled. 'Very well. He is something of a protégé of Anthony's. In the Liberals. In the town. He's making his way very well. An intelligent man . . .'

'He is not to be trusted,' said Mrs Berriman abruptly.

Miss Carmedy frowned. 'Not trusted? Why, he is the most honourable of young men. Clever. Forward-looking.'

The old woman stared at her under beetly brows. 'Sure, if I didn't know better, Miss Carmedy, I would say you had a soft spot for him.'

'Soft spot?' Miss Carmedy's right hand, stained on the forefinger with ink, curled into a fist. 'Anthony and I have a great deal of respect—'

'There are others who have a soft spot for him. He encourages it. He is very shrewd, I think.'

'This is perfectly silly,' said Miss Carmedy. 'Edward would never give cause for—'

'Edward has given me cause for great mistrust,' said Mrs

Berriman firmly. 'And, though I try not to be indelicate, encouraged a certain person's regard quite inappropriately. You and I have to do something about this, Miss Carmedy. If he proceeds, he will bring chaos in this town, more properly in this family.' She sighed and suddenly seemed older than her seventy years. She leaned forward in her chair. ''Tis a pity, Miss Carmedy, but I am driven to tell you the truth.'

So in her confidences to Miss Carmedy, Mrs Berriman made sure that Edward Maichin no longer had a place in Priorton; neither a place to work, nor a place to preen his vain feathers. Mrs Berriman loved her granddaughter, in whom she saw much of herself, in another age. She was very fond of Rhys Maichin, whom Ruth and Edward had betrayed. Banishment, in her view, was the only answer.

So here I am, wandering around the squares of London like a lost soul. My brave words to James Lytton were ill-judged. I had come across Russell Square three times and still not found Bedford Square. My feet are sore in my new Priorton boots.

I turn the same corner for the sixth time and suddenly it is there. A broad square centred on a fine garden with graceful trees. I dodge carriages and gigs to get across the square and begin to count numbers.

The office of *Judith's Journal* is in a grand-looking house but is on the very last floor before the attics. I have to knock on the door twice before a light voice calls, 'Come in.'

I am faced by a scene of chaos. There is a desk to be sure, but that is feet high with papers. There is a table, rather less burdened. On the floor, in slightly crooked piles, are stacks of magazines. A fire flickers in the narrow fireplace which has a small round hob over the grate, on which stands a lazily steaming kettle.

'Well, do we pass muster?' The woman is wearing a dress in green paisley which almost exactly matches the curtains, rendering her practically invisible. In the middle of this green mass floats a round face, fair hair swept up to emphasise the roundness. On her short nose are perched round spectacles. Through these, round, pale blue eyes survey me with evident amusement. She smiles, showing small perfect teeth. At least these are not perfectly round.

'Well?' she says.

'I . . . I . . . am Theodora Maichin. Well, Gervase, now.'

She shakes my hand. 'Ah. The wonderful stories. I am Margaret Bell, my dear, and the person hiding at the desk is the shy retiring Freddie Bannister, known in her childhood as Judith. Didn't we enjoy Miss Maichin's stories, Freddie?'

'Fine stories.' The voice emerges from the mountain of paper on the desk. Then a head appears of an older dark-haired woman. 'Fine stories, as you say.' She disentangles herself from the desk and chair and strides across the room to take my hand in a vice-like grip. 'And I believe you have something to show our friend Rupert Severine.'

They sit me down in the single chair by the fire, ply me with tea and demand that I tell them the story of the Frenchwoman who came to Goshawk Shield just after the Revolution. As I finish I look first at the fair woman who is called Margaret Bell, then at her friend Judith Bannister, for whom their magazine is named.

'A natural storyteller,' says Miss Bannister gruffly.

'I feel sure Rupert will be intrigued,' says Miss Bell happily. 'Intrigued.' She holds out her hand and I scramble to my feet. 'Come again on Friday, Miss Maichin, or Mrs Gervase, or whoever you are. We will give the novel to Rupert this afternoon. He will wish to read it before he sees you.' Her eyes twinkle at me through her round spectacles. 'We have much to do.'

Miss Bannister makes her way back to the heaped desk. 'Not least this month's magazine to assemble. Life is not all stories,' she grumbles. 'Not all family gardens, you know, Miss Maichin.'

Miss Bell leads me to the door. 'Noon on Friday, Miss Maichin. Mr Severine will be here and will have made inroads into your charming novel, I am sure.'

'This is a secret you will have to keep a lifetime, you know.' Mrs Berriman glared at her granddaughter across the silver rims of her spectacles. 'A lifetime. Unwavering.'

'A lifetime?' Ruth put the last stitch in the hem of the tiny gown she was making, and snipped it with small, gold handled scissors. 'I can't think what you're saying, Grandma.'

'Unwavering,' repeated the old woman firmly.

They sewed on together in silence for several minutes. 'Rhys seems very pleased about this child,' said Mrs Berriman. 'Never seen the boy so pleased.'

'It's not every year a man has a son,' said Ruth steadily, bringing her thread through from underneath. 'He's bound to be proud.'

'Good girl,' said the old woman. 'As I say. Unwavering.'

Twenty-six

Displacement

Edward Maichin marched up the gravel path to the Carmedys' door and banged the lion knocker very hard.

Claris came to the door in her house gown and lace cap. She peered up at him in the gloom. 'Edward! I'm so sorry but Anthony's out. Council business, I'm afraid.'

'Well, perhaps I could come in and we could talk?' His white teeth glittered at her in the dark. 'I've a matter I need urgently to discuss, Claris.' The gleaming toe of his black boot was on her threshold.

She opened the door wider. 'Come in then, Edward. Perhaps I can help you.'

In the drawing room he turned towards her abruptly. 'It's Anthony, Claris. He avoids me. I cannot see him at the pit. He never comes to hear me preach. He avoids me at meetings. I'm here to have the matter out with him.'

She did not ask him to sit. 'You must blame me for all this, Edward. I told him he must be careful of you.'

'You? Careful? Of me? I'm his loyal friend. He knows that.'

'Ah.' She looked him in the eye, her teacher's authority adding something to her diminutive height. 'Loyalty. I'd have thought, my dear Edward, that a man's very

351

first loyalty is towards his brother.'

He frowned. 'Brother? What has Caspar . . . ? Now, I know my brother is a scallywag, but—'

She shook her head. 'Caspar? No, not Caspar, Edward. It is Rhys to whom I refer.'

'What is it about Rhys? I cannot be held responsible—'

'I apologise for the indelicacy, Edward, but one would have thought that even for the gayest Lothario, one's sister-in-law would be out of bounds. Unthinkable, even.' Her words might have been chipped out of ice. 'I am surprised at you. As is her grandmother.'

The silence licked around his heels in the cluttered room. 'I can't think what you're saying, Claris . . .'

She held up her hand. 'I'd be more comfortable, Edward, if henceforth you called me Miss Carmedy. I'd not like people to think—'

'Think? Think?' His voice was thick with the effort to control it. 'People would think nothing, Miss Carmedy. Not a thing! Not even if I called you wife! They'd still take you for a dried-up, curmudgeonly spinster half or wholly in love with her own brother, which, as you and I know, is an unnatural sin against God.'

Claris walked back to the door and opened it wide. 'You'd better go, Edward. Although I will make sure to tell Anthony of your opinion of me, and him, I'd not want him to hear it from your own lips. He is far too good a man.'

He looked over her a second, his fine eyes glittering. She stared at him steadily and with loathing. 'You are mistaken,' he said through clenched teeth. 'Both of you. And you'll regret this.' His shoulder barged hers as he strode past her into the night.

Despite my earlier hesitant wanderings I have no trouble in finding my way straight back from Bedford Square to

Montague Street. At the lodgings I look for James Lytton but he is in none of the public rooms. In the dark drawing room two elderly ladies are sitting with their embroidery. In the library an old man sits at the desk, today's *Times* set out before him like a feast he is about to devour. I find myself swallowing my disappointment as I start to mount the stairs.

'Mrs Gervase! Mrs Gervase!' The pale face of Mrs Muswelhome peers up at me through the banister.

'Yes?' My voice is nice and even, I'm very pleased to say. I cannot show my disappointment that James is not here.

'Mr Lytton is in my snug, doing one of his little jobs for me. He said perhaps you would like to join him?' She leads me a long way back through this house which must be three houses deep.

Mrs Muswelhome's snug is a small room with a large round table at its centre. Piles of goods – newspapers, boxes, bottles, jars, umbrellas, tied bundles of sticks – are stacked against every wall, except the one which frames the brightly burning fire.

James Lytton is sitting at the table, poring over two rather battered violins which lie inert on the table before him. He stands up, smiling easily.

I nod towards the table. 'You've found employment, I see.'

'Mrs Muswelhome always manages to make me sing for my supper,' he says. 'Sometimes I think she goes into the highways and byways finding old violins.' He touches the battered instruments with affection. 'Now then, Miss Theodora Louisa Maichin,' he says. 'What about this venture into the great world of publishing?'

'Well, to be frank, it doesn't seem like a great world at all. More two devoted ladies, Miss Bell and Miss Bannister, at their favourite hobby, the magazine called *Judith's Journal*. Judith is Miss Bannister's name but Miss Bell calls her Freddie. They were very nice but very strange.'

'And . . .'

I take off my coat and bonnet. 'I was surprised. Theirs was no great office or library. It was just a little room piled up with papers. I thought it would be a . . . kind of . . .manufactory for magazines.'

He laughs. 'No. No. What they do is take the papers, when they are ready, to a printer's. That's where you'll find your manufactory.'

'It is very funny, I am sure,' I say crossly. 'Country girl come to town.' I plonk myself on the fireside chair. 'They are going to show my story to a certain gentleman, a Mr Severine, and we're to meet on Friday. Then we'll see.'

He glances round the room. 'Then you must needs stay here all week, perhaps longer.'

'And you, James, must needs go home to your business. It was just a whim that you came. I understand this.' My voice is very firm.

He attends to the neck of the most battered instrument, placing it between his eye and the bright window. He stares along it, like a sea captain staring through a spyglass. Captain Ahab comes to my mind, A man obsessed by a great whale. A terrible man. A terrified man. Even so, there's something very engaging about obsession, whatever the object. Memories of Captain Ahab swing my thoughts right back to Stephen. I wonder how he's coping. And how my mother and Sadie are coping with Stephen's own particular, quaint obsessions. Tonight I will write to him and tell him of my adventures. I must remember to print it, so he can read it himself.

James Lytton catches my eye. 'No,' he says. 'I will not return home. We can send Mrs Muswelhome along the highways and byways, I suppose, to find broken violins among her friends. There will be four days' work and sovereigns on the table. I can sing for my supper.'

'But . . .' I say.

'What, Theo? Do you wish me to return home, away from under your feet? Do you wish to embrace the capital on your own? To have your own adventure?'

'No. If you want—'

'The Tower! We will see the Tower, where they chopped off the heads of traitors. We will see the Palace where the old Queen stays when she can bear to be in her capital. We will go to the music hall. And I will take you to walk in the great London parks. Perhaps we can find a concert where the violin is played with the hands of angels.' He leans over the table and almost touches my hand. 'We'll have such a time, Theo. A great time. It will be as though the world up in County Durham never existed before or after.'

And so it has been. We have banished the world at home with all its responsibilities. We live for the day. When wet, in a hansom cab, when fine on our own two feet, we have tramped this city. We have skirted the grim Tower of London and run away. We have listened to string quartets sawing away at the music of the gods. We have eaten in modest restaurants and walked on paths in parks and heaths where you might blink and swear yourself to be in the country. We have read gravestones in cemeteries which were grand enough to be castles.

And – you would guess it – I am fascinated by the Thames, that broad, bustling reach of water which leads the eye through rising swell and mists towards the sea. Even among the rotting stenches of the waterside you can still smell the open sea, funnelled in by the great ships which bring the sights, sounds and smells of the whole world into this snake of a harbour side. With Seal in tow we have walked along the noisy and noisome riverside lanes and picked our way through boxes and trucks waiting to be hoisted into the gawping holds of the great masted ships, ships that lord it over the stubby steam vessels which throb rather than flaunt their power in the docks.

I tell James again of the jagged window in the Welsh castle where my father and I peered into our different futures, gazing across the salt marsh to Chester, then London, then the world. My heart plummets for a second as I think of Edward who spoiled all that, converting the lure of the sea to a source of threat. Then I have the rank burned stench of the tar-paper hut in my nostrils and I feel the strong salty arms of the tar-paper man lifting me out of the sea.

The tar-paper man!

I dig deep into my reticule and pull out a book of the poems of Robert Herrick, purloined from the pheasant room to while the hours away in the train. Tucked into its tooled leather cover is that battered piece of paper with the address scrawled on it. Lifting the scrap of paper to my nose I can smell the sea. 'I've kept this in my ribbon box for many years. The old man said I should come to London. And he said I should find his friend.' I hold the paper up and it flutters in the harbour-side breeze. 'Mr Horatio Plummer, Spitalfields. I was to remind him of Euan Barra, although I only ever think of him as the tar-paper man.'

'A quest! We'll find him.' James takes the paper from me and peers at the address. 'And we'll tell him of the fate of his friend.'

'It's many years ago,' I protest. 'He'll be long gone now, dead like his friend.'

'We'll try,' says James firmly. 'How long have you wondered about that old man? This is the week for moving towards our heart's desire, one way or another. Now we have another mission.'

I look up quickly at him, but he has been distracted by a sailor who is trying to sell him a ring from a tangle in his pocket. They haggle a little and James hands over some sovereigns and chooses a ring.

'Now then!' He comes towards me and takes my hand.

In his palm lies a ring wrought in coarse silver. It is in the form of a leaping seal. 'I'll not give you this just now,' he says, 'but will you try it for size?'

I kneel down in the dust and show it to Seal, seeing it reflected in her eyes. 'See, Seal! Here you have your namesake.' And my little seal sister flutters in and out of my mind like a wraith.

The ring sits snugly on my right forefinger. I want to keep it there for ever. Gently James takes my hand and eases it off. 'I . . . We will keep this, Theo. One day, one day . . .'

We look away from each other through the clicking forest of lines and masts. It's too hard to speak at all just at this moment. Then he coughs and takes my arm. 'Now then, Miss Maichin, we will go and seek a hansom and make our way to Spitalfields to find your old man. That will be one mission accomplished, at least.'

Numbly I trail after him. My life yawns before me, a life without James Lytton, and suddenly some old man buried in the slum lands of London seems of little importance.

Rhys clumped down Priorton High Street, ducking down his head and holding on to his hat against the predatory grasp of the wind. His head was buzzing with pride at yet another successful day in his professional life. Fifteen new customers signed on! The success had been recognised by a bluff handshake from his father-in-law, who, anticipating his grandfatherhood, saw in Rhys an ally in his over-womanised household. Ex-pitman he may be, but he certainly had a head for business.

Ruth had gone home early, feeling a little under the weather. Mrs Berriman told Rhys he was not to worry. This only happened in the early months. Rhys replied earnestly that he intended to be a good father to this child. Much better than his own father who, he confided, though very clever, was not the best of parents.

Rhys's thoughts were just dwelling on his father, wondering where his travels must have led him now, when he turned the corner of Victoria Road and bumped into his brother Edward. 'Whoa, Ed! In a hurry, is it?'

Edward adjusted his hat. 'I was just about to call on you. I knocked on the door but there was no answer.'

'No answer?' In a rush of confidence born out of his soon-to-be-father status, Rhys took his brother's arm, which stayed rigid under his hand. 'Come on in, Ed, and welcome! Ruth is home, I am sure, but has been none too well. I don't know whether you know but—'

'I know. I know,' said Edward stiffly. 'Isn't it the news of the town?' He did not add that he'd heard the news from the horse's mouth. More properly the mare's mouth. The mother in question. And hadn't he been told again by his friend Miss Carmedy who was no longer his friend? All this was not for Rhys's ears.

He did not add that he'd banged and banged on Rhys's door and had seen the curtains twitch. He knew very well that Ruth was there. He could smell her.

Rhys took out his key. 'Come in! Come in! And welcome.' He bustled into the long hall. 'Ruth! Ruthie! We have company.'

In the sitting room was a well-guarded fire and a tray of lemonade and cakes covered by an embroidered linen cloth. Rhys whipped this off like a magician. 'Well now! Even though the poor girl is ill, she thinks of me.' He poured out lemonade for his brother and went back into the hall to call for his wife.

As he sat there scenes tripped through Edward's mind, from the time his mother had a baby. A little girl. In those days Edward had been the golden-haired king of the coop, beloved of his parents and his grandparents, cleverer and more glamorous by far than his little brothers. Then the girl child, Theo, came and one day Edward caught sight of her, naked, when their mother was changing her. He was shocked at how different she was. Bulbous and bereft. Disgusting.

He had been pleased to see that his mother didn't care for the child either, moaning when the child cried and slamming her about a bit when she changed her. Then one day he had watched from the door as his mother picked up the pillow and seemed to be about to smother the baby. Edward realised this and in his mind he urged her on. *Do it! Do it!*

But something stopped her and she put the pillow aside. To Edward's disgust she picked Theo up and crooned over her, rocking backwards and forwards, backwards and forwards. After that it had been his responsibility to deal with the interloper. But he had failed down there in the marsh. He had succeeded with the filthy tramp who had helped her, and with the other one, the one who had tried to trap him. But not with Theo. Not with this one either.

It had amused him to displace his own brother for a while. To prove yet again the predilection all women have for betrayal. He had not reckoned that this one would betray him in her turn. He had been sure of his power over her. But, it must be admitted, he was mistaken.

'Lord forgive me!' he said now.

'Ruthie! Edward's here!' He could hear Rhys calling in the hallway.

'Edward?' He could hear Ruth making her way slowly down the stairs. The two of them appeared in the doorway, arm in arm. Edward hauled himself to his feet with insulting slowness.

'See, Ed. Doesn't she look well? Glossy, I call her.'

'Rhys! You would think I were a prize pigeon!'

He nuzzled her neck. 'You are! You are my prize pigeon.'

359

She suffered this for a second, steadily looking at Edward, than sat down and said, 'Rhys, my dear boy, can you get that small cushion from the breakfast room? It does so help the small of my back.' He vanished with alacrity. She looked up at Edward. 'Do sit down, Edward. You look so uncomfortable standing there.'

He threw himself on to the sofa. 'What are you playing at, Ruth?' he said. 'Letting your grandmother blacken me, losing me my friends. My job too.'

'Anything that has happened, Edward, you have done to yourself.' Ruth smiled at him. 'We did have fine times, Edward,' she said. 'A fine time together. But you were so cruel, such a boor when I told you about the baby. Should I let you get away with that? Anyway, I've said nothing in the town. I'm not responsible for what my grandmother has said to anyone. Not at all.'

'So this child is mine? Really? As you said?' he growled.

She stared at him, then shrugged. 'Who knows? Probably. Probably not. It is no matter.'

'Then why . . .?'

She shrugged again. 'I now realise I don't know you very well, Edward. Hardly at all. Except in that special way. That way of magnetism. Perhaps you had me mesmerised. But when I realised about the baby, when I thought about it, I knew it was Rhys who had to be the father or we'd all be in jeopardy.'

He stood up and was suddenly looming over her where she sat. 'Then why this business with the dratted old woman? That witch of a grandmother of yours spreading her poison? Getting her into it to make her trouble. Why?'

She sat into the chair. 'Well,' she said slowly. 'My grandmother suspected . . . the truth. And she said I wasn't to trust you. That you must not be trusted.'

'Stupid old woman. You take notice of a stupid old

woman.' His voice was wooden as he battened down his anger.

'Yes,' she said steadily. 'She's the wisest person I know, my grandma.'

Then he spoke to her through gritted teeth. 'I could kill you, you know.'

'I don't think so, Edward.'

'I killed a woman once. I could kill you.'

Ruth met glassy, rage-filled eyes with a steady gaze.

The door opened. Rhys came in, cushion in hand. The weighty silence pricked even his bland sensibilities. 'What? What is it, Ruth? Are you all right?'

'Your brother is just going, Rhys. He has a meeting.'

Edward's hand came down by his sides. 'Yes,' he said calmly. 'I only came for a moment. It's good to see you looking so well, sister-in-law. I thought the trials of motherhood would not suit you, Ruth. But I am mistaken.'

He looked at his brother. If he destroyed Rhys's smug happiness, if he revealed Ruth's perfidious betrayal, he himself would be exposed. He might be saddled with Ruth! No, let them sink in their own inferior sand. He was better off out of it. Then he strode off without speaking to his brother and the glass in the vestibule door rattled as he slammed it.

Rhys tucked the cushion behind the small of Ruth's back. 'What was that all about, Ruth?'

'Didn't you make him stop calling on me? Don't protest! I know you did that. What you don't know is he tried to tell me you were worth nothing, tales of your childhood which put you in a very bad light. Well, I disagreed with him violently and he was mad, angry at me—'

'You should have told me,' he interrupted her.

'How could I upset you? But there is more.'

'Mmmm?' he said, wondering what was coming.

'Well, it seems he was angry at you then for doing so well. The business. Work. All that. It seems he fears he is to be laid off at work.' She smoothed the flying ends of her sash down her belly. 'And I think he is even more angry with you now. You becoming a father and all that. He is jealous. The sin of envy, you know.'

'Ha!' said Rhys. 'That's Edward of old. Never liked to be bettered. Could do you harm if you bettered him. He tormented Theo over the smallest things.'

'Well then, dearest! You've bettered him and he can't do a thing about it. Not a thing!'

The post boy brought two packages for Goshawk Shield. The one addressed to Rose Clare was bulky and very heavy, but Stephen's was a slim package addressed in Theo's writing.

He watched as Rose Clare unwrapped her layers to reveal a leather box. 'A present, Rose Clare,' said Stephen, rubbing his hands, pleased at his friend's good fortune.

She held up a gold chain which glittered in the light from the window. Its clasp consisted of three pearls set in filigree. The note on which it rested said:

Dear Rose Clare,

As you see, South Africa has been very good to me. I have work with a company which deals in gold. Here there is no need to work against the law. There are rich pickings for all. But this . . . none of this . . . is anything without you. Write to me and tell me you will come. Underneath the pendant there are gold coins to pay for fare.

She looked up at Stephen. 'It is from Theo's father. From Ellis.'

He frowned. 'He took Mama's spoons.'

Rose Clare nodded. 'You open your letter, Stephen. Sure, isn't that Theo's writing?'

362

He opened it very carefully with his clumsy fingers.

'Would you like me to read your letter to you, Stephen?' said Rose Clare.

He smoothed the letter on the table. 'No. I'll read it. She writes very clear.' He put his finger on the first line. 'She is very well,' he announced. 'London is very big and there are many people. Many ships in the docks. The people are reading her story.' He paused, stricken.

'What is it, Stephen?' said Rose Clare sharply.

'She cannot come home for more days, perhaps a week.' He screwed up the paper in his big hand and threw it to the back of the kitchen fire. 'How many days in a week, Rose Clare?'

She took the paper from the fire and smoothed it again. 'There are seven, Stephen. But, sure, they pass very quickly.'

'Seven more.' He sighed heavily, hauled himself to his feet and moved towards the door.

'Where are you going, Stephen?'

'I'll go to the barn to paint the chariot. It must be really nice for when she gets off the train again.'

'But Stephen, it's wet out there. Stay here by the fire.'

He shook his massive head. 'The stove there will light well. There is much work to do. The chariot must be right or she'll not come home at all.'

An hour later, just as Rose Clare was closing the curtains in the pheasant room, the sky outside seemed too bright. Leaning over she spotted the surge of flame on the barn roof. She raced to the kitchen shouting, 'Fire, fire!'

Sadie, sitting with Susan Cornford on her knee, leapt to her feet. 'The barn!' gasped Rose Clare. 'Stephen's in there.'

When they reached the barn the fire was leaping even higher into the night sky. Crackles and detonations echoed from inside the building and the roofpoint was anointed by licks of flame.

Sadie laid the still sleeping Susan in the back of one of the farm carts and grabbed Rose Clare's arm. 'Come on. He's in there, the big gawk.'

The fire had not reached the doorway. From there they could see the chariot burning furiously, great sizzling tongues of flame leaping and reaching the roof. The dry wood exploded, shuddering and buckling like old bones.

'There! There he is!'

Stephen was sprawling face down in the dirt, coughing and choking on the smoke. Sadie heaved him over and cleared the dirt from his face. Blood was trickling from a cut on his bruised forehead. 'Here, get a leg,' spluttered Rose Clare. 'An' be quick will you or we'll all be fried to a crisp.'

They each took a leg and, gasping with the effort, hauled him to safety. They sat him up against the wheel of a cart. Rose Clare wiped his face with her apron. 'Come on now, Stephen. Wake up now, will you?'

His eyes opened and he looked at her and beyond her to the raging fire. 'The chariot,' he said, trying to struggle to his feet. 'The sticks in the fire spat on the chariot!'

Rose Clare put a hand on his shoulder and forced him back down. 'Stay there, Stephen. Sure, there's not a thing you can do.'

He shook his head. 'My chariot is gone,' he said sadly. 'And Theo will never, never come back.'

'Don't talk so silly,' said Rose Clare briskly. 'Of course she'll come back. You'll see. She'll be back. You watch.'

Twenty-seven

Circles

'Dismissed?' Edward swayed slightly, looking down at his former mentor sitting ill-at-ease before him in his office at the pit head.

'That is what I said.' Carmedy looked him in the eye.

'For what reason?'

'I need no reason,' said Carmedy. 'Lord Chase takes my advice. He rarely asks for details.'

That had not been the case when Edward first came here with his brothers to fill the gap left by the Cornishmen who had been sacked despite Anthony Carmedy's urging. Edward stared at him, looking hard at the other man's gleaming skull, trying to bore into it, fathom the under-manager's thoughts. 'But what criticism have you? I demand—'

'Demand?' Carmedy stood up and placed himself behind his chair, gripping it tightly. 'Mr Maichin,' he said, 'if you'd been anyone else I'd have had them tell you this at the pay window. I give you this courtesy because we know – have known each other outside this place. I took you for a friend. Of course, it turns out that this was my mistake.'

Edward took a step forward, his own voice softening. 'But we are friends, Anthony. Surely we are good friends. Was it Claris? Take no heed. Poor Claris. Women get themselves upset, poor things. You know that.'

Carmedy shook his head. 'Claris is not *women*, Edward! That's your mistake. Claris is *my* sister. And your words to her cause me deep offence. I must tell you this. And now it seems there is this concern she has regarding a certain matter within your own family. A delicate matter. I cannot . . . I will not ignore these things.' He looked bravely into the fierce eyes of the young man opposite. 'There is no work for you here, Edward. And no work in other pits in this district. And though you may wish to serve out your time on Priorton Council there're those there who'll be uncomfortable at your presence.'

Edward stood and watched as Carmedy picked up his pen and dipped it in his inkwell.

'Well,' said Edward quietly, 'the Lord help a man who comes between another man and his sister.'

The watery eyes of Anthony Carmedy met Edward's eyes, bright and cold as marble. 'You are a vile man,' he said. 'Like the snake in Eden.'

'Blacklisted! How can that be, Caspar?'

Caspar threw himself into the narrow chair beside Edward's fire. 'It is not fair, Ed. Not fair. A bit of gambling! Missing two shifts! Others do that and are welcomed to the fold.'

'So you're blacklisted?' Edward looked up from the sermon he was trying to write about the miracle of the loaves and the fishes and man's need to act for himself. At least the sermons had not been cancelled.

'I've tried three pits and been turned away the minute I said my name.'

Edward laughed grimly. 'Always the miscreant! Your reputation goes before you, Caspar.' He was enjoying Caspar's discomfort and would not relieve him by telling him he had been caught in the net of Edward's own blacklisting.

Caspar looked round the neatly furnished room. 'But I can stay here for a short while? I reckon I'll have to go outside the county, perhaps up to Scotland again, to get work. My bolt is shot here.'

Edward closed his notebook. 'Mayhap I'll come away with you, Cas. I feel in need of a change myself.'

Caspar's brows shot up into his thick mop of hair. 'You? With me? I thought you were well set up in this place. Leading man. Councillor and all that.'

Edward shrugged. 'This is such a little town, Cas. Commonplace. Tedious little people and little brains. Vacuous seekers after salvation. A real man needs a bigger canvas.' He pushed a letter across to Caspar. 'A letter from Father. In South Africa, he is. Riding high, it seems. Fallen in with good fortune, without stealing it for a change. He makes that quite clear. He wants me . . . us . . . to go and persuade our dear mother to join him. To share his fortune. He says there is fortune enough for all. And souls to save in the mining camps.'

Caspar held the letter close to his eyes. 'He says here that he has sent our mother money enough for the passage and more. He also says he has met Welsh miners there, although it is gold, not coal that they dig for.'

'I've read the letter!' said Edward, patiently. 'You have no need to read it out like an infant scholar.'

'And you want to go? To South Africa?'

'There'll be work to do there, Cas. Like I say. Souls to save.'

Euan Barra's crumpled paper told us his friend Horatio Plummer lives in a district called Spitalfields. James Lytton, though he thinks he knows London, has trouble finding the street, turning down alleyway after alleyway. The afternoon has dropped into that fake London night, an amalgamation of sky, soot, smoke and the swirling fog which seems to rise from the cellars and pavements and coil itself, serpent-like, round corners. We are plunging through a dark mist, which drips with fear. It bears no resemblance to the clean white mist which flows down from the moor towards Goshawk Shield. That mist may mask your path, but it does not choke your breath.

These streets pulsate with people: men and women on foot, slipping through the darkness as though in flight; some hunched down about their business, selling rags, or even their own services, with equanimity; those with time on their hands loll in doorways making laconic comments to passers-by who seem to know them. The unnatural canyons of the narrowing alleys flow all around you, invading your eyes, ears and nose to the point of suffocation. The bulging dark-eyed face of poverty shows itself, as it does in the back alleys of Priorton, but here it has a city pallor. An odd adventurer rides a horse or small cart but in this place the press and noise of the poor, crouching, leering, whistling, is everywhere.

James Lytton has his hand on my elbow and hugs me close to his side. It is worth the sense of danger to have this closeness to another human being. Only Seal, trotting along beside me, seems untroubled by the feeling (whether it is called for or not) of peril.

'Here! This is it!' says James. Above the wide, peeling door with its elaborate fanlight a gas lantern fades to a pinpoint in the gloom. James raises his stick and batters the door, which is opened immediately. A gargoyle face, all rolled-back lips and plunging side whiskers, peers out at us, opens the door wider and ushers us in, shouting behind him, 'Visitors, Ruby! Visitors, old father. We have visitors.'

I lift Seal from the greasy threshold and follow the man inside. The room is low, centred on a crackling fire of sticks and a few coals sparking up in a once-elegant fireplace. Beside it, an ancient man with a shawl around his shoulders is being fed porridge, or some such white stuff, by a very round woman who kneels at his feet, her black skirts spread around her like the sea.

The gargoyle looks at us, and his eyes glitter (I think with warmth) in the candlelight. 'To what do we owe this honour, sir, madame?'

I show him my crumpled sheet. 'A long time ago, I was given this address by a man I knew. A man called Euan Barra. The address of a friend of his. Perhaps he has left here? Mr Horatio Plummer.'

The old man by the fire turns round for the first time. He pushes the woman's feeding hand away. 'Who is it?' he says. 'Who is it who says my name?'

I place Seal on the floor beside me and she sits very quiet. 'The man's name was Euan Barra. I knew him in Wales six or seven years ago.'

The old man looks up at the gargoyle. 'Mr Barra was one of our more regular visitors,' he says. His voice, clearer now, is a surprise. His way of speaking is round, refined, unlike the guttural London talk of his gargoyle companion. 'He came here many times.' His watery pink eyes transfer to me. 'Pursued by demons,' he says. 'Though he found some peace in these walls. Many came like this to find a moment's peace here.'

The gargoyle stirs. 'The old father kept open house. That was how I came to him, fatherless, not a hope of care,' he says. 'In those days we had the whole of this house, not merely these three rooms as we have now. For many years people stayed here as they passed through. When I opened the door to you tonight, my mind went back to those times.'

'Not so,' says the woman, still kneeling on the floor. 'These two do not look broken down and poor.'

'Took anyone in. Often no pay! No questions,' the gargoyle

369

explains. 'Many people called my old father here mad, too, for his charity.'

'Loaves and fishes.' The old man's voice meanders like a broken violin string. 'The Lord will provide.' He takes the woman's hand and guides the spoon towards his loose mouth. My own grandfather comes unbidden to my mind. He had a certain goodness about him. But that might have shown itself more readily without his awful bond with my grandmother. And despite the front he puts on, my brother Edward does not have even a shred of the goodness which pervades this room. My mind searches for the barely remembered Welsh. *Rhagrithwyr*. Hypocrite.

The old man appears to sleep for a second, then his eyes snap open again and stare rheumily into mine. 'A good man pursued by demons, Euan Barra.'

I kneel beside the woman. I am aware that our skirts intermingle, like the estuary and the tide. I bring my face close to that of the old man. 'He saved me from the sea, Mr Plummer. I used to call him the tar-paper man. He lived in a tar-paper hut on the beach. I was trapped and the sea would have overwhelmed me but for him.'

'Ah. The sea! He could flee no further than the edge of the world. But he was thus blessed. To share with Christ the restoration of a life. He was truly blessed.'

I don't know whether I should tell him this, but the words tumble out. 'But . . . he died. He died in a fire. His hut burned down. Someone set fire to it.'

Old Mr Plummer's bony hand grasps my arm and he brings his face even closer to mine. I can smell sour milk and old fish. 'Ha! The flames would leap but the Lord would pluck him from the ashes. I tell you this. The Lord would pluck him from the flames just as he plucked you from the tide. The Lord would save him from purgatory just as surely as he saved you from the greedy roll of the sea. Once Euan Barra was a wicked man but you saved him from the consuming fire. Circles. Circles. Always there are circles.'

His hand falls away and he sinks back in the chair, a frail husk once more. Seal licks his hand with her soft tongue. I stand up and brush my hand down the front of my shirt.

The gargoyle claps his hands. 'There now! Isn't that fine? That is the most the old man has said in a week! Truly most of the time he babbles on like an idiot, but here you came today and show us what he was, and remind us of the joys of our duty. God bless you.'

I back off, nodding and half curtseying, anxious to be away from this room, more animal lair than abode of people. I kneel to pick up Seal, who snuggles her face towards me.

James Lytton has said nothing, but clasps me close to his side as we make our way back through the narrow alleyways to the broader thoroughfare of Whitechapel. He steers me into a chop house and orders us plain food. I am tired and hungry. This, now, is all I want. We eat in silence.

James is a neat, efficient eater and his plate is empty very quickly. Only then does he speak to me. 'Well?' he says. 'Are you satisfied with your trip into the stews of Spitalfields?'

'Yes,' I say. 'Although satisfied is a strange word. At least, in a way, it finishes the thing with the tar-paper man. With Euan Barra. At least someone who knew him knows of his death. The old man there mentioned circles. Me telling him made a circle complete. And . . .'

'And . . .'

'I fear to say this in case I sound like Edward, but it was a kind of honour to meet someone who's . . .well . . . *good*. So many people profess virtue . . .'

James drinks his ale and wipes his mouth with the back of his free hand. 'You'll not find me making such fine claims, Theo. I've been less than good in my time. Knocked heads together, told only an approximation of the truth now and then. I'd never assume the mantle of goodness round these shoulders.'

I am struggling. I'm not sure whether I have the words to say what I want to say. 'My grandfather and grandmother, my brother Edward: all these saw themselves as good. Now my father, he is a bad man – well, he does bad things – but even so I like him so much better than I have ever liked them. Despite his stealing Mrs Gervase's silver . . .' I stop to think a minute. Curiously, had it not been for that terrible theft, I'd not have met the man before me, my curious companion in this gargoyle city. 'And me, I'm not so good myself,' I finish lamely, weakened by the foregoing thought. 'Not at all.'

He slaps his hand on the stained table. 'Hard to imagine. On the one side you're a picture of independence, married, running a house, writing books, travelling the length of England alone. Or trying to.' He pauses. 'On the other hand it's as though you're just out of the egg, blinking at the world.'

I feed the last of my chop to Seal who sits expectantly at my knee. 'I must be bad. I've not loved my mother at all till very recent years. I hate one brother, despise another and only lately have I learned to tolerate my brother Rhys. I hardly like myself sometimes, or know who I am. No one meant much to me until I came to Goshawk Shield.'

He shakes his head. 'You seem to have great respect, affection even, for . . . for Stephen Gervase.'

I have to smile at this. 'That's easy, liking Stephen. I liked his mother too. As easy as loving Seal here, who loves me without question.'

His gaze is becoming intense. 'And is he truly your husband, Stephen Gervase?'

His tone stings me. 'We were married in a church near York, by a clergyman who was a friend of his mother.'

He lays a hand on mine. 'That is not what I mean, Theo.'

I stand up, button my coat and take Seal up again from the

372

dusty floor. 'I cannot think what you mean, James,' I say stiffly, and march out, leaving him to pay for our meal. I am angry, but most of all I am embarrassed by what he is trying to say.

When, breathless, he catches up with me, I am two streets away. He grasps my arm and turns me to face him. 'I'm sorry, Theo. I'm not usually so . . . direct. I've given offence. I'd not meant to give offence, I promise you.'

I look him in the eye. 'I can't think what you mean, James. Now, shall we get back to Montague Street? Shall we hail a cab?'

The magnetism between me and James Lytton is resonating in the sooty London air between us, quivering like a string on one of his own violins. But for now I want to leave it where it is, trembling in the air, recognised but not acted upon. Now is not the time.

Twenty-eight

The Honour of a Visit

Mrs Berriman blinked at the now familiar, handsome figure lounging before her. 'Edward Maichin! What brings you into Berriman's? Do you need a new poker? A new fireguard?' She looked him in the eye.

'Mrs Berriman!' He flashed his angelic smile. 'To be sure I'll have no need for a poker or a fireguard where I'm going. More a parasol or fan, perhaps.'

She looked at him warily. 'You're going somewhere, Edward?'

He shook his head sorrowfully. 'This town, this whole district has fallen far short of my expectations. Where I expected simple virtue there is shabby vice. Where I expected respect for a life well led there is banal tittle tattle from people whose own souls are stained black with hypocrisy.'

She shivered slightly and blinked away from his pale eyes. 'That's not the town I know, Edward. Not at all.'

He pointed an elegant finger at her. 'We all live in our own purgatory, Mrs Berriman. Remember that, won't you?' He looked round restlessly. 'Is my brother here?'

'Rhys? No. He had calls out at Calbeck Green, but he will be back later. Do you need to see him directly?'

He straightened his gloves on the counter. 'Urgently

enough. My brother Caspar and I will set out for South Africa within the week.' He smiled at her. 'Perhaps Rhys will wish to know that. We take our mother with us.'

'South Africa? And your mother goes too?'

'Our father is there now. Well ensconced. With a high position in a gold-mining company. We go to join him. Some souls to save there, I do not doubt it.'

'And Rhys?' The old woman watched him carefully. 'He goes too?'

That smile again. 'We will persuade him to come with us. A chance like this is too good for him to miss.'

'Africa? He'll not go to Africa,' asserted Mrs Berriman. 'He is well set here, the boy. He has a wife—'

'And a family on the way, I hear?' Edward stroked his chin. 'Well, perhaps I can persuade my dear sister-in-law to come instead. Wouldn't you welcome the notion of your great-grandchild growing up under the sun? Away from the misty vales of the cold North?'

'The child?' The old woman's cheeks blotched purple. 'Edward Maichin, if you think you can take that child . . .'

But she was talking into thin air. The bell above the door was still trembling gently after his swift exit. Mrs Berriman had to wait a long thirty minutes before Rhys came in from his journey, brushing heavy raindrops off his greatcoat.

'Go home, Rhys,' she said. 'Your brother's up to some of his tricks. Doing I don't know what mischief round at Victoria Road. Talks of taking the child to Africa . . .'

Rhys was gone before she had finished, the bell trembling after him in his turn.

Mr Severine, the publisher, is a tall, birdlike man, perhaps of my father's age. He is a man in a hurry. He shakes hands with me briskly in the office of *Judith's Journal*. 'Ah, Miss Maichin! Our chronicler of the sylvan life of a fallen aristocrat!

Nice tale, Miss Maichin. Good feeling. Natural storyteller. But come! There is much to do!' He sweeps me out of the room and down the stairs, and strides on along the broad pavements of Bedford Square with me scampering behind him. Finally I stop, breathless. 'Mr Severine! Where are we going?'

'We are going to fill the gaps in your knowledge, Miss Maichin. Your storytelling is of the first water but your facts, if I may say so, my dear, are distinctly wobbly. You need to read: Carlyle, Croker, Mahan, Guizot, and Henry Morse Stephens. Useful scholars all. And many more. We are about to mend this. You will fill in the gaps, Miss Maichin, fill in the gaps.' He draws my arm through his.

We set off again, me clutching his arm. 'But, Mr Severine, my story? Will you . . . Can it be published?'

'To be sure. To be sure. But first some facts about the first Terror in France. Get it as right as you can. That's the rule, right as you can.'

Which is how I find myself inside what is a kind of temple to learning, bigger than any church. Dusty and musty, but bright with daylight. It is a round room with desks like the spokes of a wheel, the light flooding on to the bent heads and the books from the skylights above. For an instant I am back in Mrs Gervase's pheasant room with Durham moorland light flooding the windows. I miss her. How I miss the old woman.

Mr Severine has furnished me with his bona fides in the eyes of whomever is in charge, a pile of books about the French Revolution, a broad seat to sit upon, and has vanished. This is a kind of heaven, this temple of books. He says he will be back for me at three. My hand drops to my side and I feel in vain for Seal. But she is not there. I have left her behind with James Lytton on what I knew would be a busy day. Who knew where you may be permitted to take a dog, however delicately human she may be to me?

Ruth looked up as Rhys came through the door. Young Beattie, neat in her afternoon black and crisp white apron, was handing a white china cup of tea to Edward. Ruth smiled easily at her husband. 'Here's Edward come with good news, Rhys. He and Caspar are off to South Africa to make their fortunes. And he says—'

Edward stood up. 'And I thought you might jump at the chance too, Rhys. Father is well set up and there is much—' It would be fun to upset this applecart, to get these two away from the witch of a grandmother and this smug, self-satisfied town. To tempt Ruth again under hot skies.

Rhys laughed heartily. 'South Africa? Now, Ed, there's a joke. I've everything here that I need and more. Much to be made here and it's our own soil.'

Edward looked from one smiling, complacent face to the other. 'Perhaps I should tell you, Rhys, for your own good. That child of yours— Who knows what people might say, if . . . ?'

'I was really sorry to hear you'd lost your job at the pit,' interrupted Ruth. 'My grandmother told me . . .' Then she put the back of her hand on her own brow. 'Oh Rhys, dear, I suddenly feel unwell.' And she lay back on the sofa and closed her eyes.

Rhys looked at his brother. 'Perhaps you'll excuse us, Ed. These are not ordinary times in this house. Best of luck, though, in Africa.'

Edward stood up then and almost bowled Rhys over in his angry rush to get out of the room.

The front door clashed and Ruth opened one eye. 'Has he gone? Rhys dear, I am impelled to tell you your brother is the most awful bore.' And they laughed together in a very companionable fashion.

* * *

'Three more days?' Stephen's voice was gloomy. He snorted down his nose. 'Is that what the letter says?'

'Yes,' said Rose Clare patiently. 'She's met a very important man who likes her stories and who wants her to read a lot of books.'

'There are books in the dining room, Rose Clare, and in the pheasant room.'

'So there are, but sure aren't these very clever books, London books that you can't get up here?'

Goshawk Shield was very quiet. Sadie had persuaded Rose Clare that she should take young Susan down to the farm, to see the Gomersalls. 'It's a fine day, Rose Clare. The bairn'll like to see the cows and the geese.' Sadie had stared defiantly at Rose Clare, knowing that if Theo had been here this wouldn't have been allowed. Theo was never happy about Susan Cornford going back among the Gomersalls. But Rose Clare had let Sadie go, tired all of a sudden at the web of care she had wound round herself. She wanted above all to be alone, to read again Ellis's letter, and turn over the coins which were his golden apology.

'Don't mope around here.' She spoke to Stephen with unusual sharpness. 'Why don't you go and carve some of that wood of yours?'

'I cannot carve any more. Anyway, I burned the stable,' he said mournfully. 'I burned the chariot so Theo cannot get home from the station.'

'Don't be silly, Stevie,' she said, softer now. 'Sure, Theo can hire a brake down in Stanhope. No bother at all.'

'Do you think so?'

She nodded. 'Now why don't you go and get all your tools and things and move them into the dairy? Seems there's little enough dairying going on these days. Gomersalls do the milk.'

'What will Theo say? She might say the dairy should be kept clean.'

'She'll say it's a very good idea,' said Rose Clare firmly.

As the door slammed behind him she sat down at the table and took the package out of the drawer. She smoothed out the letter and looked at Ellis's flowing, clerkly writing. Things were changing. In all those years when he was in America she had thought of him every day. The very absence of him diminished her by the hour. In those days she had to reach for the bottle to numb the despairing thoughts. But now, days, even weeks might go by and she barely thought of him. In her bedroom this morning she had taken a close look at Ellis's daguerreotype to remind herself of just what he looked like. The routines of Goshawk Shield, the company of Theo, Stephen and particularly Susan Cornford seemed to suffice now. The child, with her reaching hands and her smiling ways, was making her, at last, a mother to a daughter. But Ellis had not forgotten her. The letter was evidence of that.

A heavy clatter on the door made her jump to her feet. It surprised her that she was not surprised to see Edward, with Caspar lurking at his shoulder. 'So, Edward?' She ushered him in. 'The honour of a visit?'

Carefully, Edward placed his hat and his stick on the scarred kitchen table. He glanced around and smiled his charming smile at Rose Clare. 'Well set up here, Mother,' he said. 'You've got a good place.'

She nodded, and sat back in her chair and watched them settle themselves at the kitchen table. 'It's not my place, as you know. It's Theo's. And Stephen's.'

The fire dropped and the clock ticked. Caspar looked uneasily at Edward and said, 'We heard from Da, heard from him in South Africa.'

She nodded. 'He writes a good letter, your father. Didn't I get one myself?'

'He's doing very well,' Caspar hurried on. 'Managing some company. Not . . .'

379

'Stealing?' Rose Clare coloured as she betrayed Ellis with the word.

'He wishes us to go and join him,' said Edward abruptly. 'Said there are many chances there for us on the Cape.'

'Gold to dig, souls to save,' said Caspar eagerly. 'Diamonds, even. It says so in the newspaper.'

Edward flowed on. 'Chances for us all. He particularly wished for me to persuade you to come, Mother. He needs you there.'

'I have needed him here many a year.'

Edward stared at her. 'It is your duty, Mother. Your duty to stick by him. In sickness and health, remember.'

She looked hard at him, then slowly shook her head. 'That's over, Edward. I have duty here. Theo. Susan.'

He frowned. 'The foundling? Ridiculous.'

'And Stephen needs care.'

'He is Theo's duty, not yours. The child too.'

She looked at him carefully. 'I choose them.'

Rattles and voices in the yard heralded the subjects of their conversation. Sadie swept into the kitchen with Susan Cornford on her hip, and Stephen lumbered in behind her. Edward stood up quickly and Caspar followed suit. 'Well, Mother, if that is your last word?'

Stephen walked across to him and shook him heartily by the hand, beaming. 'I'll tell Theo you were here. She's in London with a very important bookman. Theo is very important in London.'

'Important? Theo?' Edward wrenched his hand away. 'We must go, Mother. We've got to get back to Priorton and prepare for our journey.' He reached for his hat and his stick. 'Come on, Caspar.'

Rose Clare stood easily by the fire. 'So you're really off to South Africa then?'

He looked at her. 'It seems we are, Mother. In all likelihood this is the last time—'

'Will you give my kindest feelings to your father?' she interrupted him.

'You should bring your kindest feelings to him yourself. He wants you with him. It is your duty, Mother.'

Susan was scrambling up her legs and she bent down and swept her up into her arms. Susan took the side lock of Rose Clare's hair and wound it in her fingers. Rose Clare looked quietly from one son to the other. ' I have other duties. Give your father my kindest feelings,' she repeated.

Caspar grasped Edward's arm and pulled him towards the door. 'Come on, Ed. We'll miss the train. We're off to Liverpool, remember.'

Edward took a last look at his mother, preoccupied with Susan now, as she had once been so infuriatingly preoccupied with Theo, then smiled his beatific smile. 'Right then! We can only wish you well in this Godforsaken place.' He looked up at Stephen and the smile flickered again. 'Perhaps you could take us off the farm, Stephen? Is there a less muddy way to the road?'

'And what about God, Theo? How do you find God?' James Lytton pauses over his chop and looks at me across the table, his sharp eyes peering right into me.

My brain performs an exhausted cartwheel. It aches from days of solid reading under the high lights of the Reading Room. The hand which holds the fork aches from so much writing. My brain is racing with the roar of revolution as it reaches to me through a hundred years by means of words, words, millions of words. I am wishing now I had not given Mr Severine my novel. It lacks the fire, the sheer force of those times when Pauline de la Carrière walked the earth. I am ignorant. Woefully ignorant. Mr Severine assures me this is not so. 'Just a nip here, a tuck there, my dear.' As I get more depressed he becomes more enthusiastic. 'This will be wonderful, wonderful, my dear.'

'God,' I say now, gloomily. 'I find myself sympathetic with the revolutionaries getting rid of religion. I have a problem with God.'

James yelps with laughter at this. 'Now why would that be, oh strange one?'

Each evening at supper I've been unravelling my life and adventures for James: untangling a very tangled ball of string knot by knot. In telling him all this I am knowing myself more than ever before.

'Me? God?' I try to think clearly about it. 'All that stuff about God is bound up in my mind, so much, with the pious virtue of my grandmother and the pious cruelty of my brother. In the end I have no time for it. I would rather have my father who many would see as an immoral man.'

'Well, what d'you have? Do you have no God?'

I put down my fork and close my eyes to rest them, to cool my brain. 'I have time for that old man in Spitalfields. He knows about heaven and hell and sees the balance. Or sees the patterns when the circles close. Even in his dotage he draws love to him. I have time for Mrs Gervase. There she was, building a life for her son who was scorned by the world. I have time for Stephen, who is a true innocent.' I open my eyes, wondering where to go from here.

'And nothing more? Nothing outside human beings?' He is staring at me intently and I wonder if this is some kind of test.

'When I was little I cribbed an idea somewhere about the ancient gods of Greece. I saw my grandfather as Hephaeston the god of the anvil, and the tar-paper man as Neptune, the god of the sea, because he came to save me stinking of seaweed. The sea was all to me. The tides, the swell, the driving mist, the distant, distant horizon.' I am suddenly very awake, hungry enough to attack my potatoes with enthusiasm.

'A pagan!' His smile is sweet as hedgerow jam. 'What we have here is a pagan.'

We finish our meal in silence and make our way back to Montague Street. We walk like strangers with a foot of clear space between us. To be nearer than this seems now the way of danger.

Twenty-nine

The Jagged Window

Stephen could not understand why Theo's brothers were chasing him. He'd shown them a way off the muddy track, down on to the road. Then the bulky one, the one called Caspar, had turned on him and roared like a lion, making him jump back and fall across a tussock. Then the tall fair one laughed and came across to him where he lay and started to kick him, shouting something about the mighty being fallen. He had managed to scramble to his feet then and push the tall one over before running away.

Despite his bulk Stephen was fit, and he made some headway back towards the house, losing his hat and his scarf as he went. He could hear their shouts and voices behind him. They were calling him *imbecile* and *idiot* and calling Theo names too. Tears were coursing down his cheeks and his breath started to come in sobs.

They caught him by the waterfall created by Pauline de la Carrière's workmen in the sheer fall of rock. Caspar hurled himself at Stephen and, when he fell, he sat on his broad back. 'Stop it. Stop it,' Stephen begged. 'Get off me. Please get off me.'

Caspar looked up at his brother. 'What now?'

Edward breathed heavily as he looked down at the back of

Stephen's curly head. 'The old boy stinks,' he said. 'Needs a bath. Get up, Cas.'

Caspar scrambled to his feet. Stephen lay inert. Edward put the toe of his boot against Stephen's stout side and started to kick. Caspar followed suit, saying, 'Sure he stinks, the old boy.'

Stephen could not resist any more, and his body rolled like a lumpy sack of potatoes to the edge of the cliff and over into the deep splash pool below the waterfall. Edward scraped his boot on a tussock of grass. 'That should clean him off. Get rid of the stink. Come on, Cas. We'll miss that train in Stanhope if we delay much longer.'

My time in London has stretched into a lifetime: working in the daytimes with Mr Severine; reading, writing, adjusting my pages in the evenings after supper. Always talking, only really talking to James Lytton. But now Mr Severine declares himself satisfied with the new elements in the story and has paid me for this one and given me a letter saying he will look very kindly on the next. 'I am sure there will be another one, dear girl. And more.'

So it is all at an end. Reading in the round library room in the day. Eating and talking with James Lytton in the evening. I have never talked so much or so long to anyone in the whole of my life. Untangling the string. Untangling.

Now it is time to return North. To pick up the threads with Stephen and Rose Clare and Susan Cornford. To be the old Theo Gervase. But I wonder if this is possible now. Who is the old Theo Gervase? The old Theo Maichin? Theodora Louisa Maichin? That is what will go on the title page of the book. I suddenly remember the old charlatan fortune teller, Verena Scott, and her tales of the snake who habitually shed her skins.

But suddenly it seems it is not quite at the end. As he lifts our bags out of the cab at the railway station, James turns to me. 'One more thing,' he says. 'We should do one more thing.'

I look at him, clutching Seal to me inside my coat. 'What thing is this, James?'

'One piece in the jigsaw. One more journey. One more day.'

After an hour Rose Clare missed Stephen and sent Sadie to search for him. Sadie raced back to say he was slumped on a bank on the lower reaches of the stream, 'Ah'll hafter gan down the farm to get our Reuben to haul him. No way we can lift him.'

Reuben, surly and unwilling, brought a handcart to haul Stephen back up the hill to Goshawk Shield. He manhandled Stephen's inert body into the pheasant room and lay him on the floor before the fire. Then Sadie and Rose Clare set to in a workmanlike fashion, stripped him off and packed him round with towels and stone hot-water bottles. His face was dark red, tinged with purple. His skin was icy.

Rose Clare told Reuben to dismantle the bed in Stephen's room and bring it down. 'Sure, there'll be no getting him up there in this state,' she said. 'He's a heavy lump at the best of times. Like this there'll be no lifting him. We'll have him here in the pheasant room.'

This done, she sent Reuben down to Stanhope to call the doctor. 'Tell him Mr Gervase has fallen in the water, and he's freezing cold though his brow is hot. And hurry!'

A day's bumpy travel and a night in a Lancashire inn and we end up, on a cold day, in this North Wales town, and the wind is throwing rain and sea fret at the shore in clumpy handfuls. I'd forgotten the drenching cold which comes with rain in this place. The town looks just the same: the orderly streets; the clustering houses; the rocking boats in the harbour; the

386

black tangle of factory and mine.

I tug James's arm as we move along the platform away from the puffing, grinding train. 'This way. This way. See the salt marsh.' I release Seal from her lead and she slips on ahead of us, skirting round the mountainous masonry of the castle tower through the waving grasses of the salt marsh to the seashore.

I chase after her, pulling James with me. 'See. This is where I played. Now then, if you crouch low no one can see you from the town, or the harbour. The grasses close round you like a curtain.'

I pull at his arm and he squats beside me, laughing. 'You are mad, Theo. Mad. Theo.'

Then, like a benediction, the sun breaks through the long trail of clouds and freshens the air. In half an hour the sun and the warming air has blotted up a dry patch here and there on the dark stone of the old tower.

James stretches his neck backwards to take in its full height. 'This one must be bigger than Durham Castle. That one doesn't have towers like this.'

'Doesn't it?'

'Have you never been? To Durham?'

I shake my head. 'No.'

'You surprise me. In all the time you've lived up there?'

I shrug. 'Must have had other things to do.'

'You should go to Durham City. Now that is a magical place. The cathedral. The river. Old ghosts. Magic enough, even for you, there in Durham.'

I put my gloved hand on the damp wall. 'Shall we climb the tower?' The air is funnelling raw on to my face.

'Shall we? Why do you think we came all this way to Wales? To climb the tower.'

I go first, very conscious of the heat of this man behind me. His breath rolls round the inner circle of the tower and enters me as I labour up the steps before him. When we reach the jagged window I stop and lean on the sloping sill. In the years between the view beyond has not changed; the estuary and the boats, the jumble of chimneys and tall buildings on the far bank. Beyond them the further horizons, rolling back and back into infinity.

'An amazing view.' He is close behind me. I can feel his breath again, the heat of his body. I smell the faint scent of tobacco and soap, even the spicy pomade he wears on his hair. It can't be very strong because it never stops his hair falling over his brow.

My voice trembles as I talk and talk, trying to dissipate the strength of feeling which is flowing through me at the nearness of him. 'My father brought me here. I told you. Do you remember? He brought me here and we looked out and thought about Chester and London. And America. Oh, he loved America. Stayed with my Irish aunties. Did I tell you I had aunties in . . .'

He turns me round to face him and puts his hands on my upper arm just below the shoulders. 'Theo . . .' he says.

We've been together most of the week, all our waking hours except when I was at the library. I feel I know him better than any other person except Stephen. But this is the first time he has touched me other than the normal courtesies of helping me into a cab or across a pavement. His pale face gleams down at me in the shadowy interior of the tower. 'Theo,' he says softly. 'Theo.'

Seal is winding herself round my legs, pushing hard against my skirt, as much part of me as she ever is. I take a very, very deep breath but breathe out lightly. 'You are pinching me, James. I'll have bruises on my arms as big as plates.'

His hands loosen immediately and drop to rest on my waist. Then his lips are on my cheeks and my brow and finally on my lips. This last is quite amazing. It is as though with that one soft touch a thread of fire shoots right through my being, to the ends of my toes, to the tips of my fingers, to the roots of my belly.

I pull away and say his name. 'James.' Now it is my turn. I put my hands on his shoulders and lay my lips against his. If anything, the feeling is more powerful.

When we finally pull apart it seems we have been kissing, just kissing, for an hour. I am trembling.

'You have kissed no one before.' He is saying it, not asking a question.

'There has been no one to kiss.' I breathe deeply again, to make the trembling stop. 'No one at all.'

'What a lonely girl.' He pulls me to him and rocks me to and fro as though I were a baby. At my feet Seal yaps slightly, almost mewing like a cat. He leans down to lift her up and she is there with us in a circle of three.

'This is no good, Theo,' he says. 'No good at all.'

I snuggle closer. 'It feels very good.'

'Listen! You can't go back North. We can't go back. We have to be together, always.'

I tear myself out of his grasp and Seal drops to the floor, yelping. 'What? That's stupid talk. Of course we must go back.'

He pulls me to him again. 'We will stay here. Or go to live in Chester. Or London. Or America. I can do my violins, or play them for our bread and butter. And you can write your novels. We can do that anywhere.'

I can feel danger snapping at my heels. Before, I was melting with desire; now I am melting with compliance. I so want to do this. To do what he says. How easy it would be to flow into such a life, without so much as a backward glance.

Seal barks, and tugs at the hem of my dress. 'No,' I say. 'We can't do that. I can't do that.'

He is gripping me again. Gripping me hard. 'Yes you can.

How otherwise will you be happy? You'll always be alone. A forlorn, lonely creature.'

'Being happy can't be the first thing. There is Stephen. And Susan Cornford. I have them with me. They are my . . . I have to take care of them.'

'They have your mother, and Goshawk. They will just go on as they always have.'

I pull away from him, brush past him and set off down the tower steps, calling behind to him, 'Come on. Come on. We'll check the time of the train. We may miss it. We must get the train.'

I am running away.

'We'll stay tonight and travel back tomorrow.' There is urgency and the faintest thread of anxiety in his voice. 'At least we can do that. Stay here one night.'

'No. No.' The danger is past. I'm compliant no longer, I am in a hurry now. A hurry to get away from this town and away from the dangerous idea James Lytton has planted in this head of mine. 'We must get away. A train to Chester and see how far North we can get from there.' I am running down the steps and away from him. Away from myself and my own real yearning to go, just go anywhere with him. The ends of the earth would be fine.

But I can't. I know I can't. I have dreamed some dreams but that is the most impossible.

Thirty

Sacrifice

'There! There! Take the big shovel.'

Caspar was sweating. He picked up the long-handled shovel. 'Can't think what it is you're after, Ed. Nothing gained by this.' He peered round the deserted forge.

'Shut up and do as I say.' Edward, hefting a long tool with a curled end, finally succeeded in unclipping the door on the small furnace and pushing it open. A surging gale of heat flowed over them, replacing the dusty warmth that had met them when they had squeezed through the big door into the shadowy interior of the great warehouse.

Edward surveyed the scene. It had taken these Berrimans fifty years to build up this place, to accumulate their wealth, to set themselves on the pathetic ladder which was what this town called society.

'Get some of that fire on the long shovel and come on.' Edward led the way back through the small forge into the warehouse and through to the shop. He kicked open the door which led behind the counter where Mrs Berriman always sat. He pointed to her old battered chair with its well-flattened leather cushion. 'There! Where the old woman sits!' Caspar threw the still glowing cinders on to the leather and smoke sizzled into the air.

'More! We need more.' Edward, filled with new excitement, raced back through the building to the small forge, picked up a shovel himself and plunged it deep in the coals. Caspar followed him, shouting and *hallooing* as he went. Then they careered back through to the shop, dropping hot cinders as they went.

In minutes the counter was blazing and the rows of battered cardboard boxes which held the nails and the screws were glimmering with flame here and there. They made two more trips, excited by the heat and the sense of power welling through them. On the last trip Caspar let Edward go ahead and turned back for a few moments to admire the blaze. A crack and splutter of explosions rent the air. Caspar's way to the back regions was blocked by a cabinet which had cracked and split and fallen across the doorway, burning furiously.

'Edward!' shrieked Caspar. '*Edward.*'

Edward turned back and flinched from the flames which were reaching right round the door-jamb. He ran once towards the flames, then backed off, coughing.

'Ed! Ed! For Godsake gerrus outta here! For Godsake!' Caspar roared.

Edward stood, staring at the flames with black-grimed eyes. As he watched, the speed of the leaping flames seemed to slow down and when he lifted his hand to wipe his eyes his arm moved with an elaborate mechanical slowness. Unbidden, the thought came to his head that Caspar there, poor dumb Caspar, was the only one, apart from his grandmother, who had ever cared for him at all. His mother, his father, Theo, Claris and Anthony, they all were out for themselves, caring naught for him. Selfish to the core. Selfish.

He could not sacrifice Caspar. He eyed his own long-handled shovel and started to beat at the flaming door-frame. But then the sparks leapt and danced in the air and settled on his coat, flaring for a moment then sizzling to a small black hole. The fire before him gathered force and he stepped back and back, beating ineffectually as he went. Now the warehouse was ablaze and he could hear the clanking bells of the fire engine.

That was when he turned and fled, out of the forge and down the maze of lanes behind the High Street, skirting round until he could walk easily to the railway station. He brushed down his coat as he walked, and scuffed his boots against the clumps of grass at the side of the road. At the station he collected the large bag which held his books and the small bag which held his clothes, exchanged his workman's cap for a bowler and bought a ticket for Darlington. Caspar's bag he left behind.

He was standing easily on Darlington Station when he saw his sister Theo alight from the train on the other side of the tracks. She had that ridiculous dog in one arm, a heavy bag in the other. Well, he thought, at least he wouldn't have to endure even the occasional sight of her in future. Most of all, he wished her in hell.

He settled into his carriage, sitting ramrod straight, ignoring the curious looks of people who could not reconcile his smart appearance with the faint smell of fire which clung to him.

Surely that is Edward on the opposite platform standing there like a black-clad heron. I'm sure he has seen me. I'll not speak or wave. I've nothing to say to him. I feel dull enough already, without having him cast me down further into the slough of despondency. It is not that James and I were estranged, or even surly with each other on the long way home. More, we were restrained. We had glimpsed a life we might have had and I had put it beyond our reach.

Just past York, when we knew our journey was beginning to near its end, a little tension rose between us, and he started to murmur that whatever happened we must keep in touch.

Then at last our carriage emptied at a small station just before Darlington and he took my hand in his and raised it to his lips. 'It will happen, Theo. It will.'

'Don't say this, James. It can't happen.'

He clung to my hand and slipped the silver seal ring on to my forefinger. 'Just wear that to remember this week, when we came together.'

I closed my eyes to stop the tears coming, but it was a vain action. They oozed down my cheeks. We clung together until the train stopped at Darlington. He unclasped my hand. 'I will go on to Newcastle. I've business with my uncle there. If we're to part, we'll part now.' He put a hand on Seal's head and she looked up at him with her soulful eyes. ''Bye, little Seal,' he said softly, and she yelped. He kissed me on the cheek. 'Goodbye, Theo.'

In Priorton, I enquire from the porter about the train to Stanhope. 'Yeh've got half an hour, missis. Settle in the waiting room. I've got a nice fire blazing.' He picks up my bag and leads the way. 'Quite a to-do there's been in the town this afternoon.'

'Oh yes?'

'There was a big fire. Biggest yet. Berriman's foundry. Still burning so they say. They ran out of water.'

I stand up again. 'Berriman's?'

'Yes. They say the shop was gutted. The forge itself, plenty damage there.' He starts to poke the fire.

I swing him round. 'Was anyone hurt? Was there anyone inside?'

He takes off his cap and scratches his greasy hair with painful slowness. 'They say there was a feller in there. Curled up like a rabbit. Dead as a doornail. Hey, missis! Where are you going?' He looks down at his hand, which is now holding Seal's lead, and at Seal who is staring up at him placidly enough. I start to run.

Rhys. Rhys. His name runs through my head. My racing mind contemplates life without my brother. I reflect that he is the only one of them who ever showed me kindness. It could be him. It could be him. So what about Ruth and this new baby? Who would take care of them?

The flames are still licking the heights of the building and the fire engine is standing idly by, water trickling from inert hoses. I fight my way to the front and come shoulder to shoulder with a constable and two firemen. 'What happened? Was anyone hurt?'

They glance down at me, their blackened faces hard to read. 'We got a feller out. Off to the infirmary. One of my lads knows him. Maichin is the name.'

I take a breath. 'Is he dead? He is my brother.'

They exchange glances. 'He wasn't very well, missis,' said one. 'Very poorly in fact. The smoke.'

It's a punishment. A punishment for the moment I wavered, the moment I felt I might just run away with James Lytton. The words drum through my head.

A hand grabs my shoulder and swings me round. 'Theo! What're you doing here?'

'Rhys.' I fall into his arms. 'This man says . . . he says the man they took out . . . he was called Maichin.'

'That's right,' said the fireman. 'A dog man, isn't he? My lad's a dog man too. Maichin, he said the name was. Laid bets with him.'

'Caspar,' Rhys and I say his name together.

'Caspar,' repeats Rhys. 'What was he doing here?' We look at each other. 'Edward,' he says grimly. 'Edward up to some of his devilish mischief.'

'Was there only one man in there?' I ask, terrified of the thought that I am wishing Edward dead. But no. Haven't I already seen Edward on Darlington Station?

The constable shakes his head. 'Just one. They've

been right through. Just one body.'

'Body?' I say sharply.

He stares at me through black-rimmed eyes. 'Yes,' he says. 'Just curled up under a bench.'

Then there is a disruption at the back of the crowd as Mr Berriman and Ruth's grandma arrive, driven by Ruth herself. Mr Berriman takes over and tells Ruth to get me to the house and take care of me. She sweeps me off to the station to collect my luggage and Seal, then back to Victoria Road for a cup of tea.

I am shaking as though I have a high fever and can do nothing about it. Ruth covers me with shawls and presses hot drinks on me but it makes no difference. Her face is white and strained too, even though she never thought it was Rhys there in the forge. She makes me promise to stay the night and travel on to Goshawk Shield in the morning. Rhys has gone to the infirmary to find out if it really is Caspar, but I know in my bones it is. My hand goes to Seal's head. A dog man. That's what they called him. A dog man.

Rhys is white about the gills when he returns to the house. He looks Ruth in the eye, and then nods curtly at me. 'It's Caspar all right. Not a mark on him. That's your reward for hanging around Edward.'

'Not the first time,' I say. 'Hanging around Edward has always been dangerous.'

'What?' Rhys looks at me sharply.

'Ellen Jones. Do you remember?'

'What is this?' Ruth frowns at Rhys.

He glances at me then shakes his head. 'Old times,' he says. 'Bad old times.'

'Bad new times,' I say gloomily. 'So where is Edward? I did think I glimpsed him on Darlington Station.'

Rhys shakes his head. 'Nowhere round here. I went across

to his lodgings. His landlady says he and Caspar went off to go to South Africa for good. To see our father. Bag and baggage. Both of them.'

'Caspar's going nowhere,' says Ruth. 'We can be sure of that.'

'We should tell them,' I say. 'Tell the constable. Tell him about this and Ellen Jones. Tell them about Edward.'

Rhys shakes his head. 'How can we do that, Theo? Think about our mother.'

'Still, if he was there . . . in the forge . . .'

'There's no saying he was there. He could have sent Caspar down. It could be an accident.'

'Why? Why? Why would he . . . or they . . . do this?'

Ruth goes across to sit beside Rhys and puts her arm through his. 'Edward came here beside himself at Rhys, Theo. He hates him. He hates us. My grandmother. He went to the shop and was very nasty to her.'

'Why? What for?'

'Because he is envious, a deadly sin as he would know it,' says Ruth smoothly. 'He is envious of Rhys because he is making a success of himself. Envious of us because of the baby. And Edward has lost his job because he has trodden on somebody's toes at the pit. Lost all round. He's been rude to my grandma. Rude to me.'

Out of work? He always despised Caspar, and he finds himself in just the same position.

'He must have been very, very angry,' says Rhys.

'Poor old Caspar,' say I. 'What a sacrifice. Never had more than half a life in Edward's shadow. Poor old lad.'

Rhys sighs. 'And now Edward's run off again. Just like he did from Wales. More like our dada than you'd think. Running all the time. He'll spend his life running. Prayers, ranting, none of that'll make any difference.' His tone is surprised. It's as though he is discovering these ideas as he says the words.

I have to nod, though I am not surprised. 'It seems so,' I say. 'It seems so, Rhys.'

Fogged up with the sadness of yesterday I did not reckon on the way my heart leaps as the station brake turns along the lane beside Bittern Crag Farm and starts on the last pull up to Goshawk Shield. The sky behind the fell is scored with scudding clouds, the light so clear and bright that it sharpens, outlines, highlights every blade of grass, every rolling run of heather, the lichen which clings to the dry-stone wall.

The brake rocks and jerks over the ruts and Rhys places a protective arm around Ruth. 'Not far now, sweetheart.' I thrill to their tenderness and feel an ache to my very core for James's touch.

My mother is at the door then across to help me down. 'Oh, Theo. Such bad news. Such very bad news.'

I blink at her. How can she know? We have come this way together to break the news to her. 'Bad news?' I say. 'Yes, we have bad news.'

Her gaze moves to Rhys and Ruth and she frowns. 'Theo? What is it?'

Ruth puts an arm round her and guides her back to the kitchen. It is deserted. Cold despite the heaped-up fire. No sign of Susan Cornford. Or Sadie. Or Stephen.

Ruth sits Rose Clare in the chair beside the fire and kneels beside her, careless of her fine skirts on the stone floor. 'There now, Mother Maichin,' she says. 'I fear we have very bad news.'

'It's Caspar,' says Rhys abruptly. 'He was injured in a fire at the forge. We think he and Edward set it deliberately.'

Her lips set in a very thin line. 'And Edward? Was he injured?'

I shake my head. 'No. He ran away.'

'And Caspar? Is he in the hospital? You didn't bring him

with you?' I cannot understand why she is so calm.

Ruth takes her hand. 'He died, Mother Maichin. I am so sorry but he died. He wasn't burned. It was the smoke. They said he just went to sleep.'

'And Edward?' The deadly calm is still in her voice. 'You say he ran away?'

'He was going to South Africa. To Father,' said Rhys.

'So he was.' The smallest flicker of a smile crosses her face. 'So he was.' Then she blinks and looks up into my eyes. 'They came here to tell me that, that they were going to South Africa. And then . . .' she faltered. 'Then, on their way off the farm, they tormented poor Stephen.'

I shoot to my feet. 'Stephen?' I look round. 'Where is he?'

'He ended up in the Frenchwoman's pool, Theo. He is very, very ill. The doctor has been here every day . . . Theo!'

He is lying quietly under a quilt in his mother's bedroom, his big shambling shape reduced almost to nothing in the big bed. The curtains are closed and a very small lamp stands on the bedside table. I tiptoe across and almost reel back at the sight of his face which, like his body, seems shrunk to almost half its normal size. His skin is tight and shiny, lapping over the fat folds, and is tinged faintly blue. His eyes snap open and a feeble grin struggles across his benevolent countenance. 'Theo?' he whispers hoarsely.

I sit on the bed and take both of his hands in mine and start to rub them. 'Now then, Stevie, how'd you get into this pickle?'

'I was very cold. My teeth chattered.'

'Did they? Poor you. Poor Stevie.'

His fat hand turns and grips mine. 'I thought you'd gone, Theo. That you had left me behind.'

I put a hand on his face. 'No, Stevie. I will never leave you. I promise. Never, never.'

He nods slightly and closes his eyes, appearing to go to sleep. I make to move my hand but he grasps it tighter. 'Stay, Theo. Stay with me.' Then he opens his eyes again. 'She has been, Theo. Lots of times. She brings me candles in the night, and soup. One day she brought me syllabub. I love syllabub.'

'Who? Rose Clare? Sadie? They brought you syllabub?'

He closes his eyes and shakes his head. 'No! No!' His tone is impatient. 'Mama. She is here all the time.'

Then his hand goes slack and his head goes back and he drops instantly into a deep, snoring sleep.

My mother is at the door. 'He has been like this for days. He was half dead when they brought him home. The doctor said . . . well, he said he should not have survived.'

'He says he sees Mrs Gervase. He sees his mother.'

'Ah well, Theo, if it is a comfort to him . . . She watched over him in life.'

Again I am aware of the quiet house. 'Where's Susan Cornford?'

'She's down at Bittern Crag . . . we thought . . .'

'Will you go and get her? There are two of us now. We don't want her down there. We can't have her down there.'

Downstairs the sombre looks of my brother and sister-in-law greet me.

'A terrible business all round,' says Rhys. 'Terrible.'

Ruth nods. 'Terrible,' she says.

Ruth and Rhys declare their intention to stay and when Sadie and Susan return we make some rearrangements so the household can retire to bed.

I take up vigil beside Stephen's bed. My mother offers to stay with him but I refuse. 'I'll take care of him,' I say. 'He's my responsibility. I should never have gone away.'

'Don't say that,' says Rose Clare sharply. 'That's not true. How were you to know your brothers would play the devil while your back was turned? How could you know?'

Stephen is restless, turning and muttering for whole stretches of time, then rasping out a terrible hoarse bark you can barely call a cough. Sometimes he grabs my hand and holds it painfully tight, only to let it go and thrash around as though he is still in the Frenchwoman's pool, fighting for his life.

Then as the twanging chimes of the landing clock chime three in the morning, he pulls himself half upright, his eyes wide open looking at me with his own peculiarly childish delight. 'Theo! Theo!' he beams. Then his gaze fixes behind me. 'Mama! Mama!' Then his back arches and he makes a peculiar rattling choking noise and he falls back on to his pillow, his eyes still wide and full of strange delight.

I pull my hand from his and start to shake with terror, then, taking in a very deep breath, I open my mouth and shout, 'Mother! Mother!'

She is there in an instant, her arm round me, her hand on my hair as I sob and sob against her shoulders. 'I loved him, Mam. I did love him. Poor old Stevie.'

'Sure you loved him, sweetheart. Sure you did. What? Between you and his old mother never was a man more loved.' Her arms held me close.

I don't know how many minutes we stay like this, but as the sobs ease and the tears stop flowing a thought – perhaps more a feeling – creeps into the back of my mind. My mother has never taken me in her arms like this. Never even when I was a child. Not that I can remember.

Quiet now, I am passed hand to hand to Ruth, whose thin strong arms keep me upright. We both watch as my mother approaches the bed. First she makes the sign of the cross over him, and then over herself. Next she leans over to close his eyes and flicks the counterpane straight. Then she takes out a rosary from her nightgown pocket and starts to mutter in prayer. For me, rocking there in Ruth's arms, this almost voiceless holy chatter is a comfort, although I am at a loss to know why.

The mystery of the fire at Berriman's remained a puzzle in Priorton. There was always a risk in such places. But there was much talk of the problem of the body. Brother to Rhys Maichin, married to Ruthie Berriman. What was he doing there? He could have been on some errand for his brother, perhaps. But Rhys Maichin was saying nothing. And Mr Berriman was saying nothing. And the old woman, Ruthie's grandmother, was there next day in her galoshes and an old sacking apron to clear up the mess. She said nothing. Game soul, old Mrs B.

No one from Gibsley or Priorton went to Caspar Maichin's funeral. If it had been in Priorton perhaps one or two of the dog men might have turned up, half out of respect and half speculating on the chance of a glass of port wine. But Caspar wasn't buried in Priorton. He was buried up at Stanhope alongside his brother-in-law who died of pneumonia just about the same time.

The two men shared a funeral and were laid for eternity side by side on a windy hillside. Strange that, seeing as they had never really known each other in life. That was what was said in the town anyway.

I had not thought I would miss anyone as much as I miss Stephen. I jump at shadows in the house and wait for him to come lumbering round corners. I listen for the chariot in the yard, though I know it is burned to a crisp. My mother, who was uncommonly fond of Stephen herself, has been very kindly to me.

The books on the table in the pheasant room grow dusty with little use. I cannot read. I cannot write. I go to bed early. I sleep late. I leave my mother to respond to the few letters of condolence and prickle with irritation when I hear the peal of Susan Cornford's laughter through what now feels to me to be an empty house.

Edward comes back again and again to my mind. On the high seas now, on his way to Africa. Having dealt out desolation here by water and fire and left us for dead, he is off, free as a bird. But he will never be free of his base self. And, as Rhys says, he will run and run all his life, blaming those behind him.

An odd thought occurs to me sometimes: that Edward and I are alike. We are driven by our own needs and we each have a well honed sense of our own consequence. But where Edward is driven to destroy, I am driven to create, and, without pride, I thank God for that difference. I could not speak of this to James as he would never understand. And, of course I cannot speak of any of this to my mother. This family is, as ever, enfolded on its secrets.

I cannot speak to Rhys either, who has thrown off the tragedy in practical fashion and is very involved in the rebuilding of the new forge. Ruth is very friendly these days, calling me sister and embracing me rather more than suits my fancy. She is near to her time and begs me to visit her and hold her hand during her confinement.

I have had one letter from James Lytton which remains on the mantelpiece unopened. I dare not open it in case it engulfs me with yet more guilt about being with James, kissing him in the tower, while Stephen was suffering so.

My mother dusts the letter regularly. 'Sure it's a pity you don't open it. I can't think what's stopping you. It's not right, not opening your post.' I swear there is a twinkle in her eye.

For a split second I think I will tell her about London, then I pack that secret away with the others. I think she is relieved to get rid of me, down to Priorton for my week with Ruth.

My sister-in-law is rather large now, moving like a turtle.

Her mother calls for very brief visits, but her grandmother, whom I like, comes and brings her tatting, and joins us in playing cards. She is the only one interested enough to ask about my London visit and is very charmed by my descriptions of Miss Bell and Miss Bannister and the eccentricities of Mr Severine.

She is just asking me about the next story I will write when Ruth roars and says, 'Grandma!'

After that, everything goes like clockwork as though it were written in a rule book. The midwife arrives, the doctor close after. Rhys is sent up to his father-in-law's house to smoke cigars. The little maid Beattie makes me cups of tea in the kitchen, my place of banishment. Ruth's grandma boils water.

I can hear shouts and screams and padding footsteps upstairs right into the early hours. Then at last the house is pierced with the pure, high-pitched sound of a baby's cry. I make my way to the first landing and sit on the stairs. After five minutes, old Mrs Berriman peeps out of the bedroom door and beckons me in.

Ruth is lying back on her pillows, damp hair combed back under a ribbon, her eyes puffy, her skin faintly grey. She holds up the bundle in her arms. I go and pull away the shawl and look at the neat chiselled face and the thatch of fair hair. I shoot a glance at Ruth. 'Why, Ruth! He's the very image of—'

She nods briskly. 'The very image of Rhys! Look at those eyebrows. Grandma! Has Beattie gone for Rhys? I want him here now.'

The child is the very image of Edward. Now the story is clear to me. The child's hand has escaped the blanket and as I put my finger on it he grasps me with surprising strength.

'Well done, Ruth,' I say. 'This is a very nice baby.'

'So he is!' She smiles up at me innocently. 'Don't you think Rhys will be pleased with his son, Theo?'

She is clever, this sister-in-law of mine. 'Oh yes, Ruthie. So he will. He'll be so proud.'

I am not angry with Ruth. I know about Edward. Yet I am suddenly so angry with him, so angry with the fates, or the gods, for letting him get away, that I am scalding with temper, and am very pleased to leave the cooing household and go back on the train to Goshawk Shield. I don't know whether this flood of anger has cleared my mind up in some way, but when I get back to Goshawk, I cannot wait to get into the pheasant room. I had not yet removed my hat before I was sorting the table out, dusting the books, refilling my inkwell.

My mother comes in, a smile on her lips. 'So what's this? A bit of energy are we getting now?'

'I don't know. Perhaps seeing the baby. He was a fine baby. You wait till you see him.' I wonder whether she will note the resemblance to Edward. 'But there was Ruth with her baby and suddenly I wanted to do something. And the only thing I can do is' – I look at the cluttered table – 'this.'

My mother claps her hands. 'Bravo, Theo. You get on with things.' She crosses to the fireplace and takes down James Lytton's letter. 'Sure it'd be a good thing to deal with your post, seeing as you're back in the land of the living.' She smooths the velvet cover. 'Don't waste your life, Theo.'

I leave the letter where she put it for more than an hour, while I tidy the clutter on the desk, putting the sheets of paper in order and the pens neatly in line. Around me sunshine streams into the pheasant room through every window, filling it with an unbearable brightness. Energy is flooding through me in waves and I pull my shawl from the back of the chair and make my way outside, Seal dancing at my heels.

For some reason Pauline de Carrière is on my mind, so I make my way through her garden, wandering down paths excavated for me not so long ago by Stephen. My footsteps lead me towards the waterfall, roaring full now after recent rain.

It is hot. The sun has burned off the mist and close at hand I can hear the buzz as the bees go about their work in the heather. I shake my head, pleased that my hair is loose, that I didn't bother with a bonnet.

As I climb to the high escarpment which cups the waterfall I can hear laughter. Peering over the rocks I see Rose Clare, her own hair quite loose and her red petticoats tucked up round her waist, her bare feet in the shallow water at the edge of the splash pool. She has Susan Cornford by the hand. The child, clad only in her little shift, is threshing about in the water, her fat limbs gleaming in the sunshine. An outsider would say that Rose Clare is the child's mother, so young does she look. Here in the sunshine she looks no older than my sister-in-law Ruth. The fact dawns on me for the first time that Rose Clare must only have been thirty-five or so in those days in Wales, when Edward tied me to the stake in the salt marsh. So young.

She feels my stare and glances up. Then she beams, raises her arm and seems to sweep the sky with her wave. 'Come down, Theo. Come down, won't you?' she shouts.

By the time I clamber down Seal is already there and Rose Clare has Susan out of the water and is rubbing her fat knees with a towel. She blows a strand of hair out of her eyes and looks up at me. 'Isn't it a fine warm day, Theo? Won't you try a paddle yourself? The water's a bit cool because of the fast flow, the way it swirls after the waterfall. But the air's so much warmer when you get out. There's balance in that.'

I find myself taking off my stockings, tucking up my own skirts and plunging into the swirling water.

'There now,' she shouts above the roar of the fall. 'Isn't that fine, Theo?' She starts to pull on Susan's woollen dress. 'Doesn't it wash all your worries away?'

My toes cling to the sharp pebbles and I have to rock

backwards and forwards to keep my balance in the powerful swirl of water. But I hold my own. This time I'm not tied. This time I've no need to struggle and to call up the whispering presence of my father or the saving hand of the tar-paper man. I could stay here for ever. This water or the sea. What does it matter?

My mother fastens Susan's boots, pulls her own red petticoats down to a respectable length and pulls on her boots. Seal barks at me, running backwards and forwards on the shore, unwilling to get her dainty paws wet.

'Come on now, Theo!' my mother calls from the bank. 'Come back and dry yourself, now. We'll go home for dinner. And don't you have a letter to write?'

She smiles at me.

Back at Goshawk Shield I tear open his letter. It is very brief.

> *I hear of all your sad news in Priorton. I will come when you are ready, no matter how long I have to wait.*
> *JL*

Seal jumps up on to the table and walks along it to where I am sitting with my hand on the letter. She licks my thumb and looks up at me.

I pick up the first pen in the neat line. My own letter is brief.

> *This has been an awful time, James, but thank you for your kind thoughts. I intend now to wait out the three years I promised for Stephen. I have much to do, as you must too. I look at my seal ring every day but I will keep my promise to Mrs Gervase, and Stephen. One day, though, I will welcome you with open arms.*

I don't know whether I'll last through this time, to wait out the three years. But there is much to do. The story based on Mrs Gervase's young life. Susan Cornford and my mother to care for. A new nephew to contemplate, my mother's grandson, whoever may be his father.

I know for certain now that James Lytton and I will be together one day, he mending his violins, me writing my stories. Who knows where? Here in the wide spaces of the North or down in bustling London? Or perhaps somewhere by the sea, where I can put my face up to the salt spray and feel the pull of the tides as I did as a child? No matter where, we will be content. And in our very happiness we'll rise above the wickedness that my brother Edward has tried to weave through all of our lives. In that he will be for ever defeated, wherever he is.